SPELLBOUND

"You've read *Dracula*, haven't you?" he murmured as he ran his fingertip along the exposed vee of porcelain skin between her breasts.

She nodded, her pulse racing.

"Then, you're aware of his methods," he said with a throaty laugh. "The Count never attacks his victims. He waits for them to invite him into their presence."

Celesta found her voice. "Then he hypnotizes them—renders them helpless with his powerful red eyes. He's always in control."

"And what do you see in *my* eyes, Celesta?"

She held her breath, unable to release herself from his riveting gaze. Damon's lamplit face glowed beneath chestnut hair that draped his forehead at a rakish angle.

"I see pure, unadulterated lust," she finally whispered.

"You're wise beyond your years." His fingers paused at the base of her throat.

Spellbound, she watched his lips and heard the alluring timbre of his voice, then felt the first touch of his mouth on hers. . . .

CHARLOTTE HUBBARD

MISSOURI MAGIC

Hope you find MAGIC
between these sheets!
Charlotte Hubbard

ZEBRA BOOKS
KENSINGTON PUBLISHING CORP.

For my Aunt Sandra,
who loves—and sometimes lives—a mystery.

Many thanks to Henry Sweets, historian and curator of the Mark Twain Boyhood Home, for his invaluable help as I researched turn-of-the-century Hannibal, Missouri.

ZEBRA BOOKS

are published by

Kensington Publishing Corp.
475 Park Avenue South
New York, NY 10016

First printing: November, 1992

Printed in the United States of America

Chapter 1

". . . ashes to ashes and dust to dust. We commend the spirit of our sister Rachel to your care, dear Lord. Amen."

As the preacher's words drifted away on the hot summer breeze, Celesta gazed at her mother's plain coffin, poised above its grim, rectangular grave. She was aware of Aunt Katherine on her right, dabbing her eyes and whimpering, and of Aunt Justine's stoic silence. On her left stood Patrick Perkins, unnaturally somber in his dark suit, his hand resting at the base of her sweaty spine. Eula, his mother, blew her nose with a pathetic little sob. Just the five of them, plus Reverend Case, to mourn Rachel Montgomery's passing.

And we shouldn't be here, a voice cried out in Celesta's mind. *It was just one of her headaches. She wasn't that sick, until—*

"May the Lord make His face to shine upon you and give you His peace," the clergyman murmured as he clutched her hands between his.

She nodded absently, and as he repeated the blessing to her two aunts, Celesta's mind continued its angry search for the sense in all this. Her mother had been perfectly healthy, prone only to occasional headaches that passed after a few hours' rest in her darkened room. She'd asked for her usual tea and toast, and then—

The clatter of clods on the casket brought her thoughts back to the present. Patrick, bless him, had tossed the ceremonial spadeful of dirt into the grave. His red-gold hair shone like the sun, and his anxious blue eyes met hers. "I'm not trying to rush you, but you ladies will be fainting away from this heat," he said quietly. "Perhaps we should move into the shade."

Celesta nodded gratefully. Her black suit, the only appropriate outfit in her wardrobe, was of winter-weight wool, and she was ready to collapse beneath its stifling, itchy weight.

"That's a fine idea, dear," Eula Perkins replied with a quavery sigh. "We can pay the rest of our respects from beneath those trees. No sense in falling ill ourselves, like poor Rachel did."

Reverend Case excused himself to other duties, and the mourners started toward the cluster of maple trees on the next rise, where the breeze was riffling the leaves. Seeing that Aunt Katherine was lost in thought, Celesta took her elbow.

"We'd better get you out of this sun," she murmured. "What with the strain of these past two days, you'll be all weak-kneed and—"

Her middle-aged aunt's veiled expression silenced her. "Death comes in threes," Katherine intoned. "First my Ambrose and now your mother. Who's next, Celesta? Who's next?"

The poor little woman was quaking, fresh tears streaming down her cheeks. Celesta hugged her close, wondering how to quell Katherine's notions before they became full-blown hysteria, and then Eula Perkins was beside them, patting their arms as she enfolded them in her sympathetic gaze.

"There, there, now, don't you fret over it," she clucked. Her hair and eyes were the same color as her

6

son's, only mellowed by age and muted by her dark veil. "Why, I was thinking precisely the same thing, but that the cycle began with my Tom, and then Ambrose. And now with Rachel it's ended, don't you see?"

"Superstitious poppycock!" Aunt Justine let out an exasperated sigh, her hands planted on her slim hips. Because she wore no veil, her disgust was evident as her piercing brown-eyed glare flitted among them. "Tom Perkins passed on nearly two years ago, and Ambrose disappeared last summer! How many deaths has Hannibal seen in the interim? Which proves your theory on threes as just another of your ridiculous whims! Honestly, Katherine, you do embarrass me at times."

Justine stalked off toward the shade, grasping her black skirt as though it were her last shred of sanity. Celesta glanced helplessly at Patrick. She hated to admit her spinster aunt had a valid point, cruelly as she'd made it, yet she was too upset to handle any more of Katherine's outbursts herself.

Patrick gave her a grim smile and placed his hands on his mother's shoulders. "Perhaps Celesta and her aunt would like some time alone," he suggested gently. "They've suffered a terrible shock, and we shouldn't impose—"

"Impose?" Eula rasped. The mention of her husband's passing had inspired fresh tears, and she was now approaching the same agitated state Katherine was in. "Why, Rachel and Celesta have lived with us for twenty years. They're like family! We've watched Celesta grow up, and we can't ignore the gap in our lives now that her mother's gone. I haven't the faintest notion how I'll replace her."

That was the crux of it. Eula Perkins, wealthy widow of one of Hannibal's lumber barons, had relied upon Rachel Montgomery to keep her rambling mansion in order ever since Celesta's father,

Ian Montgomery, hightailed it out of town on the eve of her birth. Celesta shifted in her aunt's embrace, hearing Eula's implied question: was Celesta going to repay the privilege of being raised with the heir to Perkins Lumber by taking her mother's place?

Patrick cleared his throat. "What Mother means to say," he stammered, "is that you have a home with us for as long as you wish, Celesta. We'd be lost without you, rattling around in that house, just the two of us."

Things had gone from bad to worse in a matter of seconds, and Celesta suddenly wished they were still hushing her aunt's hysterics. Indeed, Katherine had calmed herself and was gazing intently from beneath her veil while Eula and Patrick Perkins also awaited her reply.

"I . . . I haven't had a chance to consider—"

"Why, she's coming home to Ransom Manor, of course," Katherine interrupted. Her voice was still shaky, but her tone was quite firm. "My sister-in-law hired on with you because she was too proud to come back home after Ian abandoned her. Insisted on supporting her child, and I admired her independence. But I see no reason for my niece to continue as your domestic when she could assume her place with two aunts who are getting on—who *love* her—and who are 'rattling around' in the house that will someday be hers."

Katherine turned her attention from Eula Perkins to Celesta then, her tone softening. "And how can I endure much more of Justine's crankiness alone? As she gets older she gets worse, and with Rachel gone. . . ."

It was a compelling question. Justine was now the only full-blooded Ransom alive, and because her brother Ambrose had left no will, his widow, Katherine, was in the precarious position of being an unwanted in-law with nowhere else to go. It was a

8

situation Celesta had known all her life, but she was only twenty, with other opportunities for her future. Poor Katherine looked frailer by the day . . . had been her only connection to the family Celesta had been denied by her mother's refusal to rely upon their charity.

Leaving Katherine to fend for herself seemed the highest form of betrayal, after all the birthday gifts and kindnesses she'd shown through the years, but who *did* want to dodge Justine's barbs all the time? As though her ramrod aunt had read her thoughts and knew what Katherine was pleading for, she sent them a disdainful look from the shaded knoll several yards away.

Celesta sighed, wishing for the hundredth time her mother hadn't died. She didn't want to be at Eula's beck and call for the rest of her life, either, but where else could she go? She bowed her head wearily. Mrs. Perkins was watching her, expecting gratitude, while Aunt Katherine's soulful eyes begged her to come to a house that had never welcomed her.

Again Patrick's practicality came to the rescue. "You look absolutely done in, Celesta. When you're ready to leave, why don't we all go for a lemonade? I'm sure Katherine would be greatly comforted if you'd spend a few days with her, and you can make your decision in the meantime."

"That would be lovely," Katherine breathed.

"An excellent solution," Eula Perkins chimed in, beaming at him. "You're a thoughtful, considerate son."

Patrick's grin came out to play, dispelling the gloom for a moment. He was unabashedly handsome—and he knew it—yet Celesta had taken his golden hair and glorious blue eyes for granted while growing up with him. And where had this kindness come from? Celesta looked up at him gratefully and nodded, aware of something different in his expres-

9

sion as he studied her . . . something deeper than the devil-may-care attitude she was accustomed to.

When his gaze lingered on her lips and then dropped to her breast, she looked away, thankful her veil hid her blush. "Lemonade would taste wonderful. I—I'll think things over and let you know by week's end."

He nodded and took her elbow again. "Shall we inform Justine of our plans? Perhaps a cool drink will cheer her. . . . What the hell's *he* doing here?"

Celesta's head snapped up, not only because of the radical change in Patrick's voice, but because his grip was threatening to cut her arm in two. A few rows of headstones beyond where Justine was standing, a well-dressed man was kneeling to place a rose on a grave. He had a singularly sad air about him, and as he brushed his chestnut hair back from his face he seemed vaguely familiar.

"Why, that's Damon Frye," Eula whispered. Her hand went to the diamond brooch at her throat as she stared openly at him. "My stars, what's it been? Seven or eight years since—"

"Ten," Patrick stated, his jaw clenching. "How nice of him to visit Lucy's grave after all this time, since it's his fault she's in it. Shall we go? No doubt Mr. Frye has some soul-searching to do, and I'd hate to distract him."

As though Patrick's words had bitten him, Damon Frye turned suddenly to look at them. Celesta remembered him now: he and Patrick had been school chums, and he'd spent several afternoons at the Perkins house when they were boys. She had been only ten, which would have made Patrick eighteen, when the rumors about Damon and the Bates girl got ugly and he left town rather suddenly, chased away by wagging tongues, she guessed. Too young to be privy to the secretive talk her mother and Mrs. Perkins had shared, at the time she could only

10

wonder what horrible sin he'd committed.

Now, of course, she knew he and Lucy had been engaged, and that he'd abandoned her when he learned she was pregnant. Lucy had died after taking a potion some old crone who lived near the railyards had given her to rid her of the baby. Damon and Lucy were still the topic of conversation now and again, whenever similarly shocking events occurred.

"Do you mind if we leave now?" Patrick demanded. "It would be a slight to Lucy's memory to even speak to—"

"He's coming this way," Celesta murmured. "We can't just walk off and pretend we didn't see him."

As Frye approached she noted the strong grace of his walk when he ascended the hill, and the impeccable cut of his double-breasted blazer and trousers, all of a natty white. His clean-shaven face was dark with a masculine shadow. His coffee-colored eyes were assessing them all, and then he looked at her with a bold sultriness that was highly improper yet . . . electrifying. Patrick's arm snaked around her waist.

"I'm sorry we meet again under such regrettable circumstances," he said in a smooth baritone. Damon stopped a few paces away and looked at each of them before glancing toward the open grave. "Is this Rachel Montgomery you've laid to rest? I'm terribly sorry. She was a wonderful lady—made the best cherry tarts I ever tasted."

Celesta felt her eyes go hot, and she looked away. Just three days ago her mother's tarts had brought a record-breaking sum at a charity auction, and now—

"And this must be Celesta."

It was a statement common decency forced her to acknowledge, but when she looked up to reply, she held her breath. Damon's eyes delved shamelessly into hers, speaking with smoldering eloquence about how she'd grown and what he'd like to do

11

about it. Dear Lord, there was a cleft in his dusky chin. . . .

"Miss Montgomery has had a most upsetting day," Patrick cut in, "so if you'll excuse—"

"Miss Montgomery was always one to speak for herself, as I recall," Frye said smoothly. He stepped closer, his smile rueful. "I'm truly sorry about your mother, Celesta."

"Thank you," she whimpered.

"We'll meet again, on a happier day."

There was no question in his remark, and Celesta doubted if she could've answered coherently anyway. Damon Frye was studying her with leisurely arrogance, as though recalling her ten-year-old face and being extremely pleased with how each feature had evolved. He was ignoring the others, which made the sun beat hotter and her wool suit feel even heavier on this muggy June day. To her dismay, she opened her mouth to breathe and it came out as a pant.

Frye chuckled and slowly lifted her veil. He cupped her jaw, his palm pleasantly cool and his gaze so mesmerizing Celesta was too dazed to be embarrassed by his outrageous behavior.

"My God, you're lovely," he murmured.

It was the last thing Celesta really heard all day.

Chapter 2

"Katherine and I have chosen to do our own housekeeping because the work gives us a sense of accomplishment," Justine stated over breakfast the next morning. "I think you should find and perform certain helpful tasks during your stay, Celesta. Establishing a meaningful routine gives order to one's days and purpose to one's life."

"I agree completely." Celesta smiled, determined not to let Justine's autocratic manner spoil the delicious meal Katherine had prepared. She'd been delivering such lectures since they left the cemetery, little homilies that hinted her visit would be short and filled with the chores her spinster aunt found the least appealing. "It's not as though I have a maid at the Perkinses', you know."

Katherine chuckled quietly. "No, I can't imagine Eula allows you to sit idle. Your dear mother rarely had a moment to herself, and even with your assistance she had her hands full keeping *that* family satisfied."

"And what are your responsibilities?" Justine asked, focusing her brown eyes intently on her niece. "Katherine and I firmly believe in dividing duties according to one's particular talents."

"That's why I cook," her other aunt chimed in smugly.

Every conversation left her feeling like a spectator at a tennis match, watching the ball bounce into one court and then get lobbed into the other. Katherine felt stronger today, judging from her pert remarks, but Justine was clearly the head of the Ransom household and demanded an accounting from everyone she supervised. If she was going to stay on here, it was Justine she would have to appease, for Katherine's sake.

Again Celesta smiled at her oldest aunt, whose silver-streaked hair was wound so tightly into a bun it was a wonder she could blink her eyes. "My first chore each day is the marketing," she replied. "I go to—"

"Eula trusts *you* to shop?" Justine stared, and then dabbed her mouth with her napkin to soften her expression. "I mean, I can't imagine allowing staff the liberty of spending family money."

"Which is why your aunt Justine does all our marketing," Katherine added wryly.

"It's because you dawdle," Justine shot back. "By the time you'd get there the meat would be picked over, and on these hot days it's fly-specked before eight. I won't tolerate wilted produce, either. It's like a blouse without starch—it just won't do!"

Celesta caught herself chuckling. Her two aunts obviously enjoyed rising to each other's bait, and she suspected that this rivalry was what kept the women alive. "Actually," she said during their silence, "Mrs. Perkins has me shop because she's rarely out of bed before eleven."

"*What?*"

"No!"

Celesta shrugged and helped herself to another biscuit. "Why does she need to be up?" she asked her wide-eyed aunts. "Mama saw to breakfast and to getting Patrick on his way while I ran the errands. Eula's much nicer after she's had her beauty rest

14

followed by breakfast in bed, so we encourage her to do so. It's her routine."

"The idle rich," Justine muttered as she pushed her plate away.

"*I* couldn't live that way," Aunt Katherine clucked.

Two old ladies with the Ransom shipping fortune at their disposal could live any way they chose, Celesta mused, but she knew better than to say that. Instead she addressed Justine, hoping to build upon the point she'd just scored. "In fact, Eula often compliments my ability to dicker with the shopkeepers. So if you'd like me to take on—"

"Absolutely not." Justine stood up, looking imperiously down her nose. "I have seen to the marketing for the past forty years, rain or shine, and if I continue this chitchat your aunt Katherine will have to make do with inferior ingredients. Lord knows her cooking suffers enough with the *best* I can afford."

She went to the pegs alongside the pantry door and took down a plain straw bonnet, which she donned with military efficiency, and then she pulled on white gloves. Grasping the handle of her wicker market basket, Justine gazed at each of them in turn. "I trust you'll decide what tasks Celesta is best suited to by the time I return," she said crisply. With barely a ripple in her dun-colored skirt, she was out the door.

Celesta watched after her, her mouth clamped shut against a retort. Even in the Perkins home, her suggestions were considered worthwhile, and if Justine thought she could belittle her just because—

Katherine's chuckling brought her thoughts back to the table, where Celesta's shorter, younger aunt was brushing crumbs from the linen cloth into her open palm. The soft folds beneath her chin were quivering with mirth.

"What's so funny? First she asks what I'm capable of doing, as though I'm a four-year-old, and then she snaps like a bear trap when my answer doesn't suit her," Celesta complained. "You're right. She's even ruder than I remember, and getting worse with age."

Her hazel eyes sparkling, Katherine looked at her niece fondly. "You've gotten her goat, dear. You've upset her blessed *routine* by coming here, and Justine doesn't function well unless everything's in its proper place at the correct time. I'll tell you why she *really* does the marketing, but you must swear you'll never breathe a word about it. She'll kick us both out."

Celesta's eyes widened. Surely penny-pinching and peevishness motivated her spinster aunt more than any gossipy secrets, yet all she knew about Justine she'd heard during Katherine's visits and her mother's childhood recollections. Justine had never once come to see them at the Perkins home, and mostly looked down her nose at them during the family funerals that had brought them together through the years.

Katherine chortled, and in a conspiratorial voice she said, "Justine will tell you she takes these morning walks for her health—which she does—and that she prefers to shop because she thinks I do poorly at it. But woe unto the person who tries to unpack her basket when she returns."

"Why?" she asked, intrigued by this little mystery.

"Because her first stop is the tobacco shop, and then she buys a dime novel or two, and the groceries go on top, to hide her little habits. Sundays, when the shops are closed, can be particularly trying if she doesn't stock up enough on the day before."

Celesta's mouth dropped open. "Justine *smokes?*"

"Like a locomotive. Rolls her first cigarette on the way home—which is why she shops early," the little woman twittered, "and she puffs during the day as

16

she cleans the upstairs—which is why *she* cleans there, you see. And each evening after dinner she retires to her room, opens her window, and inhales one cigarette after another while she sits glued to some pulpy-paged western."

The thought of her extremely proper aunt being riveted by tales of Buffalo Bill or Calamity Jane, a cigarette dangling from her lips, was more than she could fathom. Celesta looked closely at Katherine, wondering if her imagination was working over-time. "And how do you know this?" she asked slyly.

"Know?" Katherine exclaimed. "Why do you think binoculars and keyholes were invented, child?"

Celesta laughed out loud, because she had no trouble at all envisioning this little woman spying on her sister-in-law. After the strain of the past few days, it felt wonderful to lose herself in such a tantalizing joke at Justine's expense. She grasped Katherine's fragile hand, both of them still giggling, and almost revealed a secret about herself that this aunt would find amazing and amusing.

But it was too soon. The writing Celesta did was a personal success she'd shared only with Mama, an outlet for her adventurous fantasies that could now occupy her empty moments and supply a small income she might need someday.

She squeezed her aunt's hand fondly. "Far be it from me to upset Justine's routine, then," she said lightly. "What can I do for *you* while I'm here? Perhaps staying out of her way and keeping you company can be my particular talent."

Katherine's eyes misted over, and the network of tiny lines around her eyes rose with her soft smile. "That would be lovely, dear. After I clear the table I usually see to the gardens, in the cool of the morning. It gets me out of this musty old house and gives Justine a chance to whisk her little habits up to her room when she returns."

Celesta smiled at the woman's sense of human nature and wondered how she'd tolerated her sister-in-law's domineering ways in the year since Ambrose drowned. She supposed it was a skill she, too, should hone, since her status as an outsider put her at the mercy of whomever she lived with.

When she stepped out into the garden, however, her gloomy thoughts dissipated like the dew that glistened in the rainbow of blossoms before her. The small stone courtyard was edged with impatiens that burst forth in orchids, pinks, and oranges, set off by the deep green foliage of red geraniums and ivy that climbed the fortresslike wall of the house. A stone path, lined on both sides with yellow-orange marigolds, led to a white latticework gazebo perched on the edge of the lawn, overlooking the wooded cliffs that tumbled down to the river.

At that moment the sun peeked out from behind a cloud, lending the whole panorama a sparkle that took Celesta's breath away. She knew immediately that this was where Katherine found sanctuary from an overbearing relative, where she sought solace for the loss of her beloved Ambrose and now for Rachel.

Her aunt came out the door tying a floppy-brimmed bonnet beneath her chin, smiling with cherubic glee. "Isn't *this* a morning?" she chirped, clasping her hands as she gazed eagerly at her flowers. "Let's see to the vegetables first. There should be enough green beans for our dinner, and plenty of onions and radishes. The lettuce has probably run amuck since I last cut any."

Celesta followed her around the corner of the imposing stone mansion, through a break in the honeysuckle hedge. Here, in a large, sunny clearing, lay the most perfectly manicured garden she'd ever seen. Along the far edge stood rows of sweet corn, staked tomato plants tied with calico strips, and potatoes just starting to bloom. Leafy bean plants rippled in the breeze, flanked by onion tops standing at attention and the lighter, brighter ruffles of lettuce and radishes. Not a single weed dared invade the rows or the hoed strips of brown earth between them!

"This is truly your calling, Aunt," she murmured. "Eula's flowers pale beside yours, and she buys her produce uptown rather than dirtying her clothes with digging."

Katherine's face lit up with pride as she handed her a flour sack she'd brought from the house. "Plants make marvelous companions, Celesta. They keep me busy, they put food on our table . . . and they refuse to produce for your aunt Justine," she added smugly.

She leaned over, gently lifting the nearest heart-shaped leaves, and gasped. "My word, would you look at these beans! We'll have a big potful to eat and enough to put up several jars for winter. We'd best get busy!"

The two of them hunkered over and picked in companionable silence for several minutes, dropping handfuls of firm, slender beans into their cloth sacks. With the sunshine soaking through her cotton blouse and the garden's earthy perfume rising around her, Celesta felt alive again, aware of colors and textures and senses that had been dulled by the shock of her mother's sudden death. It felt good to sweat. Her rapidly filling sack made the ache in her back and shoulders worth the effort.

Beside her, Katherine sighed and kept on plucking beans. "You know, it puzzles me a little, your mother's passing does. She looked fine that morning, when I stopped for a moment on my way home from sewing circle."

"She was in a wonderful mood: we enjoyed our mornings when Eula went to her charity meetings and Patrick was at his office. We'd done the laundry and hung it out, and we were beating rugs when one of her headaches started," Celesta replied quietly.

"Bright sunlight and the heat affected her that way."

"It's too early to be this warm," Katherine agreed dolefully.

"And when she asked me to bring her usual tea and toast upstairs, we assumed she'd be recovered in time to cook supper." She cleared the thickness from her throat, concentrating on the blurring beans so that she wouldn't go crazy from remembering what happened next. "You know how she heaped sugar into her tea?"

"I like my tea like I like my men—strong and sweet," her aunt mimicked, just as Mama had said it hundreds of times over the years.

"Yet she complained it tasted bitter. Had no more uttered the words than she went into convulsions." Celesta swallowed hard, blinded by tears that plopped onto the plants beneath her. "I didn't know what to do. And I didn't dare leave Mama alone."

"You poor dear, I didn't mean to upset you all over again," her aunt crooned, and then she reached over to embrace Celesta. They straightened up, hugging each other until their sniffles subsided. "She was so pink and pretty in her casket, it seemed impossible that she could be gone. Rachel used to blush that way when your father would whisper in her ear."

With a hasty knuckling of her eyes, Celesta resumed her picking. The garden was in full sun, and the dew was turning to steam already—not a day frail aunts should spend toiling in the heat. After she composed herself, she took up the thread of Katherine's conversation. "What was he like, my father? Mama never said much about him."

"There weren't words to describe the way he tore her heart out when he left." She heaved her bulging sack farther down the row and kept on picking. "Ian Montgomery came on like a race horse, fast and flashy. Your mother was the envy of every girl in Hannibal when he married her after a whirlwind,

20

high-society courtship. Your grandfather saw through him from the first; but he could never deny Rachel whatever her heart desired, so he went along with the marriage. Eleven months later you were here and Ian was gone. Vanished from the face of the earth, so it seemed."

"Was he handsome?"

"Heart-stoppingly so." A grin twitched on her aunt's lips. "Justine was green with envy—Ian was old enough to be *her* beau instead of her little sister's, you see. And she was quick to cry 'I told you so' when he left, which was all the reason your mother needed never to return home again. It broke your grandfather's heart, knowing his favorite, Rachel, lived clear across town with his only grandchild, but he understood her stubborn pride. She got it from him."

Celesta smiled to herself. The one thing no one could take from Mama was her pride, and it was a small comfort that even in death Rachel Ransom Montgomery's face radiated a serene confidence, as though she knew the solution everyone sought and refused to reveal it . . . as though she knew someone had killed her and was plotting her revenge.

The thought startled Celesta, and she stood up too quickly. Who could've possibly wanted Mama dead? And why? Something about that cup of tea—

"Are you all right, child? You're as pale as your flour sack."

Celesta blinked, forcing a smile. "I—I'm fine. Really."

"We'll be done here in a few minutes," Katherine answered as though she didn't completely believe her. "We'll cut some lettuce and put it in the ice box, and then we'll sit out in the gazebo to snap these beans. Always a breeze out there, and always shade."

She chattered on, and Celesta pretended to listen. Her thoughts were galloping, spurred by the sudden revelation that her mother had been yanked into the hereafter by a hand other than God's. But this wasn't the time to lose herself in wild conjecture. Aunt Katherine was hugging her overstuffed bag, trying to lift it without spilling any beans, and it was no job for a lady her size.

"Let me carry these while you cut the lettuce," Celesta said, quickly hefting the bulging sack from Katherine's arms. "And I'll get us some lemonade to sip while we're snapping. Justine'll come home and think we've done nothing all morning, we'll be so cool and refreshed. The idle rich, you know."

A single bead of sweat trickled from each of her aunt's silvering temples, yet the woman's laughter tinkled like a bell. "You were never short on imagination, dear! Let's hope your aunt appreciates your humor as much as I do."

Celesta scowled. "I—I do tend to fly off at the mouth sometimes, and I hope I don't offend—"

"Nonsense!" Katherine wiped her forehead with a dainty brush of her fingers, streaking it with dirt. "We need your sunshine and your smiles, Celesta. I never got to see you as much as I would've liked—didn't want to interfere, or cause trouble for Rachel with Eula Perkins. But I always thought of you as the daughter I could never have. You belong here in your grandfather's house whether Justine thinks so or not. You were his pride and joy to his dying day, the legacy of his heart and soul and irrepressible wit. Which is the very reason she resents you."

It was a lot to think about, being a flesh and blood legacy. A responsibility . . . one more subtle way Aunt Katherine had of manipulating her into staying on here at the manor. Celesta smiled to herself as she carried the sack of beans into the shaded gazebo. For all her romantic notions and apparent fragility, Katherine Ransom was every bit as brazen as Justine when it came to getting what she wanted—she just went after her flies with honey instead of a fly

22

swatter. It was a tactic she recognized easily after serving in the Perkins household all her life, because her endearing aunt and Eula were ladies cut from the same bolt of silk.

And would it be so terrible, returning to the home her mother had denied her? Celesta looked around and could only wonder. The white latticework formed a bower shaded by towering oaks and sweet gums, framed by ferny-leafed mimosa trees with feathery pink blossoms. Roses climbed the sunnier side of the gazebo, in deep shades of cerise, and around the structure's base caladiums danced in the breeze, their showy foliage reminding her of summer-bright watermelon slices. And of course, there was the Mississippi flowing below, the never-changing yet ever-fascinating lifeblood of Hannibal, Missouri.

And as she sat down in the white wooden swing, she felt the gazebo's peacefulness seeping into her. It was a serenity born not of her own need but of generations who must've sat here in seclusion, making the swing creak as their thoughts clarified, hearing the wind sift through the leaves while the water lapped at the shoreline far below. She wanted a life of her own . . . felt obligated to comfort her aunt by staying, yet realized Justine would challenge her presence at every turn . . . yearned to make a name for herself on the newsstands . . . desperately needed to know who killed her mother and why.

"So you've discovered my hideaway." Katherine eased onto the swing beside her, handing her the damp, cold glass of lemonade she'd forgotten to pour. "Many's the hour I've spent here, watching for your uncle Ambrose to return home. The *Phantom* docked just around the bend, you know. How he despised that name, but it was another of your grandfather's macabre little jokes."

"Like saying he'd return to haunt the house after

23

he died?"

"Only the ballroom alcove. Your grandmother, rest her soul, accused him of hiding a jug up there," Katherine recounted fondly, "but in truth, it was their . . . rendezvous. Ambrose Senior was a vital, affectionate man, and I imagine he felt a bit . . . frustrated after his son and I took over the suite adjoining their bedroom, as newlyweds, with his unmarried daughter in the room on the other side of them."

Celesta chuckled at her aunt's delicate phrasing. "They had a love nest? I remember him as a tall, rather forbidding man with dark hair and eyes—"

"Powerful eyes," her aunt whispered.

"—whom people considered a bit odd because he supposedly communed with the spirit world."

Katherine chuckled and sipped her drink. "He staged a séance once, as Halloween party entertainment, and he never lived it down. Loved the notoriety, actually. But your grandfather was a passionate, caring man, deeply in love with Martha, and when she died he lost his very soul. All that remained was this house full of memories, with a sharp-tongued daughter who'd never left the nest and a wild rose who refused to return to it, and a son who never quite measured up. You thought him forbidding, from your little-girl viewpoint, but I think he was just large and lonely and . . . disappointed, after his Martha died."

The words rang with tenderness, and as Katherine gazed out over the river with a faraway look on her face there was another question Celesta felt pressed to ask. "Do . . . do you think Uncle Ambrose drowned when the *Phantom* went down, or could he have been hit over the head by wreckage and lost his memory?"

"My Ambrose is dead and buried somewhere beneath the Mississippi, child," she replied. Her steady hazel eyes reflected the conviction that vibrated in her voice as she gazed at Celesta. "His captain, Bill Thompkins, confirmed it when he brought me his personal effects, but I sensed even before Bill arrived that something fatal had befallen my husband."

Katherine stroked the slatted swing seat between them, her face alight with love. "This gazebo was *our* place, Celesta, and no matter what his father thought of him, Ambrose Ransom, Junior, was a devoted husband with a lust for life and for . . . well, for *me*. Had he survived, he would've found a way to let me know. It gives me great comfort to come here of an evening and think of him . . . and at times his spirit is with me, you know?"

Celesta nodded, her eyes filling with tearful comprehension. "So when Justine implies that he disappeared rather than—"

"Justine thinks men are rather worthless, on the whole," Katherine stated lightly. She reached for a handful of green beans and began to break them into a large stock pot, punctuating her opinions with their steady, crisp snapping. "Which is precisely why men have never taken to *her*. But I know an infinitely more interesting topic than your maiden aunt to gossip about. Don't you, dear?"

Katherine's sly smile made her look almost girlish as she coyly avoided Celesta's questioning glance. Joining in her mental cat-and-mouse, Celesta reached down for a handful of beans herself. Only after she'd popped several into pieces did she end the delicious, quivering silence between them. "Who, then? Eula?"

"Bah! Enough about withered old women."

She raised an eyebrow. "Patrick?"

"Old news! Your mother always thought he was cute, but I find him rather full of himself, don't you?"

Celesta's laughter rang out over the cliff. Leave it

to her astute aunt to puncture a man's reputation with the prick of one remark!

"You can't tell me you've forgotten him, dear. My Lord, I thought your veil was going to catch fire when he lifted it."

Celesta's mouth snapped shut so fast she almost bit her tongue, abruptly silencing her merriment. And even as the telltale color tinged her cheeks, Celesta peppered her denial with indignation. "Mr. Frye's gesture was highly inappropriate—"

"Which was exactly what we all needed!" Aunt Katherine exclaimed. "Eula and I were carrying on over an old wives' tale, and Patrick was ready to smother you and—"

"It was my mother's funeral," Celesta protested. "Any *gentleman* would've refrained from—"

"Oh, I didn't call him a gentleman, but he's certainly a *man,* honey!" The little woman's eyes lit up as she playfully fanned herself. "He paid your mother a sincere compliment and expressed his condolences—which is more than young Mr. Perkins did. And a blind man could've seen his interest in *you!*"

Celesta grabbed another handful of beans, desperately wishing to derail this train of conversation. Her aunt would see right through a denial of the attraction that had flashed like summer lightning between them, or see things that didn't exist at all, in that rose-colored way she had, so there was no changing the subject. But there had to be a way to discount—

"Personally, I never put much store by people's whisperings when he left town," Katherine continued in a thoughtful voice. "Lucy Bates was a mill worker's daughter with bottle-red hair—and we all know why women hit the henna—and Damon couldn't have been more than twenty at the time. He's the dark, brooding, impetuous sort who—"

"Why did I know you'd be babbling about Damon Frye when I returned? Katherine, you do try a body's patience at times."

Celesta and Katherine turned to see Justine standing on the stone walkway behind them, grasping her basket in one hand and a hip with the other. Despite her long walk and the rising temperature, she didn't have a drop of sweat on her. Her gaze was as uncompromising as an ice pick.

"I saw your impertinent Mr. Frye in town this morning," she continued in a tone that suggested her corset was too tight. "He was just leaving the tobacco shop—"

Katherine winked quickly at Celesta.

"—and he had the *gall* to stop me on the sidewalk. Took my hand—right there in front of God and everybody!—and looked at me with those improper eyes of his and said he was sorry about my younger sister's passing."

Justine appeared highly insulted while her sister-in-law, with another imperceptible wink, sank lower in the swing and let her head loll back. "I would've fainted dead away," she said in a theatrical whisper.

"And I would've left you in a heap, you ridiculous—" Justine stood straighter, realizing her lecture fell on unsympathetic ears. She turned her attention to Celesta, her brown eyes narrowing. "And you, young lady, should take heed lest you follow in your mother's footsteps. Ian Montgomery was just such a flash-in-the-pan as this Frye is, and—"

"You can't fault him for expressing his condolences, Aunt Justine," she said quietly.

"—it's blatantly obvious to me that—what? What did you say to me, Niece?"

Celesta cleared her throat, intimidated by her spinster aunt's diatribe, yet she'd be damned if she'd kiss this woman's too-sensible shoes. "I merely stated

27

that Mr. Frye was extending his sympathies, which is certainly within the bounds of propriety."

As though Justine had been eavesdropping and knew of Celesta's switch from denying Damon to defending him, she slowly pointed her free hand like a pistol. "Mark my words, Miss Montgomery," she said in a loaded voice. "Damon Frye was dealing from the devil's deck when he left Lucy Bates in the lurch, and now he's caught *your* scent. I won't have him sniffing around here like a mutt waiting for a morsel to fall from my table. I won't have it!"

Chapter 3

I'll have her, by God! By hook or by crook, Celesta Montgomery will be mine!

Damon Frye chuckled smugly as he gazed toward town. The distance and the thick foliage kept Ransom Manor from his view, but every boy who'd grown up in Hannibal knew the place—had ventured up Holliday's Hill, heart pounding on a double dare, to sneak a peek at vampirish Ambrose Ransom and bring away proof that he'd invaded the old spook's premises. Plucking the flower that would soon reside within those walls was a mission far more daring than his childhood escapades, but claiming Celesta was worth the risks, worth the careful planning it would require to make her his own.

He stood near Lucy's headstone, recalling his first glimpse of Celesta as though minutes rather than a day had elapsed since he beheld her breathtaking loveliness. Beneath her black veil, her green eyes had challenged his impetuous gesture—eyes the color of a cat's, with the same feline hint of secrets yet to be revealed. Raven hair and well-defined brows set off a complexion with the glow of a ripened peach. A distinct widow's peak and a jawline that tapered into a defiant chin gave her a haunting heart-shaped face, and her lips. . . .

He'd spent the past twenty-four hours in a fantasy

where Celesta had finally succumbed to the flame he'd ignited within her shapely, impassioned body. Damon hadn't given a thought to the pigtailed maid's daughter with the missing teeth since he left town ten years ago, and now he couldn't get her startling beauty out of his mind. The decade between their ages meant nothing now that they were adults. Consenting adults. He'd seen it in the parting of her generous mouth and in the spark that lit up her bewitching eyes. He was going to have her, and she knew it.

And Patrick Perkins knew it, too. That alone was motive enough for stalking the delectable Miss Montgomery! And in the darkest realms of his heart, Damon realized it was his most compelling reason to steal her from Patrick's possessive grasp. To watch Perkins flush and stamp his pampered foot and then grovel . . . what a gratifying sight, after these years of his own torment. He'd returned to Hannibal to oversee the construction of Rockcliffe, but business would certainly be mixed with pleasure when the heir to Perkins Lumber paid a debt that was long overdue.

Damon glanced about Mount Olivet Cemetery, his thoughts returning to the present. Heavy, gray clouds were rolling in, and the temperature had dropped, sure signs a storm was brewing. Laying the larger of his two red roses upon Lucy's grave, he studied her plain, gray headstone. LUCINDA BATES, the block-shaped lettering declared. 1864-1889. No mention of the back-alley end she'd come to or her relationship to the people buried beside her— the parents who had disowned her.

Damon sighed with the futility of all the if-onlys: if only Lucy hadn't tried to use her pregnancy as a trap; if only she'd given him time to consider her predicament; if only her father had acted out of remorse instead of rage, perhaps his vibrant, red-haired fiancée wouldn't have downed the potion that

30

killed the baby she carried and her along with it.

"But you brought it on yourself, Lucy," he murmured aloud. He could say that with a conviction born of truth, even as the sight of her grassy grave tore into his heart. He'd done his agonizing while completing his education, and his mending while starting out with an architectural firm in St. Louis. And now that his conscience was clear he could get on with his life . . . could perhaps avenge Lucy's untimely death in a way he hadn't anticipated until yesterday, while gazing into Celesta's innocent face.

A raindrop splattered his cheek, and Damon Frye hastened to the freshly raked grave of Rachel Montgomery. With reverence he placed the second rose upon her resting place: she'd been wronged by the rumormongers, another victim of a man who had disappeared, yet she'd remained kind—generous with her smiles despite her misfortune.

"You have a lovely daughter," he whispered. "She'll need your strength and courage these next few months, Rachel. Forgive me for what I'm about to do."

As though responding to his roguish intent, lightning flashed across the sky. A gust of wind sent the trees into a swaying, frantic dance, accompanied by an eerie whistling that sounded like Satan calling errant souls back to hell. The ominous sky opened up and shot a barrage of cold, wet bullets at him.

Not a man who believed in omens, Frye turned up his collar against the downpour and strode toward the graveyard's gate, extremely pleased with his plan of action.

The bansheelike wail of the wind sent Celesta to the alcove's small window so that she could watch the impending storm. From this third-floor vantage point, Ransom Manor's stately oaks appeared to be possessed by demons, the way they shuddered and moaned. Their high, oddly formed branches seemed to clutch at the blackening clouds like skeletal hands clawing up from a grave.

She smiled at the macabre image, which was inspired by Grandfather Ransom's spine-tingling stories. One of her clearest childhood memories was of sitting in his lap listening to tales that made Katherine and her mother protest she wouldn't sleep, but that wasn't so. His greatest gift to her was his keen appreciation of the night, and of nature's grand fury during a thunderstorm. This dark-and-stormy atmosphere awed rather than frightened her: these outbursts of wind and rain and lightning brought fond memories of Ambrose Ransom, Senior, before his death. Before Justine's sharp tongue and her mother's pride ended her visits to Ransom Manor.

Glancing around the darkening alcove, with its steeply pitched ceiling and dusty plank floor, Celesta felt his presence and smiled. His walnut secretary stood beside her, a lumpy candle still drooping over its brass holder after all these years. As a girl she'd assumed the threadbare settee along the wall was a cast-off, and learning its true purpose from Katherine this morning had added a humorous, human dimension to the grandfather who'd intimidated her at times with his sonorous voice and piercing, dark eyes. Steamer trunks, old hat boxes, musty books crammed into forgotten bookcases . . . the very stillness of the heat on this floor added to the intrigue of this supposedly haunted hideaway.

She'd already decided that should she stay on, this remote room would be her retreat from two aunts who wouldn't understand—much less approve of!— the stories she wrote. This would be her imagination's nest, a place to write and recover from her mother's death—a place her manuscripts would be safe from prying eyes, because Katherine half believed the ballroom was haunted and Justine never cleaned up here. They hadn't hosted a ball for years, so there was little point.

Another bolt of lightning snaked toward the earth, followed by a bright flash and then a sharp, splintering sound. Celesta gasped. A huge tree limb was now lying across the flattened gazebo. Aunt Katherine would be beside herself—would see it as an evil force seeking to destroy her Ambrose's spirit. Justine would probably hire a man to clear away the rubble rather than rebuild her fanciful sister-in-law's haven.

The sudden deluge made Celesta pull her head inside. She should go downstairs to comfort Katherine, who feared these storms. She should perform some worthwhile task to convince Justine she deserved the food she ate and the lumpy mattress she slept on. But instead, she watched the majestic play of light and darkness and thought of Damon Frye. Surely he was the personification of such a tempestuous night!

Again she saw his dark, probing eyes, the chestnut hair that fell rakishly over his forehead, and the cleft in his shadowy chin. His blatant disregard for her grief, not to mention his brazen behavior toward Justine uptown, was reason enough to avoid his company. And such conceit, to say they'd meet again on a happier day, with no regard for her feelings on the matter!

Celesta felt the color creeping into her cheeks, just as it had in the cemetery. She pulled a yellowed envelope from the desk to fan herself, even as she realized this burst of heat had nothing to do with the alcove's stuffiness. Why did she suffer such a reaction to this self-centered man? Why did she tingle where he'd touched her cheek yesterday, when he was blocks away, his interest in her probably forgotten by now?

She had no answers. She only knew that Damon Frye's unexpected, unexplained return to Hannibal boded her ill. His wolfish intentions were quite clear.

His dusky grin was warning enough that he deserved every uncomplimentary rumor spread about his past, and his treatment of Lucy Bates proved him to be as cruel and callous as he looked.

Yet when Celesta's glance fell to the worn-out sofa she shuddered, as though she were a marionette at the mercy of a mad puppeteer. She shook her head to clear it of a brief yet powerful image of Damon's corded, masculine body pressing her into its cushions, and fled downstairs to safety.

The intense morning sun made Celesta squint as she stepped out onto the white-enameled veranda of the Perkins home. Her wicker basket was piled high with writing supplies and a few stories she needed to finish, as well as colorful skeins of yarn Katherine had asked her to buy—the perfect props to cover her most urgent reason for coming to this house on North Fifth so early. "Thanks for giving me Mr. Cramer's name. My aunt knew you could recommend a carpenter for us," she said, hoping she didn't sound jittery. "She was awfully upset when that branch crashed through the gazebo."

"And to think she was sitting there only moments before the storm," Eula replied with a shake of her head. Her strawberry-blond curls were crushed from sleep, and she was still wearing her satin wrapper. "Mort Cramer does repair work at the lumberyard, and I'm sure he'll be prompt and reasonable for you. My goodness but it's hot! That shower we had a while ago will leave the weeds in my flower beds easier to pull, but it's so *sultry* to be working outside."

Celesta nodded. She knew exactly how hot it was because the walk into town had made her dark calico dress cling to her neck and under her arms. Aunt Katherine's lament that she was short of yarn for her new sampler was the perfect excuse to follow a hunch she'd had in the night—a hunch that led her to the Perkins pantry before Eula was up to catch her sifting through the sugar bowl.

But Mrs. Perkins rose earlier these days, seeing to Patrick's breakfast. She'd raised an eyebrow when she saw Celesta coming from the kitchen, yet she seemed to accept the explanation for her visit: "I wanted my writing supplies—so I could occupy myself with my journal—and I thought I'd be sure there were no more dead mice in the pantry while I was here. I know how mice upset you."

Eula had agreed to that readily enough, but she watched Celesta closely during their conversation. Why hadn't she anticipated the change in Mrs. Perkins's morning routine and had an alibi ready? Any woman would be suspicious if her help slipped in unannounced when she was supposedly consoling her grief-stricken aunt.

And now Eula was hinting broadly about how troublesome life was without a housekeeper, and that perhaps she'd have to pay a higher wage to attract a suitable replacement for Rachel. Just her usual patter, as though she were actually glad that Celesta had stopped by and was fishing for an assurance that she'd resume her post in the Perkins home.

Celesta smiled, glancing nervously at her basket. "Thank you for allowing me to fetch a few things from my room. I—I know I've inconvenienced you by staying with Aunt Katherine these past—"

"Think nothing of it, dear," Eula replied sweetly. "The poor thing needs all the comfort she can find, living with that sister-in-law of hers. And I know how she'll miss sitting in her gazebo until it's repaired."

She paused for a moment, studying Celesta with shining eyes that suggested she was up to something. Then her hand fluttered to the neck of her nightgown. "Do you suppose Patrick could bring me to visit her, say, Saturday afternoon? He could check on

Mort's progress while I chat with Katherine—if it wouldn't be any trouble," she added quickly.

"I'm sure she'd enjoy that," Celesta stammered, "but if Patrick's too busy—"

"Oh, he'll be happy to come," Eula interrupted with that same mischievous twinkle. "Why, just this morning he was wondering how you were. He misses having you around, dear. We both do."

"Well. Thank you." Suddenly anxious to be anywhere but here, Celesta stepped toward the stairs. "I certainly appreciate your indulgence regarding my decision, Mrs. Perkins. And if Aunt Katherine's perkier by Saturday, I—I'm sure I'll have an answer for you."

"That would be fine, dear. You have a good day now, and tell your aunts we're thinking of them. Don't go to any fuss for our visit, all right?"

Celesta forced a bright smile, waving as she descended between the ornate white porch railings. Eula's suggesting a visit was a bolt from the blue, because the wealthy lumber baron's widow had always deemed the Ransom women beneath her . . . perhaps because the youngest became her maid. Saturday's visit was one she didn't relish. Everyone would be tense until she announced her decision, and either Aunt Katherine or Eula Perkins would end up disappointed with her. She couldn't win.

But her future livelihood had been the farthest thing from her mind when she'd sneaked into the Perkins house this morning. Celesta sensed the little packet of sugar she'd secreted beneath Katherine's yarn would put her no closer to solving Mama's murder, but she had to do *something*. As she'd stared out at last night's storm, comprehension had flashed like lightning: Mama had complained that her tea was *bitter*. . . . In her anxiety, Celesta had returned the tray—including a ceramic sugar bowl only she and Mama used—to the pantry with the lid still off. The dead mouse on the floor the next morning should've been an immediate red flag, but her thoughts had been fogged by shock and grief.

Mama had been poisoned.

She should've known. The research for one of her stories had told of various ways criminals had concealed arsenic and strychnine in food; accused axe murderess Lizzie Borden had laced her parents' sugar bowl with a form of cyanide, according to the police reports. Anyone could purchase those deadly powders to kill household pests without arousing suspicion.

So who killed Rachel Montgomery?

Eula and Patrick had access to the pantry, but why would either of them do away with the woman who kept their lives running so smoothly? Even Aunt Katherine had the opportunity: she knew Mama sweetened her tea, and she *had* walked through the house that day, knowing Eula was at a meeting, before finding them outside at the clothesline. But it was absurd to think Katherine Ransom had the nerve, let alone the motive, to murder her sister-in-law. The only other alternative was that Mama herself had. . . .

But that, too, seemed outlandish, and these ideas were so odious that fresh tears made Celesta mop her face with her sleeve. When she realized her mental sleuthing had taken her past houses she hadn't even seen at a pace that made the perspiration slither down her spine, Celesta stopped beneath a shade tree.

Out of habit, her feet had traveled up Bird Street, where the grandest residence Hannibal had ever seen was in its second year of construction. John Cruikshank, owner of the largest lumber company west of the Mississippi, was building a home that showcased the finest woods and most lavish appointments money could buy—at an expense that made tongues wag rapidly enough to dry the paste beneath his imported French wallpaper!

While running errands for Patrick and Eula, she'd

37

watched the house rise up from the high, rocky cliff overlooking the river, wondering how it would feel to afford such luxury. Mrs. Perkins berated her competitor's inclusion of a Tiffany stained glass window and chandeliers, and automatic electric lights in the hall closets. Such extravagances made her rambling Queen Anne mansion the *second* finest house in Hannibal now, and it irked Eula sorely.

Celesta chuckled in spite of her agitation, and wandered closer to watch the workmen. This particular crew was painting the majestic front columns on the entry porch and the woodwork around the arched palladium windows. Most of them had already shucked their shirts and were balanced on scaffolding or ladders, their sun-bronzed backs glistening with sweat. The man closest to her— probably a foreman, because he was watching the others intently from the ground—was just now tugging the tail of his shirt out of his tan overalls.

It was a provocative gesture, and Celesta watched, mesmerized. The man's muscular back rippled as he shrugged out of the blue chambray, revealing proud shoulders and a lean, compact body that disappeared into his loosely fitted pants. He gave the shirt a toss, as though he disrobed this nonchalantly every day for the curious folk who stopped to watch the work in progress, and Celesta nipped her lip. Lord, but he was beautiful!

She chided herself for staring at the man, even as she watched him brush the heavy brown hair from his forehead. He turned suddenly, catching her, and Celesta froze.

Damon Frye had sensed an observer's presence, and when he saw who it was he had to clench his teeth to keep from cheering. Fate had delivered the black-haired beauty of his fantasies! Her face was flushed, and she was trembling like a doe cornered by a cougar—and he was ready to pounce!

He advanced slowly, taking in the dark spots

38

where her calico dress clung to her curves, and the shimmering waves of steam that rose around her where the sun warmed the damp grass. Miss Montgomery was about to learn the meaning of heat, the consequences of gazing so boldly at a man who was removing his clothes.

Celesta was stunned. Once again Frye had caught her unawares, and she couldn't flee without drawing even more attention to herself. When her gaze wandered to the powerful bare chest beneath the square bib of Frye's overalls, she forced her eyes to meet his. And damned if he wasn't ogling her, fighting laughter as he realized how embarrassed she was! "Wh-what're *you* doing here?" she blurted.

Damon stopped a few steps in front of her, wondering if she'd break that basket handle, hard as she was gripping it. "Smile when you ask that," he teased, "because you're talking to the new design consultant from Barnett, Haynes, and Barnett of St. Louis, here to supervise the finishing work on the Cruikshank mansion."

Frye was an architect? That explained his return to Hannibal and his presence at this building site, but it did nothing to quell her anxiety. He was looking her over with those rakish brown eyes as though he intended to eat her alive. "I suppose I should be impressed," she muttered.

Damon chuckled, pleased that she wasn't swallowed up by her timidity. His hand ached to retrace the smooth curve of her jaw, to chuck that impudent chin, but he wanted to prolong this delectable game for as long as she'd stand up to him. Celesta's raven hair was pulled up into a becoming Psyche knot that revealed a neck so tempting and slender, with little wisps of loose hair that curled with the humidity. And those eyes . . . he'd get caught in his own trap if he didn't keep talking.

"And what are *you* doing here, Miss Montgomery?" he murmured. "Taking in the scenery, unescorted, can be risky business for a delectable young lady. Even this part of town has its share of lechers lurking in the alleys."

"Or standing right out on the lawn," she retorted, and she turned quickly to walk away from him. Bad enough that he was leering at her, but when he insinuated she'd come here to gawk at—

"Celesta, please," he pleaded, grabbing her arm. "That was uncalled for, and I apologize."

She had no choice but to face him, a prisoner in his grip. Damon's tone was polite enough, but those eyes! They mocked her, and she refused to become a laughingstock in front of his crew. "You were absolutely right, Mr. Frye. I had no business coming here alone—"

"Which is why I'll walk you back." He turned and gave the painters a wave, calling out, "Carry on, boys. I'll return shortly."

Their knowing grins only exasperated Celesta further, and she took off at a trot. The nerve of this conceited cad, to grab her in public and—

"May I carry that heavy basket?"

"No, you may not."

"May we at least slow down and talk like civilized people?"

"Civilized?" Celesta whirled around to glare at him, which was a grave mistake. Frye blocked her retreat down the street, and now that they were out of the workmen's sight she was even more vulnerable than before. "Do you call pawing at me—at my mother's funeral—civilized? And what about accosting my aunt in town—"

"She loved it. Blushed like a schoolgirl."

"—and now you're grabbing at me again!" She yanked her elbow from his grasp, but that only made the muscles in his shoulders ripple beneath his tan overall straps. What right did he have to be so blatantly male, challenging her to step around him? "And quit laughing at me, damn it! Why are you pestering me this way?"

Damon could think of several reasons, and right now finding out how her sweat-beaded, full upper lip would taste was the most compelling. He cleared his throat, trying to resume proper decorum.

"It's because I'm so pleased to see you again, after all these years, that I've forgotten my manners." He glanced down at the basket she was clutching, noting the skeins of yarn atop a stack of paper and envelopes. "I see you've been shopping. Planning to work on some stitchery and catch up on correspondence while you keep your aunts company, by the looks of it."

Celesta shifted the basket's leaden weight to her other hand. "The yarn's for Aunt Katherine's new sampler, and—"

"How is Katherine?" he asked quietly. "Your mother's passing was hard on her, and I'm sure she's been pleased to have your company these past few days."

How did he know so much about her schedule? And how could his rudeness have turned so quickly into sincere interest? She didn't trust Damon Frye any farther than she could kick him, and no matter what his intentions, she couldn't have him trailing along like a pesky pup all the way to Ransom Manor.

"Thank you for your concern," she replied, and then she started down the sidewalk again, toward North Fifth. "Katherine was the only family member kind enough to keep in touch with us these past several years. And now that her husband's gone, consoling her's the least I can do."

Damon hadn't heard about Ambrose Junior's death, and he filed the information away with an inward smile. Celesta's change of direction signaled she was up to something—perhaps a ploy as devious as his own—and her game intrigued him. "I don't imagine she slept well during the storm, then. She doted on Ambrose, as I recall."

"Then, you'll understand why I must be heading home," Celesta said with pointed sweetness. "A huge limb destroyed the gazebo, and I've gotten the name of a carpenter who . . ."

She'd just handed him the key to Ransom Manor, and Damon could hardly keep from grabbing her up and kissing her. He admired her catlike aloofness as she chatted about inconsequential matters—and damned if she wasn't planning to put him off by disappearing into the Perkins place! They were only yards away from the elegant turreted home he remembered from his boyhood . . . where Patrick might be sitting down to his noon meal about now.

". . . so after I talk with Eula for a moment, I really must be on my way." Celesta stopped in front of the white stairway and looked directly at him with a coy yet cunning gaze. "It's been a pleasure to see you again, Mr. Frye. Thank you for your escort. I'm sure your men must be wondering if you've gotten lost."

I'm not the only one about to lose his way, he thought as he studied her lovely face. It was framed by wispy tendrils that tempted his fingers, the fluttering of her long, black lashes betraying her agitation. Celesta turned toward the back entrance, but he wasn't finished toying with her. He continued along the path beside her, walking closer now so that he wouldn't step on the pansies and violets that spilled over the edge of the bricks.

This man wouldn't know a hint if I hit him over the head with it! Celesta sped up, rounding the corner of the house away from the street. Ordinarily the shady seclusion was welcome relief on a hot day, but her temperature was rising with her temper. Ignoring him—all but impossible, with his bare arm brushing against her—she bolted toward the back stairs.

But Frye was faster. Athletic from years of balancing on ladders and hoisting heavy beams, he reached the porch when she did and once more took her in a possessive grasp. "You act like you're afraid of me, Celesta," he said in a low, knowing voice. "Why is that?"

"I—I haven't the faintest idea what you mean."

His chuckle sounded wicked even to his own ears, and the tender pulse that was fluttering inside his grip only coaxed him on. "It's because I'm a man with an unsavory past," he answered. "A man who fascinates you anyway. I'm everything your family ever warned you against, Celesta, and you can't resist the . . . danger I represent."

Not only had he backed her toward the wall of the house, but he'd read her mind! He *was* unsavory, and indecently handsome, and dangerous—and all the more alluring because of it. A hundred times she'd relived his caress in the cemetery, telling herself Damon Frye could only bring her trouble and pain, yet here they were alone on Eula's back porch, in a dim corner where the clematis sheltered them from any passersby and the solid wall of the house kept their secret from anyone inside. It was a frightening moment, standing close enough to smell his musky sweat and study the shadowed cleft of his chin . . . and by far the most exciting moment of her life.

He paused, regretting that he'd forced her into a position they might regret. But the sweet cleanness of her, and the rapid rise and fall of her chest as she gaped at him, offering up her innocence despite her fear, erased any honorable way out. This was, after all, the moment he'd been waiting for: the meeting he'd promised her two days ago.

He inched forward until she was flat against the house—not that she showed any inclination to escape him. "May I ask you something, Celesta?" he demanded in a husky whisper.

She opened her mouth, but Damon's kiss stifled her reply. He pressed into her, sending all rational thought skittering like leaves before the hurricane force of his desire. The basket dropped from her hand—she heard its contents slip out across the slick wooden floor—and still he was kissing her with an intensity that stunned her.

Even more stunning was her body's reaction to him. Schoolboys had stolen an occasional kiss behind the stairs, but nothing had prepared her for the all-consuming fire this man was kindling inside her. His mouth was opening and closing, leading hers in an exchange mere words couldn't describe. His broad hands rested on her shoulders, kneading, massaging. . . .

What was that sound from inside the house? Weakly Celesta reached up to push him away, but Damon caught her by the wrists and then trapped her even more effectively by parting her thighs with his knee. With a low moan, he released her lips and gazed pointedly at her. "If you scream," he murmured, "someone's bound to come out here and see what you've allowed me to do to you."

Damn him and his arrogance! Celesta gasped for breath, glaring at him with all the wrath she could muster. "How dare you threaten me by—"

"Ah, but the threat's only just begun, Celesta," he murmured back. She was trembling beneath him, but he sensed her awakening passion was partly to blame. He kissed her fingertips, allowing her to catch her breath before his next onslaught, because now that he held her captive he wasn't about to let her go before he tasted more.

Grinning subtly, he drew her hands down over his chest, brushing the dark curls with fingers that quaked but didn't pull away. *Celesta, you'll soon be mine,* he vowed as he watched the wonder and apprehension battle upon her face. *We both know it, and we know we'll regret it. Just as we know it can't happen any other way.*

She swallowed hard. Why was she allowing him liberties no decent man would ask of her? The hair on his chest tickled her palms, and then he was dragging

44

them down the front of his twill overalls, along the firm, muscled ridge of his rib cage and the flatness of his stomach. Lord, if he went any lower—

But he sucked in his breath, shifting as though he was more caught up in this devious escapade than he'd planned, and guided her arms around his waist instead. "Who would've thought you'd grow into such a temptation?" he breathed. "Who could've guessed we'd meet again at this house, to satisfy our passions right under Patrick's nose?"

Patrick! He could be eating his dinner now, just on the other side of this wall. "Damon, please let me—"

"Oh, I'll let you," he said with a devilish grin, and he shoved her hands beneath the back of his overalls, forcing her to embrace him even more closely.

He had nothing else on! When her hands met the smooth, damp skin of his behind, Celesta jerked as though she'd been branded by a red-hot iron. Damon anticipated her yelp and stifled it with another searing kiss, this time plunging his tongue between her teeth. He was hot and virile and brutally delicious, but damn him, he was trying to get caught! Mr. Frye was as set on flaunting his prowess for Patrick as he was determined to steal the last shreds of her respectability.

Celesta thrashed, her head thumping against the wooden siding as she struggled to escape. The knee between her legs moved higher. She could feel his maleness pressing against her stomach, could feel him shaking with laughter and passion, and still she couldn't break free. Now Damon had entwined his fingers between hers and was placing the backs of her hands on the wall, sliding them upward until the full length of him was resting against her, his arms atop hers, as though their bodies were stretched flat against a mattress.

Then he raised his face to gaze at her. "Celesta," he whispered fervently, "Celesta, you've been more than sporting about all this, so I'll let you go after one more kiss—if you promise me I can see you again."

What kind of deal was that? If she agreed, she'd subject herself to these dangerous trysts for as long as he cared to entrap her. And if she refused, Damon Frye would do what he pleased with her anyway. Celesta lowered her eyes. "All right," she sighed, figuring it was the quickest way not to get caught here by either Eula or Patrick.

He smiled ruefully. "Has it been that terrible, sweetheart? Kiss me now," he coaxed in a throaty voice. "Take the lead, and I'll prove what a gentle lover I can be. Your wish is my command."

As though changed by magic, the man who held her captive waited patiently for her to take him prisoner in turn. A tiny rivulet of sweat had trailed down his cheek and pooled in that maddening cleft. His eyes were now as soft and sweet as melted chocolate . . . a treat she'd craved since she could remember.

When Celesta closed her eyes, he moaned softly and let her tender, unstudied kiss take control of him. Her tongue explored the satiny wetness of his inner lips, and now that he'd regained a fragment of her trust, Miss Montgomery was complying with his plan as playfully and seductively as he'd hoped.

When she drew away, he claimed her mouth again ever so lightly, nibbling at the fullness of her kiss-swollen lips until she sighed against him, sounding utterly content. Next time she'd surrender far more to him, but for now he was satisfied that he'd planted the seed of her desire, and that with careful, constant attention it would blossom into a passionate need that only he could fulfill.

Celesta was gazing raptly into his face when the screen door flew open and Patrick Perkins stomped onto the porch. "And what the hell's going on *here?*" he demanded.

Chapter 4

She felt her face go clammy, yet it could've been worse: it could've been Eula who found her wedged between the wall and Damon Frye's half-naked body. "I—I was stopping by to pick up a few things, when—"

"Mother said you were here earlier," Patrick challenged, his blue eyes accusing her of every sin she could name. Then he glared at Frye, who slowly lifted himself off her and knelt to pick up the papers and yarn that were strewn across the porch. "And what are *you* saying about this?"

Damon looked up from his task, shrugging. "I escorted her here, and she gave me a kiss in return. A favor few men would refuse, I imagine."

Patrick heard his smugness and suspected he'd warped the truth, probably to reopen the wound that had festered between them since they were young men. And as he took in Celesta's guilty flush, noting the extraordinary beauty of her awakening passions, he also knew he'd have to win her now or lose her, along with the ambitions he'd only recently dared to dream of. She was his ticket out of a tight spot, and he would *not* let Frye steal her away.

"I didn't mean to insinuate you were to blame for this," he said as he approached her. "Apparently ten

47

years' absence has done nothing to improve Mr. Frye's code of honor. Did he hurt you, Celesta? Are you all right?"

Celesta glared first at Damon's overalled backside and then at the blue-eyed blond before her, wondering who to throttle first. Of *course* Frye had passed the burden of guilt to her—and now Patrick was acting all solicitous and protective while his flushed neck betrayed his anger. All his life he'd been a sweet-talker, when it suited his purpose, and she wasn't falling for this change of heart.

"I'm fine, thank you," she replied stiffly. "Now, if you'll let me pick up the rest of my—"

"It's the least Frye can do for you, under the circumstances." Patrick's gaze roamed over her face, and he squeezed her elbow. "Stay here. After I send him on his way, we'll talk."

His proprietary tone didn't improve her mood, and as she watched Damon Frye stack the last of her papers in the basket, she quailed suddenly. What would he say about that packet of sugar she'd hidden? Surely it had slipped out with Aunt Katherine's yarns, and if he asked her about it, she'd have to confess her main reason for stopping by earlier.

Damon, however, placed the colorful skeins of worsted on top of her papers and then presented her with the wicker basket, unruffled. "I enjoyed our stroll, Miss Montgomery," he said with a subtle smile, "and any time you'd care to see more of the Cruikshank mansion, I'd be pleased to show you around."

Frye winked at her, and then faced Patrick Perkins with his stoniest expression. The lumber heir sported a fashionable suit and freshly cut golden waves—the essence of breeding and acceptability, as always—but he was at a disadvantage now, and they both knew it. "Is there nothing you wish to say before you send

48

me away?'' he mocked. "After all we shared while growing up, I'm puzzled by your hostility."

Patrick struggled against a retort that would make him look foolish—or worse—to Celesta. "I suppose you have a legitimate reason for being back?''

"I'm the new consultant supervising the finishing of John Cruikshank's house. The ultimate confirmation of the expertise I've acquired, through diligent study and on-the-job experience."

Perkins gripped his suspenders to keep from strangling this brazen intruder, who dared to parade his bronzed body and career achievements. He couldn't help it he'd inherited his father's lucrative lumber business, any more than Frye had chosen a humbler background to be born into. But damn it, he would *not* be slighted on his own back porch!

"Am I supposed to congratulate you?" he asked archly. "The house was well under way before you showed up. All I've seen so far is your blatant disregard for proper conduct—and for Celesta's grief. Haven't you ruined enough lives in this town?"

With a sly glance toward his conquest, who was following their exchange with wary eyes, Damon smiled. *"Au contraire,"* he replied in a silken voice, "I was paying my respects to Celesta's indomitable spirit and her rare beauty. Perhaps having lived with them all these years, you don't appreciate her attributes the way I do."

Perkins stepped forward, his nostrils pinched. "Lucy had spirit and beauty, too—or have you forgotten?" he demanded in a terse whisper. "We all know how *she* ended up, and I won't have you disgracing Celesta the same way."

The men glowered at each other, brown eyes challenging blue, and Celesta wanted to disappear between the floorboards. She resented being the object of their conflicting desires, but all she could do was watch them at war and wonder what had caused these animosities. Before Damon's return, Patrick had regarded her as part of the furniture, and now. . . .

Frye crossed his muscled arms with leisurely self-assurance. The little rich boy bristling at him had always relied upon changing the subject and wheedling his way out of trouble, which worked with his mother and most females, but that tactic was about to defeat him now.

"You, and everyone else, are quick to remind me that my fiancée died in my absence," he said in a low voice. "*I* didn't suggest she take that potion, and I would've married her anyway, given a little time to consider the consequences of her condition."

"Her *condition?*" Patrick blurted. "As though you had nothing to do with it! Her father was a hotheaded mill worker, and her mother stayed drunk and out of his way. How long did you think Lucy'd last under that roof, pregnant and abandoned?"

Frye chuckled wryly. "Bates worked for your father, Patrick, and your mother's a director at the Home for the Friendless. If you were so concerned, why didn't *you* take care of her? Or, since we were once close friends, why didn't you talk her out of that trip to the other side of the tracks, and notify me about how desperate she truly was? Two days after I returned to school, understandably shaken by her announcement, she was gone."

As his temper rose, Patrick felt his collar choking off what remained of his reasoning power. "I will *not* take the blame for any of that! Get out of here, Frye. If you come around again, or if I learn you've been meddling with Celesta, I'll notify the police. Perhaps their memories need refreshing about the sort of man you are."

Chuckling, Damon smiled at Celesta. "Miss Montgomery doesn't seem to mind my meddling," he said, his tone more pointed now, "and she's certainly old enough to decide who she'll be seen with. Take care that *you* don't overstep any bounds with her, either, Perkins. A gentleman remembers his station in life. He learns from the past rather than repeating it."

Frye descended the steps, and with a last sultry glance at Celesta he swaggered around the side of the house as though he intended to see her again at the earliest opportunity. She was watching after him, her knuckles a white, ridged ring around the basket handle and the vein above her collar pulsing visibly. So damned pretty—how had he not truly *see* her all these years?

Patrick cleared his throat to break a silence as stifling as the noonday heat, knowing he couldn't compensate for his past lack of attention but determined to anyway. "I—I'm sorry if our unpleasantness upset you," he began quietly. "Frye has an irritating habit of placing his own wishes—and his limited version of the truth—above everyone else's."

"You're right," Celesta replied, "but I have to be getting back. Aunt Katherine sent me for this yarn hours ago and—"

"Stay. We need to talk."

Even as he said it, he realized he'd have to change his attitude if he expected to win her affections. He took the heavy basket, smiling at Celesta's resistance before she relinquished it, and led her to the porch railing. Its ornate white gingerbread was the symbol of Perkins wealth and status, and as he leaned against the post, lifting a hip onto the broad railing, he hoped it was also a suitable place to declare himself.

His palms felt damp as he drew her near, into an intimate stance that immediately made Celesta brace herself. One more step and she'd be leaning against his leg, among other things, and such a position compromised everything Mama and Eula had drilled into her about proper decorum, about knowing her place. "Patrick, we really shouldn't—what if your mother—"

"I want you back, Celesta."

She stared, unable to respond. His crystal blue eyes delved into hers, highlighting his fervent expression. His grip tightened. Patrick Perkins was sought after by ambitious mothers and aspiring brides alike, the most desirable catch in town, so he had no business flirting with *her!* And Celesta had no reason to assume their lifelong association was anything other than a financial necessity, a choice her mother made shortly after she was born. "You . . . you make it sound as though I've left you, personally, rather than the housekeeping position."

He forced his gaze to remain steady. She was eight years younger but always smarter, this dark-haired waif, and he had to overcome her acuity without overlooking it. "You *have* left me," he pleaded softly. "These few days without you have shown me how much your presence means to me . . . and how blind I've been not to see you as more than a household fixture. Frye's right about one thing: you're a lovely young woman, Celesta."

Damon's name broke the spell he was weaving with his honeyed voice, reminding her that she was caught between the two rivals and didn't want to be. "It's not as though I were yours to—"

"But you could be." Patrick closed his eyes, keenly aware of his thundering pulse and the dreams she was picking apart with her damned questions. He'd wanted to woo her slowly, allow her and Mother time to get used to this idea, but Frye was forcing his hand. "We've known each other all our lives, Celesta. This has always been your home, and it still could be, with you as its mistress rather than its maid. I've always envisioned you in fine clothes, decked out with jewelry—"

"How well did you know Lucy Bates?"

He nearly toppled backward off the railing. The young woman he held so tightly by the hands wasn't falling for his sweet allusions—and she wouldn't, until he drove all other distractions from her mind. Celesta was known for her dogged persistence and her unwavering pursuit of the truth . . . and he'd give it to her, after a fashion.

"You didn't have to know Lucy to sympathize with her situation," he hedged. "Poor girl lived with a demanding, self-righteous father and a doormat of a mother, and then along comes Frye with his promises. Which turned out to be hollow, after he let nature take its course and let *her* take the blame for it."

Celesta regarded him closely, noting his heightened color as he repeated the usual rumors. There was something deeper here, infinitely more interesting than letting him paint her into pretty pictures after discovering her in Damon's arms. "I was only nine or ten when all this came about," she continued, "but as I recall, Mr. Frye came from a respectable family that was fairly well off. What did he see in Lucy?"

Why did she insist on discussing Frye when he was trying to propose? Damn her, she was flustering him on purpose! "Lucinda Bates was an attractive, vivacious woman who certainly turned other heads than Damon's," he replied impatiently. "And any one of them would've treated her better than he did."

He was sounding like a broken record. Celesta smiled coyly, teasing Patrick with the wide-eyed innocence he'd always detested. "Then, why didn't one of them take her in?"

"What man in his right mind would saddle himself with—that was ten years ago, Celesta!" he protested, moving his grip to her elbows. "I only challenged Frye about his behavior to save you from the same fate. Don't fall for his silver-tongued stories, honey. He's only using you to perturb me—"

"And why would he do that?"

Patrick let out an exasperated sigh. "Because I adored you, even when we were children, and even then he wanted to play the spoiler." In desperation he drew her closer, until her maddening, adorable grin was only inches away. "That's why I told him never to bother you again. You were too young then—and too naive now—to defend yourself against him. Forget him, Celesta. He'll only break your heart."

Before she could rebut, Celesta was pulled into an embrace that stunned her. Patrick's kiss was urgent and demanding. He smelled of fine cologne, laundry starch, and linen warmed by the afternoon sun. His hands found the base of her spine and her nape, damply urging her against his body. He was undeniably handsome and unquestionably male . . . but the fluttering of his blond lashes against her cheeks told her his flowery phrases were every bit as bogus as Damon Frye's. Sickened, she pulled away.

Patrick's eyes flew open. "Celesta—honey, I—"

Shushing him with a firm finger, she shook her head. "This'll never work and you know it. Goodbye, Patrick."

He watched her grab her basket and hurry down the steps, disgusted—with himself, mostly. She was quick and comely, and he should've gotten her into bed long ago, to establish his superiority in at least one aspect of their relationship. But Frye was forcing him to play catch-up, and he'd bungled it.

Not one to bow to defeat for long, he followed her shapely form around the corner of the house, already planning their Saturday rendezvous. Ransom Manor had several hideaways where they'd be safe from prying eyes while his mother chatted with Katherine, probably for hours. He'd be ready this time. He'd yet to meet a young lady who wouldn't get weak-kneed and naked after he plyed her with words and a trinket or two, and Celesta, sheltered as she was, would be no exception.

A rustling in the nearby bushes made him blink and suck in his breath. His mother, in her broad-brimmed straw bonnet, was coming in from the side yard, garden shears in one hand and a bouquet of daisies in the other.

"How long have *you* been out here?" he blurted.

She started up the stairs, cocking a pale eyebrow at him. "Long enough, son. Long enough."

Chapter 5

When Frye reached his hotel room that night, he closed the door behind him with a grin of anticipation. He reached into the deep pockets of his carpenter's overalls and pulled out a small, folded paper packet and then a fat envelope addressed to Beadle and Adams in New York. Thanks to Perkins, he'd been able to slide these items into his pants while Celesta was distracted by the blond's lecture. Not the most honorable way to satisfy his curiosity about Miss Montgomery, but it was a trick he couldn't resist as he'd picked up her papers.

He sat down at his small dining table and carefully unfolded the packet. Tiny white granules trickled around his fingers and onto the tabletop. Why would she be hiding ordinary salt or sugar beneath her aunt's yarn? Damon sniffed at the white mound in the paper, and then a taste from his moistened fingertip confirmed it to be sugar. She wouldn't have carried it from Ransom Manor, so she must've taken it from the Perkins pantry. But why?

Frowning, he set the sugar aside to study the thick envelope. The name Beadle and Adams sounded familiar, yet when he pulled out a stack of neatly written pages and read the top one, his mouth dropped open: *SALLY SHARPE, GIRL DETEC-*

TIVE, in "THE PEN IS MIGHTIER"—An Adventure by Montgomery C. Lester.

"Well, I'll be damned!" he whispered as his eyes raced over the page. Sally Sharpe was the heroine of a weekly dime novel series, a character whose sleuthing adventures he'd enjoyed for quite some time. And Montgomery C. Lester was none other than Celesta herself! Why hadn't he picked up on the name switch, after all the times he'd read these stories? Who would ever guess this housekeeper's daughter was a popular author?

Chuckling, Damon scanned the entire story. In this episode, the only clues to the victim's demise were two odd puncture wounds near his jugular, similar to those left by a vampire. Since the publication of Bram Stoker's *Dracula* two years ago, bloodsuckers had appeared in numerous fictional tales, but Celesta's practical-minded Sally had discovered an ingenious mode of murder rather than evidence of those nasty fangs: the victim was poisoned, and the weapon was a fountain pen, of all things!

Frye sat back in his chair, smiling. Celesta intrigued him before, but now that he knew what a clever brain she had beneath her beauty, he admired her even more. And it'd been a damn long time since he felt that way about a woman.

Did Perkins realize she was a writer? As he recalled the lumber heir's red-faced blustering this noon, he doubted it. Celesta had looked very uncomfortable when Patrick played up to her, as though startled by his advances. A few minutes of eavesdropping around the corner of the house had convinced him the blond Romeo's pleas were falling on properly deaf ears . . . which made the game more interesting. He and Perkins were both accustomed to getting what they wanted from a woman, and Damon now had the perfect ploy for making Celesta his own—

and for paying Patrick back at the same time.

He closed his eyes to envision her as she'd been this morning, her hair curling damply at her nape, her dark dress clinging to curves no man had ever explored. The memory of her soft, sweet lips answering his aroused him even now . . . the feel of her yielding to him, as mesmerized as a victim-to-be of the vampire Count's, made him chuckle and rise from his chair. It was time to make his move.

Celesta pawed frantically through her basket, swearing under her breath. *"Damn* him! What could he possibly want with that packet of sugar?" she rasped. "And God only knows what he'll do with that story—and my pen!"

She slammed her fist against Grandfather's desk and then paced over to the little window. The third floor was hot and airless, and after the uphill walk from town her clothing clung to her like a second skin. She should've *known* he had a devious motive for picking her things up from the porch, and he was probably laughing at her this very moment, thinking how she'd beg for the return of her possessions.

With a disgusted grunt she returned to the desk and began placing her writing supplies in two drawers she'd emptied. She'd intended to take the sugar to the druggist, but now her investigation into Mama's death was at a standstill. It would serve Frye right to be poisoned himself if he sampled that packet!

And how could she ask for her story back without admitting she was its author? He would've figured that out by now, would've read "The Pen is Mightier" and realized it was to appear on the stands sometime soon. She'd completed the story in the wee hours of the morning Mama died, and in the shock and confusion of the past few days she hadn't gotten it to the post office. Now it seemed too gruesome a tale to publish, and seeing it displayed in Sally Sharpe's usual space among the other dime novels would certainly upset her.

She'd fetched her supplies so that she could dash off another Sally Sharpe adventure—but Frye had also stolen her favorite pen! Celesta settled herself at the desk and stared at the small stack of blank paper before her, another fountain pen poised in her hand.

But the ideas wouldn't come. As always, she wrote *SALLY SHARPE, GIRL DETECTIVE, in*—and then stalled out. The pen's point scratched across the paper, the barrel felt foreign to her hand, and instead of a title for a new story, tears were all she could produce.

Her black fountain pen, edged in gold, had been a gift from Mama. Ink and ideas had flowed from it for hours on end, those late nights she spent penning her detective's bold exploits. Mama had saved for weeks to present her with such an expensive instrument on her twentieth birthday, and it had immediately become a talisman—a symbol of her mother's pride in the writing no one else knew about. Not even her editor suspected that Montgomery C. Lester was a girl in a third-floor bedroom who wrote to fill the hours most young ladies spent trying to catch a husband.

Creating nasty villains and dire, mysterious straits for Sally Sharpe was a lot more fun than enduring the cowlike gazes of the men who eyed her around town. When they learned she was domestic help in the Perkins home, the ones of modest income were too intimidated to call on her, and the wealthier ones didn't give her a second glance. Sally Sharpe, her prim, blond heroine in nondescript clothes, had become her closest friend, a girl whose daring escapades filled her empty hours with derring-do Celesta could never imitate in real life. And now that Mama was gone, Sally would be her comfort, her means of staying sane in a life that suddenly had a gaping hole in it.

Celesta wiped the wetness from her eyes and focused again on her paper. What if . . . what if Sally herself were the victim of a crime? What if some devious, dangerously handsome client engaged her services and she later discovered he'd made off with her most important files—information that would put her at the mercy of a ruthless criminal who'd murdered her mother, for instance?

No good. Sally was an orphan, like most female protagonists in the pulps. And it hit too close to home right now.

Heartened by the adrenaline this idea had pumped up, Celesta gripped her pen again. Perhaps Sally had a crochety aunt, an old maid who didn't approve of how she made her living—and who died at the hands of a crook who stole the will that grudgingly named Sally as the sole heir to her estate. Of course the aunt wore her hair in a bun and had a forehead furrowed from scowling at Sally—Nadine, her name was!— and . . . was that cigarette smoke she smelled? Miss Sharpe herself would certainly be the killer's next target, unless. . . .

Celesta chuckled low in her throat. She saw a dark, fashionably dressed villain with a line for every occasion, now wooing Sally after years of being away from her. Aunt Justine was in for a real jolt if she picked *this* story off the newsstands!

Alive with anticipation, Celesta crumpled the top sheet and began again. *SALLY SHARPE, GIRL DETECTIVE, in "THE CASE OF THE PURLOINED PAPERS,"* she wrote with a bold flourish. It was going to be a long, productive evening.

"Celesta, dear, you look like you didn't get a moment's sleep," Aunt Katherine fussed the next morning. She placed another pancake on Celesta's plate and tapped the china with her fork. "Eat one more, and then perhaps you should go back to bed. Rest is the only cure for that pale face."

Stifling a yawn, Celesta obediently drenched the flapjack with syrup. She'd seen the purple half-moons under her eyes when she looked in the mirror, so this loving lecture wasn't unexpected—just as Justine's next comments came as no surprise.

"She wouldn't have this problem if she'd gone to bed. What on earth were you doing in the ballroom at all hours?" she asked tersely. "And don't deny it. I heard you up there, making the floorboards creak with your snooping!"

Celesta took a large mouthful of pancake as an excuse not to answer immediately. She'd been pacing, making the details of her story dovetail as tightly as they must to keep her readers worried about poor Sally until the final paragraphs.

"And why on earth were you *mumbling?* All that racket!" Justine complained. "You could've at least shown the courtesy of staying in your room so the rest of us could sleep."

"Perhaps she was talking to her grandfather's ghost," Katherine teased. "Now that Celesta's returned home, he's probably come back to comfort her in—"

"I should've known you'd devise such a ridiculous defense!" Justine rose from her chair, glaring at each of them before going to the pantry door to fetch her market basket. "I might as well be on my way. Something tells me the shopping may be all that gets accomplished in this house today. And don't think it's going to become a habit!"

Celesta knew this remark was directed at her, so to infuriate Justine more, she didn't offer any apologies. She merely watched, her fork in her mouth, as her maiden aunt stepped briskly out the door and then slammed it.

She'd have to be more careful. Caught up in Sally Sharpe's dangerous dilemma, she'd forgotten that Justine's bedroom was directly below the ballroom, and that vents in her aunt's ceiling allowed the unwelcome heat to rise up into the alcove . . . and the sound of her voice to drift down to her aunt's ears.

"Think nothing of it, dear," Aunt Katherine said as she began stacking the dishes. "Justine's especially crochety when she doesn't sleep, and—"

"Justine would be crochety if she slept night and day," Celesta blurted. "You can't blame it on the heat and you can't blame it on *me*. She was born with a peevish streak, and that's that."

Katherine appeared startled by her tone, but then her face softened into a smile. "You're catching on, dear. But I can't help wondering why, if you couldn't sleep, you were up there on the third floor . . . unless you truly were communing with your grandfather's spirit."

Celesta couldn't admit she'd written the most exciting story of her career in six hours flat, so she played upon Katherine's own fanciful suggestion. "I . . . I just felt compelled to go up there, as though something—or someone—were calling to me," she answered in a mystical tone.

Then she chuckled, to relieve the horrified fascination on the dear lady's face. "Actually, I just *like* it up there, where it's so quiet you can hear the heat. And the view of the river from the alcove window is comforting, somehow."

Katherine nodded wisely. "You need time alone to sort out your feelings. And with Eula and Patrick coming tomorrow, expecting your answer, I imagine you're a bit nervous. They're not accustomed to anyone declining the privilege of being associated with them, you know."

Seeing the sparkle in Katherine's hazel eyes,

Celesta chuckled. She washed the dishes while her aunt dried and put them away. This woman wasn't used to being refused, either—assumed she'd stay on at Ransom Manor, even though she hadn't discussed it. After bluntly rejecting Patrick's hint of marriage, it hardly seemed wise to return to a house where she'd be under his constant watch, yet she wasn't sure how long she could endure Justine's nit-picking if she stayed here.

Since the green beans were now preserved in rows of sparkling jars in the cellar, Katherine had declared today a holiday. Celesta followed her into the parlor, because she couldn't make up an excuse to walk into town and mail her story if she went back to bed. This was the coolest room in the house, shaded by the same oaks that had dropped a branch through the gazebo ceiling, so this was where her aunt had assembled the yarns and canvas for the new sampler she was stitching.

"Your other aunt thinks needlepoint is a worthless occupation," she was saying as she settled into a wing-backed chair. "And I already have a clutter of samplers on the walls, but I find the challenge of counting out these stitches in just the right shadings a rewarding pastime. And I *have* something when I'm done. Justine claims she listens to language lessons when she isn't reading upstairs, but I have yet to hear her utter a word of French."

"Justine's learning French?"

Katherine giggled. "She has the lesson cylinders and the latest machine for playing them, anyway. For all I know, she sneaks recordings of bawdy sailors' songs upstairs in her basket, and listens to those instead."

Celesta joined in her laughter, thinking sea ditties incompatible with her spinster aunt's tastes—but French lessons? She watched Katherine lean forward and crank the gramophone on the table next to her chair. After a few scratchy seconds, the graceful opening strains of *The Blue Danube* filled the air, and she sat back with a dreamy-eyed look.

"Your uncle Ambrose always requested that tune at balls, knowing how I loved to waltz," she explained with a sentimental smile. "He was a magnificent dancer, tall and robust though he was. Sometimes after Justine retired for the evening, he and I would dance in this very room. They were wonderful times, Celesta."

Her eyes misted over, and Celesta couldn't bear to watch her wipe away tears. How had she even considered this lonely little woman as a possible murderess?

Celesta's thoughts drifted with the music, and she sat back in the chair opposite Katherine's. *Someone* had poisoned Mama—she was sure of it, after reviewing the horrible telltale symptoms that had left Rachel Montgomery lifeless. Yet without that sugar packet she had no proof, and she couldn't risk sneaking another sample.

Damn that Damon anyway! Perhaps the walk to the post office would clear her mind and she'd think of a way to confront him before he exposed her as the creator of Sally Sharpe. Her Hannibal readers—not to mention her editor in New York—would lose all faith in the dauntless Girl Detective if they knew Sally was created by a sheltered young woman writing out her adventurous fantasies.

She scooted forward, about to ask if Katherine needed anything from town, when the clatter of the brass doorknocker summoned them above the sounds of Strauss. "I'll get it," she said, eager for the distraction, and she smiled when she heard Katherine's footsteps behind her.

When she opened the massive door, however, her smile fell flat. Damon Frye was grinning at them, his brown eyes alight with a mischief she knew not to trust.

"Celesta," he crooned with a slight bow, "and Mrs. Ransom," he continued in his suavest voice. "I hope I'm not interrupting or—"

"How nice to see you!" Aunt Katherine chirped. "Why, we weren't doing a—oh, my," she breathed as he tenderly kissed the back of her freckled hand. "You *are* a direct young man, aren't you?"

"Quite," he replied, his eyes roving to tease Celesta. "When I saw your dear niece yesterday, she mentioned you'd lost your husband, and I came to express my deepest sympathy."

"Why . . . thank you," she murmured, her hand still wrapped in Damon's broad, browned one.

"And since she also said your gazebo was damaged in the storm, I took the liberty of bringing materials to fix it for you." He gestured behind him, to where a horse-drawn wagon loaded with lumber stood waiting. "But if this is a bad time, or if you've hired someone else—"

"Don't you even *think* of leaving," Katherine replied, her gaze flitting coyly from her niece to Frye. "This is the most thoughtful thing anyone's done for me since Ambrose's memorial service. Why didn't you tell me you took so long in town yesterday because you were talking with Mr. Frye, dear?"

Celesta gave the rogue in the doorway a pointed, warning glare as she replied, "It didn't seem worth mentioning, Aunt Katherine."

Chapter 6

Damon chuckled. Despite her pallor and pink-rimmed eyes, Miss Montgomery looked determined to confront him the moment Katherine was out of earshot. And since that was what he came for, he played along. "It was so hot, and she was so eager to get your yarn home, I doubt she heard a word I said," he replied smoothly. Then he smiled at the little woman, nodding toward the partly stitched fabric in her hand. "You've already worked this much of the design? What's it say?"

Katherine beamed as she held the sampler up. "Home is where the heart is," she replied with a girlish smile. "It's nothing fancy—"

"But skillfully done. I don't recall ever seeing some of these stitches," he said as he ran an admiring finger over her handiwork. "And the sentiment has always intrigued me. It seems that those without a home often lose heart, and those without a heart seldom find a true home. To have both is to be doubly blessed."

He was dangling some sort of hook, and Aunt Katherine was gazing at him, about to snap up the bait—and Celesta didn't like it one bit. "We appreciate your thoughtfulness, Mr. Frye, but how is it you can spare us your time from overseeing the

Cruikshank construction?" she asked coolly.

Katherine's mouth dropped open even farther. "You're an architect? And quite a fine one, if John Cruikshank's put you in charge of his new home!" she exclaimed. "I would *so* like to hear about it! Such a palace it must be."

With a quick, victorious glance at Celesta, he bowed slightly. "And I'll be pleased to tell you all about it, but as your niece has pointed out, my time's a bit short. I'd better get started on your gazebo."

Frye strode to his wagon, leaving Katherine gaping after him, her needlepoint clutched to her bosom.

"Really, Aunt! You're gawking like a schoolgirl," Celesta muttered.

"Yes, and I can't imagine why *you* aren't. He's kind and generous, and he's obviously made something of himself these past ten years," she said, her hazel eyes fixed intently on her niece's. "You shouldn't be so short with him, dear. Now that you're out of Eula Perkins's employ, you'll need to think about your future. You could do worse than be wooed by Damon Frye."

"I'm not so sure about that," she replied, steering the little woman back into the house. "And besides, it's hardly the proper time to encourage—"

"Your mother wouldn't want you to be alone, dear. Lord knows how much easier her life— and yours—would've been had she landed a dependable man." Katherine studied her for a moment, and then her face softened with a smile. "And since we'd be remiss not to repay Damon's kindness, we should prepare a special dinner, don't you think?"

Objecting to her aunt's matchmaking would raise questions Celesta didn't want to answer, so she followed Katherine to the kitchen. Damon's interest in her was one more reason not to return to the Perkins home, as Katherine saw it—one more way

68

her aunt had manipulated her into a tight spot, unknowingly and with the best intentions.

But Damon Frye's intentions weren't the least bit honorable—flattering an old lady's needlework so that he could taunt her niece! He was too damn clever for his own good. And he had no business wearing those overalls. His deep pockets had obviously provided a hiding place for what he had stolen from her, and the way the tan fabric hugged his backside was so shameless only a—

". . . so I think we'll make—Celesta, are you listening?" her aunt's voice cut through her thoughts. "We'll need a head of cabbage and some onions from the garden, and fetch a big pan of lemons from the cave. Lemonade's the best refresher for the hot day's work Mr. Frye will be doing."

"Yes, of course," she replied, and hurried out the pantry door before her aunt could ask what she had been daydreaming about. It was insane to be so infatuated with a man whose strut betrayed his colossal conceit, yet her eyes were drawn toward the gazebo as though they had a mind of their own.

Damon was lifting the last sawed section of the huge branch from the crushed white latticework, heaving it to one side with the effortless grace of a man twice his size. And he'd already removed his shirt.

When Celesta returned to the house, ignoring his wave, she was relieved to find Justine back from her marketing. Ramrod straight, fist on her hip, she was injecting the situation with her usual dose of sour practicality.

". . . so of course you've invited him to dinner, and this one paltry chicken in my basket won't be enough," she was complaining. "And what possessed him to volunteer his services, unless—" The spinster's brown eyes took aim at Celesta.

"I did *not* invite him here," she insisted as she laid

her vegetables in the sink. "And it wasn't my idea to cook for him, either."

"How could we not feed him?" Katherine objected with a wounded look. "It would be unheard of not to—even if we paid him—"

"Which we won't," Justine stated dryly. "Must you pander to anything that wears pants, Katherine? Put these perishables in the ice box, Celesta, and let's hope the poultry man has another bird when I get there."

The door closed sharply behind her, and Katherine's lips twitched with amusement. "Perhaps she'll have to stop two or three places, and smoke two or three more cigarettes," she said lightly. "It'll give me time to make my pie and biscuits without her hovering, telling me I'm using too much butter or too many peaches."

Celesta stifled a laugh. Surely Frye would finish repairing the gazebo in a hurry when these two geese got to hissing at each other over every little thing. It would be amusing to watch him dodge Justine's barbs and defend poor Katherine's seemingly innocent ploys—

"Squeeze the lemons first and let them soak in some grated rind and sugar," she was saying as she opened her flour cannister, "and then you can cut the cabbage for slaw and set the dining room table with our better plates. Isn't it nice to entertain company? I miss the conversations we used to have when Ambrose and his parents were alive."

Celesta chided herself for thinking only of her own predicament. Aunt Katherine was being the perfect hostess, and if anyone deserved relief from a sister-in-law's endless criticism, it was she. As they worked side by side, she reminded herself that this sheltered little woman had no way of knowing about Damon's devious nature: she saw only his highly polished veneer, which reflected her own kindheartedness when she was in his presence. Celesta knew that if she was to be free of Mr. Frye, she'd have to discourage his attentions herself—which she fully intended to do as she walked down the stone path a little while later, carrying a tray of lemonade and cookies.

Hearing footsteps, Damon turned from his work to watch Celesta approach. Her upswept hair was bouncing loosely with each step, and her mouth was fixed in a forbidding line. She looked ready to throw that lemonade at him, an obstinate expression he remembered from when young Patrick used to order her around. The rose-colored dress she wore beneath her apron flattered her complexion, but she looked pale—and he knew exactly how to bring the color to her cheeks.

"You're a thoughtful hostess, Miss Montgomery," he said as she walked toward the wicker table. "Only one glass, though. How . . . intimate."

She set the tray down so hard the ice clattered against the glass pitcher. "I don't plan to share your refreshments, Mr. Frye. I only brought this because you have something of mine."

"The key to your heart, no doubt."

Celesta slapped him, but then he caught her by the wrist, his face alight with a devilish grin. She watched, heart pounding, as he slowly, slowly pressed her palm to his lips. "You are the most underhanded—"

"You smell like lemons, sweetheart," he murmured, inhaling deeply as his mouth brushed her pulse point and continued up her bare forearm. "All tangy and tart, like the spirited woman you are. I like that."

"You're changing the subject," she muttered, sounding much less irked than she wanted to. "You stole an envelope and my best pen, and I want them back."

Damon paused halfway up her lovely arm. "There

wasn't a pen in your basket when—"

"Was too!" she blurted. She tried to jerk her arm away, but he held her fast, taking in her agitation with teasing brown eyes. Although he was freshly shaven and tanned, the shadow of his beard along his taut, square jaw made something quiver in the pit of her stomach . . . and he knew it, too.

Celesta was trembling, yet her spitfire eyes never blinked. The color was indeed flooding her cheeks with a pink akin to the showy blooms of the mimosa trees that whispered in the breeze around them. "If you want your story back, you'll have to ask me very nicely for it," he murmured, glancing suggestively at her mouth. "I've enjoyed Sally Sharpe's adventures since she first appeared in print, and I'd hate to miss an issue because Montgomery C. Lester didn't meet her deadline."

His praise was sweet, but so infuriating! "I wrote another story last night," she jeered, "no thanks to you, thief! Mama gave me that pen for my—"

"I'm telling you, there wasn't any pen—"

"You're lying!"

When she tried to jerk away, he caught her around the waist and held her so close he could feel her pulse racing against his stomach. "No, I'm pouring us some lemonade," he said as he lifted the pitcher, "and we're going to toast your literary success. I gather your aunts don't know about your writing?"

"Heavens no!"

"And what about Patrick?"

"NO! And if you breathe one word—"

"Then, it'll be our secret, Celesta," he murmured, raising the cold glass to her lips. "I consider it an honor to be privy to such information, because I truly admire your way with a story, sweetheart. And as long as you give me what I want, your identity's safe. A woman with your cunning mind surely understands what I mean . . . and what I want."

72

Her heart was pounding so loudly she wasn't sure she'd heard him correctly. "That's blackmail."

"Of the sweetest kind, Celesta—the kind lovers engage in to keep each other interested. Now drink up," he coaxed. "Here's to your continued success, and to a passion as deep and compelling as your wildest imaginings."

Frye tipped the glass until she had to swallow the sweet, tangy lemonade. Its coldness trickled down her insides, a startling contrast to the heat of his arm across her back. All she could do was watch as he solemnly sipped the drink himself, tilting his head back until his Adam's apple throbbed with his enjoyment.

When he looked at her again, Celesta stared, fascinated, as a drop of pale liquid ran from the corner of his lips.

"Catch that," he breathed.

She gaped at him, too stunned to move.

"Better hurry. The farther down it drips, the more of me you'll have to kiss."

Infuriated, she again tried to free herself but his other arm caught her behind the head, and her tongue slithered out of its own accord to halt the progress of that single, tantalizing drop. He tasted sweet and salty. His low moan spurred her on until she'd rounded his chin, reveling in the virile roughness of his face—such a difference from the silken lips that now closed over hers.

This was insane; Justine could return home any moment! Celesta resolutely clamped her teeth together.

Damon pulled away slightly to smile at her. "One more kiss," he whispered. "No one'll see us. Open your mouth this time, honey."

She almost protested but caught herself: talking would give him the opportunity he wanted! She tried to back away, but her wily captor touched his cold, wet glass to the back of her neck.

When Celesta gasped, he claimed her again. Lips sweet with lemonade coaxed him to drink deeply of her soft helplessness, until she went limp against him and savored the leisurely kisses he bestowed upon her like gifts she'd someday repay in kind.

Celesta pulled away, dazed by his magic. "Damon, we can't—I want my story back!"

"We *can*," he breathed into her ear. "And you'll get what you want as soon as I do, Celesta. I'll make it easy for us, perfectly discreet. Leave it to me, sweetheart." He released her, sending her up the path by playfully swatting her behind.

Dizzy and giddy—and appalled at how quickly she'd succumbed to him—Celesta teetered up the stone walk as though she'd guzzled whiskey. Leave it to him, he said! How stupid did he think she was?

She stopped outside the pantry entrance to smooth her apron and take a deep breath. His threats meant nothing: she didn't intend to publish "The Pen is Mightier" anyway. But the thrumming of her senses . . . the tickle of the hair on Damon's chest, the scent of sweat and lemonade as he whispered they'd be lovers, the dark eyes that held promises she should never keep . . . these images would taunt her every time she saw him. Every time he wore those overalls, she'd know he had nothing on underneath them, and she'd be more frantically aware of the power he already held over her.

As dinner progressed, Celesta watched Katherine and Justine fall victim to Damon's charm as well. He'd worked until he was called to wash up, had put his blue chambray shirt on again, and was now complimenting both ladies profusely, with a smile that appeared maddeningly sincere.

"I can't recall the last time I shared such a

wonderful meal with such delightful company," he said as he reached for his fourth piece of fried chicken. "Home-grown vegetables, good talk—and a bird so tender it must've been specially ordered," he said with a purposeful glance at Justine.

"And there's peach pie for dessert," Katherine piped up. "It's a joy to cook for someone with your appetite, Mr. Frye."

When Damon's gaze flitted suggestively to Celesta she choked on her last bite of biscuit. His appetites were no secret to *her*, and she couldn't understand why Justine wasn't cutting into his flattery with her knifelike tongue. As she and Katherine carried the dirty dinner plates to the kitchen, she was amazed to hear the spinster sounding as cultured and polite as a society matron.

"I had no idea you'd gone into architecture, Mr. Frye," her voice floated in from the other room. "No doubt you've noticed the fine craftsmanship and detail here at Ransom Manor."

"It's a proud house," he stated. "I'm a little embarrassed to admit this, but when I was a boy it was the badge of bravery to sneak up here and take a chunk of loose mortar from your retaining wall. Or better yet, to steal a peach from your trees."

Katherine was chuckling as she lifted slices of pie from the glass plate, and then she gaped at Celesta. Justine was *laughing* out there, as though Damon were a beau she sought to impress with her wit!

"You were no doubt trying for a glimpse of Father," she was saying with mock sternness. "His reputation as a riverboat pilot made for some fascinating gossip, not to mention his rather eccentric ways."

"We were in awe of him and his adventures aboard the *Phantom*," Frye agreed. "And whenever I saw these solid stone walls I thought of a castle in King Arthur's time. Couldn't help but wonder what sort of priceless treasures and princesses I'd find inside."

"You're a shameless flatterer, Mr. Frye," came Justine's twitter, "but since you have an appreciation for such things, I'd be pleased to show you around the house—if you're interested, of course," she added hastily.

Celesta nearly dropped the plates she was carrying. And as she reached the table, Damon was plying her maiden aunt with an appropriately awed gaze.

"I would be honored," he said quietly. "Why, until John Cruikshank commissioned his current home, Ransom Manor was the finest example of architectural excellence in northeast Missouri."

"It still is. If you ask me, Mr. Cruikshank's taste tends toward the excessive."

"Don't let Justine's frugal streak offend you, Mr. Frye," Katherine insisted as she placed his pie before him. "With the loss of our men, we haven't maintained our home's original splendor as we should, and we truly appreciate your time and labor today. We'd be delighted to show you around."

He wasn't sure why these two old girls were suddenly treating him as long-lost kin, but he wasn't about to let this opportunity pass him by. "I'd like nothing better, but I should complete the gazebo repairs—"

"Which gives you the perfect excuse to stay for supper!" Katherine perched daintily on her chair, a fragile smile on her face. "You're the ray of sunshine we need in the wake of Rachel's untimely demise. I hope we aren't boring you with our gloom."

He honestly couldn't remember feeling more welcome, but Celesta's simmering scowl warned him not to press his luck. Her aunts had unwittingly invited him to take advantage of her vulnerable state, and if they guessed his motives, he'd be out of her life—and probably out of a job—before nightfall.

*　　　*　　　*

Frye returned to his repair work, aware that three pairs of eyes watched him from the house now and then. It felt good to perform these manual tasks, because his position as a designer and supervisor made him more an administrator than a carpenter these days. He replaced the damaged upright supports and then the beams that met in the gazebo's peak. If he pushed himself, he could hammer the new latticework in place and have it painted by sunset.

But with prudent pacing he could return tomorrow, to finish this job while Patrick and Eula were visiting. What a treat, to watch Perkins plead his case and lavish gifts upon Celesta—maybe kiss her when he thought they were alone—only to have her refuse his offer of marriage. It was a rejection he richly deserved. Miss Montgomery outshone him in every respect, and her keen intelligence would compensate for her lack of social status when she stood up to him. It was a showdown he didn't want to miss.

And as Celesta watched from the alcove window, she sensed Frye's mind was working much faster than his muscled arms. He was lithe and confident with his tools, pure pleasure to watch as he reconstructed Katherine's gazebo without seeming to think about what he had to do next.

His presence these past few hours had left her terribly confused. She'd been so sure her fountain pen had been in that wicker basket, yet thinking back, she'd been scrambling so frantically through her desk at Eula's that she might have overlooked it. Frye seemed certain that Mama's gift hadn't been among her papers, but who could believe him? He was a smooth-talker of the highest order, and even Justine was now caught up in his spell. His kisses. . . . Celesta touched her fingertips to her lips, fearing he'd opened a Pandora's box of emotions it

77

was already too late to shut the lid on.

And after Damon allowed himself to be coaxed into supper and a tour of the house, the situation became even more exasperating. Both her aunts were escorting him, pointing out Ransom Manor's unique if eclectic beauty, so she would appear impolite if she retired to her room. Celesta saw the huge old home through the eyes of a duly impressed visitor—a visitor who noted the repairs two old women couldn't see to, and who would use them to his advantage.

"You've seen our kitchen and dining room, and this is the study where my father and brother conducted their riverboat business," Justine said with a wave toward the doorway.

Frye looked into the masculine den, with its paneled walls and leather furniture, knowing Ambrose had chosen this rounded tower room for its view of the river. The white roof of the gazebo was barely visible through the blossom-studded mimosa trees that surrounded it.

"And of course the other dining room door leads us to the vestibule," his elderly guide continued. She paused so that he could take in the grandeur of the carpeted stairway and the glossy floors of dark marble, covered with a Turkish rug that was showing some wear down its center.

"When I first came to this house, I thought it was designed backward," Katherine said with a faraway chuckle. "Since the pillared porch is on the other side, most people assume that's the main entry rather than the back hall."

"Father wanted it that way," Justine said crisply, "because the breeze from the river would cool the kitchen, and because he wished our home's magnificence to be most evident from the water."

"So he could see it every time he came home from a trip," Damon ventured.

The spinster gave him a tight smile. "Precisely, Mr. Frye. And here we have our main parlor, where my mother used to hostess her church committees and teas."

It was a quaint, flowery room, and its focal point was a baby grand piano that glowed in the light from the bay window. "Do you play?" he asked. It was a fine instrument, and his fingers itched to caress its keys.

"No. The piano was Rachel's eighth birthday present, and since Mother was gone by then we used this as a music room," she answered stiffly. "And this door leads to the library."

Celesta heard the resentment in her oldest aunt's voice and sensed the questions Damon wanted to ask because of it. He was gazing at the fireplaces and decorative details of these rooms with a keen interest, as though he would like the chance to linger and learn more about the family that once lived here. She took Aunt Katherine's arm as they entered the library, hoping Mr. Frye would refrain from exhuming too much of the Ransom past.

His smile widened as he stepped into the cozily furnished room, with its striped chairs and settee arranged before a stone fireplace. The collection of books was impressive, but the reason he circled the room was to stand before the large portrait of Ambrose Ransom, Senior, noting how the old fellow's piercing eyes seemed to follow him. "Celesta certainly inherited her grandfather's coloring and striking facial features. From what I recall of him, though, he was much less intimidating in real life than he looks in this painting."

"That's because he wanted you to peek in here and be scared, after sneaking his peaches," Celesta commented wryly. "He still haunts this house, you know. Better beware, lest the floorboards open up when you wander where you shouldn't."

79

That wouldn't happen—the house was only fifty years old, by his estimation—but the raven-haired Miss Montgomery was clearly warning him not to feel too much at home here. These high-ceilinged rooms with their graceful swag draperies and chandeliers appealed to him, however, and despite their faded colors, they exuded a warmth that drew him in. He was guessing Katherine was too sentimental—or not allowed—to make any improvements and that Justine was too tight, since money certainly wasn't a problem.

"And the last room on this floor is our summer parlor," his guide was saying. "Needless to say, Katherine spends a great deal of her time here."

Damon chuckled. Above the mantel, between the tall, rectangular windows—*everywhere*—hung her samplers. Most featured alphabets and simple home scenes, but some were elaborately stitched words of wisdom: Trust and Obey, Haste Makes Waste, Lead Us Not Into Temptation.

"She does lovely work," he said, noting how Celesta's gaze had followed his to that last sampler, and then she'd flushed and looked away. "This is a very homey room, with its ferns and the shaded view of the river. It's much like I remember our parlor when my mother was alive."

Katherine looked around pensively, and then ran her hand along a yellowed section of wallpaper. "Compared to the exquisite materials you're working with at John Cruikshank's, our patterns and colors must seem a little dated."

Damon shrugged. "They've retained their beauty remarkably well, just as the home as a whole has kept its structural integrity. If it hadn't, you'd be seeing stains and cracks."

As he followed the three ladies up the back stairway, he wondered if Katherine might be working up to a very bold proposition, for a woman in her place. The wall coverings and floorboards *were* worn in places, yet Justine, as the head of the Ransom family, was apparently blind to the house's fading glory.

"On the second floor we have our bedrooms—and I don't think we'll need to see those," the spinster added primly, "but I'll show you the ballroom that was once the envy of Hannibal society. You'll have to pardon our dust, as we never come up here anymore."

The air grew noticeably hotter and mustier as they ascended the last few steps. A narrow hallway took them past dormered rooms—formerly the schoolroom, nursery, and maid's quarters, Justine was saying—and then they turned the corner to enter a large, opulent ballroom with another baby grand on the dais, and hardwood floors, and a vaulted ceiling which housed a huge, tiered crystal chandelier.

Katherine let out a lingering sigh beside him. "How this room rang with life at Rachel's wedding dance, and for the masquerades and Christmas balls we used to have," she said wistfully. "The bronze sconces glimmered with candlelight, and everyone laughed and chattered above the music. It breaks my heart to see it looking so . . . forlorn. Hasn't been a child in the nursery since Rachel was born forty years ago, and now that Ambrose has passed away, I . . . I can't bear to come up here."

"You'll have to excuse Katherine," Justine said after her sister-in-law hurried down the stairs. "She's a fine one for talking about balls and Father's spirit haunting this floor, but I think her romantic notions overpower her reason at times. She should accept the fact that the past is gone and my brother's not coming back. These rooms will probably never be used again."

Damon flinched at the harsh finality of her words as he walked slowly down the center of the ballroom.

He recalled stories of the Ransoms' legendary hospitality from his youth, remembered the glow of these lights from across town, and the deep yearning to be a part of their elite gaiety. It was a damn shame to see Ambrose Ransom's third story collecting dust, but as he approached the entryway to a small arched alcove, he smiled. Besides a few old trunks and bookshelves, the little nook held only a threadbare sofa and a writing desk . . . with a fountain pen on it.

"Perhaps you have mice," he teased as he gave Celesta a knowing look. "The dust in here's been disturbed, rather recently, I'm guessing."

Justine let out a humorless laugh and walked briskly toward the stairway. "Celesta indeed scratches around like a mouse, at all hours of the night," she replied dryly. "What she sees in that cramped little room, I'll never know. We used to hang guests' coats in there when we were hosting a ball."

"Used to watch the moon rise over the river when we weren't," Katherine murmured as she rejoined them on the second-floor landing. "But we're boring you with our sad stories, Mr. Frye. You've been a patient listener."

"*Au contraire*," he replied with a warm smile. "For years I've wanted to see the interior of this house, and I've enjoyed it thoroughly. I hope Celesta realizes how fortunate she is to be residing here now."

His hooded glance suggested he was scheming something up. Surely he wouldn't mention her stories, or—

"And we're fortunate to have her," Katherine replied more cheerfully. When they'd come down the grand staircase with its glossy, carved newel posts, she stopped and looked up at him, her expression thoughtful. "And where are you staying these days, Mr. Frye?"

"At the Park Hotel. My room overlooks Central Park, but the view's nothing like what you have from these bluffs."

The silence that enveloped the vestibule hung heavy with anticipation, marked by the steady tick of the grandfather clock. Any *polite* guest would be saying good night, Celesta thought, yet Damon stood among them, still gazing around as though he couldn't soak up enough of the Ransom atmosphere. Something in the way Aunt Katherine cleared her throat made Celesta's mouth go dry.

"What would you think about staying here with us, Damon?" the little woman asked in a voice shrill with apprehension. "And instead of paying rent, you could do some painting and papering for us. These days I wonder how prudent it is for three women to live up here, so isolated and defenseless, and—well, we'd love your company, if you think you can tolerate us."

Damon lit up with a boyish grin and grasped her slender hands between his. "Mrs. Ransom, I couldn't have phrased it better myself. You've got a deal. I'll move in tomorrow."

Chapter 7

Damon was barely down the hill on his horse before Justine turned in the doorway, bristling. "How *dare* you invite him to live here—and without asking *me!* You two planned this while I was shopping. Plotting against me!"

"Celesta had nothing to do with it," Katherine said in a shaky voice. "And had we asked, you'd have said no."

"Of course I would!" Justine closed the door and glowered at them, her silver-streaked bun quivering with her agitation. "What will people *say* when they hear Damon Frye's come to live with us?" she demanded. "After they get done *snickering* at two old women boarding such a handsome young stud, they'll start watching Celesta, counting the days until she follows in Lucy Bates's footsteps."

She turned to her niece, her dark eyes aglitter. "Have you given Eula Perkins a decision yet?"

"No, I—"

"Well, it seems your aunt has left you no proper alternative but to return to honest employment at—"

"And what will that prove?" Aunt Katherine looked jittery, yet she drew herself up to her full height. "You're blind if you haven't noticed Patrick's interest in Celesta. Here, she'll have two of us to look

85

after her reputation when Damon's not working at the Cruikshank site. I did this for *her*, Justine. Ransom Manor is her rightful home. Were your mother alive, she'd be appalled at how yellowed and threadbare her lovely rooms have become."

"My mother has nothing to do with—"

"And besides," Katherine continued more firmly, "I thought you *liked* Mr. Frye. Why, he had you talking and giggling like—"

"I was not giggling."

"—a young woman again. We need some happiness in this house, Justine," she stated as her eyes misted over. "We're shriveling like two peas in a dried-up pod. Damon Frye's a competent carpenter with a sincere interest in preserving our home. And now that he's agreed to do the work, we can hardly tell him we've changed our minds."

Justine's eyes narrowed as she looked down her pointed nose at her sister-in-law. "Yes, you certainly saw to *that*, didn't you? After I offered to show him around—merely being the polite hostess—you tossed us out of the frying pan and into the fire. He'll eat us out of house and home, and he'll spend so much time making eyes at your niece one can only *guess* how little work he'll accomplish in his spare moments."

"He seems quite industrious to me," Katherine shot back. "Took the initiative of coming here to repair the gazebo—without expecting pay, might I remind you."

The old maid grunted. "And you don't know what he's trying to catch with his generosity? You *are* naive, Katherine."

Celesta's collar felt unbearably tight. Her two aunts were staring each other down, their silence as heated as their argument, and the last thing she wanted was to draw attention to herself by unbuttoning her top buttons.

Justine tired of their glaring contest and turned her

attention to her niece. "And what do *you* have to say about all this, Celesta?"

She cleared her dry throat. "Nothing."

"I suppose Frye's coming here has erased any inclination you may have had about returning to work for Eula Perkins."

"I . . . I haven't decided—"

"Your indecisive nature will cost you, young lady," Justine said with a wagging finger. "If you can't see that your aunt has invited the viper from Eden to live in our midst, you're doomed to share Eve's fate. And consider yourself warned, Celesta: if I suspect certain *behavior* going on behind my back, you and Damon Frye shall be banished, never to set foot in this house again. Do I make myself clear?"

"Yes, ma'am," she whispered.

"Fine. I'm retiring for the evening, and I suggest you do the same. I need to pray over this matter and gather my strength for tomorrow. What with Eula paying a visit and Mr. Frye moving in, it promises to be a trying day."

Justine marched up the center of the grand staircase, never looking back as her steady tread echoed in the hallway. For a moment the two of them stood watching after her, doom on their faces, until Katherine shifted.

"It'll serve her right to lie awake half the night," she said in a terse whisper. "She has no call to give us such a tongue-lashing for wanting to modernize this musty old house, as though she's the only one who lives here."

Celesta let out the breath she'd been holding. "It *was* a surprise when you asked Damon to stay here, Aunt. I can understand why Justine's so taken aback about—"

"You're on her side, then? You think I'm a doddering old fool for asking Mr. Frye to help us preserve this home—for *you?*"

She was caught between another pair of adversaries who, in their way, fought as nastily as Patrick and Damon did. She could either fall victim to Frye's dark desires, or be cajoled back into the Perkins household for dubious reasons; she could break Katherine's heart by moving out, or she could inspire Justine's constant criticism by staying. There was no neutral ground, and there was no way out of a bitter battle on both fronts.

"You're not old or doddering, Aunt Katherine," Celesta replied quietly, "but your matchmaking'll get us both into trouble. Damon could charm a snake—"

"I bet he has a lovely singing voice," she sighed.

"—out of a sack, and fixing up this house is the *last* reason he jumped at your invitation."

"Ah. So he's expressed his interest." Katherine grinned like a little girl caught spying. "I bet he's a wonderful kisser, too. He certainly has the lips for it."

Celesta closed her eyes against the image of a single drop of lemonade trailing down Damon's dusky neck. "I'm going upstairs now. I think we all need to sleep on this."

"Hmph. Justine's no more asleep than you and I. She's smoking," Katherine said with an emphatic nod, "and one of these nights she'll set the room on fire."

Saturday breakfast was a tense meal: Justine complained her eggs were broken and her bacon burnt, while Katherine retorted that no one should be expected to cook on such an antiquated stove. Celesta kept her eyes on her plate, wishing this day were over. "Someone's coming," she announced quietly, not daring to watch Damon approach on his horse.

The two women stopped bickering to peer out the

kitchen window. "Punctual to a fault!" Katherine crowed. "I told you Mr. Frye was an industrious sort."

"And he's about to be versed in our expectations." Justine rose from the table, checking her tightly pulled hair as she went to the pantry door. Then she turned, looking sour. "He'll sleep in the cellar, or he'll sleep nowhere. I'll not have my standards compromised during his stay. And he'll keep his shirt on!"

She was out the door like a whirlwind, and Celesta didn't envy Frye the lecture he'd get . . . yet it was for her own good Justine was behaving this way. Or did the spinster fear for her own moral downfall, after succumbing to Damon's pleasantries last night? She did have more of a swish in her skirt as she descended the stone path toward where he was squatting to open a can of paint.

Damon let the old girl approach without looking up, knowing just what sort of talking-to she was planning. Not until the hem of her dark blue skirt fluttered to a halt a foot away did he glance up with a polite smile.

"Mr. Frye," she stated with a businesslike nod.

"Miss Ransom," he replied, stirring his paint. There was an awkward pause while he waited for her to continue.

"Your prompt completion of this job is appreciated. We don't look kindly upon slugabeds in this household," she said hesitantly. "And if you've brought your things, we've decided to let you sleep in the cellar, where it's coolest. You'll undoubtedly appreciate that after a hot day's labor."

Swallowing a laugh, he rose to stand beside her, wearing his politest smile. "I sense Katherine's offer was as big a surprise to you as it was to me," he said in a genteel voice, "so if you'd rather I didn't board here—"

"Oh, no, we—we're proud to have you," Justine

89

stammered. She twisted her hands into a knot as bright pink spots appeared on her faded cheeks. "My sister-in-law does have a way of speaking before she thinks, but she's right about the house needing some work."

"I think you'll be pleased with the difference fresh paper and paint will make," he replied suavely. "I hope it's all right that I've brought some samples with me. And I'll be pleased to pass along my professional discount when I order your materials. It's the least I can do for the privilege of staying in your home while I work."

"That will be fine, Mr. Frye," she murmured.

Her bright eyes strayed to his backside when he leaned over to pick up his paint, and then he noticed she was staring at his shirt, which was unbuttoned down to the bib of his overalls. "Will there be anything else?"

She looked ready to deliver a fire and brimstone sermon, but the scowl passed. When she relaxed, or talked about her proud family past, Justine Ransom was a comely enough woman who would've made the right man a devoted, if testy, wife.

"No, that will be all. Carry on, Mr. Frye."

Indeed I will, he thought as he gave her his best smile. He set his paint brush in motion over and around the strips of new latticework, and when his landlady entered the house his eyes followed the majestic white pillars up to the third story. There, beneath the peak of the portico roof, was the rose window that bathed the ballroom alcove in its pastel lights . . . where Celesta wrote her stories now, pacing when she couldn't sleep.

Be ready to walk the floor, sweetheart, he thought with a chuckle. *You'll get no rest while Damon Frye's under your roof.*

* * *

When Celesta heard hoofbeats and carriage wheels on the stone pathway, her heart constricted in her chest. Sometime during the morning Eula and Patrick Perkins would each expect a yes from her, and she didn't want to say that. Justine had a point: her indecisiveness would only give them leverage to coax her back with. A "no" with a solid reason to decline was her best defense, yet—as Justine also knew—it was far easier to think of a clever reply than to actually deliver it.

And Damon wasn't helping matters. He was an accomplished whistler, and his light-hearted melodies floated into the kitchen while she and Aunt Katherine were arranging cookies on a plate. She knew as sure as thunder followed lightning that he was here to wreak havoc in her already turbulent world, and that it was only a matter of time before Justine caught her in his damning embrace and cast her out. Perhaps she should return to the Perkins household now and save the humiliation of begging for work when she was destitute.

Yet the twinkle in Patrick's crystal blue eyes when he stepped through the door behind his mother warned her that he, too, had questionable intentions. "Celesta, it's so good to see you," he murmured as he reached for her hands. "Pardon us for being early, but—well, I couldn't keep Mother home any longer."

Eula waved him off with an indulgent laugh and hugged Katherine. "And how are you, dear?" she crooned. "You've been in my thoughts constantly since the funeral. I imagine Celesta's presence has been an immeasurable comfort to you."

Celesta forced a smile. This was all a bit too cozy, considering the Perkins family hadn't socialized with the Ransoms since before she was born. She felt dowdy in her floral-print cotton dress—especially since Patrick was the prince of fashion in his navy blue blazer with its brass buttons. He and Eula were gazing about the entryway as though they intended to buy it, until Katherine gestured toward the music room.

"As you can see, nothing's changed since your last visit," she said with a little laugh, "but we're—"

"Just as charming as I remember it," Eula cooed.

"—in the process of redecorating. As soon as Mr. Frye finishes the gazebo repairs, he'll be papering and painting for us. You can't imagine how excited we *all* are."

Mrs. Perkins dropped into a wing chair near the piano, thunderstruck. "You've hired Damon Frye?"

Katherine looked deliciously pleased that she'd caught both Perkinses off guard. "It's barter, actually," she said with a catlike smile at Celesta. "We're giving him room and board in exchange for his labor. So much nicer for him than a hotel, you know, and we couldn't ask for a more congenial carpenter. He's a fascinating man, with a genuine passion for preserving Ransom Manor's distinguished heritage."

Eula fidgeted with the lace bow at her throat. "Well, I declare. . . ."

"And Justine's going along with this?" Patrick asked. "She had nothing good to say about him after Rachel's service."

"And who *does* she like?" Katherine replied with a roll of her eyes. "She expresses her regrets for not joining us, as she's preparing Mr. Frye's . . . quarters."

Silence. Celesta took her aunt's cue and stood facing their flabbergasted guests with her most polite smile, until she could stifle her laughter no longer. "I'll get our tea," she murmured, and quickly left the room.

Bless her, Katherine had yanked the rug from under Patrick and his mother, and it was the funniest thing she'd seen in weeks. By tomorrow, everyone in Hannibal would know about their unorthodox arrangement with Damon Frye, because Eula couldn't keep this scandalous news to herself. Her aunt had also implied that she was staying on here during the redecorating and after, preparing them to look for a different domestic.

Celesta glanced at the tea tray and went to the dining room for the silver sugar bowl and creamer. She was glad the ice had been broken concerning her employment, yet she had to be even more careful dealing with Patrick now: he'd want her back, if only to keep her away from Damon Frye.

The sugar bowl was nearly empty, so she squatted to find the correct container in the dark cupboard . . . spice jars, oatmeal, a lard tin, a sticky honey crock. She opened a jar of white crystals and quickly replaced the lid when she smelled a peculiar almond odor, then finally spooned sugar from their everyday bowl into the silver one. Then she poured boiling water over the tea in the china pot and let it steep while she thought of what she'd say to Patrick.

From the cellar came the sound of heavy furniture being dragged across the floor . . . a futile effort, because Frye wouldn't be content to stay down there. Voices drifted in from the music room, and Celesta held her breath, listening. That was Justine fussing at somebody—yet she was in the cellar! She hurried through the dining room with the loaded tray to see what was going on.

She was greeted by the ladies' high-pitched giggles as Patrick turned to face her, his fist on his hip. "Slow as you were, we thought you had to harvest those tea leaves," he quipped. "Surely Eula Perkins didn't tolerate such tardiness."

Celesta flushed but couldn't help laughing. She'd

93

forgotten his talent for imitating voices, and her spinster aunt's was his latest achievement—one of his best. "She didn't tolerate making fun of one's elders, either," she replied, "but you could always make your mother and her friends laugh with that trick, couldn't you?"

Patrick's auntlike frown became a subtle smile. "You enjoyed it, too, Celesta. Don't tell me you've forgotten how I used to read fairy tales to you, with a different voice for each character."

She swallowed hard. He was reminding her of a pastime that had kept them occupied on many a rainy afternoon . . . and he was doing it in a resonant baritone that was somewhere between her grandfather's and Damon Frye's. Celesta blinked and set the refreshments on the table beside her aunt, who was chatting with Eula. "That was years ago," she mumbled.

"We go back a long way."

Knowing where this conversation would lead, she looked him straight in the eye. "Which means I also recall how obnoxious you could be, repeating the villains' lines outside my door at night," she said in a low voice. "This is not the place to discuss—"

"Then, we'll go to another room. This house must have dozens of places we can be alone, honey."

His grip on her hand told her there was no escaping him. "I—I was going to pour the—"

"Katherine and Mother were serving tea before you were born," he whispered, his blue eyes delving into hers. "Take me where we can talk, Celesta. I have something for you."

Her pulse pounded weakly, and as she started toward the library she felt Eula and her aunt's curious gazes. Patrick followed, still holding her hand, and the insistent caress of his thumb made her stomach churn. Surely he hadn't bought an engagement ring, after the way she'd walked off last time—

after he'd caught Damon kissing her! The striped settee in the library looked dangerously intimate, even with Grandfather's portrait looking on, so she opened the outside door.

"Ah, the porch," he murmured with a chuckle. "You have a penchant for porches, don't you, honey?"

Celesta whirled around, scowling. "This is ridiculous," she hissed. "I told you I couldn't possibly—your mother will never go along with—"

"It was Mother's idea for me to come, remember?" Patrick asked with a sly grin. "And now that you're apparently staying here instead of returning to work for us, my love for you will seem more suitable. Much better for me to court the Ransom niece than the maid. Though I'd be thrilled to call you my own either way."

It would never do to have Eula or Katherine overhear any of this, so she hurried past the porch furniture and down the steps. His *love* for her—*suitable!* Couldn't he hear his own duplicity?

"Celesta, please, I—I apologize," he pleaded behind her. "I've kept my feelings to myself for so long, dreaming of the day you'd be my wife. I must sound terribly presumptuous to you, spouting off this way."

She stopped beneath the nearest trees. They were within sight of the house but wouldn't be heard, far safer than if she walked into the orchard. The garden and honeysuckle hedges were between them and the gazebo, yet she could run that direction if she needed Damon's protection. Depending upon him was like Little Red Riding Hood trusting the wolf, but his presence calmed her now. Celesta breathed deeply, allowing the shade's coolness and the sweet smell of honeysuckle to soothe her.

She turned to him, determined to end this outlandish game. "And why on earth would you want to marry me, Patrick Perkins?"

He blinked. "Why *wouldn't* I? You're witty and caring and terribly—it's not like you to fish for compliments, Celesta."

"I need answers, so I'm asking questions," she stated. "Most girls don't learn someone's in love with them while standing in another man's arms. Most girls are taken to dances or treated to picnics or—do you realize I've known you all my life, and you've never once sent me a Valentine or passed a note under my door?"

The evidence was damning, and as he watched her closely, Patrick sensed his plan was as mindless as it appeared to Celesta. She was gazing calmly at him, her head high and her proud shoulders back . . . ebony hair that would spill to her waist if he removed the pins, lips that would surely surrender if he could only get close enough to claim her.

He reached into his blazer pocket and pulled out a present he'd chosen with great care. "I'm trying to make up for my past oversights," he said in a husky voice. "Even if you keep refusing me, even if you ridicule me and say you can never love me, I want you to have this, honey. I want you to wear it with the same pride I'll feel when I take you all those places we haven't yet been together."

As he pressed the gift into her palm she felt warm, smooth metal and softest velvet. Celesta's eyes widened. It was a choker, a heart-shaped locket fashioned from gold that shone with burnished elegance on a crimson ribbon. Patrick was known for sparing no expense to impress his lady friends—of which he had several, she reminded herself—and this trinket was by far the most exquisite piece of jewelry she'd ever owned. And yet. . . .

"Perhaps this makes up for a few paper Valentines?" he asked quietly. "Let me put it on you. I thought the red would flatter your coloring and your

96

lovely neck."

She held her breath as he fastened the choker with agile, warm fingers. Patrick's hands lingered on her shoulders; his breath teased at her cheeks when he slowly leaned down to kiss her. His lips were sweet and gentle this time, undemanding now that she wasn't fighting his advances. "I love you, Celesta," he murmured, running his tongue along the edge of her ear. "Please give me a chance to show you how much. Please don't shut me out because I've been blind to you all these years."

It was the whistling that brought her back to her senses, a melody accented by rhythmic hammering from the other side of the honeysuckle. Celesta pulled away, desperately trying to think of a graceful way out of this. "I—I'm just not ready," she stammered. "Aunt Katherine needs me to—"

"She was too much in love with her husband to expect you to forfeit your own happiness for her," Patrick pointed out. He slipped his arm around her and held her chin, gently forcing her to look up at him. "Why do you insist on moving into a house that's never welcomed you? A house that's faded and cold as a tomb."

She understood his comparison, because he'd never been to Ransom Manor when it rang with her grandfather's laughter or sparkled with light from the fine chandeliers. Yet something about his words made her shudder, which jarred another thought loose. "Perhaps I'm a little afraid to return because Mama . . . it was so sudden, and we don't know why."

He pulled her close, blotting her tears against his shoulder. "Honey, I can understand that. She was a mother to me, too—a rational, kind woman when my parents were too concerned about their own affairs to bother about mine."

This much was true, and her mother had returned

Patrick's affection. Celesta forced herself to listen with all her senses, though. To observe Patrick carefully through her tears.

"Since it was apparent that something she ate diagreed with her," he continued tenderly, "I took all the precautions I could think of the next day. I had the cistern and the pipes checked for contamination, I threw away all the open food in the house, and I boiled the dishes you used, for fear you'd fall victim to whatever took your mother."

He went on, but Celesta's heart had already sunk: she'd gathered her sugar sample too late. And as Patrick repeated his earnest plea for her return, Celesta suddenly wondered if she was standing in a murderer's embrace. His precautions were practical and decent—Eula had been too overcome to think of them—but they were also the perfect way to dispose of the poison she was so sure her mother had ingested.

Why would he kill the woman he'd poured his wounded heart out to as a child, the housekeeper who'd kept some of his pranks a secret from his stern father and his excitable mother? It made as much sense to condemn Katherine for poisoning the sister-in-law she'd adored for thirty years.

Somebody did it, though. And as fresh tears welled up, Celesta only wanted to remove herself from all reminders of the horrible crime that had ended Mama's life. "I'm sorry," she rasped. "The pain's still very fresh, and I won't be good company—"

"I understand, honey, truly I do," he murmured, silently chiding himself. Why had he upset her with morbid details, breaking her heart anew instead of winning it? "I'll walk you back—"

"I'll go through the pantry," she said between sniffles. "I hate to spoil your mother and Katherine's visit. Please reassure them I'll be fine. And tell your mother I'll come for my clothes on Monday."

He heard the finality in her voice and knew not to press her. Celesta would be her beautiful, resolute self when he saw her again, and it would give him time to choose another gift or arrange an outing . . . and as he'd mentioned before, her moving back to Ransom Manor actually made his plans more socially acceptable anyway.

Patrick smiled, placing his arm loosely around her shoulders as they passed between the fragrant honeysuckle hedge and the house. Celesta had softened visibly when he placed the choker around her neck. She would turn it over in her hands this weekend and admire its beauty in the mirror, thinking of him. If it was love notes she craved, he'd send them, along with other frivolous luxuries she'd been denied all her life. He sincerely admired her and wanted her, so it wasn't as though he were courting her under false pretenses.

She stiffened, and then he saw why: Damon Frye was stretching up from his ladder, hanging one side of the white swing from the gazebo ceiling. Even with the latticework in front of him, he looked as tawny and powerful as a tiger—and every bit as dangerous.

"I think you should go in, before things get unpleasant. He has a nasty tongue in his head."

Celesta nodded and quickly ducked through the pantry door—but not before Damon saw her. From his perch atop the gazebo he'd watched the choker change hands and knew Perkins had again failed to impress Celesta, had instead made her cry. After he looped the heavy swing chain onto its hook in the beam, he moved his ladder as though unaware that Patrick was approaching the gazebo, hands stuffed in his trouser pockets.

He was stretched toward the ceiling, balanced precariously on the ladder's top step and lifting the full, shifting weight of the swing, when Perkins accosted him. "What the hell're you doing here, Frye?" he demanded. "When I tell Katherine and Justine what sort of *clinch* you had their niece in, they'll kick your deceitful ass right into the river. You must've sweet-talked Celesta—"

"Nope," he grunted as he slipped the chain onto its hook. He descended the ladder slowly, making Perkins wait. "Katherine wanted these repairs, and Katherine invited me to board here while I renovate the inside of the house. And considering the attention my other job will require, I could be here a lo-o-ong time."

Patrick scowled, fully aware of the effect Frye's well-proportioned body and virile voice would have on three lone women. "You're full of—"

"Am I?" Damon challenged. He clapped the sides of his ladder together, making his opponent jump. "Ask Katherine yourself. Or better yet, ask Justine. And then think of me eating my meals with your beloved, flirting with her while we hang paper . . . waiting every night for two half-deaf old ladies to start snoring so I can—well, you can imagine the rest. It's great work when you can get it, Perkins," he said with a big grin. "Great work, old buddy."

Chapter 8

As Damon sat beside Celesta in church the next morning, he delighted in her fragile, sweet soprano and felt her brave pain when she prayed, her coal-black lashes trembling against pale cheeks. As he watched her serving ham and creamed peas with new potatoes, he witnessed her quiet efficiency and a true affection for her aunts. And as he sat in the summer parlor with the three of them that afternoon, to show them samples of the latest wallpapers, he suddenly realized how much he'd missed the company of good women.

Justine sat to his left, stick straight yet perched eagerly on the edge of her chair. Katherine was beside him on the sofa, fidgety as a girl at her first dance. Demure and distanced, Celesta sat on an ottoman across the table from them, making his stomach flutter with her shy smiles. There was so much more to admire about her than he'd ever liked in Lucy, which posed a problem: he couldn't live with himself if he continued to use Celesta to avenge Lucy's death. Moving into Ransom Manor had seemed the perfect way to gain control over her, yet as he looked at her now, Frye realized *he* was the one who'd been taken captive.

"I can't presume to tell you which patterns to

choose or how much to spend on these materials," he began, "so I'll let you look and ask questions, and I promise not to give advice unless you ask for it."

"Thank you," Justine said crisply, peering toward the multicolored sheets. "We're a frugal lot, yet we detest poor quality. After all, Mother's papers are still intact forty years after she chose them."

"A wise attitude," he replied with a nod.

"Which of these are the Cruikshanks using?" Katherine piped up. She ran an eager finger over a green piece with gold speckles, and then looked at him, her eyes shining.

Damon chuckled. "I brought some swatches from their first floor because I knew you'd be interested," he said as he picked them up. "They're both imported—this gold gilt one's from France, and this leathery-looking paper for the dining room's running them about a hundred thirty dollars a roll, I hear. How much can I order for you?" he teased.

"My stars!" she gasped.

"That's preposterous," Justine muttered. Then she settled herself again, smiling primly. "It's good you have a sense of humor, Mr. Frye. Dealing with such extravagance must test it at times."

"It's part of my job," he replied with a shrug. "What do *you* like, Celesta? You're being awfully quiet."

She, too, knew better than to presume anything about Justine's budget, yet the chance to redecorate came so seldom she wanted to at least express an opinion. "This speckled piece Aunt Katherine likes would look elegant in the dining room . . . and perhaps these stripes for the library . . . and what about this Jacobean floral for in here? The pastels would be very soothing, I think."

Damon gave her an encouraging smile. "You have excellent taste, Miss Montgomery—and very reasonable, too," he added for her spinster aunt's benefit. "And what about the vestibule?"

"A home's entryway makes a statement about its owner," she ventured with a glance at her aunts. "To me, this scarlet with the gilt flocking is the essence of Ransom pride. Grandfather would've loved it."

"Yes, he would've," Katherine murmured.

"But we so seldom *use* the entryway," the other aunt protested. "It seems foolish to spend money on walls that no one but us will see."

"Which is the perfect excuse for entertaining again!" Katherine countered. She stood up suddenly, quivering with her excitement. "I really must look at our rooms more closely—and I'll make us some lemonade. It's so hard to decide!"

Celesta smiled at her younger aunt, and then held her breath when she saw the way Damon was studying her. "I—it's good to see Katherine so happy and involved in a project," she stammered. "I'll help her with our refreshments so she doesn't wander through the house all afternoon, daydreaming."

"Excellent idea," Justine commented. And as Celesta walked through the library, she heard her maiden aunt say, "And now you and I can talk money, Mr. Frye. Just how much will I be set back if I go along with their choices?"

Celesta chuckled and continued to the kitchen, where she found Katherine squeezing lemons with a vengeance. She got a glass pitcher out of the cabinet and then arranged fresh oatmeal cookies on a plate. "Do you think she'll really agree to all this? She's never made—or paid for—such a decision."

Her younger aunt laughed quietly. "Which is the very reason I left the room. She's too polite to throw a fit in front of Damon, and he's diplomatic enough to suggest other papers that are less expensive, if need be. The more time we give them alone, the more he'll persuade her that she can afford our choices."

"You certainly know your way around her."

"She has her pride, and her weak spots. And if she substitutes patterns we don't like, at least we don't have to look at them for another forty years," Katherine said lightly. "Justine can't live forever, you know."

An odd sentiment, but it was obviously a joke. Celesta got out a large tray, pleased that her aunt was humming as she grated some rind into the lemonade . . . pleased that Damon Frye's presence would have a positive effect on her aunts, even if she herself had to be on constant guard. He was alluring in his tweed trousers, with his shirtsleeves rolled to his elbows. He did indeed have a pleasant singing voice—seemed quite comfortable with the hymns, though his occasional smiles in church had been anything but pious. He was an enigma—

". . . and where could I have put that sugar?" her aunt was mumbling. "Surely we can't be out."

Celesta glanced up from her woolgathering to see Katherine removing the lid from a jar half-full of white crystals. She was tipping it toward the pitcher of lemon juice when Celesta grabbed for it, nearly knocking it from her hand. "NO! That's not—"

"What on earth's the matter, child?" the little woman cried. "Without sugar this lemonade won't be fit to drink!"

"It's not—" Celesta stopped, wondering how to voice the suspicions that sprang to life when the almondlike odor from the jar reached her nose. When she was brewing tea for the Perkinses yesterday, it hadn't occurred to her to identify that distinctive odor. But now, in light of Katherine's allusion that Justine wouldn't live forever . . . that death came in threes . . . that Mama had complained of bitter tea. . . .

"Take a whiff of that," she said in a tight voice.

Katherine frowned, inhaled, and then shrugged. "Smells fresh to me. Do you think it's gotten wormy?"

She seemed sincerely puzzled—and Celesta knew from her Sally Sharpe research that not everyone could detect cyanide's peculiar aroma—but Katherine was a practiced enough actress . . . could she feign innocence while on the brink of murder?

Celesta exhaled slowly, thinking how the Girl Detective would word this. "Do you . . . keep a supply of . . . powder to kill mice with?"

Katherine gasped, her eyes doubling in size. "My Lord! Justine's been complaining that—she must've sprinkled some downstairs yesterday when she was—" Visibly shaken, she screwed the lid back on the jar and shoved it across the cabinet top. "We need to label that and store it someplace else. I—I could've killed us all—*please* don't tell her, Celesta! You know how scatterbrained she thinks I am, but this could—"

Was it genuine shock or an extremely good act? Celesta's smile felt forced as she set the jar out by the pantry door, wishing she knew. "I won't say a word. Nearly made the same mistake myself once," she replied. "Shall we rejoin the others? She'll wonder why we're not out there spending her money."

Katherine quickly stirred in sugar from the kitchen table, and then preceded Celesta back to the parlor. It seemed unlikely that she'd attempt a mass poisoning when they were finally refurbishing her beloved home, yet Celesta had to wonder . . . had she hastily stashed that jar in the cupboard, after lacing Mama's sugar bowl with the cyanide? She could've hidden it in her bag of sewing supplies that day. . . .

The details still didn't add up. And when they found Damon measuring the parlor walls while Justine wrote down the dimensions he called out, Celesta made herself think more pleasant thoughts. It wasn't hard: Frye's movements showed a confident male grace as he used his eyes and his tape measure. His wink brought heat to her cheeks.

"You ladies will be pleased to know we've reached an agreement on all your patterns," he said suavely. "Justine has also chosen this flecked design for the music room and the upstairs hallway, and I think she's decided that this redecorating isn't so costly after all."

"You drive a hard bargain, Mr. Frye," the spinster stated good-naturedly.

"And you dicker like a tradesman," he teased back.

Katherine sat down to pour their drinks with a relieved smile. "It sounds like Celesta and I missed out on some important transactions. You must be thirsty after your negotiations."

Damon chuckled and took the tall, cool glass she handed him. "Are you ready for this? When I told her that Mr. and Mrs. Cruikshank *each* had a bathroom upstairs, she agreed to install plumbing in one of your tower bedrooms."

Celesta blinked, and Katherine nearly dropped her pitcher, but Justine merely sniffed. "Winter's coming," she asserted. "At my age, it's a long walk to the privy—and since Katherine's so finicky about emptying chamber pots, I decided it was time. But only because Mr. Frye agreed to install the fixtures himself, and only because he promised not to touch my room. Actually, I see no need to redecorate any of the bedrooms. We can't see the walls when we're asleep."

Frye flashed a smile at Katherine and Celesta. "We'll see how it goes. Once the first floor's complete, she may change her mind."

"Well, it seems to me we should celebrate," Katherine said with a girlish laugh. She handed the rest of the glasses around and raised her own. "With many thanks to Mr. Frye for working miracles, and a toast to a bright, happy future to all of us within these dear walls."

"Hear, hear," Celesta murmured, watching her

favorite aunt, hoping her doubts would pass with time.

"It's my pleasure to be a part of this august occasion," Frye said. And as he clinked his glass against Justine's and took a long, slow drink of his lemonade, Celesta thanked God that Sally Sharpe had averted an unspeakable tragedy today.

It was as pleasant an afternoon as Damon could remember. They finished measuring the first-floor rooms and the second-floor hallway, and as he suggested layouts for the round bathroom, pacing out places where the tub, sink, and the enclosed toilet could be, Katherine's eyes shone with her excitement. Justine was a meticulous secretary, displaying her enthusiasm by noting each room's dimensions alongside a description of the paper pattern, figuring and refiguring the square footage—and probably each room's price, but she kept that figure in her head.

As they started downstairs, the two older women asked numerous questions about the mansion he was overseeing, but it was their niece he wished to draw out. "As I recall, you were taking piano lessons when you were a girl—much to Patrick's chagrin, because you were more talented than he," Frye added. "Would you play for me? That's a beautiful instrument in the sitting room."

"Oh, I—" She blinked, brought out of her reverie by his direct, dark-eyed gaze. "It's been years since I sat down—"

"Would you mind if I played, then? Just to see if I remember anything?"

Katherine clapped her hands together and lit up with delight. "We'd *love* to hear you, Damon. What a perfect end to a lovely day."

Justine stayed behind them on the bottom step,

clearing her throat. "I believe I'll retire now. Thank you for your help and advice today, Mr. Frye. I feel we've made great progress."

Damon watched her slender form ascend to the landing, wondering what had caused such a turnabout in her mood. "Did I say something wrong? Perhaps my playing will disturb—"

"Don't think a thing of it, dear," Katherine insisted as she took his arm. "The piano was Rachel's birthday gift when she was just a little girl—Ambrose lavished the best on her because her mother died when she was a toddler, you see—and Justine, being nearly twenty years older, always felt . . . slighted. Always walked out when Rachel sat down to play, too. It's no reflection on you."

"And you've done remarkably well with her," Celesta commented as they entered the music room. "I thought she'd go through the roof when she learned you were coming, yet now she's following you around like a puppy."

Frye laughed low in his throat and slid onto the piano bench. "I have that way with women, you know. Better beware, ladies."

Celesta flushed and Katherine giggled her approval, but when he played his first thundering chords with a flourish they watched in awe. Damon Frye was an accomplished musician even as he warmed up with brilliant runs and arpeggios. And after glancing thoughtfully at Katherine, he eased into three-quarter time and played an introduction they all knew well.

"'Tales of the Vienna Woods,'" her aunt whispered, and she sank down into a chair to enjoy the graceful, lilting waltz with her eyes closed. Celesta leaned on the top of the piano, fascinated by the tanned, masculine hands that possessed such lyrical power.

Frye mentally thanked his mother for making him

practice when he was young, because Celesta's dreamlike expression was exactly what he'd been searching for . . . for more years than he realized.

"You're so lovely," he breathed, and when he saw that her aunt was lounging in the wing chair, he ended the Strauss piece with a bridge into another familiar classic. "This one's for you, Celesta. Only for you."

She listened, spellbound by the singing tonal quality of a song that went straight to her heart, because she'd played it herself years ago. "'Liebestraume,'" she whispered.

"A dream of love," he murmured back, smiling tenderly. "A dream of you . . . and I don't imagine I'll get much sleep while I'm staying here. Be mine, Celesta. Tonight."

Her heart raced wildly. Could this be the same man who had stolen her manuscript and forced her to kiss him on Patrick's back porch? The music seemed to transform him from a conniving blackheart into the handsome prince of a hundred fairy tales.

But she knew better than to fall for his seductive repartee: her aunt had made the consequences of getting caught very clear. "Justine'll hear me—"

"Not in the cellar, she won't."

She closed her eyes against visions of him pulling her close, murmuring daring, dangerous phrases as he unbuttoned her blouse. "Damon, I can't—"

"You can," he insisted, punctuating his whispered command with a compelling brown-eyed gaze that made her legs go rubbery. "I'll show you all you need to know . . . though I suspect pleasing me will come as naturally to you as breathing."

Celesta clung helplessly to the polished piano, knowing she should leave yet craving more clandestine promises that could only get her into trouble. "We shouldn't. . . ."

"Ah, but we shall. It's only a matter of time for us,

Celesta." Sensing she was about to turn away, he leaned forward until his face was directly beneath hers, still playing softly so that Katherine wouldn't hear him. "Don't forget that I still have something of yours. You know my terms of surrender, sweetheart."

Her pale green eyes flashed with resentment, and she stalked from the room; yet he knew she was already his. Damon brought the sonorous serenade to an end and discovered Katherine watching him with a knowing, secretive expression.

"You have a charming niece," he said with a dapper smile. "Temperamental, but charming. I believe I'll retire now, so I can arrange my room before I go to bed. Good night, Katherine."

"Good night, Mr. Frye. Sleep well."

Celesta shifted in the hard wooden chair, staring at the flickering candle on Grandfather's secretary. *Like a moth to the flame*, she mused, *and you're going to burn in hell for listening to his pretty lies*.

Unable to sleep in her hot, airless room, she'd come to the alcove to write. Her cotton nightgown clung damply to her back, and her pen lay atop a stack of clean white sheets—so preoccupied she was, she hadn't even written her usual Sally Sharpe heading across the top of one.

It had been a momentous day: Justine had agreed to redecorate the manor—and to install indoor plumbing! In the room below, she was still reading. The glow from her lamp and the scent of cigarettes drifted up through the ventilation grate in the floor. Katherine had nearly spiked the lemonade with rat poison, an event that still made her shake to think about it. And tomorrow she'd fetch her possessions from the room she'd lived in since she could remember, trying to close one chapter of her life so that she could start another.

The story was just beginning, but already Damon Frye had signed his name across her soul, much as she penned her pseudonym at the top of each tale about Sally Sharpe. She didn't always know how events and clues would fall into place when she started an episode, but she had implicit faith in the Girl Detective's ability to lead her through the plot's twists and red herrings to a satisfying conclusion. It just worked that way, and she didn't question the intuition behind her talent.

Celesta sighed, sensing she was on the brink of her life's most treacherous yet exciting journey, an adventure like those she wrote about because her real life was so predictable and boring. But not anymore—not with a handsome, sensual man waiting for her in the cellar even as she sat here trying not to think about him!

Damon scared her witless. And unlike a fictional thief who would stop badgering her once she wrote of his capture by her blond detective, Frye would continue to haunt her until she wrote the ending *his* way . . . and then he'd demand more, until he'd stolen her very being.

What would Sally Sharpe do with a man like Damon? How would she bring him to his knees?

Celesta smiled in spite of a conscience that cried out her doom, in spite of willpower that flickered like the flame before her.

There was only one way to find out.

Chapter 9

Poised at the top of the cellar stairs, Celesta let out the breath she'd been holding since she crept down from the third floor. The wooden steps from the ballroom had creaked beneath her bare feet—and they ran right alongside the master suite Justine slept in!—but her maiden aunt's snores hadn't missed a beat, as far as she could tell. It was hard to hear, with her heart pounding this way.

She gazed into the velvety darkness below, knowing Damon waited like a wolf in his lair—knowing this descent to her own damnation marked a point of no return. *It's only a matter of time for us, Celesta . . . you know my terms of surrender*. Damn his arrogance! But what bothered her more was his accuracy, his uncanny ability to know that she, too, sensed this rendezvous was their destiny.

Why wasn't he burning a lamp? For all she knew he was crouched at the bottom of the stairs, ready to pounce. . . . She'd scream and waken the aunts—which would be her salvation. The only sign of his presence was a faint fragrance that masked the cellar's mustiness . . . tobacco, with a hint of cherry.

Swallowing the anxiety that rose in her throat, Celesta groped for the first step with her foot, and then the next, and then the third. Still there was no acknowledgement of his presence, yet every fiber in her taut body vibrated to his silent call. Damon would play the tune, and she would dance . . . on Lucy's grave and probably on Mama's, if that was what he demanded.

Despite the drop in temperature, she felt clammy. A cold prickle of fear coursed through her when the door behind her swung shut. She was trapped down here, and it was really Damon who'd slipped that cyanide into Mama's—

Sally Sharpe would get a hold of her racing imagination, Celesta reminded herself desperately, as she closed her eyes to regain composure. *Sally wouldn't stand here quaking in the dark, waiting for something horrible to happen to her.*

She took a deep breath and opened her eyes. Up or down? The choice was hers, and since it looked like Mr. Frye was making a complete fool of her, playing upon her unsophisticated nature, the only intelligent move was to turn around and—

A *pffffft* made her gasp. In the center of the blackness below shone the light of a single match, with which Damon was lighting his pipe. The flame illuminated his shadowy face, and as he inhaled, the embers of his tobacco cast a satanic glow over his dusky features.

"Come into my parlor, said the spider to the fly," he quipped.

"Damn you, give me some light!"

His low laughter echoed in the cavernous room, and she knew in her heart she should run while she still had the chance. But she stood there, crawling with gooseflesh, too fascinated by the mystery that was Damon Frye to move.

And when he lit a small lamp on the table beside him she was amazed at the sudden ambiance. He was seated in an old overstuffed chair that had been a favorite of Grandfather's, beside a bed—already turned down, she noted—from what had been her mother's room. Behind him, Mama's cheval mirror reflected the inviting light, turning this part of the cellar into a homey den for a host who was smiling cordially now. Two other large, freestanding mirrors were arranged to either side of him, camouflaging the old armoires, trunks, and other castoffs behind it, relics that had accumulated through the generations.

The smoke from his pipe formed a mystical frame around his face. He was watching her intently, as though anticipating her every thought and move, and she suddenly realized that in her flustered state she'd left her wrapper draped over the alcove chair.

She was a vision of heartrending innocence in her flowing white gown, and yet . . . the ebony hair tumbling around her shoulders peaked on her forehead, lending a decidedly wanton air to her pale face. She was an angel about to fall, unflinching despite his piercing gaze. His heart ached with admiration, but he couldn't save her.

"I'd almost given up on you."

"You underestimate me, Mr. Frye." Celesta surveyed the dim corners of his abode until she found the envelope he'd taken, with the folded packet of sugar on it. "Do you have a habit of stealing other peoples' personal effects?"

"Only when it provides the means to get better acquainted. The folded paper full of sugar intrigues me, though."

"You tasted it?"

"I wanted to be sure you didn't take a powder before I had the chance to—" Her stricken expression brought him out of his chair and confirmed a few suspicions her detective story had raised. "I'm sorry, sweetheart. I didn't mean to make light of—"

"Just give me my envelope and my pen, so I can—"

"Wait." Damon reached up to grasp her arms, chiding himself for spoiling the mood he'd so carefully created. A tear glistened on her dimly lit cheek, and the lowest of lechers couldn't continue to seduce this grieving child. "Celesta, forgive me. With what you had to know about poisons to write that story, it's just now occurring to me that you think your mother might've taken—"

"No, I think it was mixed into the sugar bowl only she and I used."

Frye studied her closely. Her shining eyes reflected her conviction that Rachel Montgomery was murdered, and if what Celesta said was true, she could've been the next victim! "So how do you know—"

"I have no proof," she replied with a sigh. "But in retrospect, I realize that Mama's complaint about bitter tea, followed by her convulsions . . . and her pink complexion afterward, all point to cyanide."

Frowning, he urged her down the last two steps so that they could talk more comfortably. "Didn't a doctor or the undertaker offer any suggestion about the cause of death?" he asked quietly.

"She was a maid, Damon. Buried in a plain pine box."

He shut his eyes, wishing the magic of her presence hadn't rendered him so insensitive to her painful circumstances. "What did the Perkinses think it was?"

"Patrick had the water supply checked, and threw away all the open food and boiled our dishes, thinking it was some sort of contamination," she said in a quavery voice. "By the time I thought to check the sugar bowl, that day you cornered me on their porch, any evidence of the poison had been disposed of. I—I'm sorry I'm blubbering. It's really not like me."

Damon took her in his arms, sorely wishing she were standing against him, wearing next to nothing, under happier circumstances. As he rocked her, he considered her comments carefully, for Celesta

116

wasn't some goose of a girl pointing a hysterical finger at everyone in town. She was well-read and rational, with the analytical mind of a detective and a writer . . . but it seemed unlikely that anyone hated her mother enough to kill her.

"Come here, sweetheart," he murmured against her ear. "We're going to to sit down and sort this out. Perhaps there's an angle you haven't thought of, that I, as an outsider, will see more clearly."

Celesta nodded—Sally Sharpe would say that, too—and allowed him to cradle her on his lap in the large, comfortable chair she'd been held in as a child. Was this gentle, protective man the same rogue who had lured her into this tryst with threats of blackmail? He set aside his pipe and settled her against his chest, his dark eyes intent as he listened to the facts about everyone who had access to the sugar bowl. In these shadows, with his chestnut hair and low, soothing comments, he was reminiscent of the Ambrose Ransom who'd counseled her about her childish concerns so many years ago.

And as Damon listened to her thorough, if sniffle-ridden account, he reached the same conclusions: Patrick and Eula and Katherine each had the opportunity to lace the sugar with cyanide, but why would any of them want to? Rachel Montgomery had been a second mother to Patrick, an indispensable housekeeper to Eula—and her constant companion since Tom's death—while Katherine had maintained the only ties she and Celesta had to the family Rachel forsook years ago.

He blinked and held her closer. There was another party to consider, someone who appeared to have less access to the Perkins pantry but whose feelings toward Rachel couldn't be overlooked. "What about Justine?" he whispered, as though voicing this possibility might make it true.

Celesta raised her head from his shoulder, frowning. "She never visited Eula—"

"How do you know she didn't slip in while Eula was at one of her committee meetings?" he asked quietly. "You just said Katherine came through the house to find you that day, so why couldn't Justine have dropped by while she was in town doing the shopping?"

All the air escaped her lungs at once. "But Justine shops so early, I don't see how—oh, my."

"What?"

Celesta focused huge eyes upon him, and he felt her shivering. "At that hour Eula's still in bed, and on that particular morning Mama and I were rolling up rugs in the upstairs hallway. I—I guess she could've come in. . . ."

"And after Katherine's comment today about Justine feeling slighted because Rachel was the favorite, one has to wonder," Damon pondered aloud. "Your mother hadn't lived at Ransom Manor for more than twenty years, yet only now, when Rachel can no longer inherit the house, does Justine agree to redecorate it."

Scowling, Celesta knuckled a last tear from her cheek. "But it was Katherine's idea to have you come—"

"Which is just juicy enough to divert everyone's attention from your mother's mysterious demise, and exciting enough that Katherine won't dwell upon the details, either." He shrugged, brushing a midnight lock of hair from her shoulder. "Just a thought. No more feasible than suspecting anyone else, I suppose."

It set her imagination to churning, though. Justine had never reconciled herself to her little sister's favored status, even after Grandfather was gone. She never visited . . . didn't cry at the funeral or offer to pay for it, and stood apart from the rest of them in the cemetery . . . and hadn't Aunt Katherine

118

said she'd been sprinkling rat poison down here, and had probably left it in the kitchen cupboard, unlabeled . . . could easily have concealed it in her market basket. The possibilities were endlessly frightening.

"Do you realize," she said in a weak voice, "that everyone I know—everyone I'm close to—is a potential killer?"

Damon hugged her to his chest again, weaving his fingers through the silken strands of her fragrant hair. "Everyone but me, sweetheart," he reminded her. "You and I will figure this out, and—"

"How long have you been in town, Frye?"

He was momentarily stunned by her icy demand. "Two weeks, but—"

"So you *could* have gone to the Perkins pantry, not realizing those crockery dishes were ours, figuring to get back at Patrick by—"

He slipped a firm thumb over her mouth. "Your writer's imagination will drive you crazy if you don't keep things in perspective," he warned in a low voice. "I *could* have gotten into the house—anyone in town could've, apparently—and Mr. Perkins and I have our differences, it's true. But I had sincerely hoped to avoid him altogether while I was on this Cruikshank job. Trust me, Celesta. It was pure coincidence that I saw him in the cemetery."

Damon's baritone was silky-smooth, very convincing, but again there was the issue of trust. As she studied his lamplit features, he returned her gaze with eyes as dark and uncompromising as midnight. It *was* farfetched to think he'd poisoned Mama . . . but his desire to avenge some previous grievance against Patrick Perkins was as evident as his determination to possess her. And the two causes were connected, for some reason. "I—I'd better leave—"

"It was also coincidence that I saw *you* there. Quite

119

a happy one, I must say," he murmured. His hand found the firm curve of her jaw beneath the curtain of her hair, retracing its initial course. "Tell me what I said when I lifted your veil, Celesta. I know you remember."

Of all the underhanded ways to—of *course* his words were emblazoned in her mind, but only a hussy would beg for compliments by repeating—

"Tell me, sweetheart," he whispered against her ear. His fingers freed the top button of her nightgown and then the next one. "I won't let you go until I know you listen to me, and believe what I say."

Her heart pounded weakly beneath the hand that whispered over her cotton gown while he crossed a leg to hold her more tightly. She was like a turtle turned onto its back, yet the danger Damon represented held her captive as surely as the arm that supported her shoulders. "You . . . you're going to force me? Is that what you did to poor Lucy?"

"Absolutely not," he replied more curtly than he intended to. She couldn't know the circumstances surrounding Lucinda Bates's demise any more than he could dispell the rumors by revealing them, so he continued in a low whisper. "Seduction's far more enjoyable than rape, for both of us. You'll know that before you leave me tonight, sweetheart."

He felt Celesta's pulse racing, took his time unfastening the rest of her placket and then ran his fingertip along the exposed vee of porcelain skin between her breasts. "You've read *Dracula*, haven't you?"

She nodded, puzzled.

"Then, you're aware of my methods," he said with a throaty laugh. "The Count never attacks his victims. He always waits for them to invite him into their presence—can't enjoy a beautiful woman unless she leaves a window open or goes for a late-night stroll. Which makes his pursuit much more sporting."

Celesta grunted. "That's true as far as it goes. But he hypnotizes them—renders them helpless with his powerful red eyes. He's always in control, and he knows it."

As usual, her astute observations pleased him. Damon continued to stroke her, edging his hand beneath her nightgown until it ached to close over her trembling breast. "And what do you see in *my* eyes, Celesta?" he breathed. "Evil intent? Blackmail? Or are these the eyes of a man who's falling prey to *your* powers?"

Celesta held her breath, unable to release herself from his riveting gaze. They were enveloped in absolute silence, save the exchange of their accelerated breathing. Damon's lamplit face glowed beneath chestnut hair that draped his forehead at a rakish angle. His dark brows and virile, shadowed jaw were poised only inches above her as he waited . . . to be invited in. "I see pure, unadulterated lust," she finally replied in a tight voice.

"You're wise beyond your years." Frye's fingers paused at the base of her throat, and he lightly brushed her temple with a kiss. "I have no heart to offer you, Celesta—I gave it away once and never got it back. But I can show you the splendor a man and a woman share when they truly understand one another. And once you've experienced the undeniable force that's brought us together, you'll be safe from men who want to steal your soul and give you nothing in return."

Spellbound, she watched his lips and heard the alluring timbre of his voice, which promised no real protection at all. Like the vampire Count, he was in control and he knew it: he was offering to claim her virtue before anyone else could while sacrificing nothing of equal value. When his fingers finally found the nipple that strained against her gown, she gasped.

And when Celesta's firm, rounded breast quivered inside his palm for only a moment before she struggled up out of his lap, Frye wasn't disappointed or surprised. He let her go, knowing her body would succumb after her mind did . . . after she realized that he, too, was in peril of losing himself.

She cowered a few feet away, at the edge of the lamp's flickering light, clutching the front of her gown in one fist. Damon stood up, gazing steadily at her. If curiosity killed the cat, Celesta with the feline eyes was too far gone to leave now, so he began to undress. He disrobed slowly, folding his clothes over the chair to accustom her to the sight of him.

Unaware that she licked her lips, Celesta watched the most powerful body she'd ever seen being offered to her, one delectable section at a time. Square, broad shoulders . . . the chest she'd peeked at before now fully revealed, with its masculine swirls of hair tapering over a firm, narrow waist. Damon's hips and thighs flexed as he bent to remove his shoes and then his trousers. And when he turned to face her, confident yet questioning, her eyes lingered on the proud, male part of him that beckoned to the very core of her being.

Damon stood silently, knowing his next move might send her skittering to the safety of her room. "I'm going to bed now," he said softly. "You may either join me, or you may take the lamp upstairs and forever wonder why you didn't."

He stepped toward her, and she held her breath. Damon Frye was everything her mother had warned her against, and if Justine was eavesdropping, his words were condemnation enough. No virtuous girl would've wandered down here. No female in her right mind could expect to escape him unscathed. Sally Sharpe had dared her to investigate, but it was her own traitorous hand that clutched at wildfire rather than at the cool, solid handle of the lamp.

When her fingertips skimmed his bare hip, Damon's heart danced. He gazed solemnly at her, giving her one last chance to redeem herself. Celesta's eyes were wide, her lips parted in uncertainty, her breasts rising and falling beneath her thin cotton gown as she weighed the consequences of lingering here.

She lowered her head, causing her raven hair to drift around a heart-shaped segment of her face. "I . . . I'm afraid. I don't know what to do."

Her kittenlike cry made him close his eyes against a wave of intense longing. She stood there quavering in her white-clad innocence, and he realized as never before what a high price he'd demanded . . . what a momentous gift she was giving him. "Kiss me, Celesta," he murmured. "The rest will come of its own accord."

Damon's broad palm caressed her jaw, bade her look up at him, but she stepped into his embrace of her own free will. He blessed her with the dearest smile she'd ever seen, and then she closed her eyes and offered her lips to him.

With a moan he enfolded her, vowing that when she left his arms Celesta Montgomery would be his, freely and forever. Perhaps her tender, trusting affections would reawaken the soul that had lain dormant for so long. And perhaps he'd only wish they could.

Damon's lips moved firmly and fervently, and as his tongue asked hers to dance, Celesta's head spun. The warmth of his bare skin penetrated her threadbare gown along the entire length of her body. Her arms encircled him, and then her inquisitive hands explored the smooth, velvety expanses of his muscled back as though they couldn't get enough of his sleek splendor.

He ran his tongue along her sensitive jawline, delighting in her low laughter when she squirmed against him. As he kissed her supple neck, he parted the halves of her nightgown with feverish hands, eager to know every inch of her awakening body. When the gossamer fabric fell away from her shoulders, he paused to gaze at a pair of tiny pink rosebuds afloat on pert, perfect breasts. "You *are* lovely," he breathed.

Celesta flushed with shy pride. "So are you."

His pleasure rumbled in his chest as he pulled her close again, inhaling her wholesome, natural scent. "I'm going to kiss you all over, Celesta. If you get bored, glance in the mirrors," he murmured against her ear. "We'll make a fetching sight. My darker arms clutching your fairness . . . your midnight hair rippling over us like a waterfall."

When his mouth brushed lightly down her throat and then descended upon one unsuspecting breast, she was too stunned to watch in the glass. Somehow her gown was slipping off her arms. As he massaged one aching nipple and then the other with his thorough, reverent mouth, Celesta arched against him, gripping his shoulders as her head lolled back in the utter ecstasy of his wet caress.

Could anything be finer than this madness he sent racing through her? The bare skin of his stomach seared hers. His manly, musky scent was a new sensation, as was the insistent ridge that was prodding her midsection. No longer afraid, Celesta savored the feel of his agile hands as they eased her gown over her hips just ahead of his eager mouth.

As he neared the alluring mass of curls above her legs, Damon glanced toward the mirror. Her abandonment was beautiful to behold: the sight of her shimmering black hair swaying behind her arched body . . . the slender fingers that followed the curves of his arms, probably without her conscious knowledge . . . her indented waist as it ripened to lush, firm hips that appeared with the slow descent of her nightgown. Celesta's eyes were closed, and her mouth was slack—until he knelt to caress with his tongue the little salty-sweet knot that would be her undoing.

A provocative moan slipped out of its own volition, and Celesta felt as though she might burst into flames. "Damon, I can't—please don't hurt me!"

"I wouldn't dream of it, sweetheart," he said. "These are new sensations that only seem like pain because you've never felt anything so intense. You'll come to love them, I promise."

Then he was standing, slipping behind her and encouraging her to look at their reflection in the oval glass. Three times, from three slightly different angles, she watched Damon's hand come around to cup her breast while his other arm slithered possessively around her waist, a startling contrast to her pale skin.

Celesta stared, mesmerized, as his hand inched toward the dark mound of her womanhood, about to reveal yet another intimate secret she'd shared with no one else.

"Celesta, you're truly celestial," he quipped, "with two stars for eyes and white, round moons for hips, and a body that glows like the Milky Way. It's a miracle I can stand behind you and not be lost in your wondrous light, honey."

She knew he was distracting her with his words even as they watched his fingers part her tight curls. This time she was prepared for the shock of his touch, yet she shuddered against him, amazed that her body followed the compelling rhythm of his caress without her willing it to. He made her smolder and sigh. From out of nowhere came a voice she didn't recognize as her own.

"Damon, lie with me now," she breathed. "Take me slowly—but don't you dare stop before we're all the way there!"

"All the way to paradise?" he asked, nuzzling her warm neck.

"If that's what you're promising, that's what I expect."

Her dark eyes challenged his in the glass even as she was slipping beyond the realm of control, and as her lips parted with her rapid breathing she was by far the most alluring woman he'd ever held. "Your wish is my command," he replied in a husky voice. "But once you're mine you can never belong to anyone else, Celesta. It's all or nothing. Are you ready for that?"

All she could do was inhale desperately, trying in vain to stay above the wild, whirling cyclone of emotions and feelings he was conjuring up with a single finger. Then he turned her in his arms and kissed her with an unbridled passion that made her reel, spiraling up toward dizzying heights she sensed she'd regret yet couldn't refuse.

The sheets felt slick and cool when he pressed her into them. Damon's gaze bored into hers as he paused, suspended above her, his dusky face alight with a sweet, maddening smile. "Breathe with me, Celesta. Moan and sing with me as we become one," he instructed. "Lovemaking is a duet best played to the fullest, a song we'll want to share again and again."

He rubbed lightly against her, teasing her with the hair on his chest to make her smile away the apprehension lurking behind her wide, green eyes. No doubt her women had warned her against this moment, calling it a sin if she wasn't wed and a duty if she was, but he sought to free her from those spinsterish notions. A beauty like Celesta was born to soar on the wings of grandest passion, and he would show her how.

His voice vibrated deep and low, entreating her to hum along . . . *Liebestraum*, a dream of love. Celesta joined in, shyly at first, until his tender kiss reassured her. Damon stretched out, braced on his forearms to spare her his weight, all the while easing away her anxieties with his lips as he caressed her body with his. When his manhood found the slick, warm groove between her legs he rocked against her, still humming near her ear. "You feel wonderful, honey," he whispered. "Moan with me now. Crescendo with your instincts. Don't fight it, and you'll understand why I've wanted to make love to you ever since I saw you, sweetheart."

Too enthralled to reply, Celesta stroked the backs of his powerful legs with her feet. This was torment of the highest, sweetest degree, and when her lover's moan told her she'd pleased him, she, too, joined in the primal song that thrummed between their bodies.

She was wet and warm, writhing beneath him, and since his probing fingers caused her no pain, Damon claimed her mouth and then quickly slid inside her. "Lord, you're tight," he rasped.

"I'm sorry, I—"

"Don't be," came his throaty command. "Wrap yourself around me and squeeze as only a woman can, Celesta. It'll drive us both crazy."

His deep thrusting made her cling to him until she realized there was no reason to brace herself, no reason to expect anything but the paradise Damon had promised now that the barrier between them was broken. She relaxed and followed his rhythmic lead, ecstatic when her tentative squeeze made him moan as though he were losing control.

"Sweet Celesta," he murmured, sounding as incoherent as he was beginning to feel. "Take me now. Take all of me, honey."

She arched against him, allowing him to reach the

depths of her body and soul before he led her to a mind-shattering release that left her gasping beneath him. For a few moments she didn't know where she was or who she was. There was only his heart drumming against hers, and the light film of moisture between their sated bodies, and his warm breath tickling her neck, answering her own respiration.

Damon raised up to look at her, wishing her Valentine of a face didn't have such an angelic glow in the lamplight. "Damn you, Celesta," he muttered, sorry as he said it. "Why'd you have to be so good? So perfect this first time?"

Too new at lovemaking to know whether he'd paid her a compliment or called her a slut, she lowered her eyes. "I . . . I think I'd better go upstairs," she whimpered.

"Run along," he grunted as he rolled onto the other side of his bed. "And by God, don't ever ask me for any more rides to paradise. I'll never take you there again."

Chapter 10

Celesta stumbled up the last few steps to the third floor, retreating like a whipped pup. Discovering that Frye's "all or nothing" speech was all *for* nothing stung like no humiliation she'd ever known. Despite the little room's stale heat, she shrugged into her wrapper, shuddering at how foolish she'd been to fall for his lies.

Why hadn't she bolted up the cellar stairs? He'd been spinning his silken lines, knowing—like the spider awaiting the fly—that she'd get caught in his web, doomed to be devoured. Damon had admitted straight out that he had no heart, and she'd been too entranced to heed his warnings. He was probably lying in bed laughing at her this very moment.

And now that she'd succumbed, now that his vampirish nature had claimed another victim, how could she ever face him again? It would take him weeks to complete the redecorating he'd promised Justine and Katherine. She couldn't return to the Perkins household . . . dreaded collecting her clothes and Mama's things, but it had to be done.

So she was trapped here, with two aunts who might've killed her mother and a demonic man determined to ruin her for his own questionable reasons. And she'd never felt more frightened or alone.

Celesta dropped onto the straight-backed chair at Grandfather's writing desk, wishing he were here— wishing Sally Sharpe could undo the mischief she'd caused. Surely Aunt Katherine would know at a glance that Damon had claimed her, and Justine would be showing her the door before breakfast. Her bun would quiver with her indignation as she pointed a bony finger toward the back exit, condemning her to a life of shame and drudgery even more degrading than Mama's had been.

Her nose crinkled at the scent of . . . Celesta stared toward the ventilation grate in the floor, appalled. How long had Justine's lamp been lit? How long had the ghostly threads of cigarette smoke been curling up into the alcove? Justine *knew!* She was fortifying herself with a smoke, preparing a stinging lecture before she came up here to—

Or was she too restless to sleep? Too bothered by her conscience, after killing her little sister?

Holding her breath, Celesta listened intently. Nothing. Not a sound or a movement, except when Justine shifted or turned a page.

Suddenly consumed by curiosity, she lowered herself onto the plank floor and slid on her stomach until she could peer through the metal grating. There, just below her, sat Justine Ransom, turning the last page of a dime novel. Her silvery hair fell straight down the back of her plain muslin nightgown. The hand resting on the arm of her rocking chair held a cigarette, which sent a thin thread of smoke spiraling upward to where Celesta lay spying on her. And lo and behold, as her aunt turned the dimer over to read its back cover, Celesta recognized it as one of her own Sally Sharpe stories! The rocker creaked slightly, and Justine let out a soft, satisfied chuckle as she read the final paragraph.

"Thatta way, Sally!" she declared under her breath, and with a contented sigh she doused the lamp, leaving the red glow of her cigarette as the only evidence she was awake.

Was this the picture of a murderer? Or was Aunt Justine a poor old insomniac who just happened to fit into the scenario Damon had sketched out?

At breakfast, Celesta still didn't know. Her maiden aunt appeared at the table in a starched shirtwaist of striped broadcloth, looking unusually pert. She raised an eyebrow at their three plates. "Mr. Frye's not joining us?"

"He left a note," Katherine replied as she lifted ham slices from the cast-iron skillet. "Said he wanted to be on site early to line up the day's assignments for his men so he could return here and start our papering while there's still some daylight."

"A practical man. Moreso than I'd imagined." Justine's brown eyes focused on Celesta as she spread her napkin over her lap. "And what are your plans for the day?"

"I—I'm clearing out my room at Eula's. Bringing everything here," Celesta mumbled.

"You look flushed. I hope you're not coming down with something, because I'm sure Mr. Frye could use your assistance with the papering," she commented matter-of-factly. "Since you're the only one of us spry enough to climb a ladder or fetch his tools, that would be a worthwhile contribution to our project."

After Justine left to do her marketing, a glance at the hallway mirror confirmed her aunt's assessment: her face was rosier than usual, as though she'd been permanently branded by the heat of Damon's passion. The young woman gazing back at her was familiar yet foreign; her shoulders sagged slightly and her red-rimmed eyes appeared sadder and older. Celesta hoped she looked the part of the sleepless, grieving daughter today, because she felt certain everyone on the street would know at a glance how far she'd fallen last night.

Damon had avoided her this morning, thank God. Surviving Eula's inquisition and her son's plans for matrimony would require what little emotional reserve she had left. She had no idea how she'd survive this evening, when she was expected to work so closely with Frye while not letting on that anything had changed between them.

Checking to see that no one was watching her from the counter, Celesta slid the envelope containing "The Case of the Purloined Papers" into the slot marked OUTGOING MAIL. Then she checked the post office box in the far wall and slipped the envelope addressed to Lester Montgomery into her skirt pocket. There was rarely anything else in the box, since all of her family and friends lived here, and today was no exception.

"Good to see you out and about," a familiar voice hailed her.

Smiling, Celesta approached the counter and the stout, bearded gentleman behind it. "Good morning, Bill. How are you?"

He peered intently through his spectacles at her, his smile tempered with tenderness. "Well, I was right sorry to hear about your ma, Celesta," he replied in a concerned voice. "And I hear you've moved in with the Ransoms. Katherine bearing up all right? I worry about her since the shock of Ambrose's passing, you know."

Bill Thompkins had performed the gruesome task of reporting her uncle's death to the family; he'd been the captain of the *Phantom* for years before the boiler exploded, and had accepted a job as a postal clerk because of an injury he'd sustained in the accident. He always patted his sandy hair back from its center part when he mentioned the Ransom widow. Celesta suspected he was sweet on her, but too polite or timid to do anything about it.

"She's fine, thank you. Excited about the redecorating Justine finally agreed to."

Bill's eyes widened, and his laugh came out as a hoot. "Plenty of tongues waggin' about *that*, now. You ladies better watch out for that Frye fellow. He gives you any trouble, I'll be happy to check on you now and again."

Too late for that, she thought ruefully, but she maintained her smile. "That's thoughtful of you, Bill."

After an awkward moment of silence, Thompkins cleared his throat. "Will you be keeping the box you and your mother had, or shall I just put your mail in with Justine's?"

"I'll keep my own, thank you."

Bill nodded with a conspiratorial smile. "Wouldn't want her nosing through my letters, either. Might get the notion those payments from your New York uncle should be put toward your board, tight as she is."

Celesta smiled but was glad to be on her way. Bill knew what everyone in Hannibal got for mail and was inclined to chat about it, so when her Sally Sharpe stories started selling, she and Mama had created the New York uncle: he was supposedly her father's older brother, rich enough to compensate for the years Ian Montgomery had forced them to fend for themselves, and feeble-minded enough to think she was a nephew named Lester. As fibs went, it seemed awfully thin to Celesta, but as long as the Beadle and Adams payroll clerk honored her request to send cash in plain envelopes, addressed last name first, Bill couldn't expose her as dime novelist Montgomery C. Lester, and she'd have no trouble at the bank with endorsing checks.

Telling Patrick Perkins a convincing tale would be

another matter, though. As she walked slowly toward the opulent house on North Fifth, Celesta prepared herself for what she might encounter there. Ordinarily Eula met with other board members who supported the Home for the Friendless on Mondays. Would she have stayed home today, thinking her silver might leave the house in her former maid's suitcase? Patrick's schedule at the lumber company was flexible, and it was he who would ask the most pressing questions . . . would he guess that Damon had claimed her right to be a blushing bride?

These anxious thoughts made sweat trickle down her back, adding to the oppressive mid-morning heat. Celesta paused before the mint green Queen Anne with its ornately carved white railings, a lump in her throat. She hadn't expected such a welling up of emotion—wanted to pack quickly and leave, before things got sticky. But this had been her home for nearly twenty-one years, and now that Mama was gone, this visit felt like a final goodbye to the only life she'd ever known.

Holding her breath, she turned the knob and entered the back door, only inches from where Damon Frye had first kissed her. The interior of the house rang with silence. The rooms, shuttered against the summer sun, welcomed her with their cool dimness. No one was home. She could take her time and cry a little, if she needed to.

The stairway creaked in all the right places, the glossy newel posts on the landings had a special shine, and the warmer air as she ascended past the second floor smelled of Eula's rich perfume. Celesta paused in the doorway of the large dormer room she and Mama had shared, drinking in the cleanness of the white enameled woodwork and the way the sunlight glowed behind the pink floral curtains. Better to gather their clothing quickly and be gone, rather than be caught up in the wave of sorrow she felt washing over her.

As Celesta walked to the simple white armoire, it occurred to her that she should've borrowed a valise or two from Katherine: she didn't own one, because she'd never stayed overnight anywhere until this week. But when she swung open the wooden doors, the air rushed from her lungs. The armoire was empty!

She hurriedly checked the storage boxes under the beds, and her desk drawers, and the vanity where they'd kept their underthings, her panic rising. Not a single item that belonged to her or Mama remained! Eula must've cleared the room, preparing for new help, and given her few possessions to charity when she learned Celesta was so *ungrateful* as not to return!

A low chuckle from the doorway made her jump and whirl around. "Patrick! You scared me half to—"

"I'm sorry," he said, shaking his head good-naturedly. "I couldn't resist startling you, like I did when we were little."

"Well, you did *that*, all right! And just what the hell did you do with—"

"Ah, ah, ah," he teased as he braced his hands on either side of the doorjamb. "Only a few days with Frye under your roof and you're swearing like a stevedore. Sounds like another good reason to come home, doesn't it?"

Could he tell that his rival had affected much more than her vocabulary? Patrick's blue trousers and striped shirt showed him off to perfection—accented blue eyes that were twinkling at her beneath his strawberry-blond waves. Compared to Damon's darkness, he was pure, golden sunshine, a man whose teasing had always made her laugh . . . a lifelong friend.

"I—I'm sorry. I got carried away when I saw the

135

armoire was empty."

"I should've warned you when I heard you on the stairs, but I thought you'd want a few minutes alone," he replied quietly. "Mother and I knew how difficult this would be for you, so we boxed everything up ourselves. It's waiting in the carriage—unless you've decided to stay."

Celesta glanced toward the window so that he wouldn't see her tears. He and his mother had done the thoughtful, practical thing, considering she hadn't any means to convey her possessions to the Manor. They knew she'd be too proud to borrow Justine's wagon and too wistful to want Katherine's help with this heart-wrenching chore. "Thank you. You've been very kind."

What was it about her that looked different this morning? Her glossy black hair was upswept as always, with those endearing tendrils that escaped on sultry days. He'd seen her olive green skirt and checked blouse dozens of times and thought they became her despite their simplicity. Her eyes were puffy—perfectly understandable, in her situation.

No, it was her stance . . . her attitude. Celesta always looked at him straight on, challenging his every white lie, yet now she stood with her hands clasped before her like she had when they'd been caught misbehaving as children. Perhaps she had second thoughts—was realizing how much she'd miss this place, after all. Whatever the reason for her downheartedness, he couldn't let the moment pass.

"It's as though she's still here, isn't it?" he whispered. He remained in the doorway, watching her, so as not to startle her into her usual belligerence. "Your mother made this house a home for me, too, Celesta. She made us cocoa on cold mornings, and read us bedtime stories, and gave us her special smiles when we were sick. Mother's always been happiest playing the socialite—wasn't

136

terribly tolerant when our milk got spilled or when our pet toads got loose in the house. I sometimes wonder if she wouldn't have been happier without children around."

Celesta's eyes widened. This was quite a revelation from the sole heir to Perkins Lumber, a confession showing insight and sensitivity she hadn't thought Patrick capable of. He smiled wistfully and stepped toward her, as though he was about to confide something even more startling.

"It was also Rachel who counseled me as I got older, warning me about where I . . . sowed my wild oats," he said in an intimate tone. "She said Hannibal was teeming with young ladies eager to catch a husband with my looks and inheritance, who might go to great lengths to secure the lavish life the Perkins name carried with it. And she was right."

Celesta allowed him to clasp her hands between his, wondering what this story had to do with her. His grip was firm as his thumbs traced warm circles on the tops of her hands.

"I think that's why I've always liked you, Celesta," he continued. "You've seen me at my worst, yet we've always been friends. You had no designs on my money, like the girls I used to take around. Since my father died, I've become extremely tired of their wiles, and now that the future of Perkins Lumber rests on my shoulders, I must choose a wife carefully."

"Patrick, we've discussed this," she said with a sigh.

His grip tightened. "And I rushed headlong into my own plans without considering yours—a mistake I hope you'll forgive," he said earnestly. "You need time. And you deserve to be courted and escorted to dances and parties, so you can decide for yourself if we'd make a good team. I want a love match, Celesta. I want a woman who shares my dreams yet has her own aspirations, too."

This was a marked change in his attitude, and even though she suspected Patrick's motives were no different than before, Celesta heard his plea more patiently. The handsome blond holding her hands represented the comfort of a home she'd always loved, a chance to live as a wife and partner rather than as a beholden niece. But most of all, Patrick might clue her in about why Mama died—and he provided the quickest, most satisfying escape from Damon Frye. "What are you suggesting?" she asked demurely.

Patrick grinned. "I thought we'd start by attending the Fourth of July celebration in the park next week. After the concert, there'll be the picnic and games and fireworks . . . perhaps a stroll along the river, so we can get better acquainted. It'll be a fine evening, Celesta."

And it would be a safe one, with everyone in town watching them. A smile twitched at Celesta's lips. "All right. It sounds like fun."

"You'll go with me?" Patrick almost grabbed her up to whirl her around. She would never know what a lifeline she'd just tossed him, and he vowed that the new Mrs. Perkins would suspect his reasons for this match no more than his mother did. "Thank you, honey. You won't regret this, I promise. You deserve to be treated like the special woman you are, and the timetable about getting more serious will be totally up to you."

"I'll hold you to that, Patrick," Celesta replied slyly.

"And I'll hold *you*, my love," he murmured in a husky voice. He longed to seal the bargain with a kiss, but instead he gave her a smoldering look that parted her full lips with expectation, and then he added, "I'd better take you back to the Manor before I forget myself, Celesta. You've made me a very happy man."

She walked to the door and then turned to look at him. "I haven't agreed to marry you, Patrick. I still see obstacles—"

"And we'll overcome them, one by one. Together." He ushered her down the stairs and out to the carriage house, lightly grasping her elbow as he savored her surrender. A woman of Celesta's charm and family background would make any man a splendid wife, and the beauty of it was that she didn't understand *why*.

"Join me up on the seat, honey," he said, interlacing his fingers to give her dainty foot a boost up. "The carriage is full, and you're much too pretty a parcel to hide among the trunks and boxes."

Celesta smiled to herself. He would take several side streets through town, showing her off like a prize he'd won at a carnival, but she could put up with that. There were worse things than being squired about by a wealthy, winsome man who wanted to marry her—and she'd experienced some of them last night.

Patrick chatted amiably as his matched pair of bay horses clip-clopped along the brick streets, about the business mostly—no allusion to maids or mice who'd met their Maker while under his roof. And then, as though he'd forgotten something, he pulled the carriage to a halt at Broadway and Main, the very center of the business district, and pulled a prettily wrapped package from under his seat.

"For you," he said with a boyish grin. "I—I'd hoped you'd attend the festivities on the Fourth with me, and wear these. But don't open it *now*," he added when she reached for the bright red ribbon. "Save it for when you're alone, thinking of me, Celesta. I can't wait to see you wearing them. You deserve fine things."

Intrigued, Celesta held the package the rest of the way home. It wasn't large enough to hold a new dress

139

or deep enough for shoes, and even though she knew Patrick was plying her with another gift, coaxing her toward the altar for reasons she hadn't figured out, she had to admit she enjoyed his game a lot more than Damon's.

Frye watched Patrick hand the package to Celesta—obviously a bribe, since he was so damned public about it—and swore under his breath. Her eyes were sparkling as she hugged the box, and even though he alone knew how two-faced and reprehensible Perkins was, he had to admit the lumber baron's boy was no lower a snake than he himself. The noon meal in front of him suddenly tasted too much like remorse, and he shoved his plate away, staring morosely after the carriage as it headed toward Holliday's Hill.

Why had Celesta's lovemaking stirred him so? He'd intended to steal her innocence and capture her heart without making any emotional investment, to purge himself of Lucy, who'd treated him the very same way. He was playing upon her grief and vulnerability, expecting her to become clingy and demanding—as Miss Bates had when she announced her pregnancy—so that he could cast her aside without regret when his work in Hannibal was complete.

And she'd played along, an enchanting victim who knew better yet succumbed . . . until Celesta herself took control. *Damon, lie with me now . . . don't you dare stop before we're all the way there!*

All the way to paradise?

If that's what you're promising . . . that's what I expect.

From that moment he was hers. The bold, romantic lines he'd caught her with were now binding him as well: *Once you're mine, you can*

*never belong to anyone else, Celesta...take me
now. Take all of me, honey.*

And she had. And in return he'd made her feel like
the cheapest of whores by betraying the most
elemental trust a virgin gave her first lover. Compar-
ing her to Lucinda Bates was like calling a diamond a
chip of glass, and his vengeful ploys had trapped
them both. How could he continue to live under the
Ransom roof as though he deserved Justine and
Katherine's confidence? How could he face Celesta
without embarrassing her further, which would
surely lead her aunts to draw the obvious conclusion
about what he'd done to their niece?

Damon tossed some money on the table and left the
cafe, too disgusted with himself to remain among
decent people. But he would have to resolve this
problem, and soon—before Perkins discovered Celesta's newest secret. He could only guess how
Hannibal's most sought-after bachelor would retaliate for coming in second. If he'd laced Rachel's sugar with cyanide, who could tell how he
might harm Celesta?

Chapter 11

"Are we finished?"

"Yes. Thank you."

At last, she could quit keeping up appearances with Damon! Never had Celesta spent a more horrendous evening, helping Frye remove the paintings from the entryway and then preparing it to be papered. He'd politely insisted that he could manage alone, but Justine was determined that she would *contribute* to this project.

The dark-haired carpenter's aloofness infuriated her. He'd made the most inane conversation, and pointedly avoided letting their fingers touch as they worked, and he'd looked at her as though she were an unknown, unskilled apprentice who'd been foisted upon him. Now that her maiden aunt had retired for the evening Celesta, too, desperately needed time alone to untie the knots in her stomach.

Katherine was working her needlepoint in the summer parlor, and Celesta bade her a quick good night, escaping up the stairs before her aunt could ask any embarrassing questions. The light still shone in a line beneath Justine's door, but she crept by silently anyway, to the bedroom on the other side of the tower room. All day she'd pretended things were normal, all evening she'd acted excessively polite, and she was worn to a frazzle.

Closing her door behind her, Celesta then slipped Patrick's package from its hiding place beneath the bed. She'd need a better spot to stash these daring unmentionables, because Justine no doubt got nosy when she cleaned. God alone knew what the old maid would say if she saw what Mr. Perkins had given her!

The delicate garments whispered seductively as she pulled them from the tissue wrapping: a ruffled, lacy corset cover and matching drawers, a hose supporter with a satin waistband, and five pairs of patterned stockings—all of silk, and all in fiery scarlet. Patrick must've gotten them at a St. Louis bordello or from a French mail-order house, because none of the shops in Hannibal sold such brazen apparel!

Did he suspect she was already a wayward woman? Damon's conquest? Or did he plan to seduce her himself, after the concert in the park? Both thoughts disturbed her. She was asking for more trouble if she wore these to the picnic!

Yet the intricate lacework and the soft elegance of these underthings lured her like a siren's song— never had she owned anything so fine. Everyone in town would attend the Fourth of July festivities, watching her and Perkins . . . not even her aunts would know what flaming lingerie her plain broadcloth dress was hiding. And now that she knew about the deceitful ways men had of stripping a woman's dignity, Celesta could anticipate Patrick's moves and avoid situations that would lead to another humiliating encounter. If her blond admirer thought this gift would render her defenseless against his advances, willing to do his bidding, he'd better think again!

So after leaving her everyday clothing heaped on on the floor, she slipped the shimmering underthings on, one by one. She checked the mirror often, noting the way the hosiery hugged her calves, the crimson supporter belts that blazed up her white thighs . . . the buoyant, feminine flouncing of the silken drawers over her hips . . . the provocative way the corset cover nipped in at her waist—even though she wore no corset—and made her seem bustier because of its strategically arranged ruffles.

Celesta stared at her reflection, a secret thrill racing through her veins. Was that really the maid's daughter gazing back at her? Too bad Damon had sent her away, saying he never wanted her again! She smiled smugly and began to pull out her hairpins, imagining how the startling contrast of ebony waves and scarlet silk upon creamy-white skin would affect him.

Frye gaped at her, breathless, through the keyhole. He'd been mildly surprised when he'd peered at Justine the same way, noting her cigarette and the stacks of pulp westerns around her room as she rocked in her chair, listening to something on an Edison phonograph with earpieces. He'd suspected Celesta would pore over Patrick's present when she was alone, which was one of his reasons for slipping upstairs. But he'd never expected this vision in scarlet openly admiring herself. He had to step away for a moment so that his manhood wouldn't thump against the door like a happy dog's tail.

His other reason for risking this trip was to apologize—or try to—for the beastly way he'd treated her last night. Celesta's tormented expression as she helped with the papering preparations had stung as badly as if she'd raked his flesh with her fingernails. It was his place to make amends, to promise her he'd never again take advantage of her physical beauty, because such trysting was too dangerous, given their situation. But how the hell was he supposed to take a vow of chastity while she was parading around in lingerie that was begging to be torn off her?

Katherine would be coming up to bed before long. He would surely lose his job if two of Hannibal's most respected ladies threw him out for peeping at their niece. The longer he loitered, the better the chances he'd stumble over his tongue and alienate Celesta even further. Yet if he went into her room—

A creak on the stairway made him grip the doorknob, slip inside, and fall back against the wooden panel with lightning speed. Celesta pivoted, glaring with the ferocity of a cornered panther—and Lord Almighty, with her raven hair tumbling over that frilly scarlet lingerie, she was the uninhibited wanton of every man's dreams!

"What in God's name are you—get out!" she commanded in a hoarse whisper. "Justine's just a room away, and if she hears—"

"Then, you'd better listen to me without any fuss. We don't want either aunt to find us this way, do we?"

Only Frye would have the nerve to hold her captive in her own bedroom, knowing she wouldn't dare scream. Too enraged to respond, Celesta planted her fists on her hips and glared at him, vowing to throttle him if he came one step closer.

Damon waited until he heard a door close across the hall, willing his heart to cease its runaway beat. Had he ever been this agitated before? He doubted it—unless it was when he'd rushed back to the university after Lucy had begged him to stay engaged to her. He'd made some horrible mistakes in his anger, and he couldn't afford to repeat them now.

"I . . . I said some things last night that I deeply regret, Celesta," he pleaded in a barely audible voice. "I can't erase my words—they've haunted us both, I suspect—but I can try to compensate for my cruelty.

146

I . . . hadn't expected to enjoy you so much, but—"

"But *what?*" she demanded. All evening he'd snubbed her as though she were a poor relation. He'd had plenty of time to grovel when they were both properly clothed, yet here he stood leering at her, no more a gentleman than he was last night.

Her challenge meant she was forgiving him—or listening, at least—and as he drank in her lush, ruffled loveliness, Damon wanted nothing more than to hold her attention this way long into the night. But, oh, she was peeved! The blaze in her light green eyes warned him that only contrite humility would get him any farther.

"You're a bewitching sight, Celesta," he breathed, and he stuffed his hands into his overall pockets to keep from reaching for her. "And you're a more compelling lover than I've known for years. I—I hadn't anticipated being so *taken* by your—"

"That implies you have a heart," she retorted with a raised eyebrow, "and I'm not so sure I believe that, after last night. Never have I been so humiliated, and never again will I fall for your lies, Mr. Frye. Get out of this room! Crawl back to your cave before I call my aunts."

He deserved this tongue-lashing, and he admired Celesta for venting her rage rather than sniveling about being ruined, like most girls would. She wore her wrath like a glorious gown, and he couldn't resist stepping closer, pressing the point he was about to make as he changed his strategy a bit.

"Since you confided your fears about Patrick having the chance to kill your mother, I owe you the favor of a warning, sweetheart," he said in a low voice. "Call it insight from one man who has no heart about another."

She swallowed hard. "And what's *he* got to do with this?"

Frye gave her a wry smile. "Everyone on Main saw

147

him hand you that package...a gift you wear extremely well," he added with a suggestive once-over. "But a man who gives a woman such intimate apparel is after only one thing. And since I've already claimed that, I can't in good conscience allow Patrick's pursuit to continue."

So his arrogance was alive and well, masquerading as humility only when it got his foot in the door. "Are you threatening me? Planning to brag about what you did to me last night, so you can rub his nose in it?"

Her frown was truly menacing, but he stepped closer. "What will he think if he discovers I claimed you first? He'll accuse you of leading him on, of trying to fool him into believing you're still pure as—"

"You tricked me out of my innocence, so now I'm *impure?*" Celesta demanded. Her scowl turned into a sneer as she riveted those pale green cat's eyes on him. "I'm surprised you can still associate with me, Mr. Frye. This apology has turned into one more reason to—"

Damon grabbed her as she marched toward the door, chiding himself for mentioning his competition. "To me, your coming to womanhood only makes you more alluring, more . . . provocative," he whispered, allowing his gaze to linger on her quivering lips, on breasts that bobbed loosely beneath their crimson covering. "You weren't ashamed of your desires when you were in my arms last night, and I never want you to feel cheapened or less a lady for letting your sensuality run its course. You were born to bring a man pleasure, Celesta. You certainly please *me.*"

He glanced toward the door, still gripping her soft shoulders. "When you want to continue this discussion in private, come downstairs and we'll—"

She'd wanted to believe him. His words had

148

soothed her bruised soul like a salve at first, yet he was now trying to snare her with them. "You're insane if you think I'll fall for that again!"

"Am I?" Damon looked her over, a new plan already formulating as he smiled slyly at her. "Sweet dreams, Celesta. God knows I'll be sleeping better now that we've kissed and made up."

"But we haven't—I won't—"

Frye pulled her to him for an intense kiss that made her resistance snap. When he released her, she staggered backward, shocked at how quickly her desires had been rekindled even as her mind tried to shut him out.

"You'll be back, sweet Celesta," he murmured as he eased toward the door. He turned the knob with a burglar's silent expertise, and after he checked the hallway, he flashed her a wink. "Like a moth to the flame, sweetheart. I'll be waiting."

Chapter 12

And wait he would, by God! Celesta saw through every line of his apology, but he'd renewed her confidence. Each time she was with him that week, whether seated across the table or watching his shapely behind strain against his overalls as he hung paper, she smiled smugly. No more marionette acts. *She* was pulling the strings from here on out; and Frye could make eyes at her until the Second Coming, but it would do him no good.

The aunts watched—and waited, she sensed. On the first of July she and Damon rehung the mirrors and family portraits, which appeared much less dark and dour now that they were set off by the elegant crimson paper with its gold flocking. When the ladders and leftover paper and buckets of paste were cleared away, Katherine stood in the center of the hall, her face glowing.

"Isn't it *gorgeous*," she gushed, her hands clasped at her bosom. "Oh, Damon—why, this calls for a celebration! A special treat! What would you like for dessert tomorrow night?"

Frye glanced surreptitiously at Celesta as he considered his answer. "Cherry tarts," he murmured. "I've been hungry for a tart all week—if it won't be too much trouble, that is."

"No trouble at all," Katherine twittered, and the next morning she and Celesta were rolling the dough as soon as they cleared the breakfast dishes from the table.

Justine sniffed at them, grasping her market basket. "You're pandering to him, Katherine. Lord knows we feed him like royalty, without giving him choices."

"Go to town, Justine." The younger aunt looked up from stirring the thick, red filling, a smudge of flour on her cheek. "It was a simple enough request, and he's worked very hard. You like the new paper as much as Celesta and I do—you just won't admit it. I saw you in there this morning, grinning like a girl in love as you looked at it."

The spinster slammed the pantry door, and Celesta couldn't help laughing. "Was she really?"

"Absolutely moony, she was," Katherine clucked. She took the bubbling, sweet-smelling cherry sauce from the stove, her expression sly. "Of course, Justine's not the only one who looks enamored when Mr. Frye's working his wonders. And it's no secret to me what he was insinuating, asking for a cherry tart."

Celesta's face burst into flame. "I—I don't know what you mean."

"Of course you do, dear," she said with a chuckle. She looked up, her hazel eyes sparkling. "I was young once, you know. I remember those secret glances . . . how they make your heart hammer and what they lead to. Ambrose was a hot-blooded swain, and I—well, we were discreet, but we certainly weren't shy, bumbling strangers on our wedding night."

Sighing, she cut the pastry rounds that would hold the filling. Why did Katherine's every conversation center around sex? This was her most blatant effort yet at matchmaking, and it couldn't have come at a more awkward time.

"Is he taking you to the picnic on the Fourth?" her aunt asked coyly. "If he's not, I'll have to speak to him about—"

"I'm going with Patrick."

Katherine's spoon fell handle-first into the filling. *"Why*, for heaven's sake?"

"Because he asked."

Her aunt hurriedly pressed the circles of dough into the muffin tin, gasping with exasperation when two of them tore. "You watch yourself, young lady. It's one thing to strike a match, but it's another matter entirely to light your candle at both ends. I don't trust Patrick."

"And you trust Frye? After what he did to Lucy Bates?" It was a relief that Katherine didn't suspect what had flared like a fever between them, but this conversation still felt mighty tight around her collar.

"Damon has a sense of perspective that comes from making a serious mistake and enduring its aftermath. He'll not err that way with a woman again." She regained control over her emotions and finished the tarts with delicate latticework, painstakingly perfect for her dear Mr. Frye. "Does Eula know?"

"I—I don't know. I haven't seen her since they were here."

It was the end of that topic, but it was by no means the end of her troubles concerning Patrick Perkins. Celesta woke early on the morning of the picnic, smiling confidently at the rays of sunlight streaming through her bedroom window. She'd waited a week to feel the caress of that silk lingerie against her skin . . . was eagerly anticipating Patrick's furtive, questioning gaze when he came for her, and the challenge of not letting him have so much as a peek at those scarlet ruffles all day.

But when she went to the steamer trunk, where she'd layered the underthings between Mama's clothes, they were gone!

Celesta let the lid fall shut with a *whump*, totally bewildered. Surely Justine wouldn't have the nerve to . . . and Katherine wouldn't have rifled through her things to. . . .

Her mouth pressed into a grim line. If Damon Frye showed his face today, he'd get the trouncing of a lifetime.

Central Park was alive with children shrieking as they sack raced, and polka dotted with ladies' parasols, and ringing with the *clang!* and cheers as men competed at horseshoe pitching. Never had Celesta seen a bigger crowd or more festive decorations for this annual event. The fence railings and light poles were festooned with red, white, and blue streamers that flapped in the breeze, and the United States flag rippled proudly over the arched pagoda that served as a place for patriotic speeches and a band stand. She herself was wearing a blue dress with a white sailor's collar and red trim, which set off the red choker she'd put on to please her escort.

Patrick, in crisp white linen, gazed at her as though he could see red silk through her clothing while they walked between the various contests and events. His hair glistened like gold beneath his jaunty boater, and his smile, too, was radiant. He had his eyes on a prize, and Celesta smiled secretively, knowing it would egg him on . . . knowing he'd never get close enough to discover she wasn't wearing the finery he'd given her.

"I should call you Mona Lisa," he said as he put an arm around her waist. "Is that little grin because you liked my present?"

"Yes. Very much," she replied coyly. Celesta glanced around, wondering where Damon was hiding himself in this crowd.

Perkins also looked at the jovial faces around them, nodding proudly to his friends when they gawked at the woman on his arm. "Was Frye peeved that you came to the picnic with me?"

"We didn't discuss it."

"Oh." Patrick saw a shady spot ahead, near a vendor selling iced drinks, and steered her toward it. "Well, he by God better behave himself if he's here. This is our day together—the first of many—and I won't have him spoiling it for you."

She, too, sensed that the roguish architect was lurking behind the scenes, watching them, but as the afternoon glare softened into the first rosy shades of evening, Celesta relaxed. Damon hadn't appeared, everyone else had gotten over their initial surprise at seeing her with the illustrious Mr. Perkins, and they were ready to enjoy the hamper of chicken, biscuits, and cherry tarts she'd packed. All that remained was a concert by the Thompkins Troubadours, a local group Patrick played the string bass in, and a fireworks exhibition. Perfectly public. Perfectly safe.

After he spread a blanket beneath a tree, Patrick sniffed appreciatively at the packets she was pulling from her basket. "I do miss your fine cooking, Celesta," he said, "but if I have my way about it, you'll soon be out of the kitchen for good. I can't understand why your aunts don't have help, at their age."

"Katherine's hardly ancient," she teased, taking a crispy chicken thigh, "and Justine will do her own cleaning until she drops. They live that way by choice." She could tell the conversation might get intimate now that they were out of the crowd, so she distracted him with a different topic. "Has your mother found anyone yet?"

"She's hired a bedraggled young girl who sought shelter at the Home, on a trial basis, but I can't think

155

it'll last. Mother's not the most patient teacher, you know."

Celesta nodded, sympathetic. After spending her life under his mother's hawklike supervision, she still quailed whenever Eula criticized each minor flaw in the food or laundry. "If you find a black fountain pen trimmed in gold, I'd like it back," she said, watching his reaction. "It wasn't among the writing supplies you packed from my desk, and it was a special gift from Mama."

"Well, of course I'll—I can't imagine where it could've gotten to," he replied with a puzzled frown. He chewed on his chicken, as though sincerely perplexed, and then brightened. "I'll find it, though. And if I don't, I'll take you to select a new one. You'll need a fine pen to write notes for all our wedding presents, you know."

His boyish grin endeared him to her, and as they recalled previous Fourths and picnics in their lives, Celesta wished she could forget that her mother had died under unsettling circumstances in this man's house. Patrick was generous and charming; they knew so many childhood secrets about each other and shared some of the best memories she could ever make. Every unattached female in the park had eyed her with disdain when they saw him keeping her such close company. This was a fairy tale in real life, so why shouldn't she take advantage of the luxuries and elevated station he was offering her? It meant security for the rest of her life—decency rather than decadence, which was all Damon Frye had offered her.

Patrick interrupted her reverie by reaching across her for a tart, laughing low when his boater nearly skimmed her breasts. "I'll have to leave you after I enjoy this. Bill and the others are setting up," he said with a glance toward the gaily decorated bandstand. "And after our concert, I know a special spot where we can enjoy the fireworks."

It was probably the same spot he'd ushered other girls to over the years, and she looked into his sparkling eyes. "You're a rake, Patrick Perkins. If you thought about it, you'd know that Ransom Manor's by far the best vantage point for—"

"I will *not* take you where Justine can watch everything we do," he stated, tweaking her nose. "How you can live with that busybody is beyond me. Just because nobody ever kissed her, she thinks everyone else should suffer chastity as well."

Celesta raised an eyebrow. "And how do you know she was never courted? Mama's album has a few photographs of her that are surprisingly good. She wasn't breathtaking when she was young, but Justine was by no means ugly."

He grunted and tucked the last large bite of tart into his mouth. His clean-shaven cheeks glowed golden in the sunset. He was shaking his head good-naturedly as he chewed—until he grimaced, grabbing his jaw. "Did *she* make these tarts?"

"No. Why?"

Patrick slid his thumb and forefinger gingerly between his lips and pulled out a large cherry stone. "Chipped a tooth on this sucker. Damn, that hurts!"

"I—I'm sorry—"

"Never mind, honey," he said, regaining his smile as he brushed her cheek with a kiss. "Better me than you. After the concert, I'm sure you'll find a way to make it feel all better."

Celesta picked up the remains of their meal, chuckling. By rights, it should've been Frye whose tongue would scrape a jagged tooth for the rest of the evening, but he'd apparently found a better way to spend his day. People were spreading their blankets in the grass closer to the pagoda now, preparing to listen, while Bill Thompkins and his small orchestra set up their chairs and music stands.

157

The burly postal clerk's brow glistened with sweat as he tapped his baton against the top of his stand and gave a few last instructions.

At the sound of his pitch pipe, the instruments squawked to life. It was a cacophony Celesta always enjoyed. She stood to the side of the audience with a few others, where she could watch each musician tuning up. Cornets ascended showy, brassy scales while the violins droned on open fifths and then burst forth into bits of melody. Flutes, like shrill birds, twittered at the front, and beneath this chaos throbbed the heavy tones of Patrick's bass fiddle as he plucked out a syncopated passage. He winked mischievously at her, and Celesta felt herself flush despite her misgivings about him.

There was a hush as Thompkins raised his arms. He marked a silent four beats with his wand, and then the spirited strains of "Yankee Doodle" filled the air. People nodded happily, but it wasn't until the medley moved into "Dixie" that these Hanna-balians, still southern at heart, began to clap in time. A few men sang the chorus, and by the second time through everyone in the crowd was joining in with a gusto brought on by patriotic fervor, or perhaps a sip of whiskey taken on the sly.

"I wish I were in Dixie—hooray! Hooray!" Celesta sang out. And then she sucked in her breath when a broad hand closed around each of her shoulders.

"If you don't want to see your crimson drawers flying like a flag from the Cruikshank mansion, you'll come with me," a familiar voice crooned near her ear.

"You—*demon!*" she exclaimed in a hoarse whisper, turning to glare at him.

"Damon's the name, demon's my game," he replied with a chuckle that smelled like liquor.

"Where have you—? You wouldn't *dare* take my underthings to—would you?"

Frye's face assumed a Cheshire cat grin as the last rays of daylight dimmed around them. "There's only one way to find out before my men do."

"You—"

Her protest was stifled by a quick kiss that tasted of spiked lemonade, and Celesta quickly pulled away to see if anyone was watching. By now people were on their feet, accenting their hoorays! with uplifted fists, and Damon grabbed her hand. He led her behind the crowd until they were passing through the park gates, walking so fast she could barely keep up with him.

"Of all the—let me go! I came here with Patrick, because he was gentleman enough to *ask!*" she hissed.

He turned suddenly so that she would run into him. "Surely a woman who revels in red underwear has time for a little scandalous behavior. And afterward, if you're still worried about your reputation with Mr. Perkins, I'll return you to him. Underwear and all."

"You have no intention of—"

"You're right. I'll keep you for myself," he breathed, and he pulled her close for a kiss that was a prelude to the night music yet to come.

Celesta gasped for air when he released her. "You're drunk!"

"No, merely intoxicated after watching you all day from my former room." He nodded toward the Park Hotel, which overlooked the festivities, a chuckle rumbling in his chest. "You were hunting for me, gazing about like a little girl lost, while poor Perkins looked half-afraid you'd find me. I couldn't bear to let you continue that way—not when the view from the Cruikshanks' observatory will take your breath away, once the fireworks start."

They already had. Celesta's temper threatened to flare like a rocket, and her breath was hissing like a

159

fuse in her dry throat. His dark hair fluttered in the breeze as he gazed down at her with eyes that shone wickedly, reflecting the street lights around them. His shirt was unbuttoned nearly halfway, and he smelled of citrus and alcohol that hadn't come in a cologne bottle.

"You went into my room, stole my underwear, and now you're telling me you've stashed it on the topmost level of John Cruikshank's house?" she demanded tersely.

"That pretty well describes it, yes."

"Don't you get tired of setting these little traps?"

Damon chuckled, pleased she was warming to the subject. "About as tired as you get falling for them, sweetheart."

He massaged her shoulders, savoring the lamplight on her face and the defiant gleam in her eyes. "If you can tell me, *honestly*, that you'd rather spend the rest of the evening not letting Patrick find out you've lost your underwear, I'll let you go. You'll have a lot of embarrassing questions to answer, but if that's what you want, I'll—"

Celesta pulled away from his embrace and stalked up the street ahead of him, muttering. Only Damon Frye would treat her this way—and he *would* fly her unmentionables from atop Rockcliffe, probably with a banner proclaiming their ownership!

Behind them, the Thompkins Troubadours launched into a magnificent rendition of "The Star Spangled Banner," but Frye barely noticed. He allowed Celesta to remain several feet ahead of him as they ascended the long hill that led up to the mansion, his eyes following her strident sway. Even though she was accustomed to this vigorous pace, she'd be panting by the time they reached the door—and she'd have to wait until he was good and ready to guide her through the dark, unfamiliar house. All day he'd been planning this escapade, and the thought of holding her firm, agile body against his again made him suck in his breath.

Celesta turned, gasping for air. "Was that a sign you're ready to quit this ridiculous game, old man? At this rate you'll be having heart failure when we reach the top floor."

"Yes, but not for the reason *you* mean," he replied huskily. "The choice is yours, though—as always. If you want to go back, I can think of a couple men on my crew who'd get quite a hoot from finding those silky underthings. You've worn them, so they'll still have your scent. One can only imagine what sort of scene must've taken place, if a young lady became so . . . agitated she forgot to put her drawers back on."

"Agitated? I'll show you agitated!" Celesta stalked on up Bird Street until she topped the knoll and was on Cruikshank grounds. A huge, golden moon cast a shadow in the shape of the house, and an evening breeze stirred the trees around them. It was a perfect summer night, but if Frye thought he was going to seduce her with this little joke, he was in for a big disappointment.

"We'll enter through the back," he said quietly. "Don't go tearing ahead of me, or you'll crash into things. We obviously can't turn on the lights."

Celesta grunted. "It would serve you right to get caught, Frye. This is even more despicable than luring me to the cellar with my manuscript."

"More exciting, too," he teased, as he swung the door open. "We've got the whole place to ourselves. With more than twenty rooms, we could make love a different way in every one of them, if we have the stamina."

"Only in your dreams," she retorted. "Let's get my things and get out of here. This is trespassing."

"Forgive us our trespasses," he intoned, shutting the door behind him. After his eyes adjusted to the dimness, he groped for her hand. "Let me lead you on, sweetheart. Can't have you getting hurt or frightened, now can we?"

Whatever he'd been drinking had certainly lubricated his tongue. Since he was twisting her phrases into the most damning innuendo, Celesta decided to keep quiet rather than fueling his lewd imagination. She'd be out of here faster.

They'd entered what must be the kitchen, and as he led her into a large, rectangular room—the dining room, she assumed—the odors of varnish and freshly sawed wood floated around her. All the rooms seemed cavernous, and the moonlight spilling through the large palladium windows cast eerie shadows around the ladders and scaffolding.

". . . and this little nook's Moorish in flavor," Damon was saying, gesturing toward its arched doorway. "We copied it from a room in the Waldorf Astoria. If it were light, you could see the domed ceiling. And this is. . . ."

If it were light, we wouldn't be here, she thought, yet the rooms he described as he led her around the entire ground floor astounded her. Rumor had not done the mansion justice. Rockcliffe exceeded all her expectations even though it was far from finished and too dark to be fully appreciated.

Frye paused before a massive staircase that dwarfed Ransom Manor's. Celesta had made no effort to free her hand, her breathing had returned to normal, and she was as awed as he hoped she'd be. No reason to waste any more of this night touring sawdusty halls and empty, echoing rooms when the object of both their desires awaited them beyond the third floor.

"We'll skip the bedrooms—this time," he teased, "and climb on up to the observatory. If we're lucky, the music's still playing and we'll have the best seats in town for the fireworks."

Her mouth dropped open. "But we can't stay—"

162

"Why not?" He stepped closer and brought her hand to his lips, caressing each knuckle as though he had all night to please her.

She had no answer. By now Patrick would realize she was gone, and she couldn't rush back to the park clutching her silk underwear for the whole town of Hannibal to see—couldn't tell anyone, least of all Perkins, where she'd disappeared to so suddenly. It was a long walk home alone, along deserted streets where worse types than Frye might be lurking in the shadows.

"I'm trying to show you, away from prying eyes and eavesdropping ears, that our first time together was only the beginning," he explained. "Sending you away with such harsh, uncaring words was the worst mistake I've ever made. Well—one of them. Despite what you might think of the way I treated Lucy, I was shocked and deeply wounded by her death. There are things I can't tell you now, Celesta. But until the truth comes out, you'll always have the choice of accepting my affections or walking away."

It was an eloquent plea for her understanding, mysterious and incomplete though it was. Damon might be a bit under the influence, but the liquor had mellowed his arrogance and allowed him to confess flaws he wouldn't admit to in bright, sober daylight.

Celesta sighed. Mama hadn't taught her how to read a man's mind or look into his heart. "Are you asking for another chance, even though you tricked me into it? Again?"

He nodded solemnly.

"All right. But the choices *are* mine," Celesta warned, "and if you hurt me that way a second time, I won't wait for Justine to throw you out, whether the papering's complete or not. Understand?"

"Yes. Thank you," he said with a serious smile. "And just so you'll know, I'll tell you that Lucy always had the same options I'm giving you. It was I

163

who was betrayed."

He'd gone farther than he intended, and he felt fortunate that Celesta accepted his words without questioning them. Losing another woman, especially this one, would be more than he could stand. Even though he'd spent the past ten years steeling himself against feminine wiles, Celesta was like a painting he couldn't study only once . . . a young woman who attracted him in more ways than he cared to admit.

Damon glanced toward the stairway, which glowed softly in the darkness. "If you'd rather have me fetch your lingerie and then escort you home, I will. It was a petty trick, stealing your underthings to get your attention."

"It worked, too," Celesta said with a slight chuckle. She followed his gaze up the steps toward what she knew would be another point of no return, her pulse quickening. Damon Frye might be underhanded, but he was by far the most intriguing, complicated man she'd ever met. Appealing, because he was such a challenge. "I . . . suppose now that we're here, it'd be a shame to miss the fireworks."

"And maybe light a few of our own?"

He could feel her smiling in the darkness, and again he kissed her delicate hand. She was truly a treasure, this forgiving young lady, and he vowed that once her mother's murder was explained and his own past was brought to light, Celesta Montgomery would have every reason to rush into his arms and never let him go.

He was leading her upstairs now, his footfalls echoing his eagerness. Was it Damon's magic that had once again changed her no to yes, or her own wayward heart that couldn't deny him?

It was too late to wonder. They were both breathless when they bypassed the ballroom, and he hurried her up a short flight of stairs into a small windowed cubicle that seemed to be perched on top of the world.

Celesta stared around her in all directions. The river glistened like a wide silver ribbon behind the business district and outlying residential areas, which appeared smudgy and indistinct, like a nocturnal watercolor. Central Park was easy to find, surrounded by the glow of its triple-globed gaslights, yet it seemed so far away and insignificant. When Damon raised a few windows, the orchestra's song drifted in with a lazy, dreamlike breeze that relieved the little room's airless silence.

Then he stood behind her, his hands resting on her shoulders, his warm breath falling on her neck. The moment was ripe with anticipation, bathed in moonlight and that aching madness she recalled from going to him in the cellar. Would he always arouse her this way, teasing and coaxing her beyond reason before leaving the final move to her?

Celesta turned to him, her lips upraised, and his kiss continued the spell he'd begun by saying she was free to leave him. The tang of liquor and lemonade made her thirstier for him. She clung greedily, drinking in his heady male essence and refusing to release his mouth until her own was sated, for now.

"I'm getting dizzy," she whispered.

"Must be the altitude—or the fumes from the lemonade I sipped all afternoon," he said, nuzzling her nose with his. "Drove me to drink, watching Perkins parade you around. He's told people you're engaged, you know."

"He has?" Celesta scowled up at him, hesitating. "What's he after, Damon? I'm not casting for compliments here; I suspect you know things I don't, being male and all."

Frye chuckled and rested his head against hers. "A man would be crazy *not* to be after you, sweetheart. What was your answer when he proposed?"

"I refused him. More than once."

"Then, trust your instincts."

Celesta pulled away slightly to gaze at his moonlit face, wondering how he always came up with such pithy replies. Was it instinct or recklessness that had driven her into Damon's embrace again? He probably knew, but she didn't dare ask him. "Where's my underwear?"

"Hanging on a nail behind us. Shall I get it for you?"

"No. I will."

He released her, his breath catching in his throat when Celesta began to unbutton her dress. Her wide, white collar caught the moon's glow as it slipped past her shoulders and hips, revealing underthings that were drab by comparison. As though reading his thoughts, she plucked her hairpins out one by one, with a seductive slowness that made his pulse race. She knew exactly what she was doing. And she was enjoying every second of it!

"I . . . I thought you'd like to see me in that scarlet finery again," she mumbled, sounding like a jittery little girl, yet so, so provocative.

"It's all I could think about today," he breathed. "That, and how good it would feel to have you peel my clothes off and ravish me up here."

Celesta's throat went dry, but it was too late to change course. "All right. But turn around until I'm ready. I'm not exactly used to this, you know."

He squeezed his eyes shut in a moment of exultation and did as she asked. The lights below seemed to brighten. He felt himself stiffening, just listening to the hurried rustle of clothes falling to the floor behind him. Damon peeked once, in time to see two lush, ivory hips pointed toward him as she stretched a red stocking over her knee and fumbled with the fasteners on the elastic supporters.

To keep from mumbling endearing obscenities he

faced the park again and hummed along with the song that rose on the breeze. "America, the Beautiful" it was, and when a new verse began he chuckled to himself and sang softly.

"So beautiful in ruffles red, and drawers the shade of flame," he crooned. "The sight of you brings out in me a lust I cannot tame!"

Celesta's eyes widened. This wasn't really happening—such a perfect parody on a moment's notice! But now he was performing the chorus with a fervor that if not patriotic, was inspiring all the same.

"Celesta, sweet! Celesta, mine! Come warm my lonely bed. Join me tonight in passion's flight—or Hannibal sees red!"

She whirled around, trying not to laugh as she struggled into the lacy camisole. "You did *not* just make that up! Did you?"

When Damon smiled so devilishly, the cleft in his chin taunting her, he couldn't be trusted. "Of course I did. You're not the only writer who ever lived in Hannibal, you know."

She crossed her arms. "Maybe not. But Sam Clemens didn't steal my drawers and threaten to make a flag of them, either."

He nearly choked on a laugh, because Celesta had forgotten to put that particular garment on in her excitement. With her ruffled breasts protruding over her arms and her long black hair pointing to a triangle that matched it, flanked by deep crimson strips which hugged her delectable thighs, Celesta was every man's fantasy come to life. And she belonged to him, whether she'd admit it or not.

"All right, I confess," he said in a husky voice. "I made it up this afternoon. Figured they'd play that song sometime tonight."

That he'd gone to such lengths to arrange this seduction was somewhat amazing, for she'd heard women complain that their men hurried so when it came to romance. Frye was obviously different. "I suppose you know others? Surely that one song, and swilling lemonade, didn't take the whole afternoon."

"Presumptuous little tart, aren't you?" He stepped closer, guiding her hands to the front of his shirt. "If you're lucky, they'll play 'The Battle Hymn of the Republic.' Meanwhile, I want my turn. Take my clothes off, Celesta. Take your time about it."

Chapter 13

Celesta hesitated, unable to stop gazing into his hypnotic dark eyes. Beneath her hands, his heart was pulsing like a powerful engine, and she realized its beat had taken over the rhythm of her own body's respiration. They were breathing together, holding each other captive in yet another fateful moment. It was potent magic.

"Speaking of tarts," she mumbled, "poor Patrick found a pit in one this evening. Chipped a tooth."

"Serves him right, for taking something meant for me." She was trembling, afraid of her own reactions as well as his, so he gently guided her hands into his half-open shirt. "Caress me, sweetheart. You have wonderfully sensitive hands, and I can't wait to feel them exploring every inch of my body."

Beneath the downy hair on his chest she felt warm skin and tiny, hardening nipples, and Celesta came undone. Her fingers flew over his buttons while her lips found their delight along every curve of his upper body. His moans vibrated against her mouth as together they removed Damon's damp shirt.

So beautifully bold she was, brazen in scarlet and driving him wild with her eager explorations. Her feathery touch sent goose bumps racing up his back, and her fumbling with his fly buttons was endless, mind-boggling torture. Perhaps it was the liquor making him feel years younger, yet Frye suspected that Celesta herself was the potion to cure the ills he'd suffered in Fate's fickle grasp before.

When Damon stepped free of his pants he could wait no longer. He clasped her face between his hands and kissed her deeply, matching her undulations as she kneaded the halves of his backside. This was moving much faster than he'd intended, because Celesta, in her innocence, didn't realize how powerful an aphrodisiac she was.

He released her lips and pulled her close, taking long breaths of the fresh air drifting in the windows. "Let's slow it down, sweetheart," he murmured. "There are so many sensations to enjoy, and we don't want to miss a single one."

Celesta held him tightly, dazed by the druglike effect of his virility. "Wh-what do I do now? Do you want me to take these underthings off?"

"No. This sort of clothing is sometimes more erotic than bare skin . . . the whisper of it between us." He ran the tip of his tongue behind her ear and along the base of her neck, relishing the way it made her writhe against him. Then he chuckled. "They're playing our song. Can you stand another silly stanza or two, or shall I shut up?"

She grinned, straining to hear the melody . . . "The Battle Hymn of the Republic." "Sing for me. I like you when you're silly."

Pleased yet feeling a bit awkward, Damon hugged her so that she couldn't see his expression as they swayed together. "Mine eyes have seen the glory of Celesta's blooming lust . . . she has such a tempting fanny, she has such a lovely bust. When she wraps her legs around me . . . then I simply have to thrust. She's driving me insane."

Her giggle was highest praise, and as she kissed him playfully he didn't mind skipping over the chorus. "You're quite a poet, Mr. Frye. Is there more?"

"I saved the best for last, pretty lady," he replied in a husky whisper. "As I recall, this is the verse they play more slowly, with a little more expression. I hope you don't think I'm a horse's ass."

"I think you're wonderful."

The moonlight made soft stars appear in her eyes, and Damon gazed at her, his heart so full he could barely speak. "I'll watch your green eyes smolder as your love for me unfurls," he sang in a solemn baritone. "Stroke your skin so soft and ivory, like a moonlit string of pearls. Now I want to run my tongue inside . . . your scented nest of curls. You're driving me insane."

Celesta gaped, suddenly nervous. "You . . . want to kiss me there?"

He ran his finger along her cheek. "Very much," he breathed. "All the perfumers in Paris can't concoct a more subtle, intoxicating fragrance than you can, just because you're a woman, Celesta."

Damon nuzzled her breasts through the silk ruffles, running his hands lightly down her sides until they rested on her bare hips. "Balance yourself on this window ledge, and let your head fall back against the pane, if need be," he suggested in a voice thick with anticipation. "Rest your heels on my shoulders—"

"But I'll fall out," she whimpered, glancing fearfully at the distance between them and the ground.

"I'll hold on to your bottom," he reassured her with a grin. "That little bit of danger makes the pleasure more extreme. But if you really want me to stop, just say so."

He was guiding her backward, lifting her slightly so that she was resting on the wooden ledge. The cooler night air was a startling contrast to the heat of his hands, and when he knelt in front of her, his gaze roaming hungrily over her most secret parts, Celesta felt a fierce, wanton decadence coursing through her.

Her feet found his shoulders. Damon ran his

171

tongue along her inner thigh, his eyes taunting her when he nibbled at the edge of her stocking. She was gripping the windowsill, watching in fascination as he kissed his way slowly up her leg. Her heart was hammering so hard she thought she might die on the spot. And when his tongue found the sensitive nub he'd introduced her to before, she sucked in her breath.

"Relax, honey. Open for me."

Celesta closed her eyes and obeyed, and when the first gentle strokes became more insistent, inching farther inside her, she abandoned herself to the most delicious, quivering pain she'd ever experienced. Her head rolled from side to side on the window glass. Her fingers found Damon's thick, warm hair, and the moment she put herself entirely in his hands, trusting him not to let her fall four stories, she was overtaken by a wild, primitive throbbing that made her cry out.

Frye knew her exquisite predicament and pressed on. She was balanced on the precipice, ready to fall over that magical edge into mindless ecstasy—and leading him rapidly down the same path. Celesta's whimpers echoed in the little room, accelerating as his kisses deepened.

She shrieked and then exploded—or was that the first of the fireworks? Celesta was beyond caring as she gave in to shudders that made her head thump against the glass and her hips rock uncontrollably. "Damon . . . Damon, stop! I'm falling!"

He chuckled and grabbed her more tightly, continuing his torture until he was sure she was spent. She could only pant his name now, out of her head, and it was a sweeter set of lyrics than he could ever compose himself.

When she resurfaced, she realized she was limp against Damon's broad chest, supported by his strong arms. When had he picked her up? He was rocking her, whispering how lovely she was and how she pleased him, in a voice that could well have come from her own imagination. From behind them, muted and distant, came the keening of rockets and then the muffled *pop* when they exploded into stars.

Celesta gazed at Frye, shaking her head. "How is it that the music plays when you want it to, and the fireworks start at your command? Are you a sorcerer, come from another place and time?"

He kissed her nose, adoring the glimmer of awe in her still-unfocused eyes. "It's magic," he whispered playfully, "but I can't take full credit. It only happens so perfectly when I'm holding you, honey. Believe me."

Her grin felt lopsided, but it didn't matter. "That was an . . . overwhelming performance."

"I'm glad you enjoyed it." He kissed her lightly and let her slide down until her feet found the floor. "The architect in me thinks of that particular opening as a keyhole. There's more than one key, as you know . . . but I'm just vain enough to think they all belong to me."

Was he saying he loved her? She doubted it. Damon *wanted* her—that much was plain in his dark-eyed gaze and subtle smile. And as she kissed his chin and lightly stubbled neck, Celesta knew in her heart that his declarations, no matter how far astray they led her, were the words her heart was destined to hear. Patrick's proposals, though seemingly honorable, would always fall short.

She ran her hand down the contours of his arm, marveling at how perfectly he was proportioned—how sleek and manly he was, bathed in the moon's golden glow. Damon stood absolutely still, allowing her to study him without seeming the least bit embarrassed about her curiosity. When her palm paused tentatively over his proud, stiff manhood, he rubbed it against her, encouraging her grasp.

He'd been patiently considerate, pleasuring her first, so it seemed only fair to repay him. "Is this a key

173

in search of a keyhole?'' she asked, trying to keep a straight face.

Frye laughed aloud and hugged her. ''Do you know where it might find one?''

Celesta parted her legs slightly to guide him between them. ''I think you're in the neighborhood. What can I do to make you feel totally incoherent, the way you did me?''

Her question, whispered in a voice that hinted of her reawakening passion, sent a thrill through him. Not only was she willing to accept his advances, she wanted to initiate her own—a trait few women possessed. He smiled as two colorful starbursts flared in the sky behind her. ''You're missing the fireworks. Turn around, and we'll watch them together.''

Celesta faced the window again, reveling in the warmth of palms that stroked her sides and then firmly enclosed her breasts. He was rubbing against her bare bottom, teasing her sensitive nape with kisses so soft they might be an illusion. A muskiness enveloped them, perfume as heady as he'd claimed, and when his tip prodded for an opening she instinctively leaned over to grasp the casement.

As he slid inside her, Damon wished this precious time alone with his woman would never end. He found himself caressing her feverishly, propelled toward a climax he couldn't stall for long. ''Celesta . . . oh, honey, how do you do this to me?''

He was kneading a breast with one hand, wrapping his other arm around her abdomen as though he couldn't let go. Their breathing accelerated, echoing in the little room like the puffing and groaning of a steam engine climbing a hill. Sensing his desperation, Celesta gripped the wooden casement and bucked backward, her own frenzy returning.

Frye rocked against her, driven by a desire like none he'd ever known, until he shot with the blinding force of a cannon. He staggered into her with a groan, and they collapsed against the wall.

And yet, when he regained some sense of where they were, he realized Celesta was whimpering, frustrated and too shy to ask for help. "Tell me what you want," he commanded in a whisper. "Anything, and it's yours."

She was too far gone to make light of such an open-ended offer. "Touch me . . . hard. Make me scream again, Damon."

Was there no end to the surprises this angelic vixen would come up with? He obliged her gladly, overjoyed that Celesta shared his compulsive need for physical affection. She was smacking the wall with the palm of her hand, her neck arched back so that her silken hair caressed his face. And she was breathing his name desperately.

"Fly with it, Celesta," he urged beside her ear. "Float on the current and then soar higher . . . higher . . . until you burst into a thousand stars. Squeeze me, honey. . . ."

His words took over, and her passion surged until she shattered with it. Where had these powerful forces come from? Twenty years she'd lived and never suspected herself capable of enduring, much less producing, such glorious shock waves.

As she caught her breath, she glanced down toward the park and the riverfront, where a showy burst filled the night sky with showers of red, green and white firefalls. It occurred to her that she'd left her picnic basket in the park, and that she certainly couldn't go down there and retrieve it. Yet, as she relaxed in Damon's embrace, she knew she'd left something much more important behind tonight: never again could she call her soul her own. With his sorcerer's power, this man had transformed her into someone she scarcely recognized, and she hoped she wouldn't regret it for the rest of her life.

Damon kissed her long and tenderly at the cellar

door. "I wish you were sleeping with me," he whispered. "I live for the day I'll wake to find you in my arms."

After all the passion they'd shared, his words still made her flush and feel like a wobbly-kneed schoolgirl. Celesta smiled nervously and then slipped through the silent, dark kitchen. She paused, listening. The thin strains of a waltz were floating down the hallway, and the glow of lamplight edged the partially shut door of the summer parlor.

Celesta crept quietly toward the stairs, thinking to escape Katherine's questions. Yet her sense of duty got the best of her. The old dear was probably waiting up to see that she got home safely.

When she peeked into the parlor, Celesta's eyes widened. A single lamp cast its soft light into the center of the room, while the gramophone played "The Blue Danube," slightly scratchy from use. Aunt Katherine was dancing with a phantom partner, dipping and swaying gracefully around the room, her face alight with the sweetest of smiles.

Some would've thought her so far gone she could never return to reality, but Celesta realized how she must ache for her husband. Her romantic fantasies were all she had left, and she'd cling to them until she died. A sad, strangely moving thought, and it made Celesta's throat tighten.

Katherine opened her eyes, letting out a short, self-conscious laugh as she came to a stop in front of her niece. "And how were the fireworks, dear?" she asked in a wistful voice.

She was frightfully aware of how hastily she'd repinned her hair, and how flushed she must look, with lips as red as they were sore. Did her aunt notice the intimate fragrance of the love she and Damon had made? She surely must reek of it. "Fine," she rasped. "Unlike anything I've ever seen."

Her aunt nodded, as though in a dream. "I thought they might be. Good night, dear."

Chapter 14

Celesta drifted downstairs in a state of euphoria the next morning. Damon was already eating, discussing which rooms the aunts wanted him to paper next, and only his businesslike tone kept her from breaking into a give-away grin each time she glanced in his direction. She hardly tasted Katherine's omelet, and as she helped clear away the plates she caught herself before her hand landed on his broad shoulder. How on earth could she keep her love for him a secret, with both of them living under Justine's eagle eye?

Her spinster aunt's return from town jolted her back to reality. The handful of mail she pulled from her market basket included a note for Celesta, in a cream-colored envelope that had no return address.

My dearest Celesta, she read from the angular scrawl on the page. *Seeing your stricken expression, I naturally assumed Frye was fetching you because one of your dear aunts was ill. Then I realized, to my great disappointment, that you were rushing off in the opposite direction. . . .*

Imagine my embarrassment when I face my friends, whom I've told of our betrothal. We must reconcile this indiscretion immediately. You know how Mother despises any scandal concerning the

177

Perkins name. Come and see me.

He signed off with oversized P's, which reminded her that she used to tease Patrick about having initials that denoted a bodily function—and that he deserved them. She'd expected some reaction about her disappearance last night, but his note's presumptuous tone made him look all the more ridiculous.

When Celesta folded the page back into its envelope, however, she realized that Patrick Perkins had set her up: he'd purposely sent it to Justine's mailbox, unsealed. Had her aunt read it and filled in between the lines? It was impossible to tell, because the spinster had already gone upstairs to do her cleaning. A slow burn worked up from her collar, because now the older Ransom would be lying in wait to catch her and Damon in the slightest secretive exchange.

"Are you all right, dear? If you don't feel up to it, I can take down the pictures in the music room myself, while you rest," Katherine's voice interrupted her musings.

Her aunt's bright eyes had an innocent shine to them. "I—I'm fine," Celesta blurted, stuffing the note into her skirt pocket. "It's just an invitation from Patrick to come see him. I'd rather get the music room walls cleared, so Damon can work in there tonight."

The little woman smiled knowingly, and they spent the day preparing both the music room and the library. Celesta was on pins and needles, trying not to gush about Damon Frye to an aunt who undoubtedly knew what was happening between them. And that evening, when their resident carpenter was working with his usual confidence, sneaking her an occasional wink, it was all but impossible not to throw her arms around him and demand a kiss.

Each time she handed him a measured, cut strip of

178

the gold-flecked wallpaper, their fingers lingered together. Though he didn't repeat his sensual, intoxicating phrases from the previous evening, his deep brown eyes silently assured her they were true. He was humming "The Battle Hymn of the Republic" in a resonant baritone that spurred her pulse into a gallop. Such phrases as *skin of ivory like a moonlit string of pearls,* or *run my tongue inside your fragrant nest of* . . . made her feverishly aware that Damon, too, was reliving the glory of the Fourth.

It was impossible to sleep that night, knowing he was downstairs—wanting him so desperately she thrashed about in bed, not daring to sneak past Justine's room to go to him. Instead, Celesta waited until she could stand it no longer, and then tiptoed up to the third-floor alcove. Another Sally Sharpe story was due soon, and she might as well set her wide-awake mind to some useful task.

How could she have foreseen the effect her reuniting with Frye would have on her fictional heroine? She picked up the pen, went through her ritual of stacking the paper just so, and wrote *SALLY SHARPE, GIRL DETECTIVE, in*—

And her next image was of the prim blonde peeling off her shirtwaist, slipping out of her sensible shoes, and beckoning Damon Frye with a come-hither look that made Celesta's mouth drop open. Suddenly Sally, too, could think of nothing but the dark magician! It was a shock to watch her heroine throw herself into Frye's arms, wearing the scantiest of underthings, murmuring the brazen phrases she wished she could be mouthing now.

This would never work! From her editor's rare, cryptic comments, Celesta knew he expected the same fast-paced, hardboiled sleuthing Sally was famous for—undercover adventures that got nowhere near a bed with a man in it! Anything risqué

179

would surely get returned with a rejection letter, and she would've wasted the hours she spent writing the story. Better to focus her thoughts on safer subjects, to keep those checks arriving from her New York uncle.

But every time Celesta closed her eyes to visualize a dangerous crime or a villain Sally could pit herself against, she saw Damon in a sorcerer's flowing robe, waving a wand to kindle her desire . . . Damon in a black cape with a red lining, his eyes glowing like Count Dracula's as he enticed her . . . Damon naked, bathed in moonlight, as fireworks exploded into colorful stardust behind him.

The moment she resigned herself to frittering away a sleepless night in fantasy, an idea slapped her, and she had to stifle a laugh. If Frye could compose lyrics for her enjoyment—just for fun—why couldn't she toss off a tale for his eyes only? A story that would make him chuckle as he raced along the pages. A piece that would say she, too, was inspired by their lovemaking, hoping it would grow into something deeper and everlasting.

Grinning, Celesta wadded up her original page. She could see a lone, broad-shouldered rider atop a magnificent stallion, searching relentlessly for a thug who wooed dance hall girls into his hotel room with gifts of lacy finery, only to kill them. A grisly premise, but this . . . bounty hunter!—Damon Dare!—would help Sally apprehend the murderer. Probably rescue her from the demon's clutches, before riding off to his cabin with her in his arms.

Sally hadn't taken a western case for a while, and this one made Celesta shift with anticipation. Wrapping her ankles around the legs of Grandfather's straight-backed chair, she thought for a moment and then wrote *SALLY SHARPE, GIRL DETECTIVE, MEETS DAMON DARE in "The Golden Bounty."*

Her pen flew across the paper. The bounty, of course, was Sally Sharpe herself, but Sally was too busy analyzing clues along the killer's trail to notice this, until she met up with Dare. He was a loner who shunned civilization except to check the Wanted posters and collect his money when he returned to the marshal's office, criminal in tow . . . which meant he was hungry for an unsuspecting yet uniquely appealing innocent like Sally.

The repartee flashed like lightning between them. Celesta's hand could hardly keep up with her rapid-fire thoughts, and she stopped writing only to refill her fountain pen before racing off across the Wyoming plains with Sally again.

Dare, concerned for Miss Sharpe's safety, had taught her how to shoot his rifle—mainly as an excuse to get his arms around her. Sally was justifiably flustered when, as the villain came charging into their camp, knowing Damon was out gathering firewood, the Girl Detective had to grab Dare's gun to defend herself.

The blast of the rifle sent Sally flying backward, her shoulder clutched by a sudden, fiery pain. She landed against Damon with a gasp, stunned by the solidness of him, by his unrelenting maleness as he wrapped a steadying arm around her. There was only their labored breathing and the dying groan of the brute who lay sprawled before them.

"It's so long and . . . hard," Sally panted.

Dare cleared his throat, his breath riffling the hair at her ear. "What's that, Miss Sharpe?"

"Why, your gun, of course."

"Oh. Of course." He smiled, taunting her with coffee brown eyes. "Perhaps with a little more practice, you could handle it . . . quite expertly. I'd be happy to help you."

181

"I'm sure you would, Mr. Dare." Sally stepped away from his embrace, trembling now from something besides the kick of his rifle. "I—I have my own weapon, thank you."

The bounty hunter's low chuckle left no doubt about what was on his mind as his gaze raked over her. "I'm sure you do, sweetheart. And I bet you know how to use it, too."

Celesta stopped writing to fan herself, because Damon Dare was making the little alcove even hotter than usual. She laughed, picturing Frye's grin when he found this suggestive tale in his room tonight. As she scribbled a final page, she left Sally and Damon on horseback together, in sight of his cozy cabin, just as the first flakes of a blizzard hinted they might be stranded there for a long while. If Frye liked it, she would write a sequel, some other night when her mind wandered too far afield to compose anything Beadle and Adams would publish.

The clock in the entry hall boomed solemnly, its deep tones drifting up the open stairwell. Three o'clock. With a yawn and a sleepy grin, Celesta crept downstairs to bed.

Frye found his thoughts wandering that day, and when his workmen went into town for their noon meal he climbed up into the observatory to ponder his predicament. What had begun as bald-faced flattery had turned into sincere admiration for Celesta Montgomery. What had started as vengeance was now a dangerous dilemma: If he dropped the whole matter—let his grudges die with his memories of Lucy Bates—then Celesta would be crushed and Perkins would probably win her for his own underhanded purposes. And if he allowed his feelings for her to flower, he'd provoke Patrick's wrath and place her in greater danger.

Celesta deserved better than either of them. Yet she was trapped between them, and he could see no painless way out for her . . . a regrettable situation, and Damon shook his head as though this would clear the heaviness that shrouded his heart.

Had he really sung to her in this unadorned cubicle? Had they made the wild, passionate love that still sent his pulse skittering whenever he thought about it? By the harsh light of day the little room felt anything but romantic, yet its walls and windows seemed to whisper to him of the magic that had transformed them both on that mystical evening.

Celesta had called him wonderful—a sorcerer—and visions of her arched back as she slapped the wall in her ecstasy made him want her all over again. Such a wanton she was! He doubted that Lucy, in her most brazen moments, had ever been so swept away by passion. And suddenly, as he looked out over Hannibal basking in the bright sunlight, he couldn't recall what Lucinda Bates looked like, or the sound of her voice.

It was progress, but it wasn't enough. If he was to do right by Celesta, he had to do more than make love to her. He had to protect her from the fate his fiancée had suffered—and from the truth that lay buried in Mount Olivet with her.

Damon returned to Ransom Manor that afternoon determined to keep Celesta at arm's length until it was safe to love her as he truly wanted to. The sparkle in her eye should've warned him. When he was changing into his overalls, he found a thick sheaf of papers stuffed into the pocket. He sat on the edge of his bed to read—only for a moment, he told himself—and became riveted by her wit, captivated by a story that caricatured his feelings for her while giving Sally Sharpe another challenging case to solve.

While they worked together that evening, he savored their secret glances. Celesta's face was lit by a demure, expectant smile: she was waiting for him to comment about Damon Dare. But with Katherine popping in to admire their progress and Justine pausing at the door before she retired for the evening, there wasn't a good time to discuss the western hunter and his bounty.

He left her with a quick kiss that night—and left her to wonder, knowing it would sharpen her need for him. After reading the adventurous tale again, Frye smiled. Celesta had written the story as a surprise for him, and now he had a bigger surprise for her.

The week came to a close and he *still* hadn't said anything! Celesta's patience wore thin, and the fun had gone out of waiting for his response. Damon had had plenty of chances to comment about the story she'd written for him, yet all he did was wink and grin. Was she supposed to read his mind? She'd be damned if she'd beg for compliments about her work!

And to top her problems off, Katherine received a note from Eula Perkins saying she wanted to visit on Sunday afternoon. Patrick would no doubt drive his mother over and then corner her about why she'd been avoiding him. It was an embarrassing situation—all Damon's fault—and by the time the Perkins carriage rolled up outside the main entryway, Celesta was in no mood to speak with Frye or Patrick, either one.

As the polite niece, however, she opened the door while Aunt Katherine hurried out of her apron. They'd just finished the dinner dishes, and Damon had gone downstairs to change into his work clothes while Justine made herself scarce. She was in a better

184

mood these days, but she still refused to tolerate Eula's company.

The lumber baron's widow wore a dress of deep green lawn that flattered her golden complexion yet looked frumpy, somehow. Eula's smile was bright—until she paused in the doorway to study Celesta.

"My goodness," she murmured, "since you've left us, you look even more like your mother—don't you agree, Patrick?"

A smirk passed quickly over his face. "She looks quite alive to me, Mother."

"Why, what a horrible—" Eula masked her shock by smiling too kindly and clasping Celesta's hands between her damp palms. "You two will never stop antagonizing one another, will you? It was an annoyance I had hoped you'd grow out of—*Katherine!* You look wonderful, dear, and this wallpaper puts everything in my house to *shame!*"

Celesta sighed, watching the older women share a brief embrace as Eula continued to rave over the redecorated vestibule. Even though her aunt had never been overly fond of Mrs. Perkins, her excitement and pitch were rising until the ladies' voices echoed shrilly in the hall and then faded into the library.

Patrick was standing woodenly beside her. He had indeed come to antagonize her, and despite the afternoon heat his eyes looked like iced-over ponds. "Shall we talk?" he asked brusquely.

"About what?" she retorted. "If you intend to continue your snide remarks, you may as well stay with your mother, because I won't put up with it!"

"*You?*" He gripped her elbow, his golden face hardening. "You stood me up—ran off with Frye in front of all my friends—and by God, I'll have an explanation! I'm giving you another chance, Celesta, because I sense he led you away under false pretenses."

Damon had made no pretense at all about where

185

he'd stashed her red underwear and why—and Patrick Perkins was the last man she'd explain that to. She could hear Frye shifting his scaffolding in the summer parlor, so she shook herself free of her guest and stalked down the hallway.

"Where do you think you're—"

"Do you want him to hear every word we say?" Celesta challenged, pointing toward the parlor.

His scowl relaxed a little when he realized his nemesis was working in there, and he followed her out to the shaded backyard. The fool didn't seem to notice that the parlor windows were wide open, and Celesta intended to keep him facing toward the river so that he wouldn't catch on. It was her strategy for when things got nasty.

And, knowing that the smartest defense was a surprise attack, she struck first. "I suppose you think your lavish gifts entitle you to boss me around this way?"

Patrick blinked and then pointed an angry finger. "Those *gifts* signify my intentions, Celesta. And I'll be damned if I'll watch Frye—"

"What about *my* intentions?" She crossed her arms, returning his glare. "How do you think I feel, knowing you've told everyone we're engaged, yet you've neglected to ask *me* about it?"

"We've discussed this subject—"

"*You've* discussed it. I've had no choice but to listen while you babbled on about letting me remain in my home, and elevating me to a higher station—expecting me to feel so damn *grateful*—"

Damon glanced out the window, snickering. Perkins had never once out-sparred Celesta, and it was doubtful he'd ever learn to avoid such situations. That his raven-haired adversary had staged this quarrel outside the parlor had escaped Patrick, too, and if he thought marriage would mellow her contentious nature, he was stupid indeed.

186

". . . but what annoys me most is that it's Frye you choose to degrade yourself with," Perkins was saying in a strident voice. "Over and over I've reminded you how he sent his fiancée to her grave, and still you fall for his lies."

Celesta sucked in her breath, and before reason could stop her, she blurted, "And how about *you*, Patrick? Have you ever felt responsible for someone's untimely passing?"

Perkins jerked—and Frye himself gaped at Miss Montgomery. How the hell did she expect him to answer such a blatant question? Neither of them had a graceful way out of this confrontation now, unless—

"Eavesdropping, Mr. Frye? Idleness doesn't become you—or have you decided to rest on the Sabbath?"

Justine was behind him, her staid tone as damning as her questions. He'd overextended himself, and even though he hadn't made any overt advances toward Celesta lately, the spinster had a sixth sense about such things and sounded ready to call in her markers for his previous offenses. He turned to her with a contrite smile, aware that he had no shirt on and that she was studying him very closely.

"I thought perhaps your niece would need my assistance," he said suavely, "but she seems to be handling Mr. Perkins quite well."

"He has his mother's ingratiating ways while Celesta inherited Rachel's rapier tongue. How he thinks he'll survive marrying her escapes me."

Her remark was uttered in a matter-of-fact manner that made him raise an eyebrow and then chuckle. Justine's face softened, if only slightly, and she stepped into the parlor so that she could look out the window at the squabblers.

Patrick had sidestepped the issue of Rachel Montgomery's death by heaping the blame for Miss

Bates's predicament elsewhere, as usual. "This story's getting tiresome," Frye commented. "After ten years, you'd think people could let Lucy rest."

"Is it true? Did you get her with child and then abandon her?"

"No." He looked directly into Justine's unwavering brown eyes. "I don't suppose we'll ever know all of Lucy's circumstances, but my regrettable reaction came out of anger rather than guilt."

The woman's focus dropped to his bare shoulders, yet rather than preaching about where such a breach of proper attire would lead, she turned her attention to the couple outside the window. "I gather those disgraceful underthings in Celesta's trunk came from Perkins, then?"

"Yes, ma'am. Looks more like bribery than betrothal, if you ask me."

Somehow he kept a straight face. If she asked him how *he* knew about the lingerie, he'd be hard-pressed to answer truthfully—and so would she, the snoop! Justine studied him again, her head held high on her slender neck, and then she let out a low, conspiratorial laugh that he couldn't help joining her in.

"Well, it suits her, I suppose," the spinster commented wryly. "Her mother had a similar wild streak. Beauty can be such a bane."

Damon knew better than to comment about *that,* but while the head of the Ransom family was letting her guard down he couldn't resist asking a few more questions. Outside, Perkins was on the defensive again, the sweat running freely down his face as he gripped Celesta's arms.

"What do you suppose he sees in Celesta?" he asked quietly. "I mean, she's a wonderful young woman, but he's always chased after wealthy men's daughters. Perhaps his tastes changed while I was away."

Justine grunted softly, still watching out the window. "Where there's a vein there's a vampire. My father used to say that, and for all his macabre sense of humor, he was usually right about people."

Her answer teased at him until his eyes widened. Why hadn't he considered that angle? It would be just like Perkins to—

"And what do *you* see in her, Mr. Frye? Lord knows you look at her enough."

There was no escaping the old woman's astute comment. Frye thought for a moment, composing a reply he hoped wouldn't get him banished from Ransom Manor. Only the truth would do, because Justine already knew the answer to her question.

"Celesta's a delightful, witty young woman," he said quietly. "Her talents and intelligence impress me, but I'd be lying if I said I noticed nothing else. Your niece is quite an eyeful, Justine. And she knows how to kiss, too."

Her eyebrow arched slightly, and she took a step back. "Well, that was a . . . forthright reply, Mr. Frye."

"You're entitled to it." He gave her a subtle smile, hoping his luck held. "A lady with enticing brown eyes like yours surely understands the magnetism between a man and a woman. I'm betting someone in your past is very sorry he let you get away, and I don't intend to make that mistake with Celesta."

For a moment Justine's face took on the delicate pink of a sunlit rose. Then she coughed self-consciously and looked out the window again. "I—I think we've seen enough of this mindless exhibition," she muttered, and she marched toward the parlor door.

Then she paused, her head cocked almost coquettishly. "I appreciate your candor, Damon. I was determined not to approve of you when you came here, but I was wrong."

Before he could thank her, the spinster bustled out the back door, her footfalls purposeful beneath clothing as starched as her voice. "Mr. Perkins, I believe you'll have to leave now. We're all quite weary of your arguing, and you're keeping my niece from her afternoon's activities."

Celesta's mouth dropped open, and Patrick took a full red-faced minute to find his voice. "What activities?" he asked, glancing suspiciously toward the house.

"Why, she's helping Mr. Frye with his papering," Justine replied pertly. "We each do our part in this family, so that no one falls short when the account of our lives is reconciled. Care to join them, Mr. Perkins?"

Swearing under his breath, Patrick strode into the house to fetch his mother.

Chapter 15

The summer parlor, usually the coolest room in the house, felt stifling after the Perkins carriage clattered down the hill behind its matched bays. Frye noted a tightness around Celesta's eyes, a pout to her sensuous lips that he knew better than to ask about. When she tore a strip of the wallpaper, however, he had to challenge her heated silence.

"What's wrong?" he asked in a voice her aunts wouldn't hear. He rolled up the ruined paper and set it aside, watching her closely. "Surely you don't blame Justine for sending Perkins home. His story sounded as tedious as a broken record."

"At least he had one. Another man I know was content to let him humiliate me until an old lady came to my rescue," Celesta whispered vehemently. "Where's Damon Dare when I need him? Is chivalry dead after all?"

Frye fought a smile and then climbed the ladder with a fresh strip of the floral paper. "I never claimed to be created in your hero's image, sweetheart," he replied. "Can't help liking him, though. Have you heard from him lately?"

"What do you mean?" His subtle praise left Celesta with a peculiar sense of foreboding as she watched his backside strain against his overalls.

191

Damon chuckled. "Dare's the perfect match for Sally—and that was the best story you've ever written. Your editor will think so, too."

"My *what?* You didn't mail—"

"Certainly I did. I got the feeling you didn't want to publish 'The Pen is Mightier,' so I used its addressed envelope to rush the Dare story to Beadle and Adams," he said with a casual glance. "Unless I miss my guess, your readers will be clamoring for one sequel after another. You'll soon be notorious for your steamy stories, Miss Montgomery."

"Damn you to—" Yanking the ladder out from under him would cause too much commotion, so Celesta stalked outside instead, squinting in the afternoon glare. Of all the *nerve,* to send in a story that any respectable man would keep private! Rather than forwarding letters from enthused Sally Sharpe readers, her editor would no doubt send her notice that the Girl Detective met with sudden death before she got to press.

She lifted the heavy wooden door that led to the underground cave. Celesta descended carefully into the cool dankness, which was ripe with the scents of wet earth and the peaches they'd picked earlier this week. Large blocks of ice, cut from the river during the winter, loomed ahead of her, ghostly white.

She let the door drop, and the darkness wrapped around her like a velvety quilt. A few steps more took her to the square mountain of ice, and because the blocks were layered with sawdust, she felt its wet roughness as she groped for the nearest basket of fruit. The aunts would come looking for her if she stayed here for long, but she needed time alone to contemplate Damon's latest betrayal. Everything he did seemed designed to ruin her life or sabotage her writing career!

The peaches were balls of sweet-smelling suede beneath her hand. Celesta chose one and then brushed it against her skirt. As she took the first juicy bite, she froze. Someone was entering the cave—and of course, it was a pair of tan overall legs descending in the slash of daylight from the door.

"Leave me alone."

Frye glanced at her and then plunged them into total darkness. "Why didn't you tell Patrick the same thing? You knew he'd badger you about the other night."

Celesta chewed a flavorful bite of peach, not wanting to reply yet knowing she'd have to. "I'm trying to see if he'll let something slip while he's angry, maybe admit to Mama's murder."

"That's a dangerous game, young lady." He fumbled for the candlestick that was kept near the bottom step, and then reached into his pocket for a match. "I can understand your wanting to know the truth, but forcing it from Perkins during a confrontation can only lead to trouble. *If* he did it."

"I can handle him. And I knew you'd come to my rescue—or *thought* you would—if he got nasty." His presence in the damp darkness was unsettling. Was he coming toward her, silent as a cat? Or was Damon Frye going to stand there, blocking her exit, until she played out whatever devious fantasy he had in mind when he followed her here? "You . . . don't think he did it?"

"I'm not sure he's smart enough. The Patrick Perkins I know gets too flustered to cover all his tracks when the stakes are that high." He struck his match, watching the tentative flame lap at the wick. Celesta, peach poised at her lips, was a tantalizing Eve eyeing him as though he were a serpent not to be trusted.

Frye laughed. "You're quite a wordsmith, Miss Montgomery. I can't wait to see what'll happen to Damon Dare and Sally Sharpe, now that they're finally alone together."

His voice seemed to resonate from all sides of the low-ceilinged cave while his smile looked diabolical in the sputtering candlelight. He was alluding to reality rather than fictional characters. He stepped closer, his dark eyes shining.

"What do you want?" she mumbled.

"You."

Celesta took another bite of her peach, as though eating it would be her defense against him. But what would protect her from her own impulses? His skin glowed in the flickering flame while the hair on his forearms shone in golden contrast to the dark smudge of beard along his jaw. "Why'd you follow me down here?" she demanded tersely. "Isn't it enough that you've turned my editor against me and made Patrick even angrier. You—"

"I came after you because I'm intrigued, sweetheart," he replied, running a finger along her soft cheek. "Lay all the blame you want, but you must see *something* in me, to write such a provocative tale. I'm fascinated by your wit . . . your tongue-in-cheek sensuality."

"You're conceited, or you'd never presume I was writing about *you*," Celesta retorted, though her voice was huskier than she liked.

His laughter echoed around the dark walls, and his dimly lit face suddenly reminded her of their cellar rendezvous. Was that a weeks-old memory now? Anticipation made her stomach flutter, just thinking about the night he'd first seduced her. Surely he wouldn't be so brazen as to—not when either aunt might—

Damon took a bite of the peach suspended between them, knowing Celesta would taste as intoxicatingly tangy when she kissed him. She was an oasis of warmth in the heavy dankness, and her alluring scent set her apart from the lemons, vegetables, and other perishables stored down here. He set the candle on

194

top of the ice. "Touch me, Celesta," he breathed. "All week I've wanted to feel your fingertips stroking my skin."

She swallowed hard, resisting. The ice block was cold against her back, starting to soak through her blouse, yet she felt a fever sweeping over her.

"Taste me, honey," came his hoarse command. "If you think that peach is delicious—"

Celesta gasped, letting the half-eaten fruit fall from her hand. His face was shading hers, his lips hovering, lighting like a butterfly on a tender flower, a gossamer caress that he repeated once . . . twice, until her eyes closed and she reached hungrily for him.

Her mouth was sweet peach velvet beneath his as he pressed her against the block of ice. Desire hit him like a heat wave. He guided her arms around his waist and chuckled when they slipped beneath the yoke of his overalls. "What's so fascinating back there?"

"You, silly," she replied with a giggle. His firm, rounded halves were bare, yielding delectably to her massage. "I should've called you Damon Derrière in the story. It's your best side, you know."

Sheer happiness crested inside him, and he kissed her firmly. It was a thrill to know this dark-haired temptress found him attractive and desirable, and he desperately wanted to make love to her. But something warned him to pull away.

"We'll finish this another time, honey," he whispered as he separated from her. "I'll love you when it's safer."

When would it ever be safe to love Damon Frye? She nodded, muddled by his hypnotic kiss, and made a cradle in her skirt for the lemons he was passing her.

"You go first. Just in case."

Celesta nodded. And after the bright sunlight

stunned her momentarily, she saw that Justine was puttering in the geranium bed. Or pretending to, anyway.

"I—I thought lemonade would taste good, hot as it is," she offered weakly.

Her spinster aunt scrutinized her with hawklike eyes. "And I suppose Mr. Frye's fetching the ice?"

"Why, yes—he is!"

Ducking into the pantry, Celesta prayed he'd follow through. She was frantically reaming lemons when she heard the back door open quietly, and Damon set a pan of ice chunks on the table beside her. He then brushed her backside vigorously, making her glance behind them when his hand cupped her hip.

"Sawdust," he whispered with a wink. Her sweet, peachy essence taunted him, but he walked quickly out of the kitchen, only moments before Justine entered it from the pantry door.

When Frye stepped into the main building of the Perkins Lumber Company the following week, the first thing he noticed was the quiet. Like the other lumber barons in Hannibal, Tom Perkins had made his considerable fortune milling the huge logs that floated down the Mississippi from Wisconsin and Minnesota, and then selling the boards he produced. Other mills Damon passed today had been alive with the whine of giant saws, bustling with workmen who drove wagonloads of logs in from the riverfront or carted fresh boards to the lots in back, to be stacked for temporary storage.

The only person he saw here was a willowy secretary seated in the small office near the rear, reading a book. The rest of the warehouse was stocked with building supplies, and from his spot in the main aisle he noted all the latest equipment on her desk: a shiny black typewriter, an adding machine, and a battery-operated Edison phonograph with which Patrick could dictate correspondence. Either she had no work, or the young lady was doing a fine job of ignoring it.

Damon checked his watch—twelve-eighteen, which explained Patrick's absence and fit his plan perfectly. As he strolled slowly along the shelves he recalled how clean and fully stocked they'd looked when he came here as a boy to fetch something for his father. Was his memory enhancing the past, as a man fondly embroidered his first passionate encounter, or had the Perkins store slipped into shabbiness while he was away?

The secretary turned a page and then gasped when she saw him. "H-how may I help you, sir? I'm sorry—I—I didn't think anyone was here!"

He smiled kindly at her. "All I need's a bag or two of wallpaper paste mix. No hurry."

She was studying him as she stood, her fascination apparent on a comely face framed by chestnut curls. "Aren't you . . . Damon Frye?"

"Yes, I am." Her smile was a sudden burst of sunshine which then waxed sly and subtle . . . and vaguely familiar. She would've been several classes behind him in school, so he tried to imagine her with shoulder-length ringlets and a starched white pinafore. "Joy?" he asked softly.

"You remember!" Beckoning him to follow her, she swayed down the aisle with a decidedly grown-up gait and stopped a few shelves away. "Notorious heartbreaker that you've become, I didn't expect you to recall the little girl who had a colossal crush on you. But I guess there were several, weren't there?"

"Only one who sent me four Valentines one year— anonymously—and then mailed initialed notes swearing eternal devotion," he replied with a chuckle. "How are you, Joy?"

"Well, I'm—"

"She's busy, Frye. What're you doing here?"

Damon turned slowly, masking the anticipation that rushed through him at Perkins's pointed demand. "I'm here to pick up some paste mix, and Miss Holliday seems to be the only employee present to—"

"The others are at dinner. Up-to-date, caring boss that I am, I allow them an hour," the defensive blond continued. "A happy work force is a productive work force."

It was bluster and they both knew it, a warming-up for the inevitable confrontation that had been brewing these past weeks. The secretary's gaze bounced eagerly between him and Patrick, so he dismissed her with a polite smile. "Good to see you again. I need to discuss some business with your boss."

"And I haven't gotten those letters I dictated, concerning our new credit policy, have I, Miss Holliday?"

"No, sir. I was just finishing them."

With a resentful lifting of her slender, freckled nose, she walked back to the enclosed office, and then Patrick blocked her view by shifting to Frye's left. "Don't tell me Cruikshank can't supply your little papering project," he said in a venomous voice. "Lord knows you wouldn't even have to pilfer paste, as much as you're bilking the Ransoms to work for them."

"I have my faults, but petty thievery isn't among them."

The lumberman's golden complexion reddened. "No? Then, what do you call trifling with Celesta, trying to steal her from me? She's my fiancée, and if you don't keep your hands—"

"Does *she* know that?"

Perkins sucked in his breath. "By God, you are *not*

going to ruin her the way you did Lucy! Perhaps we should step out back and settle this like—"

"I don't want to dirty your suit," Damon replied, and to irritate Patrick further he brushed imaginary dust from his crisp linen lapels.

Perkins slapped at him, flushing as he stepped back. "Damn you! I registered a complaint with the police the night you abducted Celesta from the concert, so you're a watched man, Frye. One more—"

"Yes, Celesta does seem to have eyes for me. Among other things."

The blue orbs before him narrowed ominously. "Get out! And if I see you with her again, you're a dead man!"

His threats rang with such an empty defiance that Frye laughed out loud as he turned to walk away. He paused at the door, though, unable to resist getting the last word in—as he'd done all their lives. "You'd better order the wood for my casket, then," he taunted. "Something in cherry would be nice. And so appropriate."

As Damon stepped out into the noonday sun he saw the mill hands sauntering back to their idle saws, casting curious glances his way. He'd seen all he needed to, and he needed to be more protective of Celesta than ever. Cornered prey like Patrick could be fatal when he lashed out.

Chapter 16

Celesta hurried from the post office, burning with curiosity. The unmarked envelope from Beadle and Adams was thicker than usual, and because Bill Thompkins was working behind the desk she dared not open her mail here. It was probably a letter from Mr. Victor, her editor, terminating her writing relationship, and she didn't want to cry hysterically while cursing Damon Frye. Bad news was best endured in the privacy of the alcove, where Grandfather's spirit might comfort her.

When she spied an empty bench in Central Park, however, Celesta succumbed. As she slid onto the slatted seat, she tore into the envelope and then gasped. Along with the larger-than-usual check for "The Case of the Purloined Papers" was a letter written in bold, flowing script:

My Dear Mr. Lester,

Heartiest congratulations, sir! We felt "Purloined Papers" was your finest work to date, meriting a higher rate of pay—until we met Damon Dare! Our readers are hungry for just such an adventurer, and Sally Sharpe followers are sure to demand more of his derring-do . . . not to mention the sultry innuendo that smolders between him and the Girl Detective.

Continue to present this pair in such a suggestive yet tasteful way, and we shall be pleased to pay you half again as much as Sally earns you for a regular case—and we'd like to keep putting her on the stands as we always have, thrice a month. Best wishes for your continued success!

Celesta's mouth dropped open. She read the letter again, her excitement rising until she wanted to shout out loud. Was this real, or had Frye written it? But he couldn't have! There was Orville J. Victor's distinctive signature, just as it always appeared on his correspondence.

She squeezed her eyes shut against sudden tears, wishing she could share this success with Mama. When her poignant mood subsided, Celesta walked resolutely into the heart of town, to the Hoskins drugstore, where dime novels were sold. Sure enough, there were the Beadle and Adams pulps for the last week in July, and beneath the bright orange masthead, Sally Sharpe was sketched with wide-eyed confidence, cornered by an ominous, well-dressed scoundrel who wielded a knife—and who bore an uncanny resemblance to Damon, just as she'd written him! It was too good not to share with someone, so she bought a copy of "The Purloined Papers" and hurried back to the Manor with it concealed in her skirt pocket.

That evening when Damon found the dimer in his overalls, along with the letter Victor had written, he slapped his knee and chuckled. His first inclination was to remind her who mailed Damon Dare to the publisher, but when he saw Celesta's pretty flush and the grin she couldn't suppress, he realized the success was hers alone.

She was waiting for him in the dining room, the

202

last first-floor salon they had to paper, and when he was certain the aunts were out of earshot, he grabbed her up and kissed her jubilantly. "I hope you're happy, young lady," he whispered. "You certainly deserve to be."

Celesta giggled, loving the gentle strength in his arms and the hint of cherry tobacco that lingered from his after-dinner pipe. "I suppose I should be humble and admit you were right to send my story to New York."

"No need. I've already patted myself on the back." He set her down, aware that Katherine was still in the kitchen. "Besides, it was *your* tale, sweetheart. I just recognized its potential for greatness."

Her cheeks must've been ruby red, by the feel of them. "Thank you," she murmured. "You don't know how good those words sound to me."

Frye stroked her cheek, and it struck him that he hadn't felt this ecstatic—for himself or anyone else—in years. As the two of them took down the gilt-framed mirrors and paintings, he watched her with growing pride. Who would ever guess that cotton-clad Celesta Montgomery, a maid's daughter—his woman!—thrilled thousands of readers across the country with her tales of suspense and adventure?

"Are you going to tell Justine and Katherine?" he asked softly. "I bet, when they realize the extent of your success, they'll be impressed rather than appalled. They're both more open-minded than you might think."

She unrolled the wallpaper, considering this. "Maybe. But for now, I just want to enjoy this little victory—share it with you. All right?"

"Certainly." He glanced toward the kitchen to be sure Katherine wasn't listening. "When do you think it'll be in the stores?"

"In a few weeks. Mid-August, I'm guessing."

"Perfect. We'll pace ourselves so that the upstairs

hallway is all finished, and celebrate," he suggested, tweaking her nose. "If you wish to declare yourself then, it'll be appropriate, and your aunts will be in high spirits anyway. If not, well . . . we'll find a way to mark the occasion."

His provocative wink left no doubt as to what he had in mind, and during the next two weeks he teased at her with dozens of little gestures that were nearly as exciting as making love to him—which, she sensed, he was avoiding so that she'd go mad with anticipation. One morning she awoke to find a perfect red rose on her nightstand. Other days she received scandalous notes in her post office box, detailing exactly what he wanted to do to her when they were alone. Gone was the darkly dangerous beast who'd lured her to his lair, and in his place stood a gallant, proud suitor with just enough rogue in him to keep Celesta wondering.

Did he love her? Would he declare himself soon? Such daydreams had Celesta floating through the days, oblivious to Justine's barbs and patient with Katherine's attempts to bring their budding romance into full flower. Patrick had apparently decided she was too much trouble to pursue, after Justine's humiliating send-off, and that in itself made early August a pleasant time for all of them.

As though arranged by Fate, "The Golden Bounty" appeared on the stands the morning after the upstairs hallway was completed. Mr. Hoskins always put his new dimers out on Tuesdays, so Celesta found an excuse to go into town whenever she thought Sally's latest would be out. She was gazing at her magazine from an aisle away, forcing herself not to jump up and down when Wilbur Lyons, who managed the green grocery next door, bought one.

She was about to take one for herself when a shirtsleeved arm darted from behind her and plucked two copies from the display. Celesta pivoted and nearly knocked Damon off-balance, laughing with nervous pride when she realized who he was.

"Let me treat you to a keepsake copy," he said in a low voice, "and I'd like you to autograph mine tonight—perhaps after we read the story aloud, assuming our respective parts?"

His suggestion made her mouth go dry. All she could do was nod.

"Then, I'll see you when we have the moonlight to ourselves and no one can keep us apart," he murmured. And after placing a chaste peck on her temple, he went to the front of the store to pay for his novels.

Celesta stood trembling, alive with anticipation as she gazed at the sketch of the Girl Detective in her bounty hunter's arms. Dare was teaching Miss Sharpe to fire his rife, so their position wasn't overtly sexual, but compared to the other dimers around it, "The Golden Bounty" looked quite provocative. And the artist had followed her description of Damon Dare so closely she wondered if anyone here in Hannibal would recognize her hero's real-life counterpart.

Justine *did* seem to be watching Frye more closely at dinner that evening, and Celesta suspected her aunt had already secreted her dimer upstairs and was impatient to start reading it. Katherine sat giddily at her end of the table, soaking up Damon's compliments on her pork cutlets and potato salad. The conversation was lively, as though the renovation of Ransom Manor had rejuvenated all their spirits.

"We really must hold a reception or a tea," the younger aunt said as she stood to scrape the dirty dishes. "These walls look too lovely to keep just to ourselves."

Justine coughed. "Let's not be hasty, Katherine. Mr. Frye has cleared away the scaffoldings, but soon he'll be installing pipes and fixtures for the new bathroom. Why not wait until we can show that off, too?"

Damon smiled and was about to speak when the spinster looked at him with brown eyes that almost had a sparkle in them.

"In fact," she continued demurely, "I was wondering if you could possibly build us a water closet on first floor, as well. The way I understand it, the pipes will come upstairs through the study, which means we'll have to enclose them somehow. Seems perfectly logical to make efficient use of that space."

"If Justine gets a second commode, I get running water in the kitchen!" Katherine piped up.

Frye laughed and stood beside his chair, grinning slyly. "Ladies, your requests will be easily carried out, and I'm flattered that you're so confident of my work. In fact, I have an announcement about that very topic."

Celesta's eyes widened, and she could feel the excitement coursing through her two aunts as they leaned forward to listen.

"I've arranged for a crew to begin digging the trench for the pipes by week's end," he began, pausing to tease them a bit, "and I've received word that your porcelain fixtures—the sink, the flush commode, and the claw-footed tub—have finally arrived."

Katherine clasped her hands at her bosom. "I can't *wait* to see them! They'll have the loveliest white shine, and—"

"Every bit as fine as the Cruikshanks' fixtures," Justine added smugly, "because I had Damon order them from the same company."

206

"They must've been terribly expensive," Celesta murmured in surprise.

The eldest Ransom smiled as though she'd been hoarding this secret ever since Frye's work began. "We can't have the Manor falling behind the times any longer. We're a small family now, but we still have our pride."

"Oh, my," Katherine replied breathily, and then, with mist in her eyes, she said "oh, my" again.

It was one of the most touching moments Frye had ever witnessed, and he let the euphoric silence gladden their hearts for a few moments more before he cleared his throat. "I'm truly honored to be a part of this occasion," he said in a reverent voice, "and I hope you'll allow me to contribute tonight's dessert as part of your celebration. If you'll excuse me, I'll fetch it from the cave."

When he'd passed through the kitchen, both aunts babbled at once.

"Bless his heart, what's he—"

"What a thoughtful young man, to—"

"Celesta, has he asked for your hand, dear?"

Celesta's breath caught in her throat, and the silence was as sudden as her aunts' exclamations had been. They were both gazing expectantly at her. "No, Damon hasn't said a word about—"

"Oh, he will, though! I just *feel* it!"

"Katherine, that's hardly for us to say," Justine reminded her crisply. "His intentions seem honorable, but let's not forget he lives in St. Louis. If they marry, one of them will have to uproot."

Aunt Katherine's smile crumpled, and she was about to protest; but the footsteps approaching from the kitchen kept her quiet. Damon strode to the table with a frosted silver cylinder in the crook of his arm, carrying a tall green bottle and a flat, rectangular box. "I thought a taste of champagne was in order," he said in a lilting voice, "and I had fresh ice cream made, and here's a box of chocolates. I'll pull the cork if you'll get us some bowls, Celesta."

"I'll clear away these plates."

"And goblets," Justine said as she rose from her chair. "Mother's stemware was made for just such an occasion."

Moments later a bright *pop* rang around the dining room and four elegant champagne goblets were fizzing in the center of the table. Katherine spooned up generous portions of the strawberry-studded ice cream while Celesta inhaled the heavenly scent of the imported candies.

Damon handed around the bubbling glasses and then raised his own. He'd planned to say something jaunty and light, but the glowing faces around him and the new luster of the room where they'd shared so many dinners made him suddenly sentimental. "I—I propose a toast to three of the finest ladies I've ever known," he said solemnly, "with many thanks for allowing me to share your home these past weeks."

Her heart pounded as Celesta sipped the cool champagne, because Damon was now gazing at her, hinting at the more intimate celebration to come.

"And I wish to toast the future of this family," Justine said in a stately voice. "May we prosper and grow in the coming generations."

"Hear, hear," Katherine replied, her gaze flitting pointedly between Frye and her niece.

It was embarrassing to be the topic of their toasts, yet Celesta's insides fluttered all during dessert. Two months ago, she'd thought any hope for happiness had died with Mama: the prospect of being imprisoned with these elderly aunts had seemed the end of her own life as well. And now Justine acted as though she, too, had renewed her interest in living, and Katherine spent much less of her time pining for Ambrose. All because Damon Frye, the rake who gained admittance with a load of lumber and some timely flattery, had forced them to stop wallowing in their misery.

After the dishes were washed and put away, Damon invited Celesta to join him at the piano for some duets, and since her two aunts had *please!* in their eyes, she couldn't refuse. Katherine settled into her favorite chair with her needlepoint, and Justine chose a seat near the window. The padded bench was full of songbooks and sheet music her mother had once played, and since her partner was the more accomplished musician, Celesta chose to sit at his left and play the bass parts.

His shoulders were so broad she perched on the very edge of the bench and still rubbed against him. His sleeves were rolled to his elbows, revealing two powerful forearms as he flipped through a book of old favorites . . . arms that would soon hold her, hands that would soon caress her to ecstasy. The heat between them increased, and they hadn't yet begun to play.

"How about 'Annie Laurie,'" Frye said softly. "That's a good one to warm up with."

"I'm warm enough, thank you."

Her reply was muted, yet Celesta's voice made him pray for the evening to pass quickly . . . for Justine to retire to her reading and then fall soundly asleep. After he played a few introductory bars, she joined in, timidly at first, but competently. By the second time through she was improvising on the simple bass line, adding flourishes that prompted him to embellish the music as well.

"Camptown Races" was on the following page, and after a rousing first verse, Damon urged her to sing with him. "Oh, de camptown races, sing dis song—"

"Doo dah, doo dah," she joined in. It was sheer happiness to sit beside him this way, heartbeats accelerating with their cheery song as they tried to outdo each other's playing. When they ended the tune by racing to a loud chord, both aunts applauded enthusiastically.

Frye turned the pages until he came upon a piece that would be more of a challenge. "This'll be for you, Katherine," he said. "I'm sure you know it."

Celesta smiled fondly at him, and as they began the graceful "Tales from the Vienna Woods," she let the three-quarter time woo her, just as Damon was with his glances and whispered comments.

"I want you naked," he murmured.

"Keep it in your pants or Katherine might attack you," she replied with a muffled giggle. "Just look at her."

Indeed, Katherine was dreamy-eyed, her needlework lying in her lap as she nodded her head to the music. The other aunt, he noted, was watching them with keen interest, yet he also sensed . . . approval in her gaze. How far they'd all come, considering petty bickering had once been the sister-in-laws' main mode of communication.

When the waltz ended, Katherine expressed heartfelt thanks, and the elder Ransom stood up. "It's been an evening of rare loveliness," she said a little awkwardly, "and I'll retire to sweet dreams, I'm sure. Good night, all."

After another song, the younger aunt also pretended to be sleepy, leaving the two of them alone in the music room. The evening shadows were soothing, and as Celesta snuggled against the arm Damon slipped around her, she felt blissfully complete. "You *are* a magician," she whispered.

He kissed her softly. "And for my next trick, I'll make your clothes disappear."

"It's been a long time."

"I've made myself wait," he replied as he pulled her closer. "I want you desperately, Celesta, and now I bet I could stumble up the stairs to your room and

210

no one would stop me."

Her heart thudded uncontrollably. "I don't think we should risk—Justine's room is only—"

"I'll take care of everything, sweetheart," he promised, hushing her by caressing her delectable lips with his fingertip. "Wait for me in the alcove, wearing the white gown you wore the first time. I can already see the moonlight glowing in its folds as I peel it off you."

"But Justine'll be right underneath—"

"Think again," he said, and then kissed her lightly. "The alcove is directly above Justine's *balcony*. The ballroom wall is where her bedroom actually begins, so the groaning of the sofa—and your screams of wild abandon—won't be a problem. Besides, she's just getting started on 'The Golden Bounty.' She won't notice *anything*."

"But she'll hear us through the grate in the floor, and—"

"Trust me, love," he murmured, and with a final, lingering kiss he scooted the bench back. "I want to see you drenched in moonlit splendor tonight, feel the evening breeze wafting over our bodies. See you in white, in the alcove. I'll be there shortly."

Chapter 17

An hour later, Celesta was still waiting, wondering if this was Frye's idea of a joke. The house was absolutely quiet, so she would've heard the secretive creak on the stairs if he were coming. What was taking him so long? Surely he hadn't removed his clothes first! Maybe Katherine had slipped down to the cellar and quizzed him about his future plans: she'd been upset when Justine suggested he might wish to remain in St. Louis. Maybe his expensive dessert had been a farewell, despite the discussion about installing the two bathrooms. Maybe . . .

Maybe his romantic ramblings about the moonlight were just pretty lies—he'd been known to tell some—and the whole evening had only been a wishful dream where everyone had played along because they *wanted* it to be so. Celesta sighed, gazing at the pastel patterns of light on the board floor, a muted mosaic created by the full moon beaming through the open rose window.

She glanced toward the ballroom. Pale light and a wisp of smoke came up through the floor grate, whetting her curiosity. What a twist, to imagine Justine glued to the suggestive repartee in "The Golden Bounty" while the real Sally and Dare made love in the room above her!

Setting her disappointment aside for now, Celesta knelt and then slowly crawled over for a peek down the grate. Sure enough, her aunt's hair draped her shoulders in silver while she stared spellbound at a sketch of Damon and Sally setting up camp. And, as before, Justine was listening to something through the earpieces of her phonograph, her cigarette in the fork of her fingers. Her rapt expression gave Celesta goose bumps. Here was a loyal reader!

Frye shuffled very, very carefully along the ledge that passed beneath the portico's rose window, praying the wood wouldn't give way under his weight. The glass panel was raised, so he didn't have to knock on it, thank God—but the sight that greeted him made the strenuous climb worth the effort. Celesta was on her knees, framed by the arched entryway to the ballroom, and her shapely, night-gowned behind was pointed directly at him.

He couldn't laugh, or she'd cry out. So he carefully lifted one leg over the casement, balanced, and then dropped to the alcove floor with a soft thump.

Celesta stifled a gasp and turned to find him grinning at her. She remained crouched by the grate, watching him. By God, she refused to throw herself into his arms until he knew how upset she was!

As he removed his shirt, Damon saw the sparks in her eyes and wished he'd taken the more dangerous route up the stairs. "I wanted to surprise you," he said softly, "but I didn't realize how difficult it would be to climb that tree by the balcony and then shinny up to the window, with a bottle stuffed down my pants."

It sounded totally unbelievable, but he *was* setting a champagne bottle on the secretary, and he *had* come through the window! She walked toward him, feigning indignation. "That's your excuse?" she said in a harsh whisper. "And I suppose you didn't remember to bring goblets? If you think I'm going to drink out of the bottle like some common drunkard—"

"Common drunkards can't afford this champagne," he replied as he caught her by the wrist and pulled her against his bare chest. "Nor do they generally wear such translucent nightgowns, or—oh, come here, you!"

His mouth overtook hers, and Celesta forgave his tardiness with a ravenous kiss that left them both panting. "You've been eating chocolates," she accused.

"I brought the rest up for you."

When he reached behind him to pull the candy box from his waistband, Celesta gaped. That was a new bottle of champagne on the desk, and a copy of her story was rolled into his hip pocket, and—

"How on earth did you make that climb with all these things stuffed into—why, you couldn't possibly bend at the waist!"

"I realized that, halfway up the damn tree," he said with a chuckle, "but the real problem was that other thing in my pants. It started misbehaving the moment it realized we were sneaking up to see you, and now there's no controlling it."

Slipping her hand between their bodies, Celesta smiled slyly. "We'll see about that, Mr. Frye."

When her warm palm closed around him, Damon shut his eyes. "Slow down, honey. I thought we'd enjoy a little champagne and literature before we—"

"There's a time and place for all that culture, and it's not now." To drive her point home, Celesta crouched and began to gnaw gently on the ridge in his pants while she unfastened his belt.

Her bold advance made all thoughts of a slow seduction evaporate. She'd played many parts in the weeks since he'd claimed her, and now the hot-blooded wanton who was peeling down his pants was too compelling to be denied. He shoved her gown over her shoulders, sending the little buttons skittering across the floor. Their clothing trailed between the window and the old settee, and then they were at each other, writhing and entwining their limbs like impassioned snakes.

It was swift and primal, made more intense by the confines of the couch and the silence they forced upon themselves. Awed before, Celesta now realized how powerful such lovemaking could be as her body arched and responded without waiting for her mind to instruct it. Release came in a cataclysmic rush, and she stifled her scream against Damon's heaving chest. He was unable to unwrap himself for several minutes.

Neither of them spoke. He gradually became aware of the soft breasts pressing rhythmically against him and of silken ebony strands teasing his cheek, and he inhaled the glorious scent of her sated body. When he opened his eyes, Celesta's sweet, girlish smile made him tingle all over with the realization that he loved her.

She shook the last wisps of fog away and breathed deeply to still the rapid staccato of her heart. He had her pinned beneath his solid weight, yet she'd never felt freer—and she didn't want to stir for fear she'd break the spell he'd cast over them. A blanket of contentment warmed her clear through, and she might have been dozing lightly when Damon shifted to make her more comfortable. When he stroked her hair back, she awoke to find his brown-eyed gaze filled with all the tenderness and wonder she herself was feeling.

Celesta cleared her throat. "Perhaps Damon and Sally will seem anticlimactic if we read them now."

"They'll be good for an encore." He stroked the bridge of her nose with his lips. "The champagne's got possibilities, too, you know. Have you ever felt those cool pricklies exploding on your bare stomach?"

"Can't say that I have," she replied with a chuckle.

"Me neither. But I'd like to."

She stroked his thick, dark hair, knowing he'd shown her only a few of the marvels in his sensual repertoire and that years from now she'd still be pleasuring him just for the joy of it.

"I love you, Damon." From out of nowhere the words came—the most irrevocable of phrases, and the most damning if the sentiment wasn't returned. Celesta studied his reaction, heartened when he didn't so much as blink.

"And I love you, sweetheart." He enfolded her again, hiding his doubts in the silken pillow of her hair. The young woman in his arms had restored his soul these past weeks, but there was still a void where Lucy Bates had lived. It might take months more to regain his confidence in himself as a marrying man.

Celesta, still starry-eyed, needn't know that, how-ever—at least not now, while she was cradled in his embrace. He prayed she'd never suffer the agonizing degradation of a life driven awry by tainted love . . . yet the darkest recesses of his soul seemed to echo with laughter, as though it knew *he* would be the very one to ruin her.

"I could use some of that champagne. How about you?" he whispered.

She nodded, and as he unwove himself to fetch the bottle, Celesta watched his agile body. Had she been a fool to press the issue, knowing he'd been hurt by the betrayal he refused to tell her about?

It was too late to save face, and the words could never be erased. His smile and gentle kiss as he sat down beside her suggested that Damon Frye truly cared for her. And for the moment, that was enough.

They sat on the settee in companionable naked-ness, passing the cool green bottle between them, gazing at each other in the glimmer of the single candle. The champagne went to Celesta's head quickly, adding to her giddiness when Damon held a chocolate between his teeth, offering her half. She nipped playfully at it, leading into a kiss that tasted sweet and smeary and delightful in its spontaneity.

Damon raised his head to look at her. When her pale green eyes caught the candlelight they shone silver, slightly unfocused. Her lips were smudged, her midnight hair hung in disarming disarray, and she was grinning like a child who'd sneaked candy to bed and was enormously pleased with herself.

He solemnly kissed the chocolate from her mouth, running his tongue around its delicate edges and into its corners. Celesta felt soft and pliable in his arms, so willing to be molded by his whim and far too trusting. When the last traces of candy were gone from her ivory skin, he gently held her heart-shaped face between his hands. "What am I going to do with you, little girl?" he murmured, only half teasing.

Celesta giggled. "I have a pretty good idea."

The huskiness of her voice reawakened his yearning for her. He'd taken her the first time out of need, but now it was desire, hot and sweet, licking at his loins. On an impulse he tipped the bottle near her shoulder and sent champagne racing down her breast in a shimmering little cascade.

Celesta shrieked and then clapped her hand over her mouth. Her lover seemed oblivious to the noise the settee made, with its groaning springs and its claw feet grunting against the floor as he shifted to kiss the liquor from her body. "Please—I—stop!" she whispered frantically. "Justine'll hear—"

"She's listening to an Edison record. When I paused on her balcony to catch my breath, she was so far removed she didn't notice me looking in at her." Damon resumed his seduction, her thundering pulse warning him that stronger measures were necessary if she was to succumb this time.

Her breath caught in her throat when he suckled her. Every nerve in her body throbbed with raw hunger, yet as she slid helplessly onto the cushions beneath his insistent caress, one tiny flare kept popping up red, in the back of her mind. "Damon, we've got to—"

"Relax, sweetheart," he whispered, stroking her satiny skin. "Even if she could hear us she wouldn't rush up here. She'll never threaten us again, Celesta."

Was he hinting that he'd done more than merely peek in at Justine? Or was it the champagne making his words sound so ominous? Flat on her back now, she could do little about it, and the part of her brain that longed to be considered an irresistible *femme fatale* was quickly giving in to him. Damon was kneeling beside the sofa now, massaging her breasts with one hand and a very moist, thorough mouth.

When he slid the bottle between her legs, she gasped at the cold surprise of it. Once again he was taking her on a sorcerer's sojourn into a world of exquisite torment, and as her legs parted she writhed greedily, shamelessly, toward the butt of the bottle and the magic it was working.

Champagne sloshed onto her stomach, stealing her breath again. Damon kissed up the prickling liquid, tickling her ruthlessly, chuckling all the while. His thumb was drawing tight circles around one nipple while his other hand slid the bottle against her with mesmerizing slowness. Yet even as his tongue delved into her navel, the internal explosions he caused didn't mask a faint flutter of distress. *Something's wrong . . . stop this madness—sober up before it's too late!*

He could feel her resistance waning, and her arousal spurred him on. Celesta was pure delight, vitally alive as she wriggled and moaned. Her arm

219

fell limply across her closed eyes, and her mouth went slack to allow incoherent mumblings to tumble out. Damon desperately wanted to plunge into her, but she was so close it would be cruel to interrupt the spiraling frenzy within her. When her eyes flew open he instinctively quelled her outburst with a kiss and continued stroking her until she quaked and then stopped the bottle with her hands.

Damon slid onto the settee, but she shoved at his chest. "Up! Let me—smoke!"

He caught himself before he thudded unceremoniously to the floor, startled that Celesta was clambering over the top of him as though frightened for her life. She wasn't *that* drunk! Her clumsiness would've been comical, had he not noticed her stricken expression while she hurried over to the floor grate.

What Celesta saw when she peered down into Aunt Justine's room knocked the words right out of her. She rushed back to their clothing, grimacing at Frye and wishing he'd read her mind like he did every time she didn't want him to. "Fire!" she gasped. "On—fire!"

Frowning, Frye rolled quickly to his feet and suddenly realized he did smell something other than Celesta's smoldering passions. God Almighty, Justine was rocking and reading and listening—totally unaware that the stack of dime novels behind her had flames climbing up its rough edges.

He rushed for his pants, hoping his footfalls would alert the old woman. "Once we get her out of there, smother the flames with blankets and bedspreads—douse them with water—"

"All we'll have is what's in the washbowls," Celesta whimpered. She tugged her nightgown over her head as she ran through the ballroom, with Damon close behind her. Why hadn't she heeded that inner alarm? If her aunt was hurt, it was all her fault for following her body's wanton inclinations rather than her intuition. And if Justine escaped unharmed, she would surely know what had gone on in the alcove!

The bedroom door was locked, and as Damon pounded on it, Celesta burst into Katherine's room, yanking the coverlet from her bed. "Fire! Fire—wake up!" she screamed, until the little woman rolled from her mattress and toddled uncertainly into the hall.

"Justine! For God's sake get out of there!" Frye hollered. He envisioned the stacks of dimers that lined her floorboards, perfect food for flames that the breeze from her window would fan. He heard a weak mewling inside, and realized the poor creature might be too startled to let him in. He stepped back and rammed the door with his body, but all it got him was a pain that shot through both shoulders.

Then Katherine was behind him, whimpering, her eyes wide as she jabbed him with a skeleton key. "She fell asleep smoking, didn't she? It was only a matter of time!"

Frye threw the door open and nearly trampled Justine. She was hunched over an armload of something, coughing and sputtering in the dense smoke. "Please save my phonograph!" she wailed. "Oh, dear God, what've I done? I don't understand how—"

"With your damn cigarettes, *that's* how!" Katherine cried. "And if it weren't for Damon—"

Celesta rushed past the quibbling pair and lunged toward the nearest column of flames while Damon slammed the window shut. Following Frye's example, she first smothered the stacks of magazines with the coverlet and then beat against them until the heat scorched her palms through the fabric.

Damon yanked the burning curtains down and then splashed them with the washstand water. "This must've been smoldering for quite some time before we saw it," he muttered. "How the hell could she not know?"

"She was reading about Damon and Sally, remember?" she replied in a voice pinched with guilt. "We knew this room was a fire trap, but we couldn't challenge her about habits she denied having. Over here!"

Another stack of magazines flared from its back side, and as Damon dashed over to grab Justine's blankets, Celesta shoved the rocking chair toward the door, out of his way. Katherine came in for it, choking but determined.

"We'd best save that phonograph and her cupboard of recordings, if we can," the little woman rasped. "Justine's too shook up to help, but we'll never hear the end of it if she loses her French lessons as well as her novels."

Damon was smothering the last of the flames, so Celesta got behind the wooden cabinet containing the precious Edison wax cylinders and pushed it toward the door. When her aunt came back, the two of them trundled the case into the hallway and then stopped to breathe the clearer air.

Frye joined them a few moments later, winded but relieved. He smelled of singed hair and felt blistered spots on his arms that would bother him for a few days. "Well, it could've been worse, I suppose. She could've been asleep—"

Or we *could've been asleep*, Celesta mused, yet somehow the circumstances of spotting the fire bothered her more than the what-ifs. She and Damon could've roused the dead, thundering across the ballroom floor the way they did, and to be standing here in their disheveled state, so close their arms touched, was the ultimate incrimination. Especially when she realized her gown had no buttons left on it. She caught Katherine's eyes making that same discovery, so Celesta walked over to check on her

222

other aunt, clutching the placket with one hand.

Justine was seated on the top stair, leaning against the wall. She jerked when Celesta touched her shoulder.

"Are you all right? Were you scorched, or—"

"I'm fine!" she snapped, and then she pressed herself even closer to the wall.

Smiling to herself, Celesta sensed that her spinster aunt was even more embarrassed about the fire than *she* was about getting caught with her clothes off. She'd had the presence of mind to save an armful of wax cylinders and the dimer she'd been reading. And that cantankerous tone told her the lady huddling beneath the curtain of silvery, waist-length hair might deserve—or even welcome—a bit of needling.

She glanced back at Katherine and Frye, who were talking quietly. "Justine, do you have any idea how the fire started?" she asked cautiously. "Did your lamp tip over, or—"

"Certainly not." The spinster gazed up into Celesta's eyes, and then she looked behind them, at Frye and her sister-in-law. "The fire was *set,* deliberately. Someone in this house tried to kill me."

Chapter 18

The beady brown eyes leveled their accusation as clearly as the old woman's words, and Damon's heart stopped. Justine was dead serious . . . and she was stark, raving crazy.

"Oh, my. Oh, *my*," Katherine fretted beside him. "Is she losing her mind, or is she reverting to her belligerent ways?"

"I don't know. Perhaps after some rest—"

"You can't think *I* set the fire!"

"Of course you didn't, and neither did I," he assured her in a whisper. He slipped an arm around her shaking shoulders, still watching Justine as closely as she was watching him. "We're all upset. Let's get her settled into one of the other bedrooms and pursue this tomorrow. Maybe she'll realize by then that we all knew she smoked and none of us found it as shocking as she thought we would."

Settling Justine was another matter, however. She agreed to return to the tower bedroom—she'd slept there all her life, until Ambrose drowned and Katherine couldn't bear to occupy the master suite alone—but losing so many of her beloved dimers, and discovering that several of her French lesson cylinders were ruined by the fire's heat, agitated her greatly. She refused warm milk or a toddy, and long after the rest of them went to bed, Justine wandered the halls, muttering.

Sensing her aunt had lost more than Edison records and Westerns, Celesta lay awake. The grandfather clock in the vestibule chimed three before the floor stopped creaking and Justine took to her rocking chair. She was on the other side of the wall from Celesta's bed, and the insistent rolling of the rockers on the wooden floor sounded more like a child riding a rocking horse than an elderly lady soothing herself. It was frightening, but her concerns about the head of the Ransom family weren't all that kept Celesta awake.

Had Damon set the fire? Justine's glare had certainly accused him of it—and he'd mentioned stopping on her balcony, and how absorbed she was in her entertainment. If she hadn't heard them running down the stairs, she certainly wouldn't have noticed Frye striking a match behind her. Justine's instincts about people couldn't be discounted, either: the eldest Ransom had sharpened her tongue on many a reputation, but she never spoke without analyzing the situation first. It explained Frye's mysterious statement about the spinster never threatening them again, as well as his tardiness before their tryst.

Nipping her lip in the darkness, Celesta searched for other possibilities. Now that Damon had finally charmed her old maid aunt with his wit and workmanship, it seemed unlikely he'd try to kill her. After all, she'd asked him to install another water closet just this evening! The more projects she offered him, the longer he could lodge at the Manor and enjoy their food and company . . . which he certainly took advantage of tonight.

No, it seemed Katherine's explanation was the best: Justine's cigarette—which probably dropped during a hot spot in the Damon Dare story—had ignited a stack of dimers, and the old maid was too embarrassed to admit she smoked or read such stories, much less that she could start a fire without knowing it. She had to blame somebody, though, so Frye, as the outsider, seemed the likeliest scapegoat. Perhaps she'd even seen him outside her balcony door and just hadn't acknowledged his presence.

This line of thought cleared Damon, but it also made Celesta toss restlessly. She was far too enamored—had heard nothing but warnings, from Frye himself, that his heart had a hole in it—yet she threw herself at him every chance she got. His lovemaking had lulled her into a false reality, an altered state similar to the one his champagne had created. As Sally Sharpe would put it, she'd lost her objectivity. The facts had a dreamy, rose-colored quality because she fancied herself in love with him.

Guilt burrowed into her heart like a worm into an apple when Celesta realized how many weeks had passed since she acted upon Mama's murder. Except for trying to trap Patrick by provoking him every time they met, she hadn't done a damn thing to catch the killer. The Girl Detective had taught her how to probe the dark underbelly of clandestine situations, but she'd been too caught up by Damon Frye to heed her heroine's help. Only the most uncaring, slothful daughter would be waylaid by a handsome architect—and one with such a shady past as Damon's, no less!

Starting tomorrow, things would be different. No more falling blithely under Frye's spell every time he smiled at her! No more waiting for Mama's poisoning to solve itself while a killer—a person she knew well—walked among them!

She would resume her quest for answers just as Sally would: by taking charge of the investigation and demanding answers—by cutting so close to the bone with her questions that people got nervous.

And by stepping outside her grief for Mama and her infatuation for Frye to face the case objectively. She hadn't taken a positive step since she sneaked into the Perkins's pantry for a sugar sample, and this lackluster attitude was going to change!

Filled with resolve, Celesta snuggled into her pillow and smiled. Before her twenty-first birthday, she vowed to catch Mama's killer. No matter whom she inconvenienced . . . no matter whom she accused.

Justine pulled the rug from under Celesta's plan the next morning. She appeared for breakfast looking tired but as starched as ever, and no one was surprised that she ignored Damon completely. But when ten o'clock came and she hadn't returned from her shopping, Katherine began to unravel.

The two of them were digging the caladium bulbs from the bed around the gazebo, although her aunt accomplished little because she was watching the road that came up from town. "I had a feeling this would happen," she fretted, knotting her dirt-caked hands. "After a lifetime of controlling her emotions, Justine can weather any storm with barely a hair out of place. But this is different. She can't admit, even to herself, that her smoking might've cost us our home . . . or her life. Your aunt's losing her grip, Celesta."

It seemed ironic that after doubting Katherine's stability so many times, she was now witnessing the decline of her stronger aunt's faculties. "Shall I take the buggy in and look for her?"

"She'll be mortified if anyone sees her *riding* home," the little woman mused, "but it's our best alternative. Lord only knows where she might've roamed."

Celesta nodded and stood the spade upright in the garden. "She goes to the same shops every morning.

Surely the storekeepers will notice if she's varied from her routine; or if she appears disoriented, they'll help her."

"Would *you* ask her if she's lost?"

"I see your point," she replied with a sigh. She squeezed her aunt's shoulder, noting the way the morning sun made Katherine's crowsfeet look deeper today. "Don't worry yourself sick over it. The three of us can keep track of her."

"Poor Damon. I wouldn't blame him if he moved out."

Celesta nodded and walked toward the stable, cleaning her dirt-encrusted fingernails on her apron. She'd hoped to escape to town this afternoon to speak with Mr. Settles, the undertaker, concerning the details of Mama's burial, but Justine's safety and Katherine's sanity were more pressing issues at the moment.

She was pulling the harness from its peg when Katherine called excitedly to her. Hurrying toward the gazebo, she heard the clopping of hooves on the driveway and then saw that Bill Thompkins was bringing Justine home in a buggy. "Hello!" her aunt sang out with a little wave. "Wasn't it sweet of Mr. Thompkins to bring me home, hot as it is? I've invited him for lemonade, but he says he can't stay."

As their burly friend helped the spinster down, Celesta exchanged a wary glance with Katherine. This was definitely not the pillar of stoic self-reliance they knew, and Justine's sunny greeting made them even more sure she'd lost her grip on things. After thanking Thompkins, she hurried inside with her wicker basket as though nothing were amiss.

"Thank you," Katherine began in an urgent voice. "Celesta was just going into town to look for her. We were afraid—"

"Pardon me if I'm out of line," the postman interrupted, glancing toward the house, "but your sister-in-law seems a bit . . . odd this morning. Kept rattling on about a fire, when usually she just barks a hello before she leaves with her mail."

"She dropped a cigarette last night, and if Damon and Celesta hadn't noticed the smoke, those dime novels she reads would've burned us out," the little woman confided. She gingerly patted her upsweep with her soil-smeared hands, smiling at Thompkins despite her distress. "You can't know how much we appreciate your looking after her, Bill. I—I'm afraid we're going to have to watch her very carefully until she recovers from the shock of this incident."

Thompkins smoothed his beard, his expression thoughtful. "That explains the cigar stub she slipped into her pocket when she came in, then. I thought I was seeing things."

"Oh, my . . . are you sure I can't get you a glass of lemonade for your trouble, Bill?"

"No, no, I'd best be getting—"

"Or a cookie?" Celesta asked quickly. "Katherine made oatmeal-raisin ones just this morning."

His eyes lit up, and her aunt didn't wait for his reply to head for the pantry. Bill's girth was a testimony to his sweet tooth, a fondness all the unattached ladies in town played upon. "If this keeps up, Justine could become a problem, independent as she is," he stated quietly. "I hope you'll tell me if I can be of help. Katherine's bearing up well, but this must be a terrible worry to her."

"She's better already, now that you're here," Celesta said with an encouraging smile. "Katherine loves company, and she thinks the world of you, Bill. Feel free to come see us any time, even if Justine has nothing to do with it."

Thompkins blinked behind his spectacles, resembling a startled owl. "I—I imagine she still misses Ambrose—"

"It's been more than a year. That's a long time for a

woman who adores dances and parties to keep herself locked away," she replied quietly. "Damon's presence has cheered her immensely, but a man her own age would probably bring her into bloom again."

"Yes, well—here she comes," he breathed, seeming enormously relieved. Celesta smiled at him again and excused herself to check on Justine.

Had she embarrassed Thompkins by being so blunt? Bill didn't seem awkward around women ordinarily, but her suggestions had made him stammer like a schoolboy. Perhaps he'd been waiting for just such an opportunity, and was flustered at the idea that Katherine might welcome his company. Celesta hoped she hadn't ruined her younger aunt's chances for a little romance.

Companionship was the farthest thing from Justine's mind, however. Hearing the creak on the landing, she came to meet Celesta at the top of the stairs, glowering. "I don't need a nursemaid, if that's why you're up here," she snapped.

"No, no!" Celesta fibbed. "I was just—"

"I imagine Katherine was knitting herself into knots because I was later than usual," she continued brusquely, "but I felt compelled to apologize to Damon for my conduct last night, and we discussed the refurbishing of the master suite. Since I'm the mistress of this house, such tasks naturally fall to me."

Was Justine truly as collected as she appeared? As the three of them removed the smoke-soiled bedding from her room and rolled up the ruined carpet, Celesta sensed her oldest aunt's dourness had returned with a vengeance—as though she were peeved at herself for causing such a crisis but would never admit it to anyone.

But when Damon returned from his work at the mansion, the story took on a different light. He scowled slightly when Justine mentioned their morning conference, and then followed Celesta into the kitchen under the guise of helping her clear the table. "What's she talking about?" he whispered. "I heard from a couple shopkeepers she was behaving strangely, but she never came to see *me*."

Celesta's heart sank. "So the poor woman's missing a few marbles after all," she sighed. "The way she talks, you chose new paper for the master suite—after she apologized for her behavior last night. She thinks all's been forgiven and that her room will soon be restored."

Frye let out a long breath. "Well, I do have a few of my men coming tomorrow to repair the walls. I'll pretend to reconfirm the paper pattern she wanted, and get it bought first thing in the morning, so we don't upset her," he said quietly. "Celesta, I think you should follow her into town for a while. Just to be safe."

"I was thinking the same thing. Damon, I—I'm worried," she said in a tight voice. "There was a time I couldn't tolerate that woman's blessed *routine*, but now that she doesn't know she's gotten out of it, I . . . I hate to think what might happen."

He quickly wrapped his arms around her. "We'll keep an eye on her, hopefully without her realizing it. I brought something home that might help."

The four of them talked about the room renovation as they ate Katherine's cookies with vanilla pudding, and Justine seemed as cordial as she was before she accused Damon of setting the fire. She herself brought up the subject of the wallpaper, so everyone played along carefully.

"I think that lavender stripe-and-floral pattern we saw at Pickford's will be a nice change, don't you?" she asked sweetly. "The colors Mother and Father chose are so faded. Pity I didn't notice that until the

232

fire forced me to, and with those lace curtains and matching counterpane I ordered from Birmingham's, I'll just need a rug to have a whole new room!"

Lavender and lace, for *Justine?* Katherine, Celesta, and Damon looked at each other cautiously, and then he rose to fetch a box he'd set beside the buffet. "And while you wait for your new room, I thought you'd enjoy these to play on your phonograph. Some of them are songs, and some are the same French lessons that were destroyed in the fire."

Such a beatific expression had never graced Justine Ransom's face as she fingered each of the cylindrical cardboard boxes and read their labels. "Why, Mr. Frye, this is the most thoughtful gift, I . . . I'm just speechless."

Touched by her gratitude, by the fragile vulnerability that edged her brown eyes, Damon squeezed her hand. "Friends look after each other, Justine. And I'm pleased we're friends."

Katherine was misty-eyed, and Celesta herself felt brimming over with happiness at his gift: he'd bought the Edison records before he realized Justine had supposedly made up with him, knowing how much she loved to listen. And when he pulled a flat sack from the top drawer of the buffet, with a twinkle in his eyes for her, she held her breath.

"I saw something I thought you'd like, too," he said, offering her the sack.

Unable to suppress a grin, Celesta pulled a piece of sheet music out. "Aren't *you* the sly one, hiding presents like it was Christmas," she said with a low chuckle. The front sheet featured a sketch of a Negro she'd seen before, and she read the title aloud. " 'The Maple Leaf Rag,' by Scott Joplin. Isn't he from Missouri?"

"Sedalia," Damon confirmed. He'd hoped the gift would please her, and her smile relieved the worry that had lurked on her face all evening. "I heard him perform once, and this piece is so new you'll be among the first to play it. I predict Mr. Joplin's ragtime will be all the rage before—is something wrong, sweetheart?"

Celesta's eyes bugged as she glanced at the flurry of notes on the inside pages. "I hope—this looks so *hard*, I—"

"I was thinking we might play it together," he said softly.

"Oh, do!" Katherine piped up. "The dishes can certainly sit for a new song."

"Yes, that would be lovely," Justine agreed with unusual enthusiasm. "Probably a lot more fun than those waltzes you play for Katherine."

The sparkle in Katherine's eyes, the smug challenge that sounded like Justine used to—Damon had her cornered and he knew it! But what a cozy trap, to be the source of her aunts' excitement while she saw herself mirrored in Frye's adoring eyes. As always, Celesta took the left-hand part, and when her partner nodded the beat, she vowed to show him just how competently she could sight-read this new piece.

The bass line was relatively easy, a steady four beats to the measure, and after the first page she was too enthralled by Damon's playing to worry about her own. The melody was a sassy thing that danced all over the keyboard beneath his agile fingers, singing a playful, syncopated song that had her laughing by the time they reached the second section. She suddenly realized that her foot was tapping and her head was nodding, and once again the rhythmic rubbing of their shoulders and the subtle power that surged between them was working its magic.

The piece ended with an emphatic chord, and Damon grinned at her. "What do you think?"

"It's wonderful," she said with a giggle. "So many little melodies and—"

"Oh, just play it again! Don't talk it to death."

Celesta blinked at Justine, who was approaching the baby grand to watch them. "A command performance, Mr. Frye. Shall we?"

"Of course. But this time we'll play it up to tempo rather than being so . . . sedate."

Her eyes widened, and then Celesta looked at him accusingly. "You've played this before."

"Well, maybe a couple run-throughs, just to—"

"So do it yourself! You're a much finer pianist than—"

"Nope," he said, grabbing Celesta before she could escape from the bench. "I asked the lady's fingers to dance, and mine don't want to perform without them. Set the speed. Challenge me."

It was the most sultry dare she'd ever heard—right here beneath her aunt's pointed nose!—and the electricity that passed between them made her flex with anticipation. "All right, Mr. Frye. I hope you're ready."

"Try me." Lord, she was a minx, sitting against him with those sly eyes and the pink spots in her cheeks! He suddenly wanted her, audience or not, and he laughed low in his throat when Celesta took off at a trot. She was now embellishing the bass line, putting in the accents and playing it as though it were its own melody—edging the tempo toward a heart-pounding pace that told him she was as exhilarated by their music as he, and that she craved a much more physical duet later on.

How did he do it? She was pushing the speed relentlessly, yet still his quick, powerful hands executed the runs and accented chords with breathtaking precision—and he was grinning at her all the while! Even when their fingers fought for the same keys, Frye never missed a beat, and when the song climaxed in two loud, emphatic chords Celesta squealed with delight.

Katherine was applauding wildly beside Justine, who was saying, "Bravo, bravo! By God, that was the best—"

Damon's kiss blocked out all but his raw determination to possess her, and Celesta's mouth met his with equal fervor, sealing their fate as though God himself were binding them for eternity. When he eased away, she clutched at him to regain her bearings, betraying her desire with a telltale gasp.

When Frye saw the two sets of wide eyes watching them, he chuckled sheepishly. "Excuse me, ladies. I couldn't help myself."

Justine's brow arched, yet her lips hid a grin. "Seems to me that's the only reason to kiss her. I believe we have dishes to wash, Katherine."

"Yes, I believe we do," her sister-in-law replied wistfully.

And as her aunts left for the kitchen, Celesta could only stare at the man who still held her. "How do you do it?" she breathed. "How do you hypnotize us all into accepting such rakish behavior?"

Laughing aloud, Damon pulled her close for a lingering kiss that honed his need for her into a sharp, desperate edge. "Come downstairs tonight after they're asleep," he murmured against her sweet-smelling hair. "It'll be a night we'll neither one forget."

Reality returned with morning, and as Celesta carefully stayed several paces behind Justine, she felt torn in two. Again and again Damon had made her passions soar last night—and her heart with them—and now she felt more confused than ever about the staid old maid whose approval had been so evident at the piano. Before breakfast Justine was talking to her father's portrait in the library, muttering about the moral decay of today's young people. Now she was

236

going from shop to shop, to places she hadn't frequented before, not buying anything. Just wandering in and out, her empty basket on her arm.

And yet, when Celesta ducked into Pickford's and Birmingham's she learned that her aunt had indeed ordered the lavender wallpaper and the lace curtains and counterpane for her room. How on earth could anyone know when Justine was in control of her faculties and when she was drifting along in delusion?

It was causing talk among the shopkeepers, who'd endured her dickering for too many years to let this situation go undiscussed. And when Celesta saw Eula Perkins approaching her with a purposeful stride, her stylish magenta bonnet bobbing above her patronizing smile, she knew she was in for an earful.

"How is she today?" the stout little woman whispered, looking back to where Justine was entering Settles and Sievers—the undertaker's! "I heard about the fire, and I'm *so* sorry! It must be ghastly to see the devastation and know it was her *cigarette* that caused it."

Recalling the snuff tins Mrs. Perkins hid in her vanity and sideboard, Celesta smiled wryly. "Our habits get the best of us at times. I only wish we could wipe away the shock it gave her as easily as we can repair her room. I'm sure you've heard about her mental state."

Eula's smile dripped honey. "You know, I was wondering if perhaps she was slipping before the fire. Justine's barely acquainted with Patrick, which made her outburst during our last visit seemly highly uncalled for and . . . suspect. You know?"

"We've all wondered about her from time to time," she agreed, yet it was hard not to laugh when she recalled Patrick's humiliated flush. "How is he? I haven't seen him lately."

"Constantly busy! Working hard to make his

father's mill the biggest and best," she replied with a flutter of her hand. "Such a perfectionist he won't tolerate poor work from others—which is why he dismissed our latest housekeeper. Good help, like you and your mother, is impossible to come by these days."

It was an invitation Celesta was pleased to decline. "Oh, I can't even consider coming back now," she said. "These latest events have given Katherine a real turn—"

"Poor dear, how is she?" Eula bleated. "I've been meaning to come see her, but frankly . . . well, her sister-in-law doesn't exactly welcome us with open arms."

"Justine can be pretty blunt," she agreed, still amazed that her aunt watched last night's kiss as though she were witnessing wedding vows. Then she chuckled, whetted by a challenge. "I never knew *you* to be cowed by anyone, though. And I think it was your son's behavior she objected to, not yours."

Mrs. Perkins studied her for a moment, shifting out of the doorway to allow a customer into the millinery shop. "If Patrick's not welcome, I prefer not to—"

"You don't take him to Ladies' Aid, or board meetings at the Home," she said with a shrug, "so think of this as a mission of mercy for Katherine. Justine's not one to chat over tea, and with Patrick gone you and my aunt could have a lovely afternoon. She's starving for gossip, afraid to go to her meetings because there might be another accident in her absence."

"Why don't you like my son, Celesta?"

Eula's expression resembled a she-bear's, fiercely protective of her errant cub, and too late Celesta realized she'd overdone it. "Like him? We've been friends all our lives," she insisted. Then she sighed, hoping she sounded reluctantly honest rather than flippant. "But you and I both know Patrick could find a more . . . suitable wife. He wasn't the least bit interested in me until Damon came back to town."

"And how *is* Mr. Frye these days?" she asked dryly.

"Fine. Once he repairs Justine's room, he'll start on the two bathrooms. Hard to believe what a difference paper and plumbing will make at the Manor."

Mrs. Perkins let their conversation sink in, relaxing somewhat as she moved away from the milliner's door. "I suppose you should be watching for Justine. God knows what could happen if she has matches in her pocket."

"You're absolutely right. It's been good to—"

"And tell Katherine I'd like to visit next Tuesday afternoon, unless I hear it's not convenient," Mrs. Perkins continued in a slightly condescending tone. "And you're perfectly welcome to join us, dear. It's not like you're an outcast or a poor relation."

"Well, I—"

"Good day, Celesta. We'll chat soon."

She watched the magenta-clad socialite sway down the sidewalk, fearing she'd done more harm than good. Katherine would welcome the chance to chat over tea, yet now that her feathers had been ruffled about Patrick, Eula was undoubtedly arming herself with pointed comments and questions for her Tuesday visit—a visit Celesta was obviously expected to attend.

"Maybe by then I'll be as batty as Justine," she muttered, and then went to find her wandering aunt.

Chapter 19

By the time they were expecting Eula, Celesta was all nerves. Why had Damon chosen *today* to finish Justine's wallpapering? The spinster was so excited that after her morning shopping she walked upstairs and then down, checking his progress and then flitting from room to room plumping settee pillows and straightening mirrors, until no one could stand to be around her.

"What will Eula think?" Katherine whispered as they prepared cakes and tea in the kitchen. "I'm afraid to tell Justine to stay upstairs for fear she'll disrupt Damon's work—or get belligerent and intrude upon *us*."

Edgy as she was, Celesta was almost hoping for the distraction of an insane aunt, because the more she thought about baiting Eula in town last week, the more she feared her former employer would retaliate out of maternal protectiveness. At least Patrick wouldn't be coming—

But a glance out the window sent her heart plummeting. Mr. Perkins, resplendent in a blue plaid suit, was helping his mother from the carriage while glancing toward the house with a decidedly get-even grin. Celesta felt ill. There was no graceful way out of this situation because she'd brought it on herself.

241

Eula entered first, her gaze roving around the vestibule. "I just can't get over the *change* in this house! *So* good to see you, Katherine, dear."

As the women hugged, Celesta closed the door behind Patrick—who stood so she had no choice but to brush against him. "Don't start with me," she muttered. "I assumed you'd be so *busy* at the mill—"

"Never too busy to call a truce in a skirmish that shouldn't have happened," he replied suavely. He was carrying a small box under his arm, regarding her with blue eyes she couldn't read and looking as playfully handsome as he always did when he was up to something. "If there's not enough tea, you and I can go—"

"I'll brew some more," Celesta replied, and then she quickly retreated to the kitchen. How dare he show his face! Or had Eula put him up to it? There was no anticipating what she might say this afternoon, because she would delight in discussing the rumors about Justine's insanity, just to upset Katherine while pretending to sympathize with her.

And there was no sanctuary in the kitchen, either, because Damon was sitting at the table, his hand in the cookie jar. "Had I known you were entertaining Mr. Perkins, I'd have dressed for the occasion," he teased.

Celesta glared at his bare shoulders and overalls. "Don't *you* start! The last thing I need is—"

"Relax, sweetheart. I've suggested to Justine that we have our own little tea party, to keep her from ruining yours. She'll be here in a moment."

"Well, I—" She set the water on to boil and smiled gratefully at him. "That was thoughtful. Thank you."

Frye nodded, amused. "No sense in getting all rattled about Patrick, putting him at an advantage. Think of him as an adoring puppy, Celesta. The

242

worst he can do is wet on your shoe, as long as I'm around. Right?"

She chuckled, suddenly seeing this visit for the farce it was. And as Justine entered from the back stairway to sit down beside Frye, Celesta carried the laden silver tray to the music room, feeling supremely confident. Damon was right: what could Patrick Perkins possibly do to her while she was surrounded by all the people she loved?

The conversation remained polite during their first cup of tea. Celesta sat a comfortable distance from Patrick on the settee, listening to his mother bemoan the inefficient housekeeper they'd just dismissed and then extol her son's long hours at the lumber mill.

If he's so industrious, why's he here *at two in the afternoon?* Celesta mused, but she nodded at the appropriate spots in Eula's patter. The man beside her was indulging in lemon tarts and iced cakes as though that's what he came for, so it seemed the afternoon might pass without incident after all.

But during a lull in the conversation, Patrick leaned down to pick up the box he'd brought. He cleared his throat, glancing at his mother and then at Katherine. "You know, I—I feel badly about the fire, and now that Justine's not herself, I regret the trouble I caused last time we were here," he began quietly. "I understand she lost some of her Edison records in the accident."

"Why, yes, she did," Katherine responded hesitantly.

"Do you suppose I could apologize to her? Give her these new ones?" he asked. He appealed to Celesta with eyes the color of the summer sky, his tone as contrite as she'd ever heard it. "You and I can settle our differences easily enough, but your aunt— well, I want her to have these while she still understands why I'm giving them to her. May I see

243

her for a moment?"

"What a thoughtful—"

"I'm not sure it's a good time," Celesta interrupted with a warning glance at Katherine. "She's been agitated today, and now that Damon's got her settled in the kitchen. . . ."

It was the wrong thing to say, and her heart pounded during the lengthy pause that hung over the music room.

"If she can tolerate Frye's company, surely she could have a word with me."

She closed her eyes and heard Katherine walking to the kitchen, dreading the coming moments, though she wasn't sure why. Justine would be delighted with new records; she listened to the ones Damon gave her for hours on end. And there was no polite way to deny Patrick an apology, when he sounded so ashamed . . . and Lord, the vicious stories Eula would spread if her son's heartfelt request was refused!

When Celesta looked up, her aunts were framed in the doorway, two aging ladies holding hands, one's withered face more anxious than the other's. The sight squeezed at her heart, and she prayed this wasn't a powder keg waiting for a match.

Patrick rose from the settee, smoothing his suit, watching Justine as though she might run beserk around the room. He walked over to within a few feet of her and then held out the box, smiling gallantly. "I heard you lost some Edison records in the fire, Miss Ransom. I enjoy listening to the phonograph myself, so I thought you'd like some new ones."

Her eyes met his briefly, without registering recognition. "Thank you."

He watched her open the box and run a finger over the round tops of the cylinders. "I—won't you join us for tea?" he asked awkwardly. "Every time we come, I feel we're leaving you out—"

"No, thank you."

As dry as the autumn leaves her response was, and her second glance at him was no more encouraging than the first. Katherine patted her arm, gesturing toward a chair. "Perhaps you'd feel better if you talked awhile, dear," she suggested quietly. "This is Patrick and Eula Perkins, here to see how you're doing."

"I know very well who they are, and they only came so they can spread stories about me," Justine replied tartly. She removed her arm from Katherine's grasp, eyeing their guests. "Thank you for these records. Now go on with your gossip and I'll return to the conversation Damon and I were—"

"But I'm not finished! I'm trying to apologize," Patrick said impatiently. "I'm sorry I was—"

"You're a sorry one, all right," the spinster interrupted, her color rising with her voice. "And quite the actor, pretending it's Celesta's affections you want. But your motives are clear as glass to *me*, young man!"

Perkins tugged at his shirt collar as though it were the old woman's neck he wanted to grab. "I beg your pardon, Miss Ransom. Since you've barely given me the time of day over the years, you can hardly understand my—"

"Well, then, it's time we talked, isn't it?" she asked, her face hardening. "Now that my niece is no longer your maid's daughter—now that I'm old and will soon leave my family fortune behind—you come sniffing around here—"

"Aunt Justine! I think we should—"

"You'll not talk to my son as though—"

Everyone gasped when Justine let the box of records clatter to the floor so that she could point at Eula and Celesta, who froze in their tracks. The room got deathly quiet.

"I'll say what I please in my own home, Mrs. Perkins, and you'll sit and listen to me. Then you can go spread whatever stories your vapid little mind can spin, and I'll have had my say. Sit down. All of you."

Celesta's heart was pounding rapidly as she took her seat with the others. What her aunt was implying was probably closer to the truth than any of the polite chitchat she'd heard today, but where would it end? She sensed Justine had been saving up for just such a moment, using the rumors of her insanity as a soapbox to speak from. Damon had come through the dining room and was standing in the vestibule, watching from behind her aunt, his finger on his lips as he shook his head at Celesta.

"You probably assume that in my unmarried state I'm ignorant of men and their manipulatings," Justine resumed, gazing steadily at Patrick. "But what no one here realizes is that I once had a beau—as dashing as you are, Mr. Perkins—and after he declared his eternal love and took his liberties with me, he married my little sister. Now that you know to whom I'm referring, you also know he ran out on *her*, when Celesta was born. Sounds similar to what a certain man in this room did about ten years ago, doesn't it?"

Patrick's face was aflame, but he was too incensed to respond. Celesta held her breath, wondering what this could possibly lead to. Could Justine see Damon? Would she attack him next? It was clear that her maiden aunt was just warming up: after confessing the most shocking secret from her own past, who else would she expose?

"So you see, Mr. Perkins, my niece's history hardly compares to those of the pedigreed fillies you're used to cavorting with," she continued stiffly. "It's to her credit that her mother sought honest work and encouraged her many talents. And I'm quite proud to point out that Celesta is a widely read author. Far too intelligent for you anyway."

"I knew that," Patrick sneered, "but if you're

246

telling us those Sally Sharpe stories are worth reading—"

"I'm telling you to shut your mouth until I've finished!"

Her words echoed around her stunned audience, and the finger she was pointing at Perkins began to shake uncontrollably. "Maybe I'm wrong. Maybe it's not her money you're after, since you Perkinses certainly have your share. That only leaves one other thing you could want from a beautiful girl like my niece, and if you think you'll be the first to claim it, you're not only stupid, you're blind."

Damon saw Celesta's face go white, and he stepped forward, speaking quietly. "Justine, I think you're too upset to realize what you're—"

"Damn right I'm upset!" she cried, pivoting to aim her finger at him. "You think I don't know about you and Celesta? Who could sleep, listening to those animal moanings at all hours? Quite the Romeo, aren't you?"

He tried to take her by the shoulders, but she jerked away violently. "Justine, I think we—"

"And quite the sneak, too!" she blurted. "I knew you were on my balcony the night of the fire, just as I know you've been waiting in the vestibule in case I got out of hand! Crazy Justine, everyone thinks! But you set that fire, Mr. Frye, because with me gone you'll have access to the Ransom estate—"

"That's not why I came here, and you know it."

"—but it didn't work, did it? Celesta saw the fire in time and spoiled your little plan."

Her eyes were dilated black, and her slender body was trembling with rage, a volcano ready to erupt. Katherine was mortified, sitting with her head in her hands, while Eula was on the edge of her seat, wide-eyed. He had to stop this madness before Justine hurt anyone else—or herself—but she was backing away from him, deftly remaining beyond his reach.

247

"Justine, please. We know each other too well to—"

"Yes, I do know you, Mr. Frye! You've lied to us about Lucy Bates, you've taken advantage of my niece, you've wormed your way into our hearts, and now you're leaving! Get out of my house!" she shrieked. "You men are all alike and we can live without you!"

Katherine rose unsteadily from her chair. "Justine, you have no idea what you're saying, dear. If you'll calm down, we can—"

"It was *you* who got us into this mess, inviting him to live here," the spinster railed, "and I'm doing what I should've done then. Mr. Frye is leaving. *Now!*"

Damon thought frantically but could arrive at no solution to this drastic situation. As long as she thought anyone was challenging her power as the head of the proud Ransom family, Justine would accuse them, rightly or wrongly, of trying to dethrone her. "I'll leave when you sit down and rest," he said in a low voice, pointing to an overstuffed chair. "You can't protect Celesta or your money if you have a stroke, now can you?"

Justine's mouth snapped shut, and she looked puzzled.

"Some of the things you've said are absolutely correct," he went on in a soothing voice, "but if you kill yourself yelling at us, who'll keep us all on the straight and narrow after you're gone?"

The old woman crossed her arms. "Your point's well taken, Mr. Frye. But you're still leaving," she said with a wry chuckle.

"Fine. As soon as you're seated, with cake and some tea, I'll go downstairs to pack."

As suddenly as she'd begun raving, Justine meekly took the chair Damon was pointing at and watched him pour her a cup of tea with childlike awe. Then he excused himself, walking with unruffled grace toward the kitchen.

Celesta felt Patrick glowering at her. She made no response when he stood up and said, "I'll follow him, to be sure he's cleared out within the hour. To think that bastard could move in and then try to burn—"

"The only place you're going is home, young man," Justine commanded quietly. She sipped her tea and looked from Patrick to his mother. "You Perkinses are like vultures: we never saw your lowly faces until there was a corpse. Rachel may have passed on—under suspicious circumstances, I might add—but I'm not dead yet! So get out, and don't you be hovering around us again!"

Chapter 20

Justine appeared at breakfast the next morning looking exceptionally pert and serene—younger, Celesta thought, than she'd seemed since Mama's funeral. Her stormy speech had apparently cleared her mind of her stored-up suspicions, and swept clean of these emotional cobwebs, she chatted about the coming day's activities as though yesterday's tea had been nothing out of the ordinary.

When she saw a wagon out the window, loaded with workmen and large lengths of pipe, she rose from her place at the table. "There's our water line crew, bright and early," she commented with crisp approval. "Let's see if Mr. Frye had the gumption to come with them."

As she paused in the doorway and then walked down the stone path to greet them, Damon observed her closely. Her hair and clothing were immaculate, and her tight smile reminded him of the day he was repairing the gazebo, relegated to the cellar by a ramrod woman whose principles would *not* be compromised! He'd broken her rules—and she'd gone along with it—and now they watched each other with wary politeness. Both of them had been wrong a time or two, and both of them knew it.

"Good morning, Justine," he said with a reserved

smile. "I hope you didn't think I'd renege on our plumbing project for personal reasons."

"The thought never crossed my mind, Mr. Frye."

What *was* on her mind? As he looked at her bright brown eyes and fragile smile she seemed so collected, so like the Justine Ransom known for her perceptive, if blunt, opinions. In town, the tongues were already wagging, and he could only wonder how much damage Ian Montgomery, Patrick Perkins, and he himself had done to this lonely woman.

"If it's all right with you, I'll let these men get started on the trench, and I'll return tonight to move your furniture back into your room," Damon said quietly. "I'll work on the plumbing evenings and Saturdays, if that's acceptable."

"That would be fine."

He nodded, and with a glance toward the kitchen window—was that Celesta's shadow he saw?—he turned toward his horse. He'd just swung into the saddle when Justine's voice stopped him.

"I appreciate your coming today, Damon. As far as I'm concerned, you've earned out your room and meals, and you owe us nothing."

He studied her, holding the reins taut to keep his mount from shifting restlessly. "You've paid for the fixtures. I told you I'd install them, and I'm a man of my word," he stated evenly. "But if you've decided someone else should—"

"You're still the right man for the job," she said with a little smile. "I rather enjoy watching you work."

He hesitated, and then chuckled. By God, the old girl was flirting with him! On an impulse he reached down to lightly touch her cheek, a cheek that had been as firm and enticing as Celesta's at one time. Then he rode back to the Cruikshank mansion, whistling under his breath.

*　　*　　*

The September sun made the leaves on the pine oaks shine in shades of russet and copper beneath a cloudless blue sky. It was a day that sparkled like a jewel in the crown of early autumn, and once Justine returned safely from her shopping, Katherine insisted on working in the garden. Armed with a spade and a pitchfork, they were digging the last of the carrots, potatoes, and onions to store them away for winter.

Celesta paused with her foot on the shovel, blowing a wisp of loose hair aside. "Do you think Justine's all right in there by herself?" she asked quietly.

"She's cleaning—and smoking, I imagine," came the breathy reply. "I suspect she'll recover from what she said yesterday long before the rest of us will. If she even remembers it."

Chuckling wryly, Celesta bent down to knock the soil from a handful of long, orange carrots. "How much of it was true, do you think?"

Her aunt made a sound that was part laughter and part sigh. "Well, Damon certainly didn't set the fire—at least not the one in her room," she added coyly, "but I never suspected she and Ian Montgomery . . . just as I had no idea you were writing dime novels, dear."

She met her aunt's probing gaze with a shy smile. "That part's true enough. Ironically, it was one of my stories she was reading when the fire started."

Katherine giggled, taking ten years from her careworn face as she straightened her back. "I wish I'd known, Celesta! Your mother would've been so proud if—"

"She knew. It was a secret we enjoyed every time Sally Sharpe appeared on the racks, because only we two realized who Montgomery C. Lester actually was," she replied wistfully. "Although if Patrick claims *he* knew, that means he must've—"

"He's just the sort to go rifling through your

drawers. Pun intended," came a voice from behind them.

They swiveled like little girls caught gossiping, to see Justine watching them from the hedgerow. She was wearing her oldest skirt, and her blouse sleeves were rolled to her elbows. Her smile was proud beneath a straw bonnet that rippled in the breeze.

"I probably shouldn't have revealed your publishing success," the spinster continued as she knelt to gather the loose potatoes at Katherine's feet, "but I had to prove to that transparent cad—and his insufferable mother—how far above them you are, Celesta."

"Well, I . . . thank you."

"You're welcome." Justine glanced up at her sister-in-law, clearing her throat. "I'd be happy to loan you my Sally Sharpe collection sometime, if you're interested. You'll be amazed at the imagination this niece of ours has, and I'm certainly glad I kept her stories stashed safely in my armoire."

Suddenly overwhelmed by this unexpected praise, Celesta shoved her spade into the earth so that she wouldn't explode with joy. To think that Justine, of all people, would preserve her stories—

She frowned, and then glanced slyly at her kneeling aunt. "How long have you known about Montgomery Lester?"

Justine chortled. "I should've figured it out long before I did. The story about Damon Dare was a dead giveaway."

Celesta raised an eyebrow. "Perhaps someone besides Patrick rifles through drawers."

"Perhaps. Eula impresses me as a woman who'd stoop to that."

After a moment Katherine began to quake, and then they were all laughing, conspirators of the dearest sort. Celesta looked at her two aunts and wished this happy moment could last forever. Their eyes sparkled, and their faces glowed with recaptured youth. They felt like a family now, the three of them bound by ties more compelling than common blood or ancestors: they had something to *prove*, to the Perkinses and everyone else in this tale-spinning town. If only . . .

But they all remembered yesterday, and for several minutes the three of them worked in silence, Katherine and Celesta wielding the tools while Justine retrieved the vegetables. Finally the eldest woman sighed, tossing a rotten potato over the row of zinnias, toward the riverbank. "I suppose that tidbit about Ian has sprouted wings by now," she said softly. "Funny how easily that slipped out, after more than twenty years of keeping it locked away."

Katherine glanced briefly at Celesta, and they both kept digging. What was there to say? Justine would reveal what she wished to, in her own way, and they could only hope she didn't get upset again.

"You see, I said that piece for *you*, Celesta," she continued quietly. "I wanted the Perkinses to know they can't consider you in the hired-help class anymore. And I wanted to warn you, by my own painful example, about how easy it is to lose your heart to a handsome man. Your father was my age, but I was too young for him by half—which was why he conquered me so quickly with his bold, beautiful eyes. And lies. He was good with those, too."

She stood to stretch, looking toward the river as though expecting to see her old lover there, beckoning her. "Rachel and I had our differences, but I never wanted her to suffer my fate. And how could I have warned her about Ian's duplicity without admitting my own shame? It was unspeakably embarrassing—and she wouldn't have listened anyway. Too impetuous and outspoken, your mother was."

Celesta smiled to herself. Eula Perkins had often accused Mama of stronger traits than those—and Justine was no stranger to them, either.

"I wish I would've mended our fences, though. Rachel and I shared more than Ian's betrayal, and I find myself wondering if she wouldn't be alive today, had I invited her home." She blinked at them, a little sheepishly. "This old mind stumbles onto the damndest thoughts sometimes. I'll be quiet now, so we can get our work done."

Damon saw them strolling past when he was eating breakfast on Broadway a few days later, and he wondered who was watching over whom. His heart stung from missing them—both of them, damn it—and he watched them until they were too far down the street to see. Justine looked composed and demure, her basket over her arm, while Celesta listened to her with a sweet smile that drove him absolutely crazy.

Was that a new dress she was wearing? The deep green fabric flattered her immensely, and the billowing leg-of-mutton sleeves whittled her waist to a dainty proportion he could span with his hands—how he wanted to!

Did her ears burn with the gossip about how he'd set fire to the suite and stolen her virtue? Was she aware that Eula and Patrick had dusted off the suspicions about a crazy streak in the Ransom clan, and that rumormongers had lovingly polished the tale with their tongues? Hannibal, like most small towns, was cruel that way. In his darker moments, Damon wished he hadn't returned.

Yet he was far from hopeless. In his room at the Park Hotel, or while eating meals that Katherine's put to shame, his feelings for Celesta deepened. She kept him awake nights: God, he returned from the Manor each evening and fondled his memories of how she looked and what she said until they were threadbare! By an unspoken agreement, they exchanged only the briefest greetings when he went there to work. He saw questions in her eyes, and someday soon she would have all the answers, he vowed.

But now they both waited—for what, he wasn't sure. He wouldn't sneak her into his hotel room, and he didn't expect her to slip upstairs while he installed the bathroom fixtures. Jokes about fitting pipes into holes made him miss the sparkle in her eyes and her subtle laughter as much as he missed the way her body drove his to a frenzy sweeter than life itself.

That evening he worked alone in the round tower room, his labor accompanied by the steady creak of Justine's rocking chair from behind the opposite wall. She was listening to her phonograph, and although she was using the earpieces, he heard occasional strains of music escaping them.

Did she ever listen to those French lessons? Perhaps she hadn't originally had any: a woman who concealed dime novels beneath her groceries might switch the cylinders in the store and come home with some real toe-tappers in home-study cannisters. The thought made Frye laugh out loud.

Her rocking ceased . . . she was putting a different record on the spindle. Damon pushed the porcelain tub over to the wall, carefully aligning its faucet holes with the shiny pipes he'd just connected. He felt a presence, and turned to see Justine staring blankly at him.

"Are you all right?" he asked quietly. And after a moment he tried, "Shall we find Katherine? Or may I get you something?"

She left, her silver hair fluttering over her wrapper, her hands clenched into bony fists. Her tread on the stairs was firm and steady, yet he sensed he should follow her. And when she opened the back door to step down the stone pathway toward the gazebo, he ducked into the summer parlor. Katherine was working her needlepoint, and Celesta was reading, a cozy scene with Brahms playing in the background.

"Justine just walked outside. I think we'd better

see to her."

They were up immediately, their faces lined with worry as they followed him into the moonless night. Celesta was carrying the parlor lamp, her lips pinched grimly.

"She does this sometimes," Katherine murmured, peering anxiously into the darkness ahead. "Something upsets her, and she roams for half the night. I wish you were still here, Damon, though I suppose it's for the best."

He smiled sadly and then he stopped short. Justine was at the edge of the bluff overlooking the river, gazing out as though searching for a steamer that was long overdue. He held his breath . . . should he fetch her? Or would she slip and tumble down the embankment in her confusion?

The spinster turned, and when she saw them watching her she crossed her arms and shivered with the evening breeze. Her flowing hair caught the light from the lantern, and Damon felt a worm of apprehension crawling in his stomach. She was looking at him with the same expression she'd worn when she accused him of setting her fire.

Then she stepped closer, her gaze shifting between Katherine and her niece. Justine was shaking, yet he sensed she didn't feel the chill in the air.

"You're ganging up on me, trying to take away my home!" she said in a keening voice. With her pale nightclothes rippling around her, and her dark, piercing eyes, she resembled an eerie, avenging angel come to haunt them. "Ambrose inherited the business because he was the son, and Rachel got a man with her looks, and all I have to show for a lifetime of duty and devotion to my father is this house! You won't take it away from me! I won't let you drive me away!"

Chapter 21

Where did such frightening ideas come from? Celesta pondered this question long into the night, after Justine finally succumbed to a doctored toddy Damon convinced her to drink. His was the only voice she would listen to. The hand that supposedly set a match to her beloved dimers was the one that had led her inside and held the warm cup to her lips.

"I'll go now," he murmured when she was sleeping peacefully. "She might not want me here when she wakes up. Daylight will probably restore her faculties, and she'll be upset if I've stayed the night."

Katherine had whimpered a reluctant agreement, and was probably lying wide-eyed in her bed, afraid of what the coming weeks might bring. She who once feared being evicted by her surly sister-in-law now stood accused of trying to turn the tables.

Celesta understood her stunned, aching confusion perfectly: she, too, was part of the conspiracy to oust Justine, the way her failing aunt saw it. With the excitement of restoring Ransom Manor to the dignity it deserved, an idea Katherine began and Justine then embraced and asked Celesta to help with, it would seem impossible that any of them would want to be rid of the other. Yet the eldest

Ransom was convinced she was being forced from her lifelong home.

Where had this notion come from? Celesta stared blankly at the candle on Grandfather's secretary, summoning help from his spirit, or from Sally, or from anyone who could shed light on this perplexing, potentially dangerous situation. People based their beliefs on what they saw and heard, reshaping their convictions each day as they learned new evidence or gained new insight.

Celesta believed Damon Frye loved her, because of the way he spoke and acted and touched her . . . yet the only time he'd mentioned love was when she'd prompted him. Was she mistaken, disillusioned because her heart perceived his intentions in a way that prevented her mind from focusing on the facts?

Emotions were chameleons, changing with the circumstances to protect themselves. Who could say what would become of their passionate attachment now that they lived apart? Who could say what Justine was trying to protect—or trying to reveal—with her ravings? It seemed to Celesta that ever since the fire, they had no answers for what she did. They only had more questions.

The next week was a trying one. Justine, near normal in the mornings, would allow Celesta to accompany her into town as though they'd shopped together for years. It was a colorful walk these days, among flame-colored sweet gums and crimson maples edged with frost. They could see their breath as they descended the hill; the mist rising from the river fascinated them with its mysterious beauty. Squirrels scampered by, their cheeks crammed with acorns, and life followed its natural rhythm as the earth around them prepared for winter.

As each day wore on, however, Justine's mood disintegrated. She talked to herself, or to her father's portrait—sometimes when Celesta was present, and sometimes in French. Her schedule became erratic, and for the first time since she'd come to live there, Katherine commented on dusty tables and cobwebs in the ceiling corners.

"She's spending more and more time alone, listening to that phonograph," her worried aunt whispered as they prepared meals together. "And by evening it seems she can barely stand to look at us, as though she still believes we're going to force her out. Am *I* going crazy, or have you noticed these things, too?"

Celesta grasped Katherine's hand and could only nod. It was a terrible ordeal, to witness the fading of an intelligent woman's mind, like living inside a watch that was wound too tightly. How long before the next disaster? When—and how—would it end?

These were horrible questions to ponder, and Celesta felt herself drawn to Damon because despite his obvious concern, he radiated a comforting calmness. Justine felt it, too. She allowed him to tuck her into bed now, after he sat with her while she sipped her drugged milk . . . such childlike acceptance of his care, from a woman who refused to see a doctor, who weeks ago wouldn't have been seen in her nightclothes—by a man who wasn't family, no less!

The evening he completed the installation of the upstairs bathroom fixtures, Justine stood on tiptoe to kiss him good night. After she was asleep, he joined Katherine and Celesta in the parlor, visibly shaken.

"I . . . I don't know why that kiss upset me," he confided quietly. "We're certainly friends, and there was nothing sexual about it. I just feel funny. If only we could understand what's going on inside her mind."

He beckoned with an outstretched hand, and Celesta walked outside with him. The trees were rustling in a wind that rolled gray clouds across the azure sky, shadowing the moon and then allowing it to beam down upon them, the round, golden ruler of the night.

"It's going to rain," she murmured as she sniffed the air.

"It's going to storm," he corrected, pointing to the first jagged streak of lightning. "Are you afraid? Do you want me to stay?"

Celesta gave him a wry smile. "Oh, I'd like you to stay, but not because the weather bothers me. If it weren't for worrying about Justine, I'd be up watching the thunder and lightning, just for the joy of it. It's very . . . invigorating."

"If it weren't for Justine, I'd be peeling your clothes off right now," he said as he pulled her close. "Storms excite me—all that untamed energy unleashed with every flash and crackle. But sure as we'd come together, she'd be pounding on the door. She's got that uncanny sense about her now."

"I know," Celesta whispered. "I've noticed it, too."

He gazed at her uplifted face, pale in the moonlight, and when she closed her eyes his best intentions blew away in the wind. Damon kissed her long and hard, holding her as though he'd squeeze the life from her. She was warm and restless, answering his pent-up longings with guttural moans that made his desire run rampant.

"I need you tonight," he rasped against her ear, "but I can't take you in there to—"

"So take me out here. Katherine and Ambrose used the gazebo when they were newlyweds," she blurted.

Where was her resolve? Had she been so starved for his affection these past weeks that one kiss could make her risk such a rendezvous? It was starting to rain. The thunder was a continuous rumble now, and by the time they finished she'd be soaking wet. Katherine would be in the parlor, waiting up for her. Justine might awaken, still groggy from her nightcap, but she'd know what they'd been doing.

He watched the indecision flicker across her face and scooped her into his arms before she could change her mind. "Celesta, have you ever done something you knew you'd regret, but that you couldn't live without?" he whispered.

She nodded, her heart beating double-time as he carried her down the stone pathway.

"Have you ever felt scared and empty and worthless, knowing a vital part of your life was missing?" he asked urgently. "Knowing that what you so desperately want to give someone is the very thing that might ruin her life?"

Damon's question frightened her, but there was no ignoring the mesmerizing eyes above hers, eyes so deep and black with desire they seemed like chasms of midnight she was destined to tumble into. "Wh-what do you mean?" she mumbled.

"I mean I have to have you. Like the thunder needs the lightning . . . like the earth requires the moon to give it ebb and flow, and the sun to light it," he said as he set her down inside the gazebo. "It's not a matter of choice anymore. I need you, now and for always, Celesta."

Her mouth fell open, and then he was kissing her fervently, loosening her hair and letting the pins clatter onto the wooden floor. The wind whistled through the latticework, yet she didn't feel its chill. The swing behind them creaked on its chains as though ghosts were wrestling in it, but the wildness of the night only heightened the ache inside her. So long she'd languished without his attentions and stolen kisses! Damon Frye was all that mattered now, and the consequences of their loving would have to tend to themselves.

When he saw surrender in her eyes, he rejoiced: Celesta was as needy as he, and impetuous enough to meet the challenges of their deliciously dangerous relationship. Her fingers flew nimbly down the front of his shirt and trousers. Her lips were parted with wanting, and her glorious raven hair whipped around her naked shoulders, a sight as bewitching as any he could conjure up in his dreams. Only a woman who shared his mad passions could behave this freely—and she was his!

Their clothing cushioned them as they eased onto the floor and stretched out. She clutched him as though she might drown, and he washed over her with kisses that left a tingling trail when the breeze found its dampness. No words were needed as they came together with a flash of lightning that lit the gazebo around them.

Rain drummed the roof, and Damon laughed, burying his face in her hair. "Climb on and take me, lady," he commanded hoarsely.

Celesta obeyed, reveling in the passions that played upon his moonlit face. So darkly handsome as her hair fell around his shoulders, so virile and powerful he was, moving inside her with thrusts as urgent as her own. "Shall I take you all the way to paradise, Mr. Frye?" she quipped, no longer afraid he'd respond as he had the first time they'd talked this way.

"Farther," he breathed, and then he coaxed her forward to kiss the breasts that pooled on either side of his face. "Take me so far I won't know where I am—and I won't care, except that I'm with you."

His words shot through her like a lightning bolt. With a soundless cry, she arched against him until he filled the voids within her, so long denied, with a rush of warmth.

She fell against him, complete.

He cradled her close, whole again, until the moment they moved apart and his cycle of need for her began again, over and over.

Celesta wasn't sure how long they drifted with each other, but she gradually became aware that her back was wet and that the floor was hard beneath her knees. She shivered and started to get up, but Damon draped an arm over her and kissed her with a sweet laziness that made her want to stay here all night.

"Marry me, Celesta," he murmured. "It's the only way we'll have enough of each other. It's the only way . . . please say you will."

Her heart lurched, caught between panic and joy. Damon Frye was the answer to her every need physically, but—but she knew shockingly little about him, save that he once abandoned Lucy Bates and that he could charm anything he wanted out of any woman he met. Treacherous credentials, and yet—

"Yes, yes I will," she heard herself whisper.

He crushed her to his chest, too overwhelmed to speak. Celesta knew his demons yet she accepted him, a man who presented more problems than solutions. He kissed her tenderly to seal their vow, and then eased her up. "You'd better go in now," he said, "but if you want me to go with you, to speak with your aunt and justify your . . . appearance, I will."

She chuckled and started pulling her wrinkled clothing on. "I'll go up the back stairs. It'll be all right."

Damon rose to frame her face with his hands, gazing intently at her. "It'll be more than all right. It'll be wonderful, Mrs. Frye."

Somehow she dressed, and somehow she trotted through the rain beside him, and watched from the doorway until the clatter of his horse's hooves were muffled by the downpour, but she wasn't touching ground. *Mrs. Frye!* Damon had finally declared himself, and now everything else in her life would fall into place. There was nothing they couldn't face together, no hardship they couldn't overcome.

Celesta removed her shoes and eased up the narrow back stairs, holding her soggy, crumpled skirts. Her soaked hair was clinging to her shoulders, and she wished the water was hooked up so that she could luxuriate in a steaming tub and relive the most startling, joyous moment of her life.

A shadow moved above her, and she looked up to the second-floor landing. Justine was standing there, blocking her way. Her arms were folded, and her condemnation was plainly visible, even in the unlit corridor.

"Just like your mother," she stated, sounding as sane and judgemental as when Celesta had first come to live here.

Her long finger snaked out to take aim, and Celesta sucked in her breath. "I—you don't understand—we—"

"I understand perfectly. I've seen everything," she replied caustically. "Just like Rachel, you stole my lover, Celesta. And just like your mother, you're going to burn in hell for it."

Chapter 22

Long into the night Celesta lay awake, breathing too hard, her throat so dry it clicked when she swallowed.

. . . you stole my lover . . . you're going to burn in hell for it.

How much of Justine's accusation was true? Surely Damon wasn't her aging aunt's lover, and yet . . . they'd grown undeniably close. And even if she could attribute this part of the eerie pronouncement to fanciful imagination, Celesta couldn't ignore the implications of the final half. *Just like your mother, you're going to burn in hell for it.* Did these vindictive words reflect only the jealousy of a jilted sister from twenty-some years ago, or had Justine taken action? Had she somehow poisoned Mama's sugar to wreak the final revenge for marrying handsome Ian Montgomery?

This is ridiculous, Celesta chided herself as she slipped her wrapper on over her nightgown. *She's a half-crazy old woman, sleepwalking after drinking doctored milk. And I'm letting her drive me crazy.*

Once in the alcove, she scribbled a few characters' names and traits for a Sally Sharpe novel. Focusing her mind on a new challenge for Damon Dare and the Girl Detective settled her somewhat, but she was still too agitated to start a story. Come breakfast, she might find herself on the street for defying Justine's dictates about Damon, and she should be thinking of ways to support herself. These dimers certainly wouldn't pay her rent elsewhere!

Instead, she saw Damon Frye sweeping her up in his invincible arms, the raging storm as his backdrop, and heard his love words over and over . . . *it's no longer a matter of choice . . . it's the only way we'll get enough of each other . . . marry me, Celesta.*

As though she'd invoked his presence, the rain washed down the alcove window in sheets. Acorns pelted the side of the house, driven by a wind that shrieked through the trees. What was it he'd said about ruining her life? She didn't know—and didn't want to know, since lately there seemed so many roads to ruination.

Celesta glanced down at the sheet she'd been scribbling on, and from out of her despair came a giggle that put Justine's threats in perspective. Below a few character names and plot incidents, over and over, she had written *Mrs. Damon Frye . . . Celesta Montgomery Frye . . . Celesta and Damon Frye . . .*

What else could possibly matter?

Katherine, who quaked at the first hint of thunder, had lavender half-moons beneath her eyes at breakfast. When it took her longer than usual to roll the biscuits and retrieve the smoking bacon from the stove, Justine was quick to comment.

"Did it storm last night? Perhaps you should let Mr. Frye fix you a toddy before bed," she said as she snapped her linen napkin over her lap. "I slept like a baby. Didn't hear a thing."

Celesta busied herself carrying the jam and honey to the table, her jaws clenched. To think this infuriating woman's threats had kept her awake half the night, and she didn't even remember making them! As they sat down to eat she glanced at Katherine, but her younger aunt had apparently been too preoccupied by the storm to overhear the confrontation on the back stairs.

"You've always been deaf when it suited you, and so was your brother," Katherine replied wearily. "And by the looks of the lawn, we'll be all day raking up the leaves and acorns."

"The three of us will make short work of them after Celesta and I return from town," she said pertly. Then she smiled at them as she lavished peach jam over half of a steaming biscuit. "I don't know what sort of elixir Mr. Frye mixes into my milk, but I'm stronger than I've been in weeks. It's good he's decided to stay in town now, because I feel so foxy today I might just give Celesta a little competition if he were here."

Celesta's mouth dropped open, but she caught herself before she blurted words she'd regret. Her aunt apparently thought Damon vacated of his own free will . . . and why spoil her carefree mood, when afternoon would find her getting progressively more restless and disagreeable? "It was probably snake oil," she mumbled. "You've said many times that he's not to be trusted."

Justine laughed, which brought dozens of tiny lines to light around her eyes and mouth, yet she appeared younger—and *prettier*—than Celesta could ever remember seeing her. On their way into town, she chatted about how much she was enjoying her redecorated room and her new Edison records.

"Now all I need is a fresh Sally Sharpe story," she said spryly. Then she sobered a bit and placed her hand on Celesta's elbow just as they reached the edge of the business district. "Will you answer me honestly if I ask you something, dear? I hate to upset

269

your aunt about this."

She gazed apprehensively into Justine's bright brown eyes. "All right."

The spinster glanced around to be sure no one would overhear them. "I . . . I have a feeling I've not been myself lately, Celesta. I used to account for every activity during the days and weeks, but now it seems there are . . . pieces missing. Is it my fault that Mr. Frye's moved out, and that Eula Perkins doesn't visit Katherine anymore?"

Celesta stopped breathing. Her aunt had never sounded more sincerely puzzled, and in order to prevent hurting her feelings or upsetting her, she had to keep her own emotions in check. The woman gripping her arm didn't seem to remember railing at Damon or sending the Perkinses packing, and complete honesty wouldn't make her memory return.

"You've been a little . . . testy since the fire in your room," she replied softly, placing her hand over her aunt's. "It's perfectly understandable. We were all upset."

"Oh." Justine blinked and then nodded absently. "Damon's a dear man . . . such a compelling voice. I—I hope I haven't spoiled things between you. It's hell to grow old alone, and I wouldn't wish it on anybody."

She swallowed hard to keep her voice under control. "No, you . . . everything will be fine, Aunt Justine. I—I think Damon's finally taking serious notice of me."

"Oh, that's wonderful! Bless you, child, you've brightened all our lives."

It was the hardest thing she'd ever done, but Celesta forced her tears not to fall as they proceeded down the sidewalk toward the market. People smiled and told her aunt how well she looked, and she returned their pleasantries graciously. They chose a

270

plump chicken—and then another one, on the condition that Celesta would invite Mr. Frye to dinner after they raked the lawn. She thought he'd be picking up the second set of bathroom fixtures instead of coming over, but she agreed wholeheartedly to invite him, because only Damon could chase away the gloom that made her smile feel pasted on. Justine Ransom, despite the new bloom in her cheeks, seemed to be losing her reason even as Celesta watched.

And yet, as they raked great mounds of red, golden, and brown leaves over the edge of the lawn, Justine was more robust than either she or Katherine. She sent the acorns rolling down the stone walkway with brisk strokes, laughing when the squirrels chattered at them. When she paused to catch her breath, she looked wistfully out over the river as though searching for the memories that were lost to her now. "Perhaps Father will be home tonight," she said softly.

Katherine's smile fell as she glanced at Celesta for support. Neither of them had the heart to correct the poor woman's wish, and when she sagged onto the gazebo swing, suddenly tired, they suggested she nap so that she'd be good company when Damon came for dinner.

Justine scowled. "I thought we agreed he was no longer welcome in our home."

Running her trembling hand over her brow, Katherine tried to hide her intense frustration. "But you and Celesta brought home two hens so we could invite him—"

"We'll eat one tonight and have the other tomorrow," the spinster snapped. "It's ridiculous, walking to town every day at my age."

She left them abruptly, and although Celesta sensed she was reading and listening to her phonograph, neither she nor Katherine dared slip upstairs

271

to see. They put the rakes away and started dinner as usual, but the aromas of fried chicken and corn casserole didn't bring Justine downstairs. When Celesta peeked in on her, she was sprawled across the bed, sleeping sweetly. She pulled the lace counterpane around her and left her to her dreams.

"Maybe Damon can come tomorrow night," a downhearted Katherine said as Celesta joined her at the table.

"I'm not sure I want to burden him with this," she replied sadly. "Now that his men have the pipe laid, we just need him to open the valves for the water. Perhaps he should wait to work on the downstairs bathroom, until . . ."

Celesta didn't want to finish the sentence, and although she'd longed to share the news of her engagement all day, this hardly seemed like an appropriate time. They cleared the remains of their barely eaten meal and spent an evening of preoccupied silence in the summer parlor. While Katherine began yet another sampler, Celesta tried to concentrate on a book of Sherlock Holmes stories, but the British mastermind's brilliance depressed her. In order for him to show off his powers of observation and logic, there had to be a body . . . a distressing thought, because Justine didn't stir all night long.

And in the morning, she was gone.

Katherine's startled cry brought Celesta out of her room only half-buttoned. "What's the matter? Is Justine—"

"Disappeared!" her aunt whimpered. "The bed's made and her room's tidied, but—"

"Perhaps she's downstairs waiting for us," Celesta prayed aloud. "She went to bed so early, she must've wakened before dawn. And she's always at her best in the mornings."

But a quick search of the first floor made them even more frantic. Justine, pinched thin though she was, never missed a meal or went out before she'd fortified herself with coffee.

"I'll go into town," Celesta said, quickly slinging a shawl over her shoulders. "She always takes the same route. The shopkeepers will know she's not herself and look after her for us."

But none of the men had seen her. Most were just opening their shops, and they shook their heads in concern as Celesta hurried on through the gray morning mist. She hadn't bought cigarettes or westerns, hadn't stopped to dicker over produce, hadn't gotten her mail.

Bill Thompkins frowned behind the post office counter. "It's early enough that I haven't missed her yet, but if she comes in I'll get her home first thing. Could be she's figured out her mistake and walked back already."

Celesta paused outside the building, her breath coming in white puffs as she looked desperately up and down the street. Had Justine gone to see Damon? Proper ladies wouldn't dream of calling upon a man—especially before breakfast—but if she fancied herself as his lover . . .

She was hurrying toward the Park Hotel when Damon spied her, emergency written all over her urgent face. "Celesta!" he called out, and as he strode after her he sensed that their worst fears about Justine had come to pass.

She turned, her ebony hair spilling into the wind over a shawl that was much too light for the brisk autumn morning. Her cheeks were flushed, and her huge green eyes betrayed a fear that startled him as he approached. "What's happened to your aunt?"

"We can't—I thought she came to see *you*, so I—"

"Where have you looked?"

"Everywhere! No one's seen her, and—"

"Then, we'll head back along the riverfront, just to be sure she didn't wander over that way," he said, draping an arm over her shoulders. "She's fine, Celesta. That sixth sense we talked about has probably already guided her home."

The warmth of his body as they walked along soothed her, and as always, the unruffled confidence in his voice quieted her runaway heart. "You may be right. Yesterday she looked out over the river as though she expected the *Phantom* to show up. Suggested Grandfather might be coming home."

"Oh, Lord. I imagine Katherine's beside herself." He strode as quickly as Celesta's legs could carry her, searching the lumber yards and docks along the river, but no one there had seen Justine, either. Hoping he sounded more convinced than he felt, he said, "I imagine she's back, wishing you'd get there so Katherine can set breakfast on."

"I hope to God you're right."

They were ascending the hill that led to the Manor, and Celesta thought her heart would pound its way out of her chest, frightened and breathless as she was. The beauty of the fuschia sunrise was lost on her. The wet leaves were slick beneath her feet, and twice Damon kept her from slipping.

He pointed to the ridge of dirt that resembled an oversized brown snake alongside the road. "That'll pack down around the pipeline eventually. I'll seed it for you so the grass'll have a good start before winter."

Celesta barely heard him. She was looking ahead, to where the gazebo swing creaked tightly beneath Katherine's slumped form. She broke into a run at the same moment Damon did, so filled with dread she didn't dare call out to her aunt.

Frye slid onto the swing and wrapped his arm around Katherine, who was shivering from more than the cold. Her pale gray eyes were huge and haunted, red-rimmed from the tears that still slithered down her chapped cheeks. "What's happened?" he whispered, glancing at Celesta, who stood anxiously in front of them. "We looked everywhere, but—"

"The best I can tell, she headed for town but took a wrong turn. Got to the edge of the lawn and slipped in the—my God, what possessed her to—"

Katherine's sobs choked off the rest of her sentence, and Celesta turned toward the river, heavy with dread, while Damon cradled her aunt. Just beyond the stone pathway, where they'd raked hundreds of leaves and acorns over the bank, was a path of disturbed foliage that led all the way down the steep bluffs to the water's edge. A wicker basket dangled from the protruding root of a tree, and below it, swirling gently against the shoreline in the lapping water, floated the flower-shaped folds of Justine's black skirt.

Chapter 23

". . . ashes to ashes and dust to dust, we commend the spirit of our sister Justine to your eternal care. Amen."

As Katherine wept quietly beside her, Celesta surveyed the all-too-familiar scene in the graveyard. Damon supported her aunt on the other side while Eula and Patrick Perkins stood slightly behind them. Bill Thompkins fidgeted nearby, his eyes on the lowering casket, and other friends—mostly the shopkeepers Justine had pestered every morning for more than forty years—lingered at a polite distance to pay their respects.

There was no question that the head of the Ransom family had drowned. But had she become disoriented in the predawn darkness and slid down the treacherous hillside, or had she stepped over the edge of the lawn on purpose? Both possibilities were fertile ground for speculation, as was the future of the Ransom estate now that all of Ambrose Senior's children were gone.

Celesta, however, had other things on her mind, and as she glanced at her mother's simple headstone and the grass on the slightly mounded grave, she was plagued by the thought she'd once deemed ridiculous: *Death comes in threes.* Katherine had spooked her with that wives' tale, and now that Mama and Justine had passed on within three months of each other, the omen took on more credence.

She didn't think someone had *directly* killed Justine, but ever since the fire in her room the old maid's mind had deteriorated at a much faster rate than seemed natural, considering her exceptional fortitude and intelligence. If someone had helped her insanity along, that meant one of the two people standing beside her was indirectly responsible for her death.

She looked at Katherine, who was leaning against Damon as he offered her his handkerchief. Her aunt had endured a barrage of sharp remarks over the years and had feared Justine might put her out. Was that motive enough to drive her over the edge—to take advantage of the Ransom heir's confusion and secure her future a little faster?

Celesta doubted it. Katherine grumbled about her stiff, eccentric sister-in-law, but in truth the two were each other's closest friend. Loneliness was a far greater enemy to the little widow than Justine ever was, and it seemed highly improbable that she'd knowingly cause her physical or emotional harm.

Which left Damon Frye, her dashing, compassionate fiancé. He had no family, no fortune that they knew of, and his recent intimacy with Justine gave him the perfect opportunity to hurt her in ways no one else would suspect. These past few weeks her maiden aunt had shown implicit faith in him despite casting him out earlier . . . his hand held the toddy that made her sleep each night. Had he dosed it with something more lethal than laudanum or alcohol . . . something that killed her slowly on the inside until she could no longer bear to live?

She didn't know. They'd all three trusted him because they all loved him. And with Justine dead, Celesta remained as the one blood heir to the estate and shipping fortune her grandfather had amassed—an extremely uncomfortable position, under the current circumstances. *Death comes in threes . . .*

Her suspicious nature was putting her into a quandary, so Celesta concentrated on the mourners who were shaking their hands, offering them comfort. That was a problem, too, because with all these people saying how sorry they were she couldn't dodge her own grief any longer. Justine, crotchety and sharp as a thorn at times, had in the end given her the unconditional approval of her writing that every author craved. In her better moments, she'd been witty and gruffly warm and always aware of peoples' foibles and fortés—a soulmate of Sally Sharpe—and Celesta had loved her more than she'd ever admitted to herself before now.

She dashed away a tear when Bill Thompkins approached them, brushing back his hair with a pudgy hand. He gave Katherine a brief hug, which she clung to longer than he'd anticipated. "Justine's at rest now," he said in a low voice, "and she never wanted to be a burden. You'll be fine, and you have Celesta—"

"And we have Mr. Frye," her aunt said in a quavery voice. She looked at the younger man and reached for his hand. "I was appalled when she ordered you out, Damon, and I'd feel so much more secure if you'd come back. It's such a large, lonely house. . . ."

"Of course I will," he replied suavely. "If it'll make you feel better, I'll return tonight."

Bill appeared startled but was too polite to do more than nod and approach Celesta, who felt an inexplicable uneasiness about what she'd just seen. Katherine doted on Damon, and it wasn't like he hadn't lived at the Manor before, and they *were* engaged, but—

"Celesta, I hope you can be strong for your aunt. She's going to need it," Thompkins murmured as he

279

grasped her hands. His eyes betrayed an emotion she couldn't quite read, and he adjusted his spectacles. "I—I hope I haven't let her down. Things are more complicated than they seem."

With a smile that looked more like a grimace, he left the grave side, falling into step with a few other friends. Katherine was in the throes of another tearful outburst, and before she could offer Damon assistance, Celesta felt an insistent tug on her sleeve. Eula and Patrick, the only remaining mourners, were pulling her aside as though what they had to say was a matter of her own life or death.

"Celesta, doesn't she know how this looks?" Mrs. Perkins whispered, her lips pursed with disapproval.

"That's hardly the point, Mother," Patrick joined in. "We heard Justine accuse him of setting the fire, and I suspect he had a hand in her drowning. He might be after Katherine next—or you!"

He was pursuing a path she hadn't allowed herself to follow, but she couldn't admit her suspicions to a man whose motives were even less easily explained than Damon's. Celesta watched Frye holding her aunt, drying her tears with a tenderness she found touching, yet so . . . confusing. She'd given her heart to him in a moment of passion, and more than once she'd wondered if her wild, soaring devotion was misplaced.

"I appreciate your concern," she said, "but I can't just throw him out. Katherine—"

"It's your house now," Eula reminded her pointedly, "and your aunt's known for being easily overwhelmed, easily misled. It's up to *you* to—"

"I'll deal with it when we're all a little more rational," Celesta said with sudden firmness. "Damon was a tremendous comfort to Justine in her final days, and I won't deprive Katherine of his companionship for the sake of appearances. If nothing else, he needs to finish the remodeling we've paid him for."

Her words came out more harshly than she intended, and when she saw Eula's wounded expression Celesta regretted her tone. "Katherine needs your company as well, you know," she added softly. "Justine's unpredictability has kept her away from her meetings in town lately. I'd appreciate it very much if you started visiting her again, or asked her to the social functions she used to enjoy. Friends are her best medicine."

Did her words sound as forced as they felt? Celesta hoped not, because Katherine needed the support of ladies her own age now that she was suffering this second loss so soon after Rachel's passing. She was hoping Patrick noticed that his name wasn't mentioned in her invitation, but right now she couldn't concern herself with her own prejudices. She had an aunt to comfort.

During the next several days Damon proved himself indispensable, a long-suffering shoulder for Katherine and a pillar of practical strength when Celesta needed him. He came home for noon dinner to check on them, bringing groceries and supplies. At Katherine's request, he played the piano evenings and often read aloud, his soothing voice a balm to both their souls. How could anyone believe this man to be Death's accomplice? Celesta accepted his gentle ministrations, her doubts dissipating when she saw how essential he was to their well-being these long, trying days.

At her aunt's insistence, he now occupied one of the guest rooms rather than the cellar. "It's *cold* down there," Katherine said, "and he's so far away if we need him in the night!"

This made Frye's eyes narrow suggestively when he looked at Celesta, yet he seemed to understand that she needed his comfort more than his advances.

Katherine would go to bed with a sleeping potion, leaving them to talk quietly in the parlor, and then they'd part in the upstairs hall after a chaste kiss. Celesta knew this limited contact left Damon as unsatisfied as she was, yet she held herself in check, watching him. Waiting for the jury in her mind to declare him a callous killer or the perfect man to spend the rest of her life with.

Sensing her aloofness was more than grief, he kept his arm around her one evening when she suggested they retire. He smiled, following the ebony hairline around her heart-shaped face with a gentle caress. "Stay awhile," he whispered. "I don't want to be alone."

Celesta gazed at him with eyes that were slowly regaining their sparkle, although she often let her weariness show after her aunt went up to bed. "You've been so strong for us, I forget that you miss her, too," she said quietly.

"Yes, I do. Justine would probably be embarrassed if she knew what a hold she had on me."

She smiled and glanced away. "I'm not so sure about that. She adored you, Damon. You seem to charm the drawers off every woman you smile at."

"So why isn't my technique working on *you?*" he whispered with a boyish grin. Then his expression mellowed, and he pulled her closer. "I love you very much, Celesta. I hope you'll tell me if there's more I can do to ease your sadness, or tell me if I've inadvertently offended you. I miss making love to you, sweetheart. Very much."

Celesta felt her cheeks tingling beneath his earnest scrutiny. It wasn't as though she ever had to fight him off: he was far too understanding, too concerned, to force himself on her.

"Have you told Katherine we're engaged?"

"No. There hasn't been a good time."

Damon studied her ivory face for a moment,

hesitating. "Do you regret accepting my proposal?"

A vision of Justine at the top of the dark stairway made her pause, but that frightening scene held no threat for her now. "No, no regrets. Justine knew we made love that night, though."

Where was the impetuous, bewitching woman who'd ridden him beyond ecstasy in the gazebo? He took her face in his hands, longing for the uninhibited passion he'd once seen there, wondering what kept her from claiming the intimate comfort he so wanted to give her. "Do you think I had something to do with her death, Celesta? Answer me honestly, or your doubts will stand between us forever."

She didn't dare blink or lower her eyes. He'd asked the question she couldn't ignore, and he deserved a truthful reply no matter what the consequences. And the longer she wavered, the more obvious her answer became.

"No," she said firmly. "I'm sorry if I've seemed distant, but I know now that you'd never betray my aunt's trust. She wasn't herself when she threw you out, and God love her, Justine was never the same after you left, either."

Her answer would have to do, because now that she was crying against his shoulder he couldn't press her further. Damon pulled her onto his lap and rocked her like the heartbroken child she was, until she stopped blotting her nose on his shirt. "Perhaps we should start getting out," he murmured. "Choose somewhere we can meet tomorrow. Maybe Katherine has some errands, and she can join us afterward for dinner in town. It'll do us all good."

She smiled against his rough, virile neck as an impudent idea sprang to mind. "How about the library? I need some information for a story."

He rolled his eyes. "Sounds terribly romantic."

For the first time since Justine's funeral, Celesta laughed. "We should cultivate other common interests, you know," she murmured, and then she ran a teasing finger along the length of his fly. "I'm sure you'll rise to the challenge somehow."

From his vantage point on Fifth Street, Damon watched his intended approach the library and had to loosen his collar. Indian Summer had arrived with a vengeance, and after a brief shower, steam was rising in waves from the brick streets. Celesta had escorted her aunt to her Ladies Aid meeting and was now walking toward him, anticipation in her step as she looked around for him.

Even with his shirtsleeves rolled to his elbow he was sweating. He could only imagine how the afternoon's mugginess was affecting Celesta under all her layers of lingerie and the dark, long-sleeved dress she wore. She stopped to pat her brow with her handkerchief, and then extended her lovely neck to caress it with the lacy linen—a gesture he found excruciatingly seductive. He longed to nibble her upper lip and inhale her intoxicating essence, made more pungent with the heat, and free her from her restrictive clothing.

Was he too obsessed with her? Was he letting important details on the Cruikshank mansion slide because his mind so often wandered to Celesta? All Damon knew as she entered the brick building was that he'd never felt so intimately attuned to another person, and that it was time to tell her that. She deserved his honesty along with his affection.

As he strolled through the library door he reached into his pocket for the dozenth time today. It was still there, solid and warm, and he prayed it would erase any doubts she might have about his love for her.

Frye glanced around at the rectangular tables where silent patrons read their papers and leafed through their books. The scent of human heat mingled with the pleasant mustiness he always associated with libraries, and his own temperature rose when he found Celesta in a secluded corner behind the tall shelves. She was perusing an oversized volume, her profile inviting in the dimness. She'd undone the top buttons of her bodice and was absently fanning her neck with it as she studied.

Damon came up behind her and encircled her with his arms, stifling her gasp with a kiss. "Mmmmm," he murmured as he nuzzled her damp neck, "this is even better sport than when we were in school."

Celesta's eyes widened. "I never did any such thing in a library when—"

"Had you been a few years older, I'd have tutored you in the fine art of public seduction," he said with a chuckle. He slipped a finger inside her open placket to tease her collarbone. "Why do you think so many students came here after class?"

She was tingling from his dangerous closeness, trying not to moan when his hand closed around her breast. "Why, they came here to learn!" she whispered, feigning shock.

"And learn we did. Anatomy, stimulation technique, how to improve one's circulation by . . . oh, Celesta," he mumbled as his other hand closed around a breast. "It seems libraries aren't the only places with stacks, sweetheart."

Laughing quietly, she escaped to a nearby table, just as Miss Lizzie Lingle, the librarian, peered sternly between the rows of books at them. Celesta seated herself and propped her book open against the edge of the table. "Behave yourself," she warned, "or you'll get us kicked out."

"Hot as it is in here, that would be no great punishment." He strolled over to the newspaper display and picked up the most recent *Courier Post*, nodding suavely at Miss Lingle. Celesta had a point: he couldn't present her with the gift in his pocket, the way he'd been planning all day, if they were shown to the door. His companion's adorable flush told him she, too, was enjoying the game—even though her gaze was glued to the page in front of her—so he would continue it more discreetly.

Frye sat down across from her and slipped a shoe off. Then he opened his paper, holding it up so that Celesta couldn't see his face. She'd chosen the solitary little table well, and after he pretended to read for a few minutes, he slid his foot stealthily across the floor until it found hers.

Celesta cleared her throat to keep from laughing— and then nipped her lip. Damon's sock-covered toes was slithering up under her skirt, lightly skimming her calf. Surely he didn't intend to . . . yet the table between them was narrow enough so that . . . and his legs were long enough to—

She sucked in her breath when his foot reached her knees. "Mr. Frye, you're shameless!" she hissed.

He took advantage of her whispered outburst to wedge his instep between her thighs. "Shhh! This is a library," he replied hoarsely.

"And this wanton act is a sacrilege! You may as well be making love to me in church."

"I'll keep that in mind, come Sunday."

Still hiding behind the paper, Damon inched his foot higher, chuckling when she stopped resisting and parted her legs. His toe found its goal, and when he began to knead her, he heard her breathing become more labored.

He peeked over the top of his paper. Celesta was staring at her book in glazed rapture, until her eyes closed and she slid her hips forward to rub against his inquisitive toe. She was surging toward satisfaction, panting audibly, when Damon withdrew his foot and raised his paper to hide his smile. Miss Lingle was approaching, her footsteps ominous and heavy on the wooden floor.

She stopped at the end of their table, staring imperiously. *"Must* I remind you about proper library conduct?" she demanded, and her whisper seemed to echo around the entire reading room.

Celesta sat wide-eyed, mortified.

"Miss Montgomery suffers from a respiratory ailment," Damon said smoothly, "and this oppressive heat has triggered an attack. Surely by now you've heard she's an author of some renown?"

Miss Lingle looked doubtfully at Celesta. "I've heard rumors that she writes those—"

"Then, you wouldn't want it to get out that she couldn't complete research for her next story because she was banished by an unsympathetic librarian," he finished quickly. He held her gaze until she muttered something and stalked off toward the front of the room.

"You're incorrigible," Celesta whispered, chuckling in spite of her embarrassment.

"And you, my love, are a delectable shade of pink I'd like to research further." His foot rested between hers again, tapping with anticipation. "Shall I continue? We were interrupted at an inopportune time, I fear."

"I—I think you've gone far enough, Damon."

"Not quite."

Celesta's pulse had nearly returned to normal, but now it quickened again. The man across from her replaced his shoe and then started digging in his pants pocket, smiling devilishly, his chestnut hair falling over one sly brown eye. Curiosity made her lean forward to see what he was retrieving.

"Give me your hand, Celesta," he whispered.

She glanced around, and then reached across the table.

"Your left one."

Her heart shot into her throat. Slowly she obeyed, swallowing a cry of delight when he slipped a ring onto her fourth finger. The glistening gold band supported a large, pear-shaped ruby, and as he caressed it over her knuckle she was too stunned to speak.

It was the reaction he'd prayed for. Celesta's hand trembled in his large one, and his heart spilled over with emotion as he watched her wide green eyes fill with mist. "It was my mother's," he said in a hoarse whisper. "I—I didn't offer it to Lucy because she wouldn't have—I never felt this strongly about her, Celesta. I'm glad we found each other when I was older and knew what really mattered in life."

She gazed from his shining brown eyes to the crimson gem on her finger, and then back to his face. Suddenly she was out of her chair, surging toward him like a magnet to steel, and Damon was there, meeting her in an exuberant kiss above the table. His mouth opened and shut hungrily, plumbing the sweet depths of hers, until they heard a startled gasp and rapid, purposeful footsteps.

Frye looked the stalwart librarian in the eye, knowing his fate and grinning in spite of it. "Would you like to be the first to congratulate me, Miss Lingle? Celesta has agreed to be my wife!"

"Don't be impertinent, Mr. Frye!" she rasped, shaking a finger at him. "This is by no means the *only* time I've had to remove you from the premises for—one would think you'd have *matured* since—"

"Oh, I have, ma'am," he said as he clasped Celesta's hand. "And instead of denying my crimes like I used to, I'm inviting you to our wedding."

"And I'm telling *you* to—"

"We were just leaving," Celesta whispered quickly, and as they hurried past the agitated Miss Lingle it was all she could do not to laugh. The shade felt wonderfully refreshing when they stepped outside, and she giggled when Damon caught her up in a kiss. "I doubt poor Lizzie knows what she's missing."

"No fault but her own, for being such a battleaxe," he replied lightly. He held her against him, his eyes hooded with desire as he gazed down at her. "I know what *I've* been missing, though, and I want it. Tonight. Downstairs. After Katherine's gone to bed."

Celesta felt her heart hammering against his, and as she got lost in the depths of his spellbinding eyes, she knew she would never say no to this magical man again.

Chapter 24

Katherine, in her excitement, stayed up hours longer than usual. "This is the most wonderful thing!" she gushed, alternating between Damon's embrace and Celesta's. "If only Justine could see this ring! If only your mother were here to share this moment."

Celesta sobered a bit. "That just means all of our happiness is heaped upon you," she said quietly.

"Couldn't happen to a nicer person, either," Frye added, and when the little woman asked them to play the piano he tried not to grit his teeth. He was eager to have his fiancée to himself, to make love to her all night long, yet he couldn't deny Katherine a little pleasure. God knew she'd suffered horribly from two losses, and he felt as responsible for her well-being now as he did for Celesta's.

A rousing rendition of "The Maple Leaf Rag" sharpened his desire for her. She was challenging him with her highstepping bass beat, flirting openly with green eyes that made him smolder. Tonight would be nothing short of extraordinary, if her music was any indication of her excitement.

After an encore, Katherine coyly excused herself to bed. Frye wasted not a moment: by the time her aunt had reached the second-floor landing he was deep into a probing kiss, cradling Celesta's head in his hands. Her ebony hair fell loose, cascading around his face as he brushed his lips along the slender column of her neck. "We'd better go downstairs while I can still walk," he moaned.

He was being funny, yet she didn't laugh. The passion she felt rising from deep inside her was reflected in the coffee-colored eyes that now commanded her, silently, to follow him. As he led her past the dining room table, Damon plucked a rose from the bouquet he'd brought home in celebration. Celesta descended to the cellar ahead of him, her heartbeat echoing in the cool, impenetrable darkness.

A match flared, and then the lamplight glowed around the eclectic boudoir he'd fashioned in early summer. Nothing had changed. Justine had apparently forgotten about this room—or was too fascinated by the arrangement of the bed, the chairs, and the three cheval mirrors to move them. The fears that once lurked in these shadowy corners were now replaced by a dusky sensuality that teased at her mercilessly. The dark danger she once associated with Damon Frye drew her into his embrace, a willing victim of his mystical allure.

He stood behind her, facing the center mirror, and slowly unbuttoned her dress. Celesta watched in the glass, enthralled by the sight of his hand baring her skin. "Sometimes the least amount of light reveals the most startling beauty," he whispered. "You're a dream come true for me, Celesta, and tonight we'll make love that's more powerful than we ever thought possible. Do you feel the forces gathering, as I do?"

She nodded, mute with awe. He held the rose between his teeth and finished undressing her with an urgency he couldn't disguise. Then she turned in his arms and repeated the process, reveling in the warmth of his skin, the hint of cherry tobacco that always lingered about him, the fresh sweetness of the scarlet rose he held for her to inhale.

"How do you do this to me, Damon?" she breathed, running her fingers lightly through the dark down on his chest. "How do you transform me from a mere mortal into a heart with wings?"

He laughed low in his throat. "I suspect that power's been hiding inside you all along, just waiting to be released. But I'll certainly take credit for whatever else happens to you tonight."

As she watched in the glass, he began to stroke her with the rose. From her temple, he drew the dewy velvet petals along her neck with a lightness that made her shimmer inside. Celesta held her breath when the crimson flower circled her breast once . . . twice, enticing her nipple into a tingling peak. The utter elegance of his gesture, tripled in the mirrors, went beyond her previous comprehension of what lovemaking was all about.

Damon watched her body bloom beneath his tender touch. Her skin quivered as he teased at the curve of her stomach, circling the mound of raven curls without parting them. The sight of a red rose following her ivory thigh around the dark door to her womanhood only intensified the aching in his loins.

The sheer glory of his caress enthralled her. He moved more quickly now, as eager as she, stroking down one leg and then up the back of her calf. Celesta giggled when he circled behind her knee.

"Ticklish?" he asked.

"I'd be in deep trouble if I admitted it," she whispered, and then she sucked in her breath as the delicate flower flickered around one half of her behind and then the other. Such exquisite torture— and then he stood gracefully as he ran the rose up her spine, raising her hair so she could enjoy its caress to the fullest.

"A ruby, and a rose," Celesta murmured as she

admired her ring. "What other tricks do you have to captivate me with, Damon? What splendid gifts can I give you in return?"

He tossed the flower onto the bed. "I'm already master of all I survey," he replied softly, meeting her eyes in the mirror, "and your heart was mine long ago—a present all the more precious because you didn't know I'd give mine as well. What more could I possibly want, my love?"

Celesta watched her face light up with a sly smile as she led one of his hands to her breast and guided the other to the top of her thighs. "How about these, for starters?"

Frye let out a tigerlike growl and pulled her back against his rigid body, his lips and hands in constant motion. She was his, without reservations, and as he considered the completeness Celesta brought him he was even more determined to please her this way forever.

With his hand causing such a frenzy from the front and his manhood pressing her backside, she felt herself escalating toward the fiery madness that always made her beg shamelessly for more. Her breath was coming in whimpers now. She leaned back against her lover and gave in to the spasms that spiraled through her, her gaze riveted to the mirror. Damon's dark arm supported her, cradling her breasts, while his hand moved in a steady rhythm that drove her over the edge.

"Reach for it," he whispered. "Succumb to my fingers, sweetheart, and—"

Celesta's cry echoed around the cavernous cellar, and when she collapsed against him he carried her to the bed. He laid her gently across it, murmuring his love words until he could see she understood him again.

She gazed up into his face and wondered if his heart heard the rhapsody hers was singing. "I love you—so much—" she panted. "I just want to—"

"Shhh, relax now," he crooned. He took hold of her ankles and placed a lingering kiss in each of her insteps. "We're going to cool you down so you can do this again, and again. Once will never be enough for you, Celesta."

Her grin felt lopsided as she watched Damon nuzzle her leg, knowing quite well where he intended to work his way up to. He proceeded to her knees, delighting in her giggle, and then guided her feet onto his shoulders. "If this grows too intense, tell me. I don't want to hurt you."

Sensing she was in for yet another new experience, Celesta let him take his time and his pleasure as he worshipped her thighs and stomach with warm, thorough hands. He was kneeling between her legs, and the contrast between his lightly stubbled jaw and his silky dark hair as he kissed her sent a fresh wave of sensation through her veins.

He stopped to gaze at Celesta, his hands alongside her hips and her delicate ankles at his ears. She was arching toward him, inviting him with her rhythmic movements. It was an invitation he couldn't refuse.

With utmost care he slid into her, watching her eyes widen, allowing her to adjust to the angle that sent him into the depths of her. Damon stroked her slowly, and when Celesta discovered how best to suspend herself, he smiled his thanks.

"Hang on, sweetheart," he murmured, "I have a feeling I might get carried away."

"I've been there myself, and it's wonderful," she breathed. "Take all you want, Damon. I've got you right where I want you, and I won't let you go until you scream for mercy."

Something inside him rushed forth like water through a floodgate. Only Celesta could set him free this way, and as he moved against her he burrowed deeper and faster until they were rutting like crazed animals. Celesta gripped his muscled shoulders and felt her head slip over the edge of the mattress. Her first ecstasy had prepared the path for him, yet this time the frenzy felt more prolonged and delicious. Damon moaned her name and rocked furiously against her until she, too, had to give in to the unquenchable ache he'd created. She couldn't breathe, her head was at such an angle, but she didn't care. He gasped with his final release and fell against the backs of her legs.

"I hope I didn't hurt—"

"Do I look like I mind?" she whispered sweetly. She wrapped her arms around him, savoring his weight and the damp sleekness of his skin, and the way their bodies breathed as one.

"Good Lord, I nearly landed us on the floor," he said with a breathy chuckle. He gathered her in his arms and inched them backward, maintaining their intimate connection. Then he gazed into her flushed face, overcome by his love for her. "You're a helluva woman, Celesta."

"That's because you're a helluva man."

Her unhesitating response sent joy surging through him, and as he eased her lovely legs down on either side of him, he prayed for this blissful soaring of their minds and spirits to continue forever. "I hope I can make you smile this way when you're Justine's age."

"You'd better, or you'll find out she wasn't very crotchety at all, compared to how *I'll* be."

Damon chuckled and nibbled her earlobe. "Save your threats, woman. You're stuck with me."

Giggling, Celesta pulled him down for an abandoned kiss that told him she was every bit as happy about that as he was.

It was a long, exhausting night.

* * *

A few days later Katherine announced she was ready to clean out Justine's room. Celesta's engagement had revitalized her to the point that she hummed as she performed household tasks her sister-in-law had previously seen to. It was a special treat for her to clean the new bathroom, admiring the shiny spigots and the steamy water that rushed into the sink.

"Justine should've hung on a few days longer," she said wistfully. "Such a shame that she never got to use these fancy facilities."

Celesta sensed a few cracks in the veneer of Katherine's high spirits, so she volunteered to clear out her spinster aunt's armoire and chest of drawers. She carted boxful after boxful of dime novels downstairs, so they could sort through them later, and then lovingly folded her plain but fine-quality garments into a spare trunk. Justine had always donated generously to the church's foreign missionaries, so it seemed fitting to send them her clothing.

The vanity drawers yielded such odds and ends as tortoiseshell combs, numerous pairs of gloves, and underthings of unadorned cotton. Celesta smiled as she realized how much a woman's personal effects revealed about her: in the bottom drawer, beneath faded fans and much-mended cotton stockings, were two tins of tobacco and a package of cigarette papers, with a box of matches. Beneath those supplies was a packet of envelopes tied in a faded ribbon. Her heart beat faster as she wavered between reading the letters and allowing Justine's past to rest with her.

Curiosity won. All that climbing up and down the stairs had earned her a rest; so Celesta settled into the rocking chair, and on an impulse she wound the key of the phonograph beside it. The empty cylinder box on the table was labeled "Best-Loved Hymns," and when she donned the earpieces a chamber orchestra was playing "Nearer, My God, to Thee."

She sat back and pulled a letter from the top envelope, a page so worn from repeated readings that the folds were limp and barely legible. *My darling Justine,* the angular script began, *how I long to see you again, to lose myself in your sparkling brown eyes and stroke your gossamer hair. I'll be home soon, my love, and we can escape to . . .*

Celesta's eyes were wide as she turned the page over to see who'd signed this provocative letter. To think *Justine* had received such mail! Reading this message seemed almost as craven as peering through the keyhole of a bedroom door, yet it could do no harm to—

She swallowed hard as the strains of "Oh, Master, Let Me Walk With Thee," met her ears. *Faithfully yours, Ian.*

A bitter sadness wrapped around her heart as she stared at the signature. Justine hadn't been totally off-balance after all, that day she'd spouted off and sent the Perkinses and Damon away. Here was proof that her father, the heart-stoppingly handsome Mr. Montgomery, had first led poor Justine astray before ruining her mother's life as well. It sickened her to think that two trusting Ransom women had suffered lifetimes of loneliness, becoming a pair of chipped pearls on a necklace this Lothario had undoubtedly been stringing ever since.

Yet no one—not even inquisitive Katherine—had suspected Justine's suppressed misery all these years. Celesta was too overwhelmed to read any further and slipped the ragged page back into its envelope. Thank God her aunt wasn't so hardened toward men that she hadn't seen the admirable traits in Damon Frye. By allowing him to prove his dubious past was truly behind him, she'd brought many weeks of laughter and friendship . . . and love into this family again. What a pity she couldn't have lived until the wedding—

Celesta blinked and listened more closely. "Savior, Like a Shepherd Lead Us" had faded, and instead of its uplifting lyrics, other words were being spoken: *Come down to the shoreline, Justine, we'll share the dawn like lovers—sail away from those who taunt us, into our own eternal paradise. We were meant to be together—*

Her mouth went dry, and she forced herself to keep listening despite the horror that filled her heart. This explained why her aunt had gazed longingly toward the river, as though seeking a long-lost beau—all the hours she'd spent listening to this recording had softened her lonely old mind until she *believed* these stirring, fatal phrases.

Come with me and be my own. We'll love with the abandon of animals, away from the disapproving eyes of those who don't understand our destiny. Meet me at the shoreline, Justine. Wade out to clasp my hands, and we'll walk—

With a gasp Celesta yanked the earpieces off. Tears streamed down her cheek as an intense hatred welled up inside her: her aunt had drowned, but she'd been talked into it! The person who recorded over this wax cylinder knew precisely what heartstrings to pluck, and he knew that after the fire Justine's mind was fertile soil for such romantic seed. It was only a matter of time before the head of the Ransom family succumbed—an apparent victim of insanity. And what woman wouldn't weaken as the hypnotic words seeped into her being, beneath the gates of rational reasoning?

Gripping the wooden chair arms, Celesta frantically wondered what to do next. It was up to her to expose this insidious bastard, but it was so painful to think that a man they knew and trusted had—she herself was in so deeply she wasn't sure she could bear to—

"He's going to pay for this," she muttered as she

stalked toward the door. "He can't sweet talk his way out of it, because *anyone* can recognize his voice on that recording! If he thinks I'll—"

She stopped her ranting when Katherine came out of the bathroom wearing a puzzled frown. "Were you speaking to me, dear? I wasn't paying . . . whatever's wrong, Celesta? Have we undertaken this painful task too soon?"

She knuckled the hot tears from her cheek. "Not soon enough," she rasped. She glanced bitterly back into the master suite, resplendent in its lavender and lace. "It was *Damon* who—all along we thought Justine was crazy, saying he was her lover, but *he's* the one who—"

"Celesta, calm down, dear. I can't make sense of a thing you're saying," Katherine pleaded.

Grasping her aunt's hands, she wondered how much of the awful truth the little woman could endure. Someone else had to verify that voice, though, or her case would appear to be a figment of a distraught fiancée's imagination. And Katherine wouldn't believe the evidence unless she heard it for herself, because she'd been the first to fall under Frye's spell.

"Listen to that record on her phonograph," she said in a ragged whisper. "Remember how Damon replaced her melted wax cylinders? Remember how she practically worshipped him—*kissed* him, even— at the end? Tell me that isn't his voice, coaxing her to her death!"

Katherine paled, but she went in and sat down beside the phonograph. Too full of rage to watch her aunt's reaction, Celesta marched into Damon's room and threw the window up. As memories of his lovemaking, promises, and endearments fanned her wrath, she pitched his belongings outside. Suits, shirts, and overalls fluttered two stories to the ground, followed by his books and pipes—and that damned cherry tobacco! If she ever smelled it again, she'd probably strangle the unknowing offender!

God, he was brazen! Preying on three women, playing the oldest trick in the book by marrying into money—but of course it did him no good while the heir to the Ransom shipping fortune was alive and wise to him. Justine was right: he'd set fire to her dimers, and when it hadn't killed her, he'd used her addled state to finish the job.

What a plot! Someday Sally Sharpe was going to convict Damon Dare of the same ruthless crime, even though it would end a lucrative series. She'd created the bounty hunter—how horribly appropriate—in Frye's image, and once she wrote away her pain she never wanted to think about either of them again.

Celesta turned to find her aunt staring at her, pinched and frail. "I . . . I just can't believe it."

"It's Frye, isn't is?"

Katherine nodded. "And I was such a goose, I invited him to live here not once, but twice! If only we'd listened to Justine—"

"Well, we'll not let him get away, like he did when poor Lucy needed him most!" Celesta declared. "I'm taking that record to the chief of police. And by the time I inform Frye he's to fetch his belongings, they'll be hauling him to jail, where he belongs!"

Chapter 25

Frye sat hunkered on his cell bunk, reviewing the previous afternoon's events, but they left him as numb in the pale gray of the dawn as they had when they were unfolding like a nightmare he couldn't control.

Don't play innocent with me! I know how you drove Justine crazy now, and I'll see you pay for it! Celesta's contorted face still haunted him, and her words stung as badly as the ruby she'd flung in his face. *Conniving bastard! You set that fire, just like she tried to tell us, and we got smart far too late.*

He didn't want to think about the rest of her visit to the mansion site. John Cruikshank himself was present, checking on the progress of his nearly completed home, and the men had all witnessed Miss Montgomery's vicious attack. He and Cruikshank were trying to talk some sense into her when Harlan Jones, the police chief, arrested him. Sympathetic to his cause, his employer went to Ransom Manor to ask some questions and returned with his luggage full of soiled, crumpled belongings, but the lumber baron's pleadings hadn't convinced her to drop the charges.

He sighed for the hundredth time and rubbed his sleepless eyes. Celesta's irrational behavior stunned him. How had she discovered this *evidence* that he'd lured Justine over the cliff and into the river? Hadn't he proven his unwavering devotion to all three women time and again?

When voices echoed in the hallway, he stood up. Perhaps a night's rest had brought her to her senses—perhaps Katherine had convinced the young woman she'd jumped to the wrong conclusion and that he deserved a chance to defend himself. Chief of Police Jones, a beefy, balding man whose uniform strained against his midsection, stopped in front of the cell and glanced at John Cruikshank before speaking.

"We've come to release you, Mr. Frye," he said quietly, "but we need your word you'll comply with certain conditions."

Damon's hopes fell. This sounded more like deal-making than absolution. "What do you mean, conditions?"

Cruikshank, an immaculate, bearded little man, let out a resigned sigh. "We've listened to the recording Miss Montgomery brought in, over and over again. It *sounds* like you, Frye, but such a message could only come from a mind so twisted—well, it just doesn't fit the decent, conscientious man I know you to be."

"But we can't ignore the way you left Hannibal ten years ago, under the cloud of a scandal involving another woman," Jones joined in. "Seems Lucy Bates's death was also connected to you, and—"

"She died two days after I returned to the university," Frye pointed out harshly. "I didn't tell her to take that potion, and had I known she intended to, I would've—"

"We believe you, Damon," his boss reassured him with a shrug, "but we can't let this matter drop until we figure out who's responsible for that recording. Justine Ransom was the head of an old, respected family, and the fact that she could've gone over the edge because of this *voice* everyone thinks is yours—

not to mention the sizable fortune she left behind—can't be swept under the rug. It made the front page of the *Courier Post*."

"Any idea who could've altered that Edison record, son?" the chief asked.

He swore under his breath, stuffing his hands into his pockets. "Sure, I could give you his name," he replied bitterly. "And because he was nowhere near Justine for weeks before her death, and because he, too, is of an old, respected family, his alibi's far tighter than mine."

Cruikshank scowled. "You're not helping your case if you don't tell us who you suspect."

His patience snapped, not because these two men were quizzing him, but because Hannibal—and Celesta—had once again convicted him without knowing the facts. Only Lucy Bates could prove he wasn't responsible for her death, and poor old Justine was so feebleminded at the end she probably didn't know whose voice coaxed her into the river. The two dead women knew the culprit well, but they weren't likely to identify him.

"I suggest you ask Miss Montgomery to reconsider the evidence," he said sarcastically. "As the creator of Sally Sharpe, Girl Detective, she should be able to sleuth this one out herself. If the villain doesn't get to her first."

Harlan and the lumber baron exchanged a wary glance. "If you think Celesta's in danger—"

"I think my reputation has been sacrificed to the rumor mill once again. You said you were going to release me. What are the conditions?" Frye demanded.

Cruikshank cleared his throat. "I felt it best, under the sensitive circumstances, to relieve you of your supervisory duties—"

"You've fired me, to show your support?" Damon exclaimed. "Wonderful! What do I tell them in St. Louis?"

305

"I've already dispatched a message to Barnett, Haynes and Barnett, insisting that your exemplary architectural skills will still serve them well. In any place but Hannibal."

"And what do *you* have to add?" he asked the bulkier man. "That I may freely ply my trade, but should be forced to wear a scarlet letter—M for Murder—so decent people will know my crimes and not subject themselves to my evil presence?"

Chief Jones frowned. "We're doing this for your benefit, just until we can—"

"Then, unlock the damn cell!" Frye blurted, rattling the barred door at them. "Let me enjoy my *freedom*, starting now! Let me indulge in my rights as a law-abiding citizen, despite the big black question mark that'll hang over my head forever!"

Harlan took a key from his pocket, his jaw clenched. "You'll be the first to know when we've cracked this thing, Mr. Frye," he said tersely. "Meanwhile, I strongly suggest that for your own protection, you steer clear of Hannibal until we notify you—"

"Don't bother." His tone was icy as he left the cell with his luggage. "I should never have returned, and now there's nothing here to come back for. Good day, gentlemen."

"You *what?*" Celesta's voice rang shrilly around the police chief's little office. "I can't believe you'd let that—that murderer *go*, when it's so obvious he killed my Aunt Justine!"

Harlan Jones let out a sigh that suggested he was already weary of this investigation. "As I've tried to explain, Miss Montgomery, we had nothing solid to hold him on—"

"You want solid?" she jeered, grabbing the wax cylinder from the top of his desk to shake it at him.

"I've given you the most damning evidence against Frye—"

"And we'll both be sorry if you hit me in the head with it." Jones looked steadily at her from his desk chair, clasping his hands over his middle like a priest awaiting a confession.

Celesta exhaled slowly and lowered the cylinder. "I—I'm sorry. Mr. Frye has upset me."

"So I've noticed." He fingered the Edison record and looked at her, his strained patience showing in his eyes. "And had Mr. Frye *struck* Justine with this, we'd have him. But this is merely a recording, Celesta, not a weapon. Frye didn't force your aunt to listen to it, did he?"

"No," she mumbled. "Justine loved her phonograph long before he came to live with us, but—"

"And had she been her normal, lucid self she would've seen through the attempt to coax her over the cliff—would've accused Frye herself," he added quickly. "Unfortunately, it's common knowledge that your aunt lost her mental balance several weeks before her demise, after a fire probably caused by her careless smoking. I'm very sorry, Miss Montgomery, because I held Justine in highest regard, but I can't incarcerate a man for merely making a recording. If I could, every irate businessman who owns one of those newfangled dictating machines would be subject to arrest, for the threats in his recorded correspondence."

He had a point, but that didn't settle the impotence that roiled her stomach. "What am I supposed to do, then? That's Frye's voice on the cylinder, and if the Chief of Police refuses to help me while the wealthiest man in Hannibal ushers the suspect out of town—"

"He said you could solve it yourself. Said the creator of Sally Sharpe would sift through the evidence and figure out who dunnit."

She planted a hand on her hip. "And I suppose

he knows?"

"Says he does, but he wasn't telling *me*, either. If you've got any clues, little lady, I'll be happy to help out. Games like this can get nasty if they're allowed to continue."

Games? She straightened to her full height, realizing now why she'd never thought much of this hulking, awkward lawman who dared refer to her as a *little lady*, with his crocodile smile. "Why would I want to help you?" she muttered as she turned toward the door. "You're an incompetent, double-dealing—no better than Damon Frye! Thanks for nothing, Mr. Jones."

It seemed only fitting that as she stalked up the hill to the Manor, a gray brigade of clouds rolled in on the horizon. Of *course* Chief Jones would tease her about putting clues together like she did in her stories, as though the *little lady* was only fit to fight crime in the dimers! And Frye had put him up to suggesting that! Which made perfect sense, because Damon was once again pointing at Patrick Perkins, perpetuating their feud over Lucy Bates.

She'd thought of Patrick right off, after the initial shock of discovering the altered cylinder. He'd never liked Justine, and he *had* brought her some new Edison records, and, lover of mechanical devices that he was, he no doubt had a dictating machine in his office. And she'd known for most of her life what a mimic he was; he'd proven that the day he aped Justine in the music room!

But Perkins also knew he'd never get away with such a warped trick because she would figure him out. As the head of Perkins Lumber, Hannibal's third-largest mill, he couldn't afford to be associated with such a scandal. And he had no need to kill the woman who'd stand between him and the Ransom fortune because if he *were* financially strapped, he could've married any number of wealthy socialite daughters months ago—girls who wanted *him*. She'd certainly told him enough times that she didn't.

So, while Patrick had the motive, means, and opportunity to cajole Justine over the cliff, his case wasn't nearly as compelling as Damon's. Frye had every reason to capitalize on his closeness to the family, and he'd nearly done it—nearly married the new heir to the Ransom estate. Only he could play upon Justine's weakness for him. Only he could've orchestrated their engagement so perfectly, except he'd failed to remove the one puzzle piece he assumed she wouldn't stumble onto.

These thoughts, along with Katherine's fretfulness, made the evening seem endless. Her aunt bemoaned cooking for just the two of them, and when the thunder and lightning announced a storm after dinner, she became so nervous Celesta nearly asked her to sit on her hands. She'd stitch for a few moments on her sampler and then pull the yarn out, claiming she'd miscounted.

To avoid watching this wasted effort yet again, Celesta looked out at the turbulent sky. The rain splattered loudly against the window, drowning out the scratchy strains of Katherine's record, and the lightning looked like ragged, electrical wounds on the black face of the night. A particularly close clap of thunder made her aunt jump and then stick her pricked finger into her mouth.

"I wish we weren't so isolated up here," she whimpered. "Damon was such a comfort during a storm. Even Ambrose had his ways of distracting me when the weather kicked up, and I . . . I wish those days weren't over."

She didn't need Katherine to remind her how Frye's presence had affected them all. This was his sort of night, and a glance at the white latticework of the gazebo, illuminated by another sudden flash, brought back memories of his tempestuous love-making, of declarations she'd believed all too quickly. Since such recollections served no purpose now, she tried to direct her thoughts down a more constructive path.

"Who do you think made that awful recording?" she asked thoughtfully. "Damon, or Patrick Perkins?"

Katherine looked up from her needlepoint, startled. "There's a chance Mr. Frye didn't?"

"Certainly. Patrick brought new cylinders, as you'll recall—"

Her aunt nodded slowly.

"—and you've heard how he could imitate voices, and you know how he disliked Justine," Celesta continued.

Katherine shrugged. "He apologized for causing the disturbance that day she sent them home."

"And you felt it was sincere?"

She let out a short laugh. "Personally, I've never felt young Mr. Perkins had a sincere bone in his body. He takes after Eula, the way he touts himself as such a paragon."

"Do you think he despised Justine enough to kill her?"

She stitched for a moment, pursing her lips as she considered the question. "I don't think he feels that passionately about anything, except himself. He didn't pursue *you* all that diligently, even though Damon seemed to be egging him into competition."

"Do you think he wants our money? I certainly didn't dangle any other prizes in front of him," she said wryly.

Katherine chuckled and shook her head. "To hear Eula tell it, Perkins Lumber is neck-and-neck with Cruikshank's, more profitable than when Tom was at the helm. And frankly, I don't think he's sharp enough to put all the details, and the timing, and the . . . the words, together so perfectly."

Celesta nodded, glancing out the window at the storm. "And you think Damon could?"

"I don't think he *would*," she replied in a firm, small voice. "I—I just wish Justine would've kept their new records separate, or labeled them. I wish she'd have *told* us about that awful message instead of listening until it became too real for her to deny. I wish a lot of things that'll never come true, Celesta, and it's not getting us one step closer to the man who led her on. But it has to be one of them."

Katherine's lament echoed her own frustration. Such mysteries were so easy to solve when Sally Sharpe was investigating, even when she didn't know which suspect was the culprit when she began the story. Why did real life have to be so complicated? Celesta sensed the answer was pointing its finger, laughing in her face, yet Damon had apparently taken her powers of perception when he stole her heart. First Mama and now Justine, and she had a feeling, despite Chief Jones's unfortunate choice of words, that for someone she knew very well, this murder business was indeed becoming a game.

She scowled out the window, listening. Was that a horse approaching, or the sound of rain driving against the house?

Katherine, too, puckered her brow and rose to look outside. "Was that a whinny?" she fretted. "Surely no one would be out in this storm."

Unless he's up to no good, Celesta mused darkly. She and her aunt gasped at the rapid-fire thunderclaps and kept staring out until the next flash of lightning revealed a rider on a tall, skittish horse. He was cursing his mount, trying to keep a tight enough rein that the creature couldn't toss him off into the mud. His hat was crammed low, and his cloak, though sodden with rain, whirled dramatically as he fought for control.

Her aunt grabbed her arm, nearly pinching it off, as the horse neighed frantically and reared with the

311

next blinding flash. Its dark front legs pawed at the sky, and they could see the whites of its eyes quite clearly.

Celesta walked decisively toward the fireplace and grabbed the poker.

"Whatever are you doing?" Katherine breathed. She glanced outside again and clutched at the lace bow on her blouse. "He's dismounted, and—"

"And if it's Patrick or Damon, we certainly don't want him getting a jump on us, do we?" she replied. "Who else would have business here on such a night?"

Katherine sucked in her breath as the loud pounding on the back door echoed in the hallway. "I—I don't—perhaps it's Bill Thompkins, come to check on us. Dear God, did we lock that door? He's going to beat it in!"

"I guess we'd better find out." As Celesta approached the back entry, she could see it vibrating with the force of the man's blows, and her heartbeat sounded puny in comparison.

"Open up, damn it! I know you're in there!" came the man's muffled voice.

Grasping the poker, she glanced at her aunt, who was too shaken to nod. If only Damon were still on their side, protecting them. But it was up to her to identify their caller and hope she reacted properly, and in time. The light here was so dim—

"Damn it, do I have to break a window?"

"I can't tell who it is," Celesta said in a frantic whisper.

"I—I suppose we'd better ask." Katherine inhaled deeply and approached the crack that ran around the door. "Who's there?" she demanded in a wobbly voice.

"I didn't come all this way to be left standing out in—"

"Throw the lock and step aside," Celesta whispered, raising the poker above her head. "By God, we'll teach him to announce himself properly."

Her aunt complied and jumped back as though the lock had bitten her. With a whoosh of spray, the door flew in. The tall, dark intruder splattered them with cold rain as he clumped inside and then fell against the door to close it with a *whump*.

Celesta gripped her poker, telling herself it wasn't too late to disable him—even though he towered above her and his haughty presence filled the back hallway. Katherine stood at a distance on the other side of him, peering anxiously, as though she didn't really want to know who it was. Damon or Patrick they would've recognized by now, but this monster of a man made no effort to reveal himself. He stood, panting for breath, looking out from beneath his dripping hat brim as though their feelings of mistrust were mutual.

Finally he stood free of the door, and it was then Celesta noticed he had a peg leg. She stepped back, still clutching the poker in hands that were growing numb with apprehension.

"Put that fricking thing down before you hurt someone," he muttered.

"I'll put it down on your head if you don't state your name!" she cried. "We weren't exactly expecting guests!"

Slowly he reached for his hat, his gaze sweeping from Celesta to linger upon her aunt. Katherine paled, trembling, as the broad, black brim came up over a smooth head that was splotched with scars and had a fringe of dark hair around it. His brown eyes glimmered, unmoving, as a long, low cry escaped the little woman's throat.

"Ambrose—" she breathed, and then fainted into a heap on the floor.

Chapter 26

Celesta glared at her uncle as he shrugged out of his soggy wraps. "You could've at least announced yourself so we—"

"And I'd still be out there in the storm, wouldn't I?" he retorted.

"Then, you could've sent word ahead, rather than—"

"There wasn't time. The telegraph from Thompkins made it sound like all hell was breaking loose," Ambrose said as he let his cloak drop to the floor, "and someone had to take charge before the family fortune fell into the wrong hands."

That explained Bill's nervousness when she'd tried to encourage his attentions toward Katherine, but *this!* "So you've really been in hiding, letting poor Katherine assume you died in the *Phantom* explosion—"

"You always were perceptive, for a girl," he said with a short laugh.

"—and while you wouldn't return to take care of *her*, you've come running when your damn money's at stake?" she spat. Celesta knelt to cradle her groaning aunt, glowering up at him. "That stinks, Ambrose."

"I've missed you, too, Celesta," he replied as he

315

glanced around the hallway. "I'm going upstairs for dry clothes. Knowing Katherine, she hasn't had the heart to clear out my belongings."

She glared after him as he walked slowly past the summer parlor toward the main stairs—step *clunk*, step *clunk*. Damon Frye had once seemed the epitome of arrogance, but this haughty uncle's reappearance topped anything her former fiancé had pulled. Let him discover for himself that the armoire in the master suite now held nothing but the Sally Sharpe dimers Aunt Katherine insisted upon saving! "Be ready to answer a *lot* of questions!" she hurled after him.

Ambrose turned, his scowl intensified by the scars on his head. "I've got a few for you, too, you little schemer," he snarled.

Was this truly the man her aunt still idolized? Celesta didn't remember him being so ruthless . . . so *cruel*. Katherine was coming around now, moaning as she tossed her head from side to side. Her poor aunt was in for a rude awakening, after more than a year of pining for the only man she'd ever loved, and Celesta had a feeling they'd learn some startling, distasteful things before this night was over.

"Let's get you onto the settee in the parlor," she murmured, placing her hands under Katherine's arms. "You'd better brace yourself. The storm's just beginning, now that Ambrose is back."

"Ambrose?" Katherine's voice was high and childlike. Her eyes fluttered open, and she sat against Celesta's supporting hands. "I . . . I had the most haunting dream, dear, about—"

"It was no dream," she replied quietly. "Uncle Ambrose is home."

Her aunt's hazel eyes widened fearfully. "We've seen his ghost, then. My Ambrose died during the boiler explosion aboard—"

"That's what we all thought," Celesta said, patting her aunt's arm as she watched the confusion cloud her pale face. "He must've had some very compelling reasons for playing dead all these months—"

"Yes, he's dead," she confirmed with a confident nod. "He's in Heaven, and Justine's joined him and Rachel now. They're all together with . . ."

Celesta swallowed a painful lump of emotion as Katherine prattled on about the souls of their departed kin. No good would come of arguing about where Ambrose Junior's spirit was *really* headed, so she gently helped her aunt to her feet. "Let's sit in the parlor, beside the fire," she said as she guided Katherine's steps. "We've had quite a shock, and you need time to adjust. That's it . . . sit right here. I could use a cup of tea. How about you?"

"Tea would be lovely, dear."

She hesitated to leave the shaken woman alone, but it was the best way to confront her uncle before he upset his wife any further. Celesta hurried in to put the kettle on, and just as she was coming through the dining room she heard his uneven tread upon the stairs.

Ambrose Ransom, once graceful and athletic, hobbled down to the bottom of the stairs still clad in his damp clothes, exuding God's own wrath. "Why does my home look like a whorehouse?" he demanded. "You can't tell me my sister paid for this garish red paper! And the master suite looks like some floozy's—"

"That was Justine's room, actually," Celesta replied, crossing her arms to return his harsh gaze. "Your wife convinced her that the Manor deserved a proud, new image for the coming century, and—"

"Don't feed me that," he jeered. "My sister was so tight she squeaked, and—"

"—the bathrooms were her idea, too," she continued above his sarcasm. "Did you think our lives would come to a standstill when you *died*, Uncle?

Did you want your money to gather dust in the bank while your wife and sister rattled around in these dreary old rooms, letting progress pass them by?"

He snorted. "An interesting question, coming from the urchin who stood to inherit after Rachel and Justine passed on. You must be terribly sorry to see me, Celesta. Hope I didn't spoil too many plans."

Her slap resounded in the stairwell, and she gasped when Ambrose grabbed her stinging hand. "How can you even think—what? Are you insinuating I *wanted* them gone? That I may have done them in? *There's* a new wrinkle!"

He shoved her away to stroke his reddening cheek. "Bitch!" he muttered. "Rachel filled your head with her own romantic fantasies, and frankly, I wasn't surprised at your choice of fiancés. Thompkins has been a faithful captain, keeping me informed when something of importance happened. And when I heard you'd wormed your way into this house and brought that underhanded Frye with you, I knew it was only a matter of time before I'd have to rescue my family's good name and estate."

Celesta felt like throwing up. "How noble of you to return," she said with a sneer. "And since you've had the benefit of an informer—and since my aunt would still be in a heap by the door, were it up to you—you damn well owe us an explanation, Ambrose. Katherine thinks she's seen your ghost, so be *very* careful how you address her, or I'll—"

"My, my but we've grown presumptuous," he said with a sardonic chuckle. "Let's not forget whose home and social position we've taken advantage of since—"

"Let's not forget that only a *coward* would let his devoted wife believe him dead!" she blurted. "Katherine deserves better, and you know it! Were Grandfather alive, he'd boot your yellow ass out."

The burly man on the step above her didn't reply

318

for several seconds. He smoothed the fringe of hair surrounding his scarred pate, as though her comments had finally found a heart to hit after all. "Is that the kettle whistling?"

"Yes. I'm making my aunt some tea."

"I'll have some, too—and a sandwich of some sort. Haven't eaten since before I left St. Louis."

"There's beef in the ice box and bread on the counter," she said coolly. "I've left Katherine alone long enough. Join us in the parlor when you've prepared your explanations."

She'd won this first battle of wills and words, but as she arranged the tea tray Celesta felt the hollowness of her victory. Never a gracious loser, Ambrose would retaliate—as though he hadn't shocked and hurt them enough! Her remarks about his cowardice had struck a deep wound . . . what was it Katherine once said? That he never felt he measured up to Grandfather's high expectations?

Losing the *Phantom*, the very foundation of Ransom shipping, must've confirmed his self-doubts and driven him into hiding. Like an animal in pain, Ambrose might lash out at them any time they reminded him of his failures—as his wooden leg surely did, every step he took—and Celesta prayed that for her aunt's sake she could hold her tongue. His reasons for feigning death would *never* justify the anguish he'd caused his wife, but it wasn't her place to pick at his wounds.

She paused in the parlor doorway to assess her aunt's condition. Katherine had remained on the settee, looking like a beautifully behaved little girl with a graying upsweep. The bow at her collar was askew, but otherwise she appeared unruffled by her husband's unexpected appearance.

"Our tea should be brewed just the way you like it by now," Celesta commented as she set the sterling tray in front of her aunt. She poured two steaming cups, carefully gauging the little woman's mood. "Ambrose is eating a bite, and then he'll join us. I'm sure he has much to discuss."

No comment. Katherine stared into the swirling steam above her cup as though it were sending her some sort of message.

After a few soothing sips, Celesta tried for conversation again. As long as Ambrose was taking to eat, he must be stalling—he *should* be embarrassed, by God!—and the waiting was making her anxious. "Your molasses crisps are delicious," she said as she took a second one. "Nobody bakes cookies like yours, Aunt Katherine."

The little woman glanced blankly at her but made no move toward her cup.

Her stomach felt like someone was threading a drawstring through it. Never in her life had she seen Katherine Ransom so detached . . . so ominously quiet. "Are you feeling all right?" she asked. "Did you hurt something when you fell?"

Katherine looked toward the crackling fire as though she hadn't heard a word.

The drawstring tightened. Celesta set her cup down and slid onto the settee to put her arm around her aunt. "I know Uncle Ambrose gave us quite a shock," she pleaded, "but if something's wrong, please tell me! It's not like you to—I know! Blink once for yes and twice for no. Did you bite your tongue or bang your head when you fell?"

The hazel eyes in front of hers remained focused on her upper lip, unmoving.

"Try again—one blink is yes and two means no. Are you in pain, Aunt Katherine?"

Her gaze wandered aimlessly to the tea tray, but she didn't pick anything up.

Celesta's pulse pounded in her temples. *Dear God, no! Not another mind unraveling even as I watch.* "Talk to me!" she demanded, clutching her aunt's slender shoulders. "Tell me who I am! Tell me who you are! Tell me anything at all, just—"

"I see Katherine's retained her flair for the dramatic," Ambrose commented dryly. He was leaning against the doorjamb, watching them.

Celesta pivoted to face him. "You did this!" she hissed. "You gave her such a scare she doesn't even know who she is."

"She looks perfectly healthy. She'll come around when she gets tired of being ignored, so I suggest you and I have our chat," he said as he took the chair facing the settee. He eased down carefully, compensating for his wooden leg. "You'd better listen closely. I probably caught my death riding in this storm and I'm exhausted. Do you realize it's damn near impossible to say on a horse when you have only one knee?"

His martyred attitude made her seethe, but she held her fire. Better to get the facts from him and be done with this "chat" before it turned into another quarrel that would upset Katherine. "I assume you lost your leg when the boiler exploded?"

"Indirectly. The blast hurled me into the river, and I was battered by flying debris," he replied quietly. "Thompkins insisted a surgeon see to the gash in my leg, but I refused. Knew the doctor wouldn't respect my anonymity . . . and when I became too weak to fight him, Bill moved me to a hospital in St. Louis. Gangrene had set in, so amputation was my only recourse."

Celesta glanced at her aunt, who was lost in her own little world. "And your anonymity was more important than a grieving wife and sister?"

"At the time, yes." Ambrose shifted his weight, his eyes following Katherine's lack of reaction. "The shipping business is extremely competitive, Celesta, and it's the only trade I've ever known. Had I come home unable to work again, I'd have gone mad. My

321

friends would've patronized me, and Justine and Katherine—well, surely you know how it was between them. My sister would've harped at me constantly, and at my wife for waiting upon me, and Katherine would've smothered me in pity."

He knew his women well, but Ambrose Ransom was clearly a slave to his vanity. Despicably self-centered. "So you allowed the passage of time to bury your deceit. You figured you'd left Justine and Katherine wealthy enough to live out their lives in comfort—"

"Without the burden of a scarred-up cripple," he finished.

Celesta looked away in disgust. Perhaps it was best her aunt didn't comprehend Ambrose's hypocrisy. "You got here in one piece when you thought Damon Frye and I were making off with your money! In a storm, no less."

"Bill made it sound like an emergency. It wasn't raining when I left my apartment in St. Louis."

"Maybe Bill was tired of keeping up your pretenses," she said bitterly. "I can't imagine him being party to such a lie all these months!"

Her uncle chuckled and leaned over the side of his chair to toss another log on the fire. "He wouldn't hear of it, at first. It was he who pulled me unconscious from the river—as well he might, since he'd gone over the side before the explosion. The boiler was his responsibility, you see."

She studied the man across from her. "You're saying he jumped ship, knowing disaster was at hand? And you played upon his guilt to keep yourself hidden away—blackmailed him into silence so he could remain in Hannibal. As your spy."

Ambrose smirked, his dark eyes sparkling. "Who would've guessed my pretty little niece had such a fine mind?"

"And who would've guessed my illustrious uncle

322

was such a sham and a cheat?" she countered. "Don't think I'm going to keep your little secrets!"

"Why not?" he asked, cocking his head as though considering the possibilities. "This home's the perfect hideaway. It's removed from town; my widow won't be expected to entertain anytime soon, now that Justine's gone . . . if indeed she's capable of it."

Glancing at her aunt, Celesta felt the color rushing up her neck. She leaned forward, pointing at the man whose dark eyes taunted her . . . much as Damon's had at times. "I refuse to act as though you're the dear departed head of this household," she blurted. "When I realized how Damon conned Justine into the river, I had him arrested. And for the ways you've hurt Aunt Katherine, I could just as easily—"

"Spine as well as intellect, eh?" he cut in. "Will your talk be so cocky when you realize how much your taletelling will cost you?"

"What have I got to lose?" she scoffed. "Thompkins was concerned about his integrity, but when you've been the maid's daughter most of your life, status doesn't mean much."

"But the Ransom fortune does," he mocked. "Now that you've had a taste of life on the hill, I doubt you'll want to return to Eula Perkins's employ. Bill tells me young Patrick was none too pleased when you so brazenly broke your engagement to him by flaunting your affections for Mr. Frye. You have a lot to learn about finding favor with men, Celesta."

She stood, clasping her hands to keep from striking him. "And you have a lot to learn about me, if you think—"

"You have your price, like everyone else. You're bold enough now, but when your name's to be stricken from the will—"

"And how will you do that, without consulting the lawyer?" she demanded.

Ambrose tented his hands beneath his chin, studying her. His rumpled suit didn't hide the tough, masculine physique Katherine had always loved. His face, while not as striking as Grandfather's, still bore a regal Ransom virility and would've been handsome had his conniving not lent a weasellike sharpness to his features.

Had he always been this devious? Or had Katherine overlooked his baser motivations, as she usually did when a man paid her some attention? Frye had certainly fooled her—more than once—and Celesta wondered if her silent aunt would ever realize what sort of ogre lived beneath her husband's stunning exterior.

Her uncle's gaze shifted to Katherine, and Celesta's mouth went dry. She shouldn't have pressed him about the will. She should've humored him until her aunt—or Thompkins—was aware of the new scheme he was dreaming up.

"I'm glad you asked about the lawyer," he said after a nerve-tautening pause. "I'd have to confine you to the house—starting now, of course—and have Bill bring up supplies and check on you and Katherine, who, rumor would have it, had both fallen ill. His ministrations would lead to matrimony, and since Katherine's so obviously unfit to oversee the Ransom estate, Thompkins, as her husband, could do whatever he—under my direction—wished with her money. You'd be left penniless, dear child. The story has a few holes in it, but none that couldn't be patched by a man who's made death work to his advantage for the past year."

Celesta dropped to the edge of the sofa. He'd reeled off that story with total sincerity, and she'd never been more frightened in her life. Ambrose Ransom, Jr., had no qualms about holding a niece hostage, forcing his witless wife into a bigamous marriage, and controlling his rescuer's life even more onerously than before—all to prove how powerful he was. He hadn't so much as spoken to Katherine; seemed convinced her mind would remain fogged in—as though he'd planned it that way—and was ready to play her like a pawn without a moment's hesitation.

If only Justine were here to stand with her . . . if only Damon hadn't turned traitor. Celesta reached for her aunt's hands to quell the overwhelming loneliness she felt in the face of this evil that had invaded their lives. But Katherine's fingers merely curled up in hers, and then she frowned and pulled them free, as though she'd never seen her niece before now.

Ambrose laughed low in his throat while he scooted to the edge of his chair. "Have you reconsidered?" he asked, rising to his imposing height. "You've lost your mother, and your aunt Justine, and your handsome prince—and for all practical purposes, you've lost Katherine, I fear. Is the brief satisfaction of exposing me worth losing your inheritance, too?"

As his shadow fell over her, Celesta felt panic pumping through her veins. This madman looked ready to strangle her! His large hands flexed at his sides, and although Ambrose appeared to be awaiting her answer, she could feel him tensing like an animal ready to pounce if she gave the wrong response.

She bolted sideways off the settee, and when her uncle lunged to catch her she dove for his wooden leg.

"You goddamn—"

Ambrose fell against the spot where she'd been sitting, and Celesta didn't waste a moment of her advantage. She scrambled toward the door, not daring to look back. Her life—and probably Katherine's—depended upon finding someone who could protect her while exposing her resurrected uncle for the viper he was.

The list of heroes seemed terribly short: she couldn't trust Bill Thompkins, couldn't rely upon Police Chief Jones. And who else would believe her if she awakened them in the middle of the night with such an incredible story?

The wind chilled her, and the rain had slackened to a quiet drizzle. If she stopped to saddle a horse, Ambrose could trap her in the stable. If she ran, he'd catch up to her on horseback. The sound of his hurried, uneven clumping across the hallway tiles nearly drove her insane—until other footfalls caught her attention.

Her uncle's mount, left out in the downpour, trotted toward her with a curious whicker. Now that the storm had blown over he seemed eager for company. The stirrups were so high she had to spring toward the saddle horn and haul herself up to get a foothold, but by the time Ambrose threw the door open behind her she was racing toward town on his horse.

Chapter 27

Patrick Perkins looked up from his ledgers, scowling. Surely no one would be pounding on the door at two-thirty in the morning . . . must be the screen banging, and he'd best hook it before it woke Mother. If she saw his mathematical jugglings between these two sets of books, months of planning and patience would be for nothing. Better to let her brag that Perkins Lumber was still the second most profitable mill in Hannibal—because it soon would be again, if all went as he anticipated.

Good things come to those who wait, he thought smugly as he padded downstairs. He tied his dressing gown more securely, swearing under his breath while the racket from the vestibule resounded around the ground floor. What could anyone possibly want that couldn't wait until—

He yanked the door open and forgot the cutting remark he was about to make. Celesta stood there, quaking with the cold, her eyes wide with desperation. Patrick felt a smile warming him all the way to his bare toes: she'd finally come back to him, and his problems would soon be solved. So would Celesta's, if she played along.

"What in God's name? Get in here before—" He was all concern, questioning her with his eyes as he shut the door on the brisk wind. "Where's your coat, honey? You'll catch your death if you stay in these wet clothes."

"You've got to help me," she blurted. "I'm afraid for Katherine, and there's no one else I can trust to—"

He pulled her close, chafing her cold, damp dress sleeves. "We've been friends forever, Celesta," he reminded her. "Now come into the kitchen and tell me what's wrong, over a hot cup of tea."

"I—I'm not sure this can wait until—"

"Who was at the door? It's only—oh, my!" Eula's yawn turned to a gasp when she saw Celesta in her son's arms. "Is it Katherine, dear? I know how she frets during a storm."

Inhaling deeply to still her galloping heart, Celesta let Patrick's warmth seep through to her clammy skin. "You won't believe what's happened," she rasped, still gulping in air. "I rode down here as fast as I could. Had to tell *someone*—had to get away before—"

"Before what?" Patrick asked warily. "If Frye's after you, I'll haul Jones out of bed, and we'll put his ass back in jail, where it should've been—"

"Not Damon," she said, shaking her head emphatically. Aware of Mrs. Perkins's stare, she eased away from Patrick. Eula's face was pale with the creams she wore to bed, and her former employer was likely to turn whiter yet unless she worded her announcement carefully.

"When it was still storming, we saw a horse and rider approaching the Manor," she said urgently. "We didn't recognize him—didn't want to let him in, of course, but he kept beating on the—"

"Who?" Patrick demanded.

Celesta blinked, startled by the brilliance of his blue eyes. "Ambrose. Uncle Ambrose is home, after all this time we thought he was dead. He's been in hiding ever since the *Phantom* sank."

"My stars!" Eula exclaimed. "Katherine must be beside herself."

"She fell over in a faint and hasn't been normal since she came around," Celesta replied. "I hated to leave her, but when things got ugly, Ambrose threatened to—"

"You're sure it's him, and not some imposter worming his way into your bank accounts?" Patrick asked. He hoped his frown expressed concern rather than the sick feeling he had in his stomach right now.

"He has some scars and a wooden leg, but it's definitely Ambrose," she replied firmly. "What can I do? Katherine's speechless with shock, and when I said I'd expose his underhandedness, he threatened to hold me hostage and force her to marry Bill Thompkins so—"

"Whoa, there! This makes no sense at all," Patrick said, guiding her toward the kitchen. "We're going to sit down and hear the whole story over tea. No sense rushing over to Harlan's until I've got all this straight."

"You don't think Katherine's in danger, do you?" Eula asked, clutching the neck of her satin wrapper. "Ambrose is a burly fellow, but I never considered him capable of violence. At least not toward her."

Celesta thought for a moment. "I . . . I suppose she'll be all right for a while. He was too full of himself to pay much attention to Katherine."

"Fine. Now, start from the beginning, and I'll take over from there," the blond beside her commanded.

She allowed him to steer her toward a chair in the shadowy kitchen while Eula rushed to put the kettle on. Her teeth were still chattering from her ride in the rain, and that drawstring she'd imagined in her stomach was pulled until it would snap if she didn't settle herself.

The familiar sights and scents of the Perkins kitchen soothed her; she reminded herself that these two people had been an intimate, daily part of her life until a few months ago. Why did she hesitate to reveal Ambrose's horrible story and threats? Why did she sense, as Patrick and Eula took their places at the small table, that they would use her vulnerability to their own advantage?

It was too late to regret coming here. The high-pitched whistle of the kettle announced that tea would soon be served . . . the beverage she'd gossiped and lamented over for most of her twenty years . . . the drink that had ended Mama's life, and now marked the start of renewed ties with the house where she had died.

Celesta cleared her throat. "Well, it started when Katherine and I heard an approaching horseman," she began in a voice that sounded too timid to be her own. "He beat on the door, demanding to be let in yet refusing to identify himself. I grabbed the poker, but he was so tall and powerful he could've snapped it in two, I think."

"Oh, my," Eula breathed, glancing away only long enough to pour their tea. "I would've been petrified! And you two all alone up there in that house—why, we might not've found you for days, had it been a stranger."

"He's not the Ambrose I remember," she replied with a shake of her head. "Paid no attention to Katherine when she keeled over and . . ."

Patrick listened to her account with resigned patience, because now that the head of the Ransom household had returned from the grave, as it were, his grand designs were tumbling into a tomb of their own. As she told about Bill Thompkins's involvement and outlined Ambrose's plan to hold Celesta hostage while forcing Katherine's marriage to his spy—all to keep his holdings beyond this trembling waif's reach—he realized how frightened she was. Ordinarily Celesta would've seen the gross improbabilities of the scheme her uncle had cowed her with, but his sudden reappearance and her aunt's reaction had sent her mind into a tailspin . . . which could work to his advantage, until he found out what

Ambrose Ransom, Jr., really intended to do.

"You did the right thing, coming here to tell us about this," he reassured Celesta. He reached for her hand, so small and fragile in his own. "He never gave you or your mother a thought before the *Phantom*'s boiler exploded, and it's obvious he still considers you beneath him, even though you've cared for his wife and sister these past several months."

"Who would've guessed he had the gall to deceive Katherine so?" Eula said with a disgusted shake of her head. "She's my concern, now that you've gotten away from—"

"But I doubt he'll do her harm," Patrick insisted. "She can't challenge him, and if he's rattled off such a scheme to protect his secrets and his money, he's no doubt formulating more lies now that Celesta's gotten away. Katherine may be his ace in the hole. He won't hurt her as long as she can be useful to him."

Celesta nodded, relieved. She still didn't trust Patrick and had never felt comfortable confiding in Eula, but their influence and protection would prevent Ambrose from carrying out any of his rash plans. Their involvement meant that Harlan Jones wouldn't look the other way as he had when she produced the incriminating evidence against Damon Frye. She didn't feel entirely secure now, but at least she wasn't fighting by herself.

"What do you think I should do?" she asked quietly.

Patrick stroked her hand between his. Lord, she was a beauty with her flushed cheeks and huge green eyes, her ebony hair tumbling in windswept disarray around her shoulders. All was certainly not lost, now that she'd returned to his home.

"Why don't we all get some sleep," he suggested, "and I'll take you to see Jones first thing in the morning. Ambrose won't go anywhere—he'll wait to be confronted. And we'll be sure he's exposed for the scoundrel he is before he deceives anyone else."

331

"Thank you," she whispered.

Eula reached over and squeezed their joined hands. "You'll always have a home here with us, Celesta," she said in an emotion-choked voice. "I'll get you a nightgown, and you can sleep in your old bed. Patrick will see your uncle gets his due, and I'll be sure Katherine's out of harm's way. We've missed you, Celesta, and it's the least we can do."

As she ascended to the bedroom she had occupied for so many years, Celesta had a strange feeling she'd betrayed Mama, and Katherine, and even Justine by coming here. But where else could she turn? Ambrose was a force she couldn't handle by herself, and the Perkinses were the only close friends she had now that Damon was gone. It was frightening to be so alone.

They made an odd foursome as the carriage rolled up in front of Ransom Manor the next day. Patrick's blue eyes blazed protectively as he looked toward the windows for signs of Ambrose, while his mother fretted about what they should do for poor Katherine if she still wasn't talking. Police Chief Jones had looked skeptical about coming—seemed to think this whole story about Ambrose Ransom's return was a hoax Celesta dreamed up to infuriate him further. When Patrick chided him for letting Damon Frye escape unpunished and suggested someone else could handle his position more effectively, however, he agreed to hear Ransom's story for himself.

As she was helped down between Patrick's strong hands, Celesta's pulse throbbed weakly. "I hope he doesn't do anything impulsive. I hope Aunt Katherine's all right," she murmured, glancing fearfully toward the door.

"Everything'll work out, I promise you," he replied firmly. "He may be conniving, but he's nobody's fool when four witnesses are present."

As though anticipating their purpose, her uncle opened the door and stepped outside, his wife beside him. "Welcome, friends," he said jovially. "I imagine after what Celesta's told you, you have some questions. Please come in! Katherine's got tea brewing."

While Eula stared openly at the scarred, peg-legged man, Celesta felt the chief's eyes questioning her, felt Patrick's grasp tighten on her arm. "Be ready for anything," she murmured. "He's obviously changed his ploy."

"Why don't you and Mother help with the refreshments? Harlan and I can start quizzing your uncle."

She nodded, a lump of fear hardening in her throat. What if Katherine were behaving as the perfect wife because she'd been threatened? What if she never recovered her faculties or her ability to speak? The little woman was smiling at her now, an oddly detached expression, and it took every ounce of Celesta's courage to approach her.

"How are you today?" she asked as they preceded her uncle into the hall. "You look rested in spite of our little . . . surprise."

"You—you must've been *quite* surprised," Eula twittered with a nervous glance toward Ambrose, "but if my Tom returned, I know I'd be speechless with joy myself."

Once in the kitchen, Celesta grasped her aunt's hands and looked her over. She saw no bruises or signs of abuse, only a dear, familiar face with a faraway smile. "Are you all right?" she whispered earnestly.

Katherine nodded once.

"Thank God she understands now," Celesta breathed as she glanced at Eula. She rubbed her aunt's cool, freckled hand, wondering how to proceed.

"Can you talk to us, dear?" Mrs. Perkins asked. "If

there are things you'd rather we didn't repeat, we'll certainly understand. It must've been such a shock to see Ambrose standing there."

Again her aunt nodded, and then pulled away to arrange cookies and the tea pot on the silver tray she'd laid out.

"She can't answer yet. We'd better not press her," Celesta mumbled. Yet when Katherine picked up the tray, she took the other side of it, forcing her aunt to look at her. "Do you understand why I had to leave last night? Why I came back with people to help us this morning?"

Her hazel eyes went blank for a moment. Then she started purposefully toward the door, silently insisting the tray was her responsibility.

Celesta blinked back sudden tears as she and Eula followed Katherine to the front parlor. "She'll recover in time, dear," Mrs. Perkins insisted softly. "At least she's performing like the gracious hostess she's always been. No telling what stories Ambrose may have filled her poor muddled head with while you were gone."

When they entered the men's company, it was clear that her uncle had indeed changed his tune to suit his own purpose. He patted the spot beside him, inviting Katherine to share the loveseat as though they'd made up for more than a year apart, and she complied.

"The stories Celesta's told you have done their job," he said, smiling at each of them. "I hope my niece will forgive me for taking advantage of her flustered state. Poor dear was so agitated she threatened me with a poker! But I knew she'd be back with responsible people—people who can prepare Hannibal for my unexpected return. I can understand why my family and friends would question my motives and past actions, and I want their confidence in me to be restored."

Celesta took a seat beside Patrick, glaring at her

334

uncle. "So you're making me out as a liar? Telling the Perkinses and the police chief I was out of my head? I *know* what I saw and heard last night!"

"And I think you'd better state your case pretty quickly, sir," Patrick added emphatically. "I won't be party to some slick game you intend to pull over on—"

"Oh, it's no game! And believe me, I understand your concerns," Ambrose said, casually dropping two lumps of sugar into his cup. "My deception undoubtedly strikes you as callous and cruel, but hear me out! What man, having been robust and vigorous in every way, would willingly return to his home a cripple? I lost more than a leg in the explosion, gentlemen. At the risk of being indelicate, I'll just say that some of the qualities Katherine admired most no longer serve me. I had to face that about myself . . . had to have a plan for success in other areas before I returned to her."

Celesta could see that Harlan and Patrick were swallowing the line about his lost masculinity, but to her it sounded like a sympathy plea. "How much of what you told me was true, then?" she demanded. "Was Bill Thompkins your liaison to Hannibal and your family?"

"Yes, and he's been paid handsomely for it," Ambrose replied, his dark eyes looking directly into hers. "And now that I can take care of my own business, he no longer has to keep my secrets."

"So you're saying that story about holding your niece hostage and remaining here, in hiding, while Thompkins took your, uh, place with Katherine, was merely an idle threat?" Jones leaned forward, apparently enjoying this turn of events.

"How could I possibly get away with such a scheme?" Ransom replied with a chuckle. "I was merely rattling Celesta so she'd do something rational. And here you are!"

"I don't believe a word of this," she muttered, but

when she scooted forward Patrick took her elbow.

"And why are we so important?" he demanded. "Why the shenanigans at Celesta's expense? Any decent man would—"

"Any shrewd businessman would realize the repercussions of returning from the dead," he countered. "The plans I have require a foundation of trust, based upon my previous integrity. When people think they're seeing a ghost, in the guise of a one-legged man with scars, their reason flies out the window. Bless her, poor Katherine's proof of that, and I hope you'll bear with her. She's greatly improved but—"

"Don't change the subject. What's this plan you keep hinting at?" Perkins eyed the man across from him. Ambrose Ransom was banking upon his physical disabilities and family name to reestablish himself, and the whole story turned his stomach. He sensed Celesta's instincts were right, and that the burly coward had only returned to protect his fortune . . . which wasn't what Patrick wanted to hear.

"I'm starting up the shipping business again," Ambrose stated with boyish enthusiasm. "Never cared for my father's macabre names and outdated steamers, so now's the perfect time to begin anew. And instead of one vessel on the Mississippi, I'll have three—*King's Ransom, Queen's Ransom,* and in honor of my lovely niece, *Celestial Fortune.*"

She sucked in a furious breath, but managed to hold her tongue as her uncle continued. He was doing this to provoke her—overextending himself financially instead of easing back into business, and making a mockery of Grandfather's empire!

". . . and of course such a venture requires the unquestioned backing of my banker," he was saying, "as well as the quick completion of my three new steamers. That's where I need your help. When you return to town, I'd be forever grateful if you'd spread the word of my return—get people excited about my new venture, get a story in the *Courier Post*. My wardrobe and belongings should arrive from St. Louis by tomorrow, and then I'll be ready to answer to Hannibal society."

He gazed fondly at Katherine and took her hand. "My wife and sister have done a wonderful job of redecorating our home, as though they were anticipating just such a rebirth. When my steamers arrive, we'll host a christening party like this town's never seen—a coming-out my darling certainly deserves, for the agony I've put her through this past year. Won't that be wonderful, love?"

Katherine was gazing raptly at him, but when her smile went out of focus he looked at each of his guests. "I'm sure you'll understand that this lovely lady and I have some catching up to do," he said pointedly. "If she's to be recovered for her return to society, she'll need your understanding and support. And her rest."

"We were just leaving," Eula stated, standing suddenly, "and you can count on Celesta and me coming regularly to check on her."

Celesta blinked, but at Patrick's urging they said hasty goodbyes and were boarding the carriage within minutes. The ride was shrouded by an oppressive silence, as though each of them was stunned by what they'd seen and heard.

Celesta sat numbly on the swaying seat, wishing she could sort the truth from the hypocrisy. It wasn't her concern how Uncle Ambrose spent his money, but—any sensible person would know not to sink so much into a shipping enterprise in this era of railroads and—

"This is an outrage," Eula's muttering finally ended the silence, "and he's lost more than his manhood if he thinks people will fall for it. And the way he scared Celesta into playing his pawn! I wouldn't blame you if you never spoke to that insufferable bastard again!"

Celesta couldn't help smiling, just as she couldn't miss the way Patrick was grinding his teeth to keep from exploding. "I—I hope you don't think I made up those things I said last night just to—"

"Of course you didn't," he replied more brusquely than he intended to. He forced himself to give her a lingering look, which softened as an idea occurred to him. "I know you're concerned about Katherine," he said quietly, "but I think for your own protection you should stay with us rather than returning to the Manor. I don't trust Ambrose any farther than I could throw him. How about you, Harlan?"

The police chief grunted. "Damndest stunt I ever saw. And with his money, he'll get away with it."

"Then, it's settled," Eula clucked. "We'll fetch your things, and you'll be back in your own room, dear. It's probably best your aunt's so far gone she doesn't realize what he's up to, because the husband she adored is still buried with his father's steamer, far as I'm concerned."

Why wasn't her heart glowing with gratitude? Her friends were siding with her against a ruthless schemer, but she found little comfort in their support. Mrs. Perkins had implied she had a job again, a roof over her head—and Jones was grudgingly admitting she wasn't merely a hysterical little lady after all. And Patrick—

Well, Patrick's deep scowl suggested that today's events had upset him more than he cared to admit. And Celesta had the uneasy feeling it would affect his dealings with her.

Chapter 28

Hard work and the familiar routine of the Perkins household were balm to Celesta's soul. In addition to the cooking and errands, Eula asked her to do as much fall cleaning as she could find time for, because the two interim housekeepers had left the windows unwashed, the rugs unbeaten, and dust clusters under the beds.

Patrick was quick to praise her meals and the improvements he saw around the house, yet Celesta sensed he had other things on his mind. The third day after her return, when Eula was attending her Ladies Aid meeting, the handsome young heir to Perkins Lumber sauntered into the kitchen at noon and pulled her into a ravenous kiss.

"It's been so long," he murmured as he ran his hands over her firm, rounded hips. "This house has been like a tomb without you, Celesta. When you came to your senses and had Frye arrested, I felt a flicker of hope and prayed that—tell me you missed me, too, honey."

His blue eyes were delving into hers, and his golden hair and skin glowed with the warmth of his words. But he would never fill the void Damon left, could never mend the heart the crafty architect had shattered with his betrayal. She couldn't tell him

339

that, though—and she couldn't rebuff her gallant defender's affections until she was sure Uncle Ambrose meant her no harm.

Celesta's kiss was sweet and gentle, so innocent for a woman who'd been had by the likes of Frye, he thought. Soon she'd respond to his fire . . . soon she'd give him the satisfaction he deserved, even though her money was temporarily out of reach. Together they'd remedy that. Celesta was smart, capable of revenge against an uncle who'd made a fool of her while floating her inheritance down the river.

Patrick released her with a final brush of his lips, frowning as he noted her reddened knuckles. "Mother works you too hard," he muttered. "It's time she thought of you as her future daughter, a lovely young woman who shouldn't smell of ammonia or have chapped hands."

Celesta shrugged. "It's better than living under Ambrose's thumb. And the house does need some looking after."

"Not every waking moment. Not to the point you've got no time for your writing . . . or for me." He flashed her an ornery smile. "Meet me at the office tomorrow and we'll eat dinner in town. Wear the choker I gave you, honey. If you still have it."

"Of course I do," she mumbled.

"Ah. You knew all along I'd be the man you married—the man who's adored you all your life," he said in a reverent voice. "You won't be sorry you got rid of Frye. I'll show you what you've been missing, Celesta."

A few minutes after twelve, Celesta entered the warehouse of Perkins Lumber despite the gnawing feeling that she should run the other way. The cavernous room, stacked with sweet-smelling boards

340

and kegs of nails, echoed eerily with her footsteps. The employees were out for their noon meal, yet Celesta wondered if she was being watched. Something seemed to be lurking around the corner . . . were those footsteps, stopping when hers did?

It's your wild imagination, which needs to be exercised on paper, she told herself. *It's the beating of the tell-tale heart Poe wrote about, the narrator's own pulse driving him insane.*

Then she did hear steps, light and pert, and she gasped when a pretty young woman swayed around a tall set of shelves. "Joy! You startled me," she yelped, sounding like she'd been caught with her drawers down in the boss's office.

Miss Holliday smiled slyly and kept walking. "Enjoy your dinner with Mr. Perkins, Celesta. He's certainly . . . excited about it."

Celesta turned before the secretary could see how red her face was. Why did men have to brag about their conquests? Why did she feel like she was sneaking around, when eating dinner in public was a perfectly acceptable way to be seen with Patrick?

Or was dinner what he had in mind? Celesta's steps faltered as she reached the door to his small, secluded office, because Perkins was gazing at her as though she had no clothes on. The sunlight from the single window made his red-blond hair glimmer like a halo, yet his expression was anything but angelic. His white shirt displayed broad shoulders and a lean physique accented by his stylish suspenders. He loosened his collar.

"You came," he murmured.

"Of course I did. We agreed to meet for dinner—"

"Come here. All morning I've been imagining you with your hair done up, wearing a pretty dress," he said in a low voice, "and I'm not disappointed. Maybe, if I'm lucky, you wore that red lingerie under it. Had a devil of a time convincing Miss Holliday to

341

leave so I could find out."

Her mouth went dry. Before she could flee, Patrick grabbed her hand and pulled her close, shutting the door and then trapping her against it. "Patrick, I—somebody could barge in—"

"Not likely. They're getting double pay to stay away for the next hour," he purred against her ear. "Celesta, feel what you're doing to me, honey. I need you so damn bad."

She was momentarily stunned when Perkins pressed her palm against his crotch, but then she shoved him away. "Of all the humiliating—to tell your employees I was coming here so you could—"

"I never said a word about—"

"Well, Joy certainly knew! Maybe from experience, am I right?" It was the wrong thing to say, but she refused to become this man's plaything, the whispered-about mistress of Perkins Lumber.

Patrick sucked in his breath, catching her subtle rose perfume and the indignation that flashed in her eyes. The scarlet flowers in her dark, tapestry-pattern dress set off the velvet choker gracing her neck . . . her slender, sensitive neck where the vein pulsed visibly.

He dropped his hands and stepped away from her. "Girls like Miss Holliday pale beside you, Celesta," he whispered, watching her circle away from him. "But you're nobody's fool. You know that to keep dancing you have to pay the piper, and he's certainly played you a gracious tune. I've given you a job, a home again. A little kiss before dinner seems an appropriate reward for my generosity, don't you think? You never refused Frye when he asked."

She didn't dare turn her back on him, and her caution gave him the advantage he needed. Patrick walked slowly toward her. When she bumped back against his wooden desk, the sound rang like a knell in the stuffy little office.

"Patrick, please don't hurt me. I didn't mean to—"

"You don't have a thing to worry about, my love," he murmured, his smile tight with desire. "You know what I want, and you're no stranger to a man's needs. Used to drive me crazy, thinking about you and Frye together. But now you're mine, and we can express our passions freely and skillfully, without any shy fumblings."

Celesta leaned backward to evade his kiss, yet again he had her trapped. He held her, and while his free hand yanked her dress up over her knees he claimed her with another kiss. The fact that she *had* been with Damon proved to her what a selfish, uncaring lover Perkins was, and it gave her the presence of mind to jerk her face away. She pushed against his chest, but he only chuckled and pulled her closer.

"You know me well, Celesta, and I'm glad I never lost faith that you'd someday be mine," he murmured. "Challenge me, sweetheart—your struggle excites me. God, I hate it when a woman just lets me. Nothing less satisfying than someone who lies there and takes it."

Celesta had no intention of giving in to him, but with Patrick wedged between her legs, leaning her backward onto his desk top, she was at a distinct disadvantage. He was moaning, burrowing his head between her breasts while she thought frantically of ways to fend him off. Her hands were shoving at his shoulders, a futile effort until the heat of his palm at the top of her thigh startled her into action. Suddenly she was grabbing his neck, clutching him desperately.

His eyes widened. "Two can play that game, Celesta," he rasped, "and you can't possibly win it."

To prove his point, Patrick grasped the velvet ribbon on either side of her heart-shaped locket and pulled it so tightly it could've strangled her. For a moment, she saw bright flashes of light, and her head

343

started to spin. When her hands dropped limply to her sides, he released her.

"Don't ever threaten me," he warned. "Women who don't give me what I want are always sorry, honey. Believe that, and I'll never have to put you in your place again."

Wheezing, Celesta was too dazed to protest when he slid her back until she was lying flat with her hips at the edge of his desk. Her neck still throbbed where the metal locket had bruised it; she wondered why her captor appeared to be moving so slowly when her blood was rushing through her body at an alarming speed. If she didn't distract him soon, he'd have her drawers down . . . already her skirts were fluttering around her waist as Patrick drank in her exposed thighs and underthings.

"I'm glad we don't have to hurry," he breathed, smiling now that she was so compliant. "Most of my life I've daydreamed about what you'd look like naked . . . how lovely you must be beneath your simple dresses. It was worth the wait, Celesta."

When he leaned over her to take a tapestry-covered breast into his mouth, Celesta squeezed her eyes shut. There had to be a way—this rapist in rich man's clothing wasn't going to claim her! Pretending to stroke him, she kept panting for breath while drawing both feet up along the outsides of his legs. Once her heels reached his hip bones she could surely thrust him backward and—

A loud shattering of glass made them both gasp, and then a heavy object thudded against the side of the desk.

"Son of a—who'd put a brick through my window?" Perkins demanded, rushing toward the jagged pane.

Celesta scrambled to her feet and grabbed the timely projectile to defend herself. "There's a note attached," she said, eyeing Patrick nervously. "It reads, 'Miss Montgomery—and her money—will never be yours. I'm wise to you, Perkins. Better watch your back.'"

"Is it signed?"

"Would *you* put your name on such a note? Who knew I was coming here?"

"I could ask you the same thing," he jeered, snatching the brick from her hands. He read the message and exhaled with contempt. "Whoever wrote it's behind the times if he thinks any of your uncle's money will end up in your name. Is that Frye's handwriting?"

She wished desperately that it were. Despite his nasty habit of leading women to their graves, Damon Frye was much better company than the bully she was with now . . . and odd as it seemed, Patrick sounded peeved enough that her money might be behind his interest in her, after all. Had she been as blind to his motives as she'd been to Frye's?

"Damon writes a much neater hand," Celesta replied quietly. "Close as I can tell, that was written by Ambrose himself."

He gaped, and—as she'd hoped—lost all interest in their tryst. "From what I've seen, he has no plans to pass the estate on to—he'll be broke by the time those three steamers are in the water, and everyone knows it. That's all people are talking about."

"Perhaps he's protecting me, rather than an inheritance that wasn't mine to count yet," she said as she backed toward the door. "Or perhaps he thinks the inspiration for the *Celestial Fortune* deserves better than a tawdry desktop seduction. Or it could be that Katherine's come to herself and convinced him—"

"Get out of here," he spat, bitterness rising like bile in his throat. "Takes more than a brick through my window to sidetrack me from the woman I've always wanted. And not a word of this to Mother," he warned sharply. "We'll take up where we left off when I get to the bottom of this."

The sparkle in her green eyes as she shut the office door made him swear violently. Damn her, had she duped him again? It made no sense for Ambrose Ransom to pull such a juvenile stunt, and he doubted Frye would risk showing his face in Hannibal. Which meant that just as when they were growing up, Celesta had probably bluffed him.

He was getting closer, though. As Patrick swept the shards of glass from the office floor, he smiled to himself, whetted by the viewing of her primly clothed beauty. Frye might've been the first to win her favors, but his own victory would be more permanent—and more lucrative. Because he'd tipped his hand, the raven-haired heiress would be leary of his advances now, but by God he would find a way to claim her. It was a matter of creating the right situation—the right time and place, with irresistible bait—so that Celesta Montgomery could no longer refuse him.

Chapter 29

"What we need is a party!" Eula exclaimed. "Despite the unsettling events these past weeks, your twenty-first birthday shouldn't go uncelebrated, dear. And the fact that it's on Halloween has always been an excuse for a masquerade. What do you think?"

Celesta smiled and continued folding clothes. "We did have some memorable parties when I was in school—"

"And our ballroom's been much too quiet since Tom passed on," her employer insisted. "We need music and dancing, gossip and games! Why, I feel excited just thinking about a masked ball! We'll have a huge cake—and it'll be the perfect way to get your aunt Katherine into society again. Surely Ambrose wouldn't deny her an evening out because of that infernal leg."

She chortled. "If anything, he uses his peg to spark conversations. It doesn't keep him from clumping down the sidewalks in town, pumping hands like a politician."

"He thrives on his notoriety, doesn't he?" Eula picked her own underthings out of the laundry basket and began to fold them into piles on the kitchen table, where the two of them sat. "I hate to

347

speak ill of your kin, Celesta, but I still think he played a despicable trick on his wife and sisters, and I'll never trust him again. Patrick tells me the bankers have the same qualms, even though the Ransom fortune is considerable collateral against those three new steamers."

Mrs. Perkins always discussed other peoples' money as though it were a member of their family and subject to the same speculation, just as she always held her son's ideas up as gospel, so Celesta merely shrugged. "After the Jekyll-and-Hyde switch he pulled on me, I can't pretend to know what he's plotting. And I really don't care, as long as he's tending to Katherine."

The woman beside her nodded. "She certainly looks normal. I just wish she'd start talking again," Eula clucked. "Nearly a month it's been since she uttered a sound, and besides worrying her friends, it can't be good for her marriage. Lord knows living with Ambrose must be a strain these days . . . she surely has things to say to that underhanded husband of hers."

"She writes him notes. Nasty ones, at times."

Perhaps it wasn't proper to discuss such matters; but the past few weeks had been lonely ones, and Celesta craved female chatter. She made sure she was never alone with Patrick, but since her circle of family and friends had shrunk so drastically, she couldn't keep from discussing her personal concerns with Eula Perkins. "When I was visiting a few days ago, she seemed on the verge of laughing with me— just blurting something out. But it wouldn't come."

"Perhaps with time," the little blonde consoled her. "We can only hope and pray, and wait."

Several moments passed while they folded the clothes. Celesta was pleased, as much for Katherine as for herself, that Eula wanted to have a party. She was a lavish hostess, and she would use this as an opportunity to flaunt Patrick's successes with Perkins Lumber for the first time since his father died. It would give them something to look forward to, add a purpose to days that bored her with their predictable tasks and housework.

And perhaps the anticipation would spark her creativity again. She finished a Sally Sharpe story two days ago, but sensed the Girl Detective's sleuthing lacked its usual luster. Even though she was back in her childhood room, where her pen had first found words, the atmosphere was charged with Patrick's suggestiveness and the poignance of Mama's unslept-in bed . . . and the unshakable feeling that the solution to her mother's poisoning was right here, if she only knew where to look. Her birthday was two weeks away, yet she was no closer to naming the killer than when she'd promised herself she'd do that.

Eula's shriek brought her out of her woolgathering. "Mouse!" she cried, her gaze locked on the far corner of the kitchen. "It darted along the baseboard, a fat little gray thing—"

As Mrs. Perkins's hysterics continued, Celesta's pulse began to pound. There was only one logical solution. "I'll go to the druggist's for some crystals," she said in a mute voice. "The colder weather's driving them inside. We can't have mice taking over, right before the party."

The little widow blinked and finally dropped the skirts she'd hiked up off the floor. "Yes—yes you should, dear," she mumbled. "Where there's one mouse, more will follow. Such loathsome creatures! If you'll go right now, I'll finish this folding for you."

Minutes later Celesta was strolling into the business district, prickling with tension. What would happen, now that cyanide was once again present in the Perkins household? Patrick was being stiffly polite these says, still brooding over their interrupted rendezvous, while Eula chattered non-stop—pointedly ignoring her son's interest in the maid. Celesta felt like the little mouse that scampered into hiding, because she had a feeling that the next two weeks would reveal the identity of a bloodthirsty cat: the person who had murdered Mama . . . and who might try for her next.

That's dime novel mentality and you know it, she chided herself as she walked toward the post office. *The Ransom deaths and Ambrose's resurrection are too much in the news these days; where Justine and Mama's ends seem too dissimilar to be connected, a third heir's passing would point up a scandal demanding an investigation. Any smart murderer would know that.*

Celesta stuffed her latest Sally Sharpe story into the outgoing mail slot. It was silly to feel so nervous about rat poison! The subject would never have occurred to Eula, had that mouse not excited her; a woman planning the biggest costume ball of the season wouldn't kill the guest of honor!

Would she?

Staring blankly at the rows of metal mailboxes, Celesta tried to halt her frantic thoughts. Mrs. Perkins had no reason to want her dead: she was the finest housekeeper the niggling little widow could keep on, and despite Patrick's insistence that he wanted to marry her, she had no aspirations toward Eula's precious boy.

And Patrick—if he were truly after her money, he certainly wouldn't poison her. If anything, he'd be after Uncle Ambrose for putting the Ransom fortune out of reach.

A quiet chat with Mama, or a dose of Justine's practical insight, would certainly do her good about now. Aunt Katherine could give her no advice, and she didn't want to upset the poor woman—or let

Ambrose overhear her concerns. She had a sudden, overpowering urge to feel a strong pair of masculine arms around her, to hear Damon's low, resonant voice reassuring her that he'd see her safely through the coming days.

Celesta closed her eyes, lulled by the hiss of the lobby's steam radiators. Damon seemed very near to her right now, and as she imagined his handsome smile she heard him saying, *Nothing's changed between us, sweetheart, but you must trust me—and realize that your clouded perceptions keep you from seeing who really killed—*

"Are you all right, Celesta? Can I get you something?"

She blinked away her daydream of Damon and found Bill Thompkins standing to one side of her, peering anxiously through his spectacles. "Thank you, no—I—it's so blustery outside, I was just soaking up some of your heat before I leave," she stammered.

The postal clerk nodded doubtfully. "Awfully chilly for October."

A moment's tense silence passed. Celesta had been ready to fetch the check from her box, but even though Thompkins probably knew now that her New York uncle was really her publisher, she hesitated to raise any questions. Ever since Ambrose's return, his informer had acted extremely busy whenever she came in, and his lingering now, as though he were going to say something that was terribly difficult for him, made Celesta uncomfortable.

"Well, I have errands to run for Eula, so—"

"Please—I—can't tell you how horrible I feel about deceiving you and your aunts, Celesta," Thompkins uttered. He ran his hand through his hair and shifted from one foot to the other. "Dozens of time I swore I'd tell Katherine her husband was

351

alive, yet I was afraid to. She's so easily upset, and when Rachel died and then Justine, there hardly seemed a good time to tell her about Ambrose."

The man beside her was truly distraught, and she hoped no one else came into the post office before she heard his whole story. "What made you summon him, then?" she demanded in a low voice. "She was adjusting fairly well to Justine's—"

"Ambrose saw the obituary in the *Courier Post* and contacted me," he replied. "Suspicions of foul play were in the air—you were accusing Damon Frye of driving your aunt over the cliff—so I sent an urgent telegraph to him, under his assumed name. Had I known he'd start for Hannibal so quickly, I would've warned you."

Celesta glanced toward the window, considering his confession. "So he came charging in during the storm, hellbent on catching me with my hands on the bank accounts. He knew it was Justine who put a stop to my visits when Grandfather died, and he assumed I was getting even by killing her—or having Damon do it. I don't suppose he had any way of knowing that his sister had come to love me?"

"Probably not. Correspondence was risky, so I only notified him of important events, like Rachel's passing, and mentioned that you were living at the Manor," he replied ruefully. "I should've told him later about how well the three of you ladies were getting on—how lively Katherine was, and how even staid old Justine was loosening up because you and Damon gave them something to live for. But I doubt Ambrose would've believed his women were faring so well without him."

A smile twitched at her lips. "Proud to a fault, isn't he?"

Thompkins let out a mirthless laugh. "So proud he was ready to die of gangrene rather than live as a one-legged man. But I'm not much better. I found myself wishing I'd have let him rot, for the cruel way he was deceiving his wife. I've often regretted that I didn't remain aboard the *Phantom*, as any responsible captain would've, so I might've died with honor rather than living to have a hand in such a scheme. One mistake led to another, and once I agreed to keep Ambrose's secret, I doomed myself to carrying out his lies. It was a coward's way out, Celesta, and I can understand why you'd detest my very presence."

Bill Thompkins's abject outpouring shed new light on the tale she'd heard only from her uncle's viewpoint. Well she knew how domineering Ambrose Ransom could be, how determined he was to maintain his powerful position and reputation, at other people's expense . . . and Bill Thompkins, as an employee who'd jumped ship, was the handiest man to sacrifice.

"You couldn't have foreseen his treachery, Bill," she said softly. "The way Ambrose tells it, you saved his life—twice—which more than compensates for fleeing a boiler that would've blown anyway. And your concern for Katherine has certainly been genuine."

"Oh, yes," he said with a wistful shake of his head. "Indecent as this may sound, I was praying for the day your uncle would pass on so I could court her—as you apparently were prompting me to do—yet I had a feeling this scheme would backfire. At least her reputation's intact."

Celesta patted his arm. "From what I can tell, so's yours. No one's mentioned your part in keeping my uncle's existence a secret, or in keeping him alive."

"A crumb from the table of the almighty Ambrose," he commented wryly. "When the *Phantom* went down, we crewmen lost our livelihoods for a while, so at least the hush money bought food until I landed this postal job. Since then I've banked the cash he's sent. Can't stand to look at it."

"I'd say your earned it," Celesta said firmly, "and as far as I'm concerned, you owe no one an apology. You saved my uncle's life and then accepted terms he wouldn't let you refuse. Who could've done any differently? And who would've believed you, had you exposed Ambrose for the scoundrel he was before he showed up in the flesh?"

He grinned shyly. "You've got a point there. But I'm still concerned that Katherine'll hate me when she learns—"

"I won't tell her," Celesta insisted, "and you can be sure Ambrose won't admit needing your help, after all his ballyhoo about buying three new steamers. Confessing your part in the story would do Katherine no earthly good, that I can see . . . and if you want to tell her when she's recovered, I guess that's your business."

. Bill's eyes looked more liquid than usual as he adjusted his spectacles. "Thank you. You've been very kind," he murmured.

"My friends are precious and few these days. Can't afford to lose any to grudges and petty misunderstandings." A sigh escaped her, and then there was another awkward silence until Celesta brightened with a sudden idea. She grinned at Thompkins. "What're you doing Halloween? Eula's hosting a birthday party for me, and I'd love it if the Troubadours would provide the music."

He chortled. "No one misses a Perkins party if he can help it. We'd be pleased to play—but are you sure Patrick'll go along with this? Rumor has it he's after your hand."

"What he's after is the main reason I want him to be holding a bass fiddle that night," she replied with a wink. "Eula will see it that way, too, so we've got him outvoted."

Thompkins returned to his post behind the counter, chuckling, while Celesta quickly took the envelope addressed to Lester Montgomery from her mailbox. Now that the air between them was cleared she felt much better about buying the cyanide crystals Eula sent her after. Somehow she would solve Mama's murder, and somehow Patrick would figure out that marrying her wasn't the solution to his financial problems—if indeed he had any. She would rely upon herself, as she always had, and the pieces of her life would someday fall back into place.

A brisk wind from the river made her hurry along Broadway and into Hoskins Drugstore, where Eula always did business. She nodded to people she knew and stepped up to the counter, where Robert was counting little pink pills into a vial. When he glanced at her, Celesta reminded herself to sound firm rather than fearful. "I need some cyanide crystals, please. Eula saw a mouse in the kitchen, and she won't rest until it's dead."

The druggist smiled and handed her a fat paper packet. "Must be the weather, 'cause folks're sure buying me out of this stuff. I'll put it on her account."

She thanked him and turned toward the door, but was stopped by a familiar voice. "Are you sure the rat's name isn't Ransom, Miss Montgomery? I hear you and Ambrose haven't spoken a civil word since my visit to the Manor with you."

Celesta pivoted, aware that the store had become extremely quiet. Police Chief Jones was watching her, awaiting her answer. "I think that's our business rather than yours," she replied in a low voice.

Jones looked her over with a smirk. "The way Ambrose tells it, you and that Frye fellow were in it together, working your way toward the family fortune a little early."

"And you'd believe a man who's been playing dead for more than a year?" she challenged. "If Katherine could talk, she'd tell you what's really gone on, and—"

"Like you say, Miss Montgomery, that's Ransom business," the chief stated with a sardonic chuckle. "Just consider yourself warned before that poison gets put where it shouldn't be. I get paid to keep watch."

Celesta gripped the small sack to keep from smacking him with it. "And I bet Ambrose pays you well," she muttered, and then she whirled around and strode out the door.

Chapter 30

As the hour of her birthday party approached, Celesta felt anything but happy. All week she'd cooked and cleaned because Eula didn't hire any other help. Only the cake came from the bakery; the elaborate canapés, petit fours, and punch were her own creations. And now, as the three of them draped black and orange streamers between the ballroom sconces, Mrs. Perkins was even flightier than usual.

"Have we forgotten anything?" she fretted. "I haven't entertained in ages, and I'm so afraid I've overlooked something or failed to invite someone, or—"

"*My* concern is that we have no unpleasant encounters," Patrick said, eyeing Celesta pointedly from his perch on the ladder. "Harlan Jones anticipates a squabble, and ever since you behaved so brashly at the druggist's, he's been asking about you. If you can't call a truce with your uncle, I hope you have the sense to stay across the room from him tonight."

"It's not my fault he's such a bully!" Celesta insisted. "Every time I check on Aunt Katherine, he hovers about as though I'm going to walk off with the family silver."

"He's been terribly rude," Eula chimed in. "I

357

wouldn't have invited him if Katherine weren't so fond of parties. Lord knows she needs an outing, so I hope Ambrose behaves himself."

"Well, you didn't help matters by asking the Troubadours to play," her son snapped. "How am I supposed to intervene if he gets hostile? I'd hoped to be dancing with Celesta instead of playing that damned bass all night."

Eula let out an airy chuckle. "I'm sure you'll find a way, son. You always manage to get what you want."

Patrick glared after her until her footsteps were echoing in the hallway, and then turned to Celesta. "Mother's right, you know," he stated in a low voice. "Tonight you're mine, so don't try to avoid me by accepting offers for every dance."

Whose party is this? Celesta bit back her retort as she handed him the last of the black and orange candles for the sconces. First Eula had heaped all the preparations on her, and now Patrick was telling her not to enjoy herself. What a fine twenty-first birthday she was having! And to make matters worse, she had a nagging feeling that something far more ominous than a squabble with Uncle Ambrose would turn the masquerade into a crashing fiasco.

She dressed carefully that evening, unable to shake the sensation that irrevocable events would follow each other like falling dominoes tonight . . . and that Patrick would start the chain reaction. He'd been watching her closely, like a panther analyzing its prey—and Eula had been observing them as though she, too, expected dire consequences if things got out of hand at the party.

It was enough to make Celesta wonder if the cake's candles were loaded with dynamite . . . or if the punch in her cup would somehow get spiked with cyanide.

Celesta ran her hands over her luxurious crimson velvet gown, the indulgence her New York uncle had paid for. Its fitted bodice followed her curves down to a peaked waistline and a full, bell-shaped skirt that whispered lushly when she turned in front of her mirror. The elongated cuffs, which closed with ten tiny buttons, hugged her forearms and then flared into huge leg-of-mutton sleeves. A scalloped neckline daringly displayed the ivory hollows of her collarbone, and Patrick's choker was the perfect accessory, even if she wished it had come from someone else. She'd never looked lovelier, yet she couldn't seem to smile.

As Celesta sat in front of her vanity to arrange her hair, she pondered another unsettling circumstance. She'd been the first person downstairs this morning—or so she'd thought, until she heard a rustling in the pantry.

"Eula?" she'd called out as she walked through the kitchen. "May I get you something? If you can't sleep, I'll fix you some—"

She swung the door open to an empty pantry, and the sight of a fat mouse lying belly-up on the counter made her yelp. Were those footsteps retreating outside, or the beatings of her own heart?

When she opened the outside door she saw no one, and only when she turned back inside did she notice the sack for the rat poison lying on the floor. She and Eula had dusted the crannies of this room and the kitchen, yet Celesta could've sworn at least a third of the poison was left. All appetite for breakfast vanished as she picked up the empty sack.

The first thing she checked was the sugar bowl she alone used now . . . the bitter almond aroma she sought wasn't there. Or did the sweet spiciness of the little cakes and cookies for the party mask the tell tale scent of the cyanide? Reason told her that neither Eula nor Patrick would sprinkle the refreshments with the lethal powder, but all day she'd been wondering where the rest of it went . . . and who took it.

Now, as she put the last pin into her elaborate hairstyle, Celesta fought the tightness in her stomach. It was very hard to celebrate a birthday she feared would turn into a death day—*there's your runaway imagination again,* she chided herself.

The Perkinses weren't brazen enough to do her in while Hannibal's upper crust looked on. Were they?

And they certainly had no motive for getting rid of her . . . did they?

"Enough of this," she muttered as she stood up. From her window she saw a wagon pull up and Bill Thompkins directing his musicians as they unloaded their instruments. Soon there would be music and dancing, gaiety like none of them had enjoyed since before Mama's passing. *You've got to go, for her,* she thought staunchly. *You must pretend this is the happiest night of your life while you figure out what's happened to that poison.*

Celesta donned her mask and managed a subtle smile: the vixen in the mirror looked every bit as brazen as she'd hoped. The red velvet mask, edged in rhinestones, covered just enough of her face to render it provocatively mysterious. Everyone would know who she was, and she'd be highly visible, which certainly played to her favor tonight.

She took a deep breath and went downstairs.

Patrick saw her, and his breath caught in his throat. She was carrying trays of food from the dumbwaiter to the long refreshment table, a scarlet vision that stirred something primal within him. Then he scowled. It was Celesta's birthday, yet she was the serving girl—had received no help with preparations all week, now that he thought about it.

His mother needed a good talking to, for trotting his intended out as the maid while they were entertaining Hannibal's elite. It wasn't as though they couldn't afford a couple of girls to perform these menial tasks—

Patrick's throat went dry when he caught sight of his mother's smug smile. She wore an elaborate, layered dress of brilliant blues, teals, and greens with a feathered headpiece that also formed a mask—a peacock's head, complete with a golden, glittery beak and eyeholes. Sequins and spangles caught the ballroom's low light and made her shimmer as she flitted from the dais to the arched entryway to greet the Troubadours.

She was up to something. Eula Perkins assumed these moods when she was ready to manipulate people and events—he'd seen his father fall victim often enough to recognize the signs—and Patrick suspected that either he or Celesta would have to comply with her wishes tonight or be subjected to some bitter medicine.

The sight of Celesta's cleavage made him forget his unpleasant thoughts. God, she looked ripe in that dress, so richly attired that every man present would marvel at the transformation from the housekeeper to the host's lady. The glimmer of the golden heart at her throat made him smile: Celesta had chosen the scarlet dress to wear with his choker. She was finally learning her place.

"Put your tongue back in your mouth," Thompkins teased as he walked by with the music stands tucked under his arms.

Perkins chuckled and then grasped his elbow. "Start the evening with a couple of numbers I don't have to play in, so I can greet our guests—"

"You'll be too busy gawking down her front to notice who comes in," Bill grunted.

"—and after the intermission, I'll want to dance with her," he added. "Status has its advantages, and I intend to take every one of them."

He clapped Thompkins on the back and rushed

over to assist Celesta with a large crock of punch. "You look absolutely ravishing," he murmured as he relieved her of the heavy vessel. "Your mystique would be ruined by a stain on this magnificent gown, so allow me to refill the bowls tonight. You're the guest of honor, after all."

He couldn't read the thoughts behind her deep green eyes, because the crimson mask, with its twinkling rhinestones, covered her facial expressions. "Thank you," she replied, and went to fetch the last tray from the dumbwaiter.

The Troubadours began tuning to Bill's pitch pipe, and then the various instruments trilled through familiar passages from the ensemble's repertoire. The candles were flickering above the gracefully draped streamers, a spicy scent of mulled cider teased at his nose, and the refreshment table looked ready to collapse beneath the spread Celesta had prepared. All was ready, and his first time hosting his peers and competitors would be the most talked-about event in Hannibal for weeks . . . the hard, circular lump in his pocket assured him of that.

He guided Celesta toward the doorway. "Let's greet our guests," he said with a pleased smile. "For the rest of the evening we'll let them serve themselves so you can enjoy your party, darling."

Her hand felt clammy in his, a sign that she shared his excitement. Her ebony hair was braided around her head with strings of crimson glass beads, and her matching earrings dangled enticingly down her ivory neck. She was probably wearing his scarlet lingerie as well—perhaps had been inspired by the way it complemented her coloring—and he made a note to provide plenty of red for this splendid creature's wardrobe . . . red that made his pulse pound for her.

". . . and of course you know my son, Patrick," his mother's voice cut into his thoughts. He greeted the couple clad as a gangly hare and a ponderous tortoise, and recognized them as one of Hannibal's other lumber barons and his obese wife.

"Bertram, Agatha," he said as he clasped the man's furry glove. "And in case you haven't met our birthday girl, this is my dearest friend, Celesta."

Guests were gathering in the hallway now, admiring each other's costumes and trying to guess who was wearing them. The most prominent doctors, lawyers, and lumbermen were here, men whose ranks he was about to join as he assumed his father's social status—and they were all enthralled by the woman at his side. It was an auspicious beginning for the new era of Perkins Lumber, and Celesta deserved a reward for making it possible.

"Meet me on the back veranda during the first intermission," he whispered. "I want you to myself for a few moments. And save me some dances, all right?"

She nodded almost imperceptibly as she greeted the next guests, John Cruikshank and his wife. Damn she was a tease! She knew precisely how much he wanted her and was playing coy to arouse him.

Patrick kissed her lightly on the cheek. "The ensemble's played two dances without me. Time to get over there, to keep those fellows following a beat. I love you, my dearest."

He felt her gaze following him between the couples chatting along the dance floor, all the way to his stool at the back of the other players. It took his utmost concentration during the next waltz—not only because his Celesta was the crowning jewel in the room, but because her aunt and uncle had just come through the doorway.

Ambrose Ransom swaggered in dressed as a pirate, a red bandanna tied rakishly over his head and a black patch covering one eye . . . appropriate, considering the way he'd shanghaied his niece's inheritance. Katherine stepped shyly into his mother's embrace and then Celesta's, poignantly elegant in what he assumed was her wedding gown. Layers of lace and veiling made her appear girlishly vulnerable—also appropriate, because she was now the key to his upcoming success. When Celesta's wedding day drew near, he knew Katherine would either convince her husband to come forth with a sizable dowry, or she could be cajoled into obtaining the money herself. It would keep him afloat until he thought of a more permanent plan, anyway.

Perkins gripped the neck of his instrument as he watched the exchange between Ambrose and his niece. It was stilted, but cordial enough because his mother kept exclaiming over Katherine's gown. When the tall, burly steamship magnate thumped on into the room and greeted his friends, Patrick relaxed and found his place in the music. It was a sure bet Mrs. Ransom would want to dance sometime this evening, and he polished a few opening lines as though they were his halo.

"Ladies," Bill Thompkins was announcing above the crowd's murmur, "the next dance will be a schottische, so grab a partner! I want to see everyone having a good time!"

The director raised his baton, and after couples formed a ring around the ballroom he gave the count. Patrick dug his bow into the strings, producing the steady bass beat that would propel the dancers through this spritely song. He was secretly pleased that Celesta lingered beside the punch bowls, watching the dancers circle the floor—until her chin lifted and she stared toward the doorway.

When Perkins followed her gaze, he stiffened. A commanding figure surveyed the crowd from behind a chilling white mask that covered all but his mouth and chin. His dark hair was waxed back, and he was clad in a black suit, over which a black cape lined in red rippled with the current the dancers were creating. A vampire . . . and because he seemed so haughtily at home, Perkins racked his brain to figure out who the hell it was.

He gripped his bow until it nearly snapped when he saw the debonair newcomer stride straight toward Celesta.

Celesta, too, was so stunned by the stranger that she barely heard Harlan Jones's question. It could've been Grandfather playing one of his spooky games—he'd sported just such a cape on occasion. But the suave, eerie form approaching her was far more frightening than Ambrose Senior's ghost, and she turned toward the police chief in hopes of avoiding it.

"Pardon me?" she asked lamely. "I was preoccupied with my canapés."

Jones, whose paunch made his western marshal's gear look downright silly, gave her a hooded look. "I merely commented that Mr. Perkins hath a lean and hungry look tonight."

Celesta glanced toward the bass player, whose blond hair was concealed by a tight hood. "It's the spider costume. Black makes him look anemic."

The policeman grunted. "Is your interest in him mutual, Miss Montgomery? Such a match would certainly improve your—"

"Patrick's like a brother to me. I'm not his type and everyone knows it."

"How fortunate," came a heavily accented voice from behind her. "I sense your type is exactly to *my* tastes, however. Shall I sample your lovely neck to find out?"

Celesta felt the blood rush from her head. With Jones looking on, it was best to humor the man standing so closely behind her. "You flatter me,

Count Dracula," she teased as she turned to him, "but I don't recall mailing any invitations to Transylvania."

"We vampires have ways of procuring what we need." He reached into his inside pocket and produced a vellum invitation identical to the ones Eula sent out, but he replaced it before she could verify her employer's signature. "I believe the orchestra's introducing a waltz. If you'll dance with me, I'll tell you how I got myself on the guest list."

The Count gave her no chance to refuse. He was clasping her hand in a white-gloved grip and leading her to a place between the other dancers, infuriatingly sure of himself. Celesta's heart was pounding. Who had planned such an encounter—a rendezvous with a man who obviously knew her, but was keeping his identity camouflaged by his accent and lustrous white mask?

When he began to guide her smoothly through the three-quarter beat, Celesta gasped. She was eye-level to a strong, shadowy chin that had a very familiar cleft in it.

He tightened his hold on her. "It's to your advantage to keep my presence a secret, sweetheart," he said in his normal voice. "And it's the least you can do, considering how many times I've rescued you from Perkins lately."

"And how have you done that, Mr. Frye?" she demanded. "Wasn't it enough that Cruikshank and our lame-brain police chief turned you loose?"

Damon chuckled low in his throat. "Remember that rock that shattered Patrick's office window? A timely gesture, I thought—as was the removal of the rest of that rat poison this morning. You're surrounded by companions far more dangerous than I, Celesta. And you know as well as I do that this masquerade's the perfect place to cause you further harm."

Her head was reeling, partly because his words echoed her own suspicions, but mainly because he was holding her so closely that his magnificent satin-lined cape was enveloping her in its magical, arcane mystique. "How do I know that was you?" she challenged weakly.

"Who else is aware of those incidents? Perkins didn't see me in the alley because I was crouched beneath his window, and you've been too spooked about that cyanide to mention it to anyone else."

How did he know her so well? Celesta leaned against his arm to study the hard white mask and the dark hair that was slicked away from it. He was too handsome, too much the sorcerer even after his unforgivable crimes, and she was determined not to fall under his spell again. "And why are you protecting me? Surely I made my hatred clear after you lured Aunt Justine into the river."

His lips curved into a smile that made the gruesome mask look more human. "I'm surprised you haven't figured out who the real culprit is, Celesta. But I love you anyway, and I realize now that you're far too precious to sacrifice to Perkins for the sake of my selfish pride. I did that ten years ago, to Lucy, and I'll regret it the rest of my days."

The cool aloofness had disappeared from his voice, and she heard the Damon Frye who'd once declared his intentions so ardently, so passionately. He sounded *sorry* about leaving her—ready to open his heart about his most compelling secret—and as they swayed gracefully around the crowded ballroom, Celesta sensed he held the key to all of her unsolved mysteries. "All right. I'm listening."

He'd deftly maneuvered her into the small turret room behind the refreshment table, where crocks of punch and trays of food were waiting. "We need privacy," he said as he backed her against the wall. "Such a confession deserves your complete attention and every ounce of my courage. I don't bare my soul to just anyone."

She licked her lips nervously. "So where—"

"Meet me on the back veranda later, when you can slip away unnoticed. I'll wait a few moments and follow you downstairs."

It occurred to her that Patrick had specified the same meeting place, yet it didn't matter. Damon was gazing down at her as though he'd devour her, his warm breath teasing her forehead. Celesta was exhilarated yet confused, wanting to believe him while wondering if this was just another cruel trick to destroy what was left of her heart.

"All day I've wanted to crush you close and kiss you," he whispered. "But it'll have to wait."

She wasn't sure she could. "How . . . how have you kept watch over me without anyone knowing you were back in town?"

He chuckled and ran a gloved finger along the side of her face. "We vampires can pass through walls and disappear into thin air, remember?"

"Don't tease me, Damon, I—"

"Makes for some interesting eavesdropping, too," he continued lightly. "It seems your uncle's dramatic reappearance and Katherine's speechlessness have made people forget all about me. But you haven't, have you?"

Celesta felt her insides tighten, even as she was willing herself not to kiss him. Damn him, he'd yet to prove himself innocent of her charges, yet he so effortlessly led her deeper into his hypnotic embrace.

Frye let out a husky sigh and followed the curve of her neck with his velvety fingertip. "Don't pretend you didn't miss me, sweetheart. Your scarlet disguise can't hide your true feelings from *me*."

She held her breath, riveted by the dark eyes beneath his pale mask as his finger followed the neckline of her dress.

"That's what I thought," he murmured, so softly that only her heart could hear it beneath the frantic pounding of her pulse. "You're still mine, as you'll always be. It's the best thing that could happen to either of us, you know."

Closing her eyes, Celesta raised her face for the kiss she so desperately needed. If she knew this was real, rather than a wishful daydream—

"By the way, my love, you've never looked more stunning," he said matter-of-factly. "But I can't figure out who you're supposed to be."

Her eyes flew open. How dare he ignore her plea for—he was still the infuriating Damon Frye, and now he was humiliating her! "I'm surprised you don't know a cherry tart when you see one," she snapped, and then she wrenched herself from his grasp and stalked out of the little room.

Patrick was waiting for her. His black clothing was as tight as his smile; his extra four legs, attached to the center of his back, swayed as though they were reaching for her. His golden good looks were concealed by his hood and a mask, so only his mouth was visible, but that was enough to show her his mocking displeasure.

"It's time for a birthday toast," he said as he took her hand. "Our guests are filling their punch glasses, wanting you to cut the cake. You shouldn't let a stranger keep them waiting."

He knew as well as she did who the stranger was, but with nearly a hundred revelers looking on, Celesta couldn't challenge him. Patrick raised his glass and said appropriate words that made the audience applaud on the other side of the cake table from them, but she barely noticed. She felt a dreamlike distance from these events—went through the motions of blowing out the candles before slicing the top tier of the elaborate cake—all the while wondering how she was going to escape the downward spiral Damon Frye and Patrick Perkins were pulling her into. Damon was standing at the rear of the crowd, watching her, and she wanted to scream for his help, but—

"Here honey, the first bite should be yours," Patrick's voice interrupted her trancelike state.

She blinked. He was holding a forkful of cake a few inches from her lips, as though he'd been waiting for her to take it. She had no choice, with everyone looking on.

When the sweet, frosted morsel was in her mouth, Perkins grinned triumphantly and faced his audience. "If that looks like a hint of things to come, it is," he announced proudly. "Celesta Montgomery has agreed to be my wife, and I can think of no more appropriate birthday gift than a diamond ring."

Chapter 31

Celesta felt him slipping a warm band onto the fourth finger of her left hand and gaped: the diamond was as large as the lump in her throat, a lump that threatened to choke her as he raised her hand to show off his extravagant gift.

The applause was deafening—or was she loosing consciousness? She was vaguely aware that the Troubadours were playing another waltz, and that she and Patrick were dancing, encircled by their guests. Harlan Jones was smirking at her, and little wonder. Uncle Ambrose watched with great interest while Katherine's pale eyes mirrored her own confusion. Eula Perkins sipped her punch, her eyes riveted on them as she fingered the beadwork on her collar.

And then there was a ripple of red upon black as Damon danced alongside them with Katherine. He seemed to be goading Patrick with pointed stares while making polite conversation with his partner, and soon other couples were joining in the dance.

Celesta had never felt more frightened in her life. The room seemed to spin in its own warped circles as Patrick clutched her closer, murmuring about how he wanted to have her after the party. She had to escape somehow, before this conniving blackheart forced her into anything else.

"Forget him, Celesta. Frye's a liar and a murderer," Perkins whispered against her ear. "I've loved you all my life. Come away with me tonight—we'll be together forever, my darling."

Her throat went so dry she couldn't swallow. The voice Patrick had just used was very similar to Damon's . . . the voice on the wax cylinder, which had driven Aunt Justine to her death! Why *hadn't* she assumed it was one of his imitations all along?

She looked away from him, focusing on Aunt Katherine's euphoria as she glided in perfect time with the vampire who held her. Her eyes were nearly closed as she inclined her ear to Frye's whisperings . . . so long she'd gone without dancing, and Celesta wished the situation wasn't becoming more desperate by the second. She had to free herself from Patrick's grasp. She caught a shimmer of teal and blue beads, and saw his mother striding purposefully out of the ballroom.

There was a startled cry as Aunt Katherine stood stock-still in the midst of the couples whirling around her, staring at her partner. "Damon!" she croaked. "Damon, thank God you're back! You've got to *do* something!"

"And I intend to. If you'll excuse me—" Frye released her to tap Perkins on the shoulder. "Allow me a dance with your bride-to-be," he ordered, and when the spidery blond refused to relinquish her, he swung around behind Celesta and kept on dancing, holding her as he faced his opponent.

"We make an unfortunate trio, just as we did ten years ago when Lucy got caught between us," Frye continued in a low voice. "Be the gracious host and dance with Katherine, or escort her to her husband. If you back down, we can settle this privately. If not, I'll make it so you can never conduct business again—in Hannibal or anywhere else. And you know how I'll do that, don't you, Perkins?"

"You goddamn—if you say one word, I'll—"

"Go find your mother, Perkins. Her little secrets are just as appalling as yours—and you know how nasty things will get if everyone here finds out about them."

Patrick stepped back, grimacing like a cornered animal. Ignoring Katherine, he shoved his way through the crowd and caused a murmuring among the dancers that were gathering around her.

"You've found your voice!"

"Somebody tell Ambrose!"

"Is that vampire really Damon Frye?"

Celesta was still staring at her aunt, her joy overshadowed by the truth about Justine's death. "Are you all right now? Do you want some punch to clear your throat?"

She'd released Damon to clasp her aunt's hands, and the little woman's pulse was racing. "I—I think you'd better leave," Katherine said in a crackling voice. "Ever since Eula planned this party, I've had the most awful feeling—"

"Katherine! Is it true what they're telling me?" Ambrose demanded as he clumped between the onlookers surrounding his wife.

Celesta felt Damon's hand slip around her waist, and as the curious crowd focused on the two Ransoms he whisked her out of the ballroom and down the back stairs.

"I should've told you about Lucy long ago," Frye was muttering. "Should've trusted your feelings for me. Do you still love me, Celesta? I have to know."

They were on the back veranda now, lit by a pale moon that turned the carved pillars and scrollwork a dreamlike white. As she gazed up at him, she recalled their earlier declarations, when Damon had directed the thunder and lightning, had sealed her fate with kisses that made her ache just remembering them. She reached up slowly to raise his mask. "I could never love anyone else," she whispered. "I—I had no idea Patrick would give me this ring—"

"Another of his insidious traps, sweetheart."

"—and I'm so sorry I blamed you for making that awful recording, when I should've known—" Celesta blinked the mist from her eyes, wondering if her heart would burst right out of her dress as Damon gently removed her mask. "Can you forgive me for being so blind? So stupid?"

His smile was dark and shadowy as he leaned her against the wall. "I already have, or I wouldn't be here. Do you remember the first time we kissed, Celesta? It was in this very spot."

His resonant voice made her tremble as he took her hands and flattened the backs of them against the house. Faint strains of music and laughter drifted down from the ballroom, and a breeze riffled Damon's cape as he stood gazing at her.

She laughed softly. "You knocked the basket from my hand—stole that gruesome story about the pen with the poison in it. And I accused you of stealing my favorite pen, too, but you didn't, did you?"

"No."

Celesta sighed. "You must think I'm the most impulsive, temperamental—"

"And those are some of the qualities I admire most about you," he murmured. "Kiss me now. Remind me why I fell in love with you that day, Celesta."

She closed her eyes, and this time he didn't trifle with her feelings. Damon pressed her against the wall, seeking her eager mouth with his. She tasted like cider and birthday cake, all the sweet happiness he hoped he could bring her in the coming years—but he had more serious subjects to cover now, before Patrick made his inevitable appearance. One or both of them might be badly hurt, and Celesta deserved to know the truth, whatever happened.

He pulled away too soon, but she understood his urgency. "Tell me about Lucy," she whispered.

Damon raised up so that he could look into her eyes. "As you know, we were engaged. And when I ran out on her, she was pregnant, so everyone assumed the child was mine."

"Because it was," came a voice from the bushes beside the porch. There was a rustling, and Patrick stood up from his hiding place. He'd removed his hood and mask, and as he ascended the stairs the moonlight gave his face and hair an infernal glow. "She was a mill worker's daughter, shunned by her family and shamed into taking the potion that ended the baby's life as well as her own."

"*Your* baby's," Frye blurted.

Perkins stopped a few steps away, sneering. "That's the most ridiculous—how can you prove that to a smart girl like Celesta?"

"You sneaked Lucy into your father's office one day when he was out. Spread her flat on his desk, just like you did Celesta, only you got what you went after."

"I didn't exactly have to force her."

"So I found out. The hard way," Damon replied bitterly. "You were the heir to the Perkins throne, and Miss Bates thought she'd do a little social climbing, so she—"

Celesta listened in horror, her back to the wall as Damon railed at his accusor. All these years he'd kept his fiancée's infidelity to himself and shouldered the blame for that long-ago scandal. And now, when Frye had a true love to lose, this whining lumberman's son was determined he'd pay for Lucy's duplicity forever.

"I was only eighteen, for Chrissakes," Patrick protested. "The last thing I needed was a sniveling little, redheaded—"

"And *I* was only twenty!" Frye shot back. He

advanced toward Perkins slowly, trying to keep his rage in check. "Imagine my shock when she came crying to me, begging my forgiveness. Begging me to marry her, even though my good friend made her pregnant."

Perkins scowled and jabbed Damon's chest with his finger. "Why should anyone believe that? It could just as easily have been your—"

"No, it couldn't. And Lucy knew it." Frye clenched his fists against the same rage that had boiled within him a decade ago, the shame of a betrayal that had scarred his life forever. "She wouldn't let me love her until our wedding night, Perkins, and I respected her wishes. Lucy was a flirt, but she was a decent girl until you coaxed her into a quick roll with your pretty promises. You strung her along and then turned on her—the same way you turned on me, you damn—"

Perkins came at him, so he lunged, sending them both tumbling down the stairs to struggle in the cold, damp grass. Too long he'd kept his torment locked inside, and as he pummeled the agile blond his burden was lifted. When he felt Patrick reaching into his waistband, however, he sensed the fight was taking an ugly turn.

From the porch Celesta saw the gleam of a knife blade, but when she tried to bolt down the stairs she was blocked by a sturdy body and caught around the waist in an iron grip. A quick hand stifled her cry for help.

"We'll let them fight it out," her captor stated, "and if Frye's unfortunate enough to live, he'll watch you die, Celesta. You know too much, just like your mother did."

Celesta froze, a scream welling up inside her while Eula continued her chilling monolog. The hand clamped over her face was oddly fragrant, but her employer's perfume was hardly important at a moment like this.

"You see, Rachel found out about Patrick and Lucy, and being a responsible servant and a mother herself, she told me the girl might cause a problem. We couldn't have that, of course, so I saw to it that Lucinda Bates never had her baby."

A whimper rose in her throat when the fight in front of them became more vicious. Damon swore in pain. His elegant cape was now trapped beneath him and hampering his movements. Bright violin music filtered down to them, an ironic counterpoint for when Patrick rolled on top of Frye and slugged his jaw.

"Once Damon left town and Miss Bates was buried, we agreed the incident would never again be mentioned," Eula went on calmly. "Patrick never knew I suspected his little tryst, and no one was the wiser about the old crone who provided Lucy's potion . . . I do love to disguise myself on occasion.

"And the whole sordid affair would've remained buried had Damon not returned to Hannibal this summer. Your mother saw him in town and made the mistake of mentioning how handsome he'd become. Knowing how he'd eyed you when you were young, I couldn't risk letting the past raise its ugly head now that Patrick's running the mill. Your mother would've told you about Lucy, since you weren't old enough to hear such things when they happened. She was a dear friend, but you surely understand why my son's welfare was more important than hers."

Celesta's heart stopped. She stared at Mama's murderer, knowing now who poisoned the sugar bowl . . . and aware that the slight bitterness of almonds on Eula's hand signaled the beginning of her own end.

She forgot about the men struggling in the yard and focused upon the unlikeliest of killers: wealthy, sophisticated, donor of time and money for every

charity in town . . . a devoted mother. After penning
so many Sally Sharpe stories, she should've realized
that Eula Perkins had stronger motives than anyone
else—more to lose, so more to protect—yet the
summer's startling events had blinded her to the
obvious clues about who killed Mama.

"Patrick didn't help matters," the little widow
went on with a wry chuckle, "and his sudden interest
in you prompted me to do some research. Tom would
spin in his casket if he knew there were now two sets
of ledgers. Our son was always more interested in
flaunting his power than working for it . . . sickens
me to think how he frittered away our fortune to the
point that I couldn't afford help this week, because
that diamond drained our accounts.

"Poor boy got impatient when Ambrose spoiled
his plans to marry your money, after the other heirs
were so conveniently dying off. So once again I'm
forced to clean up his mess to keep the Perkins name
out of the mud."

Celesta's eyes widened as the woman's hand
snaked up her side, bringing with it the pungence of
cyanide.

"Ironic that you suggested this clever method in
one of your stories," Mrs. Perkins said, her grin
malignant below her feathered mask. "And when I
found your fountain pen in your desk after your
mother's funeral, I sensed I might have a chance to
try it out. If you recall, in 'The Pen is Mightier,' the
victim had two small puncture wounds in her neck,
like those inflicted by a vampire. How sporting of
Mr. Frye to dress for the part—and how convenient
that your choker will cover the wound."

All her mysteries were now solved, but Celesta was
in worse trouble than when she'd been naive and
grieving. Below her, one of the men swore violently,
and after repeated smacking blows she heard a
gurgling sound. Who was strangling whom? She

didn't dare look away from Eula, couldn't think about what would happen if it were Patrick choking the life out of Damon . . . her Damon, who'd lost the best years of his life to an unfaithful fiancée and a false friend . . . Damon, who loved her enough to come back and rescue her, despite her lack of trust in him.

The sound of Eula flicking the cap from her fountain pen brought her out of her stupor. Celesta jerked her head free and screamed, throwing her weight against the smaller woman to knock her off-balance. Still her captor managed to pin her against a porch pillar, and with the hard wooden post cutting into her backside, Celesta gasped for what she assumed would be her final breath.

Visions of Mama's last contorted, confused expression flickered before her mind's eye, memories of that fatal cup of tea that caused convulsions and collapse before—

"Mrs. Perkins, you don't want a third murder added to your record," a forceful voice declared, and then Eula was wrenched off her by none other than Harlan Jones. "Your little story clears up a lot of questions, so why don't we go on down to the jail and—"

"You can't lock my mother away!" came Patrick's protest. He was dragging himself up the stairs, yet his voice rang with defiance. "I'll pay her bail and—"

"With what? She just admitted you drained the accounts buying that fancy ring," the chief replied smugly. He gripped Eula harder to keep the lethal fountain pen from scratching his face, and finally squeezed her wrist until she dropped it. "Come with her and answer some questions. I know better than to hope you'll apologize to Celesta and Mr. Frye, so we might as well be gone before a crowd gathers."

Patrick was wheezing against the porch pillar now, his blue eyes glittering fiercely. Celesta noticed a dark, wet stain on his shirt, and when he leered at her there was a bloody gap in his teeth. "Can't apologize to a dead man," he said with a nasty laugh. Then he glared at the policeman. "Now unhand my mother, or you'll wish you never came to this party. Hurry up, before the guests see all this."

"He's got a knife," Celesta breathed, but just as Perkins raised his weapon there was a commotion in the doorway. Ambrose Ransom swaggered onto the porch, drawing his dagger from its sheath with a flourish.

"My blade's a lot longer than yours, Perkins," he threatened, "and from what Katherine's told me about Justine's death, I ought to cut your damn heart out with it! Now move!"

"I don't take orders from some peg-legged—"

With amazing agility, the burly pirate balanced on his good leg, and with his wooden one he sent Patrick sprawling backward down the stairs. "By damn, Harlan, we'll lock these two up, and tomorrow you'll have your reward. Fine job of watching out for my niece!"

Celesta stared after them as they steered the Perkinses down the sidewalk, but when she caught sight of Damon's inert form in the yard she rushed to his side. "Dear God, no! I thought Patrick was only baiting me—you can't be—"

Falling to her knees, she scooped his head and shoulders into her lap. Her mind was spinning wildly while the gash along his face smeared against her dress. He was ghostly pale, dead weight in her arms as her tears splashed onto his cheeks. "You can't be gone, Damon!" she wailed. "First Mama and then Justine and—oh, Aunt Katherine, what'll I do? I made a horrible mistake, and he died trying to make up for it. I—"

Frye held his breath a little longer and half-opened one throbbing eye. The sight of Celesta bemoaning his death made his pain worthwhile, but only a monster would let her carry on this way. She was clutching Katherine's arm, and he was vaguely aware of other voices and movement around them, and of the cold, wet grass . . . and his face rested only inches from the pale, round moons of her cleavage, which quivered with her sobs. A man could die a worse death.

He drew a shuddering breath and opened his eyes—or at least the one that was cooperating at the moment. Celesta nipped her lip and gazed fearfully at him. "Damon?" she breathed.

His lips cracked when he smiled. "Last time I checked, I was."

"Are you all right?"

"Never better, as long as your heart's not set on dancing the night away."

Her mouth fell open. "You ornery—I thought you'd passed on, and now you're making fun of me!"

"We vampires can die and come back at will," he reminded her wryly. "I was playing dead so Perkins would quit messing up my face. He always did fight dirty, but aside from that a couple of cracked ribs were all he inflicted. So quit your crying. I'll be my obnoxious self again in no time."

She let out a quavery laugh and wiped her face with the back of her hand. "I—I don't know how to thank you—"

"Sure you do. But I hope you can restrain yourself while we have an audience."

Relieved laughter rippled through the crowd around them, and her heart filled with wonder. This man, who more than once had frightened and awed and infuriated her, was now making her chuckle in spite of his pain. "It's a good thing I love you, Frye," she whispered, "because otherwise I'd be peeved that you ruined such an extravagant party. *Weeks* I worked, getting ready for it!"

"You're a fine hostess, Celesta," he agreed as he reached for her hand, "and I hope we'll soon be entertaining this lavishly in our own home."

"Oh, that'll be so lovely!" Katherine gushed as she gazed at them. "I'm so glad—"

"What'll be lovely, my dear?" Ambrose called out. He was coming back up the sidewalk with a confident step, as though his former amiable nature had been restored by the evening's excitement.

Katherine gazed fondly up at the man who towered above them. "Parties at Damon and Celesta's new home. And with him being an architect, I can only imagine what a grand place it'll be."

Ambrose smiled slowly at Celesta. "I'm sure it will, judging from his work at Ransom Manor. And until it's built, I hope you'll both accept my invitation to stay with us. It seems I misjudged you two, and I certainly owe you lodging for looking after my wife and sister. I . . . I hope we can make up for some lost time and past mistakes."

"I'd like that, Uncle Ambrose," Celesta said softly.

He grinned sheepishly at Frye. "I caught quite an earful once my wife's voice returned, and among other things she's informed me I have no business commissioning three new steamers. Something tells me the money for the *Celestial Fortune* will be my niece's dowry. Is that acceptable?"

Frye shrugged and shifted closer to her. "Do what you want. I was ready to marry her when she was the maid's daughter, and your money won't change that."

Ambrose gave a satisfied nod and helped his wife up off the ground. "Shall we go back to the ballroom while Dr. Denton tends to Frye?" he asked the revelers around them. "No sense in leaving before all that food and punch are gone!"

As the crowd dispersed to go upstairs, Celesta stroked Damon's face. John Denton, an earnest young surgeon, knelt on Frye's other side with his medical bag and handed her a slender, dark object—her fountain pen. "I stepped on this coming outside," he said. "Sorry I flattened it."

Celesta gazed at the pen Mama had given her, sighing when she realized that a dime novel manuscript could've spelled out her own demise. "It won't be any good for writing now, but it'll serve as a memento of a very eventful birthday."

Frye grimaced when the doctor pressed his ribs, but kept his eyes on Celesta. "I hope that doesn't mean you'll never publish another story. You're off to a galloping start—"

"But when I should've listened to my instincts, my imagination ran away with me," she mumbled. "I thought you killed my aunt, and I thought you were only using me to get back at Patrick, and—"

He could understand her qualms, because some of them had been true at one time. She was smart enough to know that, too, and decent enough not to hold it against him . . . and Celesta Montgomery was indeed the most fetching young woman he'd ever met. "Will you marry me anyway?" he murmured as he looked up at her. "No doubt it'll be a better cure than anything the doc here can do for me."

Denton chuckled and stood up. "We'll wrap those ribs and get you to bed. No doubt she can fix what ails you there, too—but carefully, understand?"

Damon laughed low in his throat and held his breath as Celesta lowered her lips to his. She was being too cautious—he wrapped an arm around her neck and moved his mouth hungrily over hers, ignoring the pain because the sweetness of her response was the most gratifying medicine of all. She loved him, after all she'd suffered at the hands of Patrick Perkins . . . whose foul intent surfaced only after he'd egged the blond into it. He owed her a lot, and he tried to pour his feelings into one long, lovely kiss.

Sighing blissfully, Celesta held on for what seemed like forever, sensing this was the start of the greatest plot she'd ever concocted. Here she was in the arms of the wounded hero she'd wrongly cast out, who'd returned to rescue her despite her mistakes, and she now had a dowry, and her aunt and uncle were reconciled, and the two villains were behind bars . . . Sally Sharpe should be here to enjoy all these little victories.

Damon saw the faraway light in her eyes and wanted her desperately. "Is that angelic smile because of my kiss, or because of what you hope comes next?"

Celesta's chuckle sounded sly and wanton and very, very pleased as she looked down into his dusky face. "I feel a story coming on," she whispered.

And Frye knew it would be her finest one yet.